MW00986890

Bhagavati

Tor Books by Kara Dalkey

BLOOD OF THE GODDESS

Goa

Bijapur

Bhagavati

Bhagavati

Blood of the Goddess
III

Kara Dalkey

A Tom Doherty Associates Book
New York

This is a work of fiction. All the characters and events portrayed in this novel are either fictitious or are used fictitiously.

BHAGAVATI

This book is printed on acid-free paper.

A Tor Book
Published by Tom Doherty Associates, Inc.
175 Fifth Avenue
New York, NY 10010

Tor Books on the World Wide Web:
http://www.tor.com

Library of Congress Cataloging-in-Publication Data

Dalkey, Kara, date
Bhagavati / Kara Dalkey.—1st ed.
p. cm.—(Blood of the goddess ; 3)
"A Tom Doherty Associates book."
ISBN 0-312-86003-X
1. Herbs—Therapeutic use—Fiction.
I. Title. II. Series: Dalkey, Kara, date
Blood of the goddess ; 3.
PS3554.A433B48 1998
813'.54—dc21 98-5548
CIP

First Edition: June 1998

Printed in the United States of America

0 9 8 7 6 5 4 3 2 1

Bhagavati

PROLOGUE

What, yet another story you ask of me, traveller? Truly Ganesha has blessed you with an avid curiosity. This shall be the last, however, else my throat will dry up from the talking.

But what tale shall I tell? Ah, I have it.

This story takes place long ago and far away, in a village by the sea. In this village there lived three sisters. The eldest was a studious girl, who served in the village temple. She was named for the goddess worshipped there, so let us call this sister Lakshmi, or Mahadevi, for her goddess was very like those of that name. The middle sister was forthright and brave, and watched over the family goat herd . . . so let us call her Strength. The youngest sister was patient and sweet-natured and helped her mother at home, let us call her Dreamer.

These three lived as harmonious a life as three sisters of different natures might, befriended by three cousins of equally disparate moods.

Then the day came when a mighty horde of strangers arrived from the north. They claimed they were refugees, driven from their homeland, seeking a safe place to settle.

Well. The village by the sea had known peace for many, many years, and so they welcomed the strangers with what hospitality they could offer and attempted to live beside them in harmony.

But the newcomers brought strange ways and strange gods. And they insisted upon installing the image of their god in the temple in which Mahadevi (the eldest sister, remember?) served. And after this was done, they demanded that the image of the village goddess be removed, to be supplanted by the foreign god.

This was, of course, more than Mahadevi could bear. She encouraged the priests and priestesses of the temple to refuse. Her sisters supported her in this, Strength threatening to overrun the temple with her goats, and Dreamer saying no one from her village would bring offerings to the foreign god.

Then the trouble began. The priests of the newcomers tried to slander Mahadevi, claiming she had defiled the temple by fornicating with fishermen there. They claimed that she boasted that she was more beautiful than her goddess. But these were not believed and had no effect.

So the newcomers brought forth their mightiest wizards who worked night after night to create their greatest curse. And then, as Mahadevi and her sisters and their cousins assembled in the temple for *puja*, the sorcerers emerged from behind the idol of the Mahadevi and said, "Since you and your sisters are so devoted to this idol, you three shall resemble her forever!"

They flung their curse upon the sisters. As you can imagine . . . well, the image of their goddess was much like those of ours here in Sind. Bodies and heads of animals and so forth. Imagine something that in flesh instead of stone might be hideous. To such a form were those sisters changed. On top of that, the sorcerers cried, "Since you now have divine form, no mortals may look upon you and live!" And so it was that anyone who met the sisters' gaze perished.

As for the cousins, the wizards said, "Since you think yourselves so wise in choosing to support your friends in their error, you shall be aged and wrinkled as ancient sages forever!"

And the cousins, who were just past girlhood themselves, turned into grey and wizened crones.

The sisters, because they were now a danger to their family and village, were forced to flee, and they ran off to live in caves in the mountains. For a while, the villagers would bring food and clothing for them, but as the decades passed, the sisters were no longer thought of as friends to be pitied, but as monsters to be feared.

And so they lived for year after lonely year, having only each other for companionship. Meanwhile, in the world outside, their legend spread and grew, until the day a proud adventurer from a distant kingdom arrived to slay the legendary monsters and steal the treasure they had supposedly amassed. He found only Mahadevi at home (the other sisters were off searching for food) and cunningly using a mirror to avoid her deadly gaze, he chopped off her head and took it home as a ghastly prize.

What, you say this story sounds too familiar? That you may have heard it before? I beg your pardon, then, I will bore you no further. But if you have heard it, have you never wondered what happened to the other two sisters, Dreamer and the goatherd named Strength? They were immortal as their sister, perhaps more so. And what of the cousins who had been turned into crones? What would it be like if they still lived in the world, wiser now for all the centuries they had experienced?

But I shall detain you no more. Be on your way, then, traveller, and let your steps not be slowed by such trivialities. Surely legends of so long ago have no meaning for us now. Could they?

Gandharva
Musician to the
court of Ibrahim
'Adilshah II of Bijapur

I

MYRTLE: This tree is evergreen and puts forth pale blossoms and berries of a dark blue. It is said the myrtle is the one tree Man was permitted to take from the Garden of Eden. It is the symbol of the Eye, and atonement for sinful thoughts brought by the sight of that which one desires. It is a tree of immortality and resurrection, yet also a tree of death–in particular, the death of kings. To the ancient Greeks, the myrtle was a sign of authority. But to the Romans, it was symbolic of forbidden love and they shunned it. In England, it is a tree of good fortune, but only if by woman planted....

Cart wheels rumbled like continuous thunder as the Mughul army set forth. Thomas Chinnery turned in his saddle and looked back through the dust kicked up by the horses, elephants, and Mughul foot soldiers around him, catching one last glimpse of the glimmering domes and minarets of Bijapur.

"Aye," said the burly Scotsman Andrew Lockheart, riding beside him, "Gaze upon the shining city whilst you may. Who knows when we may see its like again?"

"In truth," Thomas sighed, "I care not if I ne'er see its like again."

"I would take greater care in your wishes, were I you, Tom," said Lockheart more softly, "lest they be granted."

"How might that be worse," said Thomas, "than this journey that I never wished for?"

"That depends upon the manner of the granting, lad, for the Fates are fey, and events rarely run as Man would plan them."

"So I am learning." Thomas was far from where he'd imagined only months before. Then he had been aboard *The Bear's Whelp,* bound for Cathay, with hopes of serving as a factor in the trade of herbs and spices for his master Geoffrey Coulter, Apothecary of London. Unfortunately, the captain of the expedition was fond of piracy, and an encounter with two Portuguese ships in the Arabian Sea had left them stranded on the coast of India. The only booty of note from their encounter were two captives and a strange brown powder. One captive was a Portuguese alchemist, reputed to be a sorcerer, the other was a Hindu woman who seemed something between a priestess, a courtesan, and a spy. The powder proved to be a poison to any living soul, but could return life to the dead.

Since his discovery of the powder, Thomas had found himself on a bizarre, inadvertent journey to find its source—a quest that had already led him through the dungeons of the Inquisition in Goa and the splendours of the palace of the Sultan Ibrahim 'Adilshah of Bijapur. And now he sought the strangest place of all—a mythical city hidden within a mountain where an immortal queen, or perhaps a goddess, was said to dwell. In the span of the last several weeks, Thomas had come to feel far older than his twenty years.

The *rasa mahadevi*, or "blood of the goddess", as the powder was called, had so far proved to be more curse than blessing. The Portuguese sorcerer now lay dead in the Inquisition's morgue in Goa. And the Hindu woman Aditi . . .

Thomas turned his head again to look toward the rear of the army column. There was a gaily painted and gilded entertainer's wagon wherein, known only by a few, lay the body of Aditi who had become his lover and spoken on his behalf to the Sultan of Bijapur, preserved and awaiting resurrection when the source of the powder was found.

"Mayhap you should sit backwards in your saddle," Lockheart suggested, "and thereby spare your neck its pains."

"Your pardon," said Thomas as he quickly turned to face forward once more. "My thoughts do tend to matters behind me this morn."

"You'd do well to think on matters ahead," said Lockheart with a nod toward the men who rode but a few yards in front of them. One of them was Padre Antonio Gonsção, of Lisbon, who was envoy to the Inquisition in Goa and leader of the European contingent on this expedition. The others were three Portuguese Goan soldiers in bronze morion helmets and cuirasses.

"Methinks the Padre will have other matters on his mind than which way I turn my face."

"Think you so, when he relies upon you for the direction we must travel on this quest?"

Thomas fell silent, for it was through lies and trickery that he had convinced the Inquisition to send him on this expedition, in hopes that during the journey he would find some opportunity to escape. No good opportunity had arisen, however, and now duty to his master and to a dead woman spurred him on to a goal he had no knowledge of. Unbeknownst to all but Lockheart, his only guide was a blind Hindu musician who had been a friend of the late Aditi, and now rode with her preserved corpse in the entertainer's wagon. *And thus the blind doth lead the ignorant. What a potent lot are we.*

A gust of wind heavy with dust blew across Thomas's face, obscuring his vision and forcing him to cough. "Brother Timóteo was wiser than I knew," Thomas said when he could at last breathe clear air. "By insisting upon riding the Mirza's elephant, he is above all this dust."

"A perceptive lad, no doubt," said Lockheart. "Though his choice of masters could have been better."

"Growing up in Goa, what choice had a pious boy but to 'prentice himself to the Inquisition?" said Thomas. "I cannot blame him."

"You are more charitable than I."

"Come now, Andrew, you once thought it to your purpose to wear a monk's robe."

"Certes, though 'twas but a ruse. You will note that I wear it no longer, nor have I for some time." Indeed, Lockheart was dressed in a long *jama* jacket of golden-brown silk tied with a broad scarlet sash, and loose *shalwar* trousers. Thomas, whose English clothing had been taken from him in the Santa Casa of Goa, also wore *shalwar* trousers and a simple beige *kurta* shirt. The clothes were parting gifts from Sultan Ibrahim of Bijapur, as were the fine horses they rode. The Sultan had not been pleased with the Goans' behavior and had been eager to see the foreign visitors gone.

Padre Gonsção, however, had declined the gift of new clothes, preferring to remain in his Dominican robe of white wool, now brown with the dust of the road, and black cape.

"But did you not once say, Andrew, that a monk's guise suited you better than many another? If what you told me yesternight be true, you are as entitled to such garb as the Padre, though you might wear a toga instead of a scapular. . . ."

"Speak no more of my faith, nor mock it not," said Lockheart in soft but urgent voice. "If our Padre has slain your ladylove for her belief in her goddess, think you he will show me no less mercy?"

Thomas sighed. "I know not what to think. Time was, ere I began this journey, I would not think sane men capable of such an act. But since my own sojourn within the Inquisition, I have learned how madness may oft wear the guise of reason." He shifted his shoulders, still sore and weak from suffering the strappado while in the dungeons of the Santa Casa of Goa.

"There are those who would say our expedition is such a thing; madness in the guise of reason."

"True. My hopes demand that it not be so. If we find the source of the blood that brings the dead to life, then Aditi lives again. I care not if that source is animal or mineral or monster or immortal queen. A Brahmin I once spoke to said the powder is the blood of a goddess, but these Hindu have strange ideas about divinity. Aditi once told me she was her goddess's adopted daughter."

Lockheart chuckled darkly. "Then woe betide her murderer when the mother discovers him."

"Indeed." But Thomas took little pleasure in the prospect. *Is it that by my hand the Padre was resurrected when he was felled by the fever and I am loth to see my work undone? Or do I fear discovering that there is truth to pagan faith, I who was raised Protestant and yet was unknowingly consecrated as a child to Diana in the cult to which my father and Andrew both belonged? I who was forced to sign a confession in the Santa Casa, thus surrendering my soul to a papist God? Woe betide my poor bewildered soul if yet again I must swear new allegiance.*

Brother Timóteo grinned in rapture, looking out from the back of the *howdah*, swaying with the elephant's rolling gait. He stared in amazement at the river of humanity following behind. In all of his thirteen years, he had never seen such a marvel. Uncountable hundreds of men rode on sleek horses, whose saddles and harness were gilded and hung with scarlet tassels and oxtails. The men wore spiked helmets topped with plumes or pennants, and armor of polished mail covered with embroidered, padded coats. They carried lances of sharpened bamboo, and had bows and quivers of arrows slung on their backs, and shields made of animal hides hung from their saddles. *And the Padre said this is a small army compared to those of Portugal or Spain.* Timóteo sighed in awe of it, and wondered if such admiration was a sin.

He peered through the dust, knowing somewhere in the midst of all that rode the Padre and Tomás and the others. He wasn't sure if they could see him but he waved anyway. To his delighted surprise, some of the Mughul horsemen looked up with startled smiles and waved back. *Surely,* thought Timóteo, *the difference in the* muculmanos' *faith is merely error. They cannot be the monsters the Padre seems to think them.*

Timóteo turned and scrambled to the front of the *howdah* to look out over the *mahout's* shoulder and the elephant's broad head at the landscape ahead of them. The lush fields and groves that surrounded Bijapur were giving way to a barren, fantastic desert of red and gold dust, dotted with occasional forests of thorn trees and palms that hid mysterious villages. Outcroppings of huge, pale boulders brooded on hilltops resembling ruined, abandoned castles of giants, or the bones of the earth.

Timóteo could not understand why the bearded, turbanned Mughul prince-general, the Mirza Ali Akbarshah, who sat beside him, seemed so uninterested in the view. *Well, he is much older and surely he has seen many more wonderful places than I have.*

It happened that the Mirza spoke passable Urdu, a Persian-like language that Timóteo knew somewhat, so they could make themselves understood to one another. The Mirza had been a gracious host in allowing Timóteo to ride on his elephant—another sign that the Muslims could not be the embodiment of evil.

The Mirza held out a porcelain dish containing dates stuffed with honey and walnuts. Timóteo bowed his thanks and gratefully took some.

"So," said the Mirza, "You are enjoying this journey?"

Timóteo nodded and took another date.

"I am pleased to see that someone is."

"Are you not enjoying this, Highness?"

The Mirza sighed. "I have come a long way already, and I fear I have little enthusiasm for the journey ahead."

Timóteo regarded the Mirza's concerned, weatherworn face, feeling puzzled. "You do not? But we will see such wondrous things!"

The Mirza laughed without joy. "If you are right, then I shall be pleased. But I must please my emperor and my men as well, and that may prove more difficult."

"If we find the . . . the immortal Queen of Life and Death, will they not be pleased?"

The Mirza gave Timóteo a long, searching stare, and for a moment Timóteo wondered if he had overstepped the bounds of courtesy to his host. "Your pardon, Highness," he added quickly, "if I have offended."

"No, no," said the Mirza. "It is merely a matter that you may not comprehend because of your youth. The desires of men can follow many different paths; some hunger for wealth, some for power, some for knowledge. My Emperor Akbar is one of these last—he has great curiosity about other faiths, believing all have some validity. He will listen to any myth, any story, no matter how amazing. When he heard of this immortal queen with powers of life and death, at once he wished to know more of her. So I am here, sent to find this powerful Begum Shah. I have, at times, wondered if the Shahinshah thinks of himself as a Solomon, hoping to find his Queen of Sheba."

Timóteo nearly dropped his dates. "You . . . you have read the Bible, Highness?"

The Mirza blinked. "No. But you understand, our faiths share many stories, though they are not entirely similar."

"Then . . . then you are aware of our Lord Jesus the Christ."

"Of course. He is regarded by my people as a wise and prescient prophet."

"But how can you not see, then, that he is the Savior and the Son of God?"

The Mirza scowled down at him in silence for long moments.

Timóteo swallowed hard, knowing this time he had overstepped courtesy. "Your pardon, Highness."

A hard smile suddenly split the Mirza's face. "Let us have a bargain, you and I," he said. "I will not try to win your soul for Allah, if you will not attempt to win mine for your Christ. Is this agreeable?"

Timóteo found himself torn. It had been his duty, as an advocate in the Santa Casa, to see that lost souls were steered toward the Light. However, he knew he must not be a nuisance, or endanger the fragile alliance that allowed him and the Padre to travel escorted by the Mirza's army. "I . . . can we say that so long as we are riding the elephant, we will not talk about it?"

The Mirza's smile grew wider. "You are a bold and clever boy. Very well, it is agreed. So long as we are on the elephant."

Timóteo nodded, frustrated but aware that he must prove true to his word.

"Although you might find it better to argue philosophy with my Sufi advisor, Masum," the Mirza went on. "He is far better acquainted with the details of faith than I. But as I have told you of my emperor, will you do me the honor of telling me what king has sent you on this journey and what he hungers for?"

Timóteo looked away, knowing a dangerous question when he heard one. He had to be careful in his response. The Padre did not want the Mughuls to learn too much, or they might see no reason to keep the westerners alive and with them. "Um . . . the Domines of the Santa Casa in Goa sent us, Highness. And they, too, hope for knowledge."

"Do they? From what rumors I have heard about Goa, I did not think your Domines would listen to every fanciful story that comes their way."

This encroached dangerously into things Timóteo was sworn to secrecy about, under the Santa Casa's Rule of Silence. "I . . . I cannot speak of these things, Highness. The Domines had learned of it from . . . very important men." Brother Timóteo had, at Padre Gonsção's direction, found and read the ledgers which contained the confessions of former Governador Coutinho and Viceroy de Albuquerque. Timóteo knew he should not reveal the fact that powerful government ministers of Goa had been seduced into a pagan cult where they were given proof that a certain pagan belief was true.

"Ah. Is one of these important men among your party?"

"No."

"It would be helpful, you understand, if we could know which among you has the knowledge of where this queen is to be found. That way we could ensure he was especially protected, so that his knowledge would not be lost."

A truly dangerous question, which Timóteo dared not answer truthfully. The *inglês* Tomás was his friend, and a wise and good person, for did he not know of Timóteo's grandfather, the great herbalist Garcia de Orta? Even if Tomás made Timóteo angry sometimes, Timóteo knew he dared not betray him as the one who knew the way. *Madre Maria, forgive me for I must lie.* "I . . . I do not know, Highness."

The Mirza sighed. "It speaks well of you that you are cautious, boy. But understand, all is not so simple as it seems. We must learn to trust one another in order to be successful in our journey. Perhaps even to survive. Think on this, if you will. And if you sometime realize there is something I should know, you will find me an eager listener."

Timóteo nodded again, although he knew he would never willingly reveal anything to the Mirza without the Padre's permission.

"Good," said the Mirza. "I have always thought it unfortunate that there has not been greater peace between our peoples. Our sacred texts are similar. And now, even our stories of this fabled queen are similar, and yet we keep secrets from one another, hoping to keep the advantage. Well. This may be a simple adventure for you, boy, but understand that my responsibilities, for the lives of my men and the will of my Emperor, are heavy ones.

"The Sultan Ibrahim joined our expeditions so that my army might give your people protection and your people might give us knowledge. But I cannot protect you if I do not know what dangers face us on the road ahead, or how this Begum Shah is to be approached once we find her. You would be wise to share whatever useful knowledge you have, so that we might all survive this journey safely, and gain from it that which we desire."

And this was the most dangerous question of all, for Timóteo did know things. For Timóteo had read the ledgers in the Santa Casa. And Timóteo had been told the ancient myths on his grandfather's knee. Timóteo knew what, or whom, they would probably find. He had tried to tell the Padre, who did not understand. He dared tell no one else.

"I do not know, Highness. But I think . . . I think it will be the most amazing thing you have ever seen." Timóteo turned his attention fully on the scene ahead of them, hoping to discourage any more questions from the Mirza. Somewhere out there was a city, hidden within a mountaintop, in which lived a creature who might prove the greatest challenge to his faith, but who might also give confirmation to his dearest childhood dreams.

Prabaratma rocked back and forth, chanting softly as the sapphire prayer beads dropped one by one through his cupped hands. He sang the Hymn to Dawn, blessing the Mahadevi for life and light. He sang the Hymn to the Goddess Earth. And he sang in Praise of Generosity, to which he added a verse of his own—thanking the Mahadevi for his blindness.

Prabaratma had been born into the highest Brahmin family in the holy city of Bhagavati. His clan had served in the many names of the Mahadevi ever since her avatar, Stheno, had come to gather the chosen into Her city, at the dawn of time.

He had been a good student, learning from his father and uncles at the temple, and could recite the Vedas by heart. As a young man, he served in the Lower Temple, near the Gate of Parvati, teaching and doing his dharma as husband and father. In maturity, he had prepared for the life of a hermit monk, to devote his life to prayer. And then, at sixty years of age, a milky film grew over his eyes, and he was called to serve in the Palace of the Mahadevi, at the feet of the great Goddess Herself.

To look upon the aspect of the Mahadevi brought death. Therefore, in Bhagavati, blindness was regarded as a sign of divine favor. Only those without sight could serve the Mahadevi. Some ambitious Brahmins gouged out their eyes in hopes of becoming chosen, but this was not a certain path to service. Often as not, such men were rejected, and driven from the palace in humiliation. Far better to have the blessing fall by nature.

The most amazing thing, Prabaratma had discovered, about his loss of sight was that as his vision of the outer world became dim and distorted, his inner visions had become vivid and prophetic. The teaching was driven home to him that the earthly world was truly *maya*, illusion, and only the land of the spirit mattered.

Prabaratma had fasted for two days now, and his body felt light as air. The flames in the little braziers before him were vague, dancing saffron lights—shapes swiftly changing from one form to another, much as the Mahadevi changed in Her moods and aspect.

He raised his head, noting a change in the air around him as well—the same feeling as when a storm approaches, promising rain and threatening thunder. He caught the scents of sandalwood, cinnamon, and jambo flowers. He heard the rattle of a bead curtain and the tinkle of tiny brass bells. The Mahadevi had come.

Prabaratma smiled. "Welcome, She who is most Great and Good. What prayers shall I sing to you today?"

She laughed, her voice low and throaty. "I have been listening to your devotions, Pra. I think I heard enough prayer for today."

She spoke tiger-bold, yet Prabaratma sensed a child-shyness in her sometimes. It did not bother him—the wonder of the Mahadevi was in her variation. She walked past him, the scents of flowers, ashes, and snakeskin drifting with her. Prabaratma felt her cool fingertips brush his brow and he shuddered with joy.

"Why do you always smile like that, Pra?"

"Your presence fills me with happiness."

She walked around him like a cat watching a bird's nest. Prabaratma could dimly discern the shadows of Her garments, lamplight glistening on her skin. In his muddled sight, Her shape changed much like the flames in the brazier. Her head seemed wreathed in a nimbus of light and shadow, with occasional glints of bright reflection. He could feel Her gaze upon him and was glad he could not see it.

"Sometimes, Pra, I wish you were not blind."

"My life is Yours, Great One. Release my soul, if it is Your wish."

She laughed again. "That is not what I meant. It is good for friends to look upon one another—a pleasure Fate has denied me. I find myself out of sorts today, Pra. I have come to hear your visions. Who am I, what is my aspect at this moment, Pra? What does your inner sight show you?"

It was a game she played. Prabaratma had heard this question addressed to other priests. Each time they would name a goddess, such as Lakshmi the All-Giver, or Sarasvati the Wise Teacher, and give a flattering explanation. Each time, She would argue against their choice until the priests were reduced to silence.

"You are all things, Blessed One. You are whomever You choose to be, at whatever moment. You are like a cut jewel—many faces, but all one."

"A cautious answer, Pra."

"But a true one."

She paused in Her pacing and stamped Her foot like an impatient cow. There was something else She wanted, though he could not guess what. He counselled himself to patience.

"I have been dreaming," she said at last.

"Ah." *What do the gods dream of, I wonder? Is not the world their dream?*

"I dreamed I was a mortal, Pra. I stood on a sun-baked hillside, tending a flock of goats. There was a cool wind blowing up from the sea and my long hair fluttered around my face. . . ." Her voice trailed off into a whisper.

"You have been many things, O Mahadevi. Perhaps you were once such a woman, in such a place."

"I believe so. So long ago. The dream made me sad, though I cannot think why."

"The World Dream is full of sorrows. Only Being is true joy."

She snorted derisively. "Sometimes I wonder if you are sane, Pra."

The rapture sought by Brahmins was sometimes called madness by the ignorant. Did the Mahadevi think he was only imitating Insight? Perhaps She meant he had truths to learn. "I await enlightenment, Blessed One."

"No, Pra. This time I seek wisdom from you. Look into your brazier and your heart. Tell me what your inner vision sees."

Ah. It is a test. Prabaratma felt an anxious moment, for his visions did not come on demand, only when they wished. Still he leaned over the glowing brass brazier and breathed in the sandalwood smoke. He took up his beads again and began to chant. He was only ten words into The Creation Of The Sacrifice, when the visions smote him.

So fast, so fast, it was hard to discern their shape as they flickered by, but he tried to catch hold long enough to name what he saw . . .

. . . a white dove flying—

"There will come a message,"

. . . dark clouds blown by tempests—

"It will bring anger and sorrow,"

. . . a glowing coal became a gleaming eye, a tongue of fire a sharp beak—

"Garuda, the eagle, approaches, talons outstretched."

"Is not Garuda the enemy of serpents, Pra?"

But the priest could not answer, he was so caught within the visions. The flames flickered upright and swayed, yellow and blue, to the rhythm of his heart. "I see a dancer, perhaps it is Krishna, with his flute and crown."

"Is this Krishna in his aspect of Lover?"

"He also danced upon the serpent Kaliya until it gushed forth blood."

"This is not promising," she muttered. "Is there more?"

. . . the dark clouds again, spitting lightning.

"Indra brings his thunderbolts."

"He who split the world serpent to create the Earth?"

"He. And Shiva comes to dance."

"The Destroyer?"

"And Bringer of Gifts."

"I see. If I am to become host to so many gods, I have much to do to prepare for the festivities. I don't suppose you can explain why I am to be so honored?"

The visions faded and Prabaratma slumped, his grey-bearded chin falling onto his chest. "No, Blessed One," he sighed.

"Poor Pra. I have taxed your aging flesh. I often forget how weak you mortals are, how short-lived. Sometimes I feel I rule a colony of ants."

Prabaratma nodded. "The small is a reflection of the great," he murmured.

"You don't know what you are saying. A hill of ants can be destroyed. Like this!" She kicked over his little brazier, the blurred shape of her foot scattering the glowing coals. "There. What can you see now, Pra?" He heard her soft footfalls departing, the bead curtain rattling like old bones.

Prabaratma felt a moment of vertigo, as if the universe were shifting around him. He smiled. *The cycle turns. That is why She wished me to see whom She was becoming. No longer bountiful Lakshmi or patient Sarasvati. She is become the Mother of Creation and Destruction. Welcome, Kali. The gods come to behold your rebirth. I await the wonders you bring. Truly,* he thought with an ecstatic sigh, *the universe was created from joy.*

II

SAFFRON: This spice comes from the innermost stem of the crocus blossom. Its bright yellow color brings much delight, and it has a strong perfume, and is oft given to dispel melancholy. The Greeks used it to scent their baths, yet some ancients disapproved of its use, for it was said to make women behave unseemly. The Irish believe bedclothes washed in crocus water will strengthen the limbs of those who sleep in them. The French use saffron for the gout and rheumatism. In the East, saffron is credited with magical powers and the Hindoo write their sacred texts with it. Gerard writes that saffron makes quick the senses, but too much of it may make one mad....

Padre Antonio Gonsção stood in the shade of a withered tamarind tree, steeling his ears against the wailing of the Muslim prayers. The dusty earth around him was carpeted with Mughuls crouched upon their knees, facing the setting sun. *Five times a day I must endure this. Dear Lord, what a trial you have given me.*

The sun glowered an angry red in the west, its dimming causing no lessening of heat. Gonsção plucked at his once-white Dominican robe where his sweat made it stick to his skin. He felt disgruntled and snappish from heat-sapped weariness. It was taking great effort to ward off that greatest of sins, despair.

I should not be here, a part of him kept repeating, an internal litany that would not be silent. *I should be on a ship, returning to Lis-*

boa, with my report on the corruptions of the Goan Santa Casa. I should be preparing how I will tell Cardinal Albrecht that a cabal of Hindu sorcerers had deluded a Goan Governor and Viceroy into paganism. That they even subverted the faith of Inquisitor Major Sadrinho, inciting in him greed for a powder that could bring the dead to life.

Gonsção felt cold dread despite the heat. That was another part of the thought that he preferred not to dwell on. *I should not be here. I should be dead.* It seemed one of God's subtler ironies that the young *inglês* Tomás Chinnery should have brought Gonsção back to life with that same powder that Gonsção had sworn to destroy.

"Like the yowling of rutting cats, are they not, Padre?"

Gonsção started, not having noticed the soldier Joaquim Alvalanca walk up behind him. Joaquim was garrulous and had an annoyingly crude sense of humor, but he was one of the three Goan soldiers who remained with the expedition, the ten others of his cohort having fled at Bijapur. "They are our hosts, Joaquim. We must not offend them, however offensive they may seem to us."

"Ah, you are being diplomatic, Padre," said the small, wiry soldier. "Which is all to the good, I suppose, as we wish to preserve our lives." He removed his morion helmet and wiped his forehead with his sleeve. "Ay, Maria, but it is hot, forgive the blasphemy, Padre. Here, will you have some wine? It is not the Mass now, but you might find it a blessing nevertheless, yes?" Joaquim held out a wineskin.

"No, I thank—" Gonsção realized how parched he felt and took the wineskin. "I thank you." He squirted a long stream into his mouth, finding the taste strange, like an exotic white wine, but welcome. "What is this?"

"It is *arrak*, Padre, made from the palm tree. Not like our fruit of the vine, eh? But it will suit in this place."

"Yes." Gonsção handed the wineskin back to Joaquim. "By chance, have you seen Brother Timóteo?"

"Last I saw of him, the little brother was in deep discussion with the *muçulmanos.* He may have them all converted before this trip is over."

"Yes, well I am glad to know they have not harmed him. And Senhor Chinnery, is he behaving himself?"

"All seems well with him, although he keeps muttering to Ermão Andrew, that strange companion of his."

"Ah, yes. Brother Andrew, the monk-who-is-not-a-monk. I keep wondering what his interest in all this is." The Scotsman, Andrew Lockheart, had come to the Santa Casa in the guise of a Jesuit, accompanied by a well-known and respected monk, Father Estevão. It was "Brother" Andrew who had brought the *pulvis mirificus* to Gonsção's attention, presumably in a foolish attempt to free Senhor Chinnery from the Santa Casa's dungeons.

It should never have succeeded. But Inquisitor Sadrinho had been so hungry for information about the powder— *No*, thought Gonsção, *perhaps I am truly to blame. If I had not challenged Brother Andrew to resurrect the sorcerer De Cartago, if I had not been so arrogant in believing he would prove himself false . . . perhaps it is fitting after all that I must make this horrible journey.*

"And Tomás keeps looking back toward the entertainer's wagon," Joaquim prattled on. "You know, I think he misses his dancing girl."

"It will pass, I am sure, Joaquim." Gonsção studied the soldier's face but saw no suspicion there. *So Carlos has not told him about the woman Aditi's death. How she flung herself against a sword in the sultan's palace in Bijapur, rather than answer my questions about her involvement in the Goan cabal. What a waste of life. And now her soul must surely burn in Satan's domain* . . . And yet, and yet . . . there were those shadows of memory, dreams from the time when Gonsção himself had crossed to The Other Side. Dreams that in no way resembled what he had been taught to expect. What had Sadrinho called it, the Architecture of the Afterlife— as if Death were a new world, like that beyond the Atlantic Ocean, waiting for explorers to make maps of it? Imaginative cartographers, on maps of New Spain, would draw in monsters in those regions yet unknown. *In the Land of Death I have seen,* thought Gonsção, *how apt such renderings would be. Perhaps such visions were a warning from Heaven, that I was trespassing where I was not meant to go.*

"Padre?"

"Hm? Your pardon, Joaquim. My mind was wandering on . . . distant paths."

"I said I never thought it would be possible that I ever would miss Goa, but you know . . . a night under the palm trees by the Mandovi River sharing a betel cake with a dark-eyed meztica, ah what a sweet thing that seems."

"I understand, Joaquim."

"What is it you miss, Padre?"

Gonsção closed his eyes. "To hear the evening bells of the churches in Lisboa, to smell the fresh wind from the sea." He chuckled. "Odd. After my voyage to Goa, I never thought I would miss the sea."

"Lisboa," Joaquim said, reverently. "That is like a distant dream. I wonder if I will ever see it again."

"As do I," Gonsção said softly.

"Padre . . ." Joaquim looked down at his hands and paused before continuing. "Padre, do you think we will survive this journey? The *muçulmanos,* they are so many and we are so few. And we do not know what we will find, if anything. When I was learning to be a *soldado* in Goa, I believed I was not afraid to die. When I was imprisoned in the Aljouvar, I imagined all sorts of deaths; by the sword, by sickness, by the rope. I was not afraid then either. Perhaps I was going mad, eh? But now, Padre, I find I am afraid."

"That is only sensible in our circumstances, my son, and is no sin. But never despair, or believe that God is not with us. Remember why we are here. Imagine this," Gonsção gestured to indicate the foreigners around them, "oversweeping the world with armies of resurrected dead. This quest is not for our own glory, but to save all of Christendom. God has given us a most weighty task, Joaquim. For the sake of the future of the world, we must prove ourselves worthy."

Joaquim smiled ruefully and nodded. "Your words inspire me, Padre. I thank you. It must be you are not afraid, but, then, you have been . . . you have seen . . ."

"I have been dead, you mean."

"Tomás had said you were only sleeping, but Carlos, he had felt no pulse on you, and seen no breath."

Gonsção placed his hand on the *soldado's* shoulder. "I will not speak of what I have seen, for that is not for living man to know. But as for the question in your heart, there is nothing for you to fear in death, my son."

Joaquim's eyes widened and he sighed. "Thank you. Thank you, Padre. That takes a great heaviness from me."

There came a great rustling around them as the Mughuls rose from their prayers. The world seemed to come alive again with the cries of animals and the babbling of men.

"I am glad, my son. Feel free to speak with me whenever you wish about whatever troubles you. Now, I detect the scent of dinner on the air."

"*Sim,* the smell of their spices is heavenly, is it not, Padre?"

"That is not how I would describe it, but it does make the mouth water. Come, we must not snub the Mirza's hospitality."

Enyo walked slowly through the grove, a waterpot in her hands, the dirt cool beneath her veined and wrinkled feet. Her yellow sari whispered against her legs as she went from tree to tree, beech to oak, myrtle to fir, pouring water at the base of each. It was the dry season in the Deccan, and plants from a faraway land needed care to thrive.

Of all the duties Enyo had in Bhagavati, in service to the despoina, this was her favorite. Here in the grove, her ancient bones did not ache so much, and the air was sweet with scents that reminded her of home. At the center of the grove was an artificial pond, made to resemble a certain sacred mountain lake. If one did not look too hard through the branches, or wander far from the pond, one could forget that the garden was in the midst of an enormous stone palace that had been old even when Enyo, her sister Porphredo, and the despoina had arrived. Here one could imagine the Lady of Beasts still hunted on nights when the moon was but a smile on the dark horizon.

Enyo was startled at the sound of rustling leaves and she looked up. Her tall sister Porphredo came striding through the trees, clad in a sari of dark emerald, face weathered and creased like bark—as if she were a tree come to life. She carried long strips of palm leaf, the sort on which messages were inscribed. Her eyes seemed darker than usual, and her expression was grim.

"There is news from the Dove Tower?" Enyo asked.

"The dove keeper himself flew down to deliver this," said Porphredo.

"Gandharva sends bad news?"

Porphredo gave a solemn nod. "But not without hope, if we hurry. Where is she?"

"In her sanctum. Now is . . . not the time to disturb her."

"It can't be helped. If we are to save Aditi, Stheno must hear this now."

"Aditi? What about our little Aditi?"

Porphredo laid a long-fingered hand on Enyo's shoulder. "Our Aditi is dead, dear sister. Murdered."

"Ai!" Enyo felt her skin and stomach turn cold. "Who would do such a terrible thing?"

"Gandharva did not say."

"Could he not give her the *rasa mahadevi* and restore her?"

"Apparently not. But she is not far, and we might be able to bring her some if Stheno will permit it."

"Surely she must. And yet—the despoina is in one of her . . . moods. I heard she made a mess of Prabaratma's cell this morning. I fear for how she might react."

"Imagine her reaction if we wait and Aditi is thereby lost forever. Come, and you will hear all."

Enyo put down the waterpot with trembling hands and followed her sister to a stone archway that led into the oldest part of the palace. Here, deities too weathered by centuries of rain and wind to be recognizable guarded a dark passage that had been carved out of the black basalt of the mountain centuries ago.

The dry air in the corridor was cool, and scented with earth, cinnamon, and sandalwood. Lit rush tapers placed at intervals along the walls kept the passage from being dark as night. Beneath the tapers were small niches, each containing a stone image of a Hindu goddess; Lakshmi, Parvati, Durga, Sita, Ratri. Here and there, one of the niches would contain an incongruous centaur or harpy.

The two old women padded silently to the anteroom of the despoina's private chamber. The doorway was covered with a curtain of copper and chalcedony beads. A stone tiger, frozen in mid-snarl, stood to one side of the chamber doorway. On the other side, on a marble pedestal, sat a serene bronze bull with a sun disk between its horns. On the wall behind it was an unfinished fresco—only the hands and part of the face of the dancing figure had been fully painted in.

"This is new," said Porphredo.

"Yes," sighed Enyo. "Prabaratma tells me it is a representation of Kali, Goddess of Life, Death and Destruction. I wonder why she has chosen this one. Why now."

"Perhaps you ought to ask her."

"And hear how many more ways she can insult me? No, thank you."

Voices could be heard within the chamber—a man and a woman, speaking the beautiful Kannadan tongue.

"She has company. Alas, we must disturb her." Porphredo stood before the bead-curtain and clapped twice.

"What is it?" snarled the woman within, in Greek.

"News for your ears alone, despoina."

"Come back later."

"It cannot wait."

There was silence a moment, and then the woman murmured a gentle dismissal. The man responded with words of undying love that sounded much like Vedic prayers. Moments later, a young, naked man staggered out through the bead curtain, his face alight with an ecstatic smile that would have shone through his eyes, had he still possessed them. But there were only vacant sockets and scar tissue where eyes should have been.

Enyo sucked in her breath and stepped back to allow the man to pass. *Again,* she thought in sick dismay, *again the despoina permits this. Why will she not let her priests keep their eyes and their distance?*

Porphredo flung the bead curtain aside and stepped into the chamber. Enyo followed, fists clenched on her skirt.

A multipaneled screen of pieced ivory stood in the middle of the chamber. From behind the screen, her voice low and melodious, the despoina said, "So. This news had better be worthwhile."

"Forgive us for disturbing you, despoina," said Enyo.

"I hear disapproval in your voice, mouse. May I not enjoy what few pleasures remain to me? She of the Pointy Helmet may have withered your loins, but mine are still healthful, more or less."

"Unlike that man's eyes."

"It was his choice. Better than his dying for his devotion. I hope you haven't come just to lecture."

Porphredo said, "We would not waste our breath so, despoina. We bring news from Gandharva. Aditi is dead."

There came the sound of a wind before a storm. And the harsh whisper, "Who has done this?"

"We do not know. But you may learn it from your daughter yourself, for her body has been preserved and Gandharva brings it this way. He has smuggled her into the midst of a Mughul army, and in three days' time they should be halfway here from Bijapur. If a messenger goes swiftly with Your Gift, she can be revived with little harm."

"Ah. A Mughul army did you say? Did Gandharva mention an eagle, or a flute player?"

Enyo looked with alarm at Porphredo. The tall crone shook her head and said, "No, despoina. Why do you ask?"

"Merely some things Prabaratma said. It would seem his prophecies may have some truth to them."

"We should send the messenger as soon as possible," Enyo said. "We do not want this army coming close."

"Cease your squeaking, mouse. I will send no messenger."

"But, despoina—"

"I will go myself."

"Despoina," said Porphredo, frowning, "is this wise?"

"This is my daughter we speak of. My gift must be fresh, to best revive her. And I have not left this mountain in uncounted years. And I wish to see this army."

"Despoina—" Enyo began.

"Silence, mouse! Since you have no spine to bear you, you will remain and deal with matters in my absence. Porphredo, you will attend me. That is, if your ancient bones can stand the ride."

"My bones are no more ancient than yours," Porphredo countered, "despite appearances. I will keep up with you."

"Good. We will leave tonight."

Enyo wished she could reach through the screen and shake sense into the woman behind it. "It will take hours, despoina, to assemble a proper escort—"

"There will be no escort. Two can ride faster than many and be less visible. I can defend myself, you know."

"I know. That is what I fear."

"Shush. Be off with you. Porphredo, I will meet you at the entrance to the North Tunnel at full dark. Go about your business, Enyo. I will not have Bhagavati neglected while I am gone. Go!"

Reluctantly, Enyo allowed Porphredo to pull her out through the beaded curtain into the passageway. When they were some steps away from the antechamber, a whisper exploded from her. "This is foolishness! You mustn't let her go. Not when she is in this mood."

Porphredo put her hands on Enyo's shoulders. "There now, sister, I will be there to guide the despoina and make sure she does nothing foolish. She is right, you know. Aditi will have a better chance of returning whole if the *rasa mahadevi* is . . . fresh. Fear not. We will return in no more than seven days. How much harm can even the despoina do in so short a time?"

Enyo glanced back at the fresco of Kali. "I am afraid that is what we may find out."

III

VERVAIN: This herb is also called Enchanter's Plant, and Juno's Tears, as well as Herb-of-the-Cross, for it is said to have grown on Calvary when our Lord was there crucified. Its leaves resemble those of the oak, and are nearly as venerated. The herb has one long stalk which brings forth spears of light purple flowers in late Summer. Vervain tea will heal wounds and soothe ailments of the stomach and spleen. Mixed with wheat or peony root, it will prevent fits. Vervain is ofttimes used to sprinkle holy water and is proof against enchantment. Yet witches also know its powers and use it in charms for foretelling the future....

Thomas sat up on his bedroll, awakened for the third time in the night by the rumble of drums and the cry "Khabardar!" followed by shouts of "Ya!" from Mughul soldiers on the periphery of the army camp. He rubbed his face and said, "Must they do that upon each quarter hour? Between the watch and their prayers, when do these Mughuls ever rest?"

"Mayhap they find it soothing," said Lockheart who sat illuminated by a small oil lamp, clearly not even attempting to sleep.

"Soothing? This din?"

" 'Tis all a matter of what one is accustomed to. Were you disturbed by the calling of the hour aboard the *Whelp?*"

"At first. Then work at sea made me so weary, Neptune himself might have risen from the waves and I'd not waken. But this!"

"The cry means 'Be wary' and it ensures at least some of our expedition are alert and watchful for thieves. One of the Mughuls told me he had heard this region nigh Bijapur was infested with brigands. Though a band would need be desperate indeed to attempt to steal from an imperial army, howsomever small. So you see, the noise means we are protected, and therefore a man might find it soothing."

Thomas sighed. "Leastwise it keeps my nightmares at bay—I cannot sleep long enough to have any. What is that you are studying?" he asked, nodding at the flat piece of burnt bone Lockheart was holding.

"Attempting to divine our future, me lad, through the ancient art of scapulomancy, or spatulomancy as it is called in my homeland. This is a Speal Bone, the shoulderblade of a sheep. When I noticed we had mutton for dinner, I asked the camp cook to give it me."

"Is such augury a part of your pagan worship, Andrew, or merely an idle pastime?"

The Scotsman raised a brow and said, "Mortals have attempted to divine the future from eons past, lad, no matter the land or faith. Fair Dian has shone down upon wiser oracles than I."

Thomas noticed his question had not been precisely answered. "So. Now you are an augur as well as a tradesman, soldier, monk, and priest. Truly, your skills know no bounds. What does your Speal Bone tell you is our fate?"

Lockheart glanced at him with a rueful grin. "I have not the skill of the ancients, mind, and my methods you would not understand. Yet—" He stared down at the bone and his bearded face became blank. "Crossed and crossed again . . ." he murmured.

After a moment's pause, Thomas said, "And what does that portend?"

Lockheart blinked and shook himself. "Eh? Oh. Our path, 'twould seem, is not straightforward, Tom. Expect the unexpected. Events shall not turn as we will them to. The meanderings of a serpent, not the flight of an arrow."

Thomas laughed. "Why, this is no different than what one might hear from a card reader in 'Pauls. Truly the oracular art hath been debased since the age of Apollo."

Scowling, Lockheart said, "I allow that I have not the Delphic skill in poesy and riddles. But you asked what I saw and I have said it. Be content."

"Your pardon. You seem troubled, Andrew."

A rakish grin split Lockheart's burly face. "Aye, and surely there's no cause for that. We are as safe as Jonah in the belly of the whale, are we not?"

Thomas sighed and rolled over, pulling the blanket tighter around him. "I am too weary to match wits with you."

"Far be it from me to duel an unarmed man. Get your rest, Tom. The days ahead will doubtless try our strength."

"Doubtless . . ." Thomas murmured as he closed his eyes.

. . . and found himself in a dark pit, surrounded by fire. He heard the thunder of the beating of enormous wings approaching. *I should not have spoken of my lack of nightmares. 'Twould seem I have summoned one.*

The harpy landed on a rock shelf overlooking the pit, towering over him as a hawk would a mouse. "We have you now, murderer," she shrieked. "You cannot escape!"

"Why do you torment me?" Dream-Thomas cried.

"Fate! It is the fate you have earned, murderer!"

"I have killed no one!"

"Liar! You have and you will again."

"No! There is only my mother who died at my birth—"

The harpy drowned out his words with a horrible screech. The thunder began once more and the harpy smiled with dark ecstasy. "She comes. She will have you, murderer. She for whom beauty and death are one. She comes! Prepare for her arrival!"

The ground beneath him shook, and Thomas shook with it wondering if the earth of the pit would swallow him.

A very different voice cried, "Tomás!"

Thomas opened his eyes to find himself back in the tent, staring up at Brother Timóteo's young, concerned face.

"Tomás! *Salvatisne?*" the boy said in Latin, the one language they shared.

"In waking, I am, though not in sleep," Thomas replied in that same tongue. He sat up and rubbed his face. "It was only the nightmares come again."

"You were yelling things," Timóteo said. "Though I could not understand what you said. You seemed in pain."

"No, Timóteo. My nightly torment is more spiritual than physical. I dream of harpies who call me murderer and threaten death. I have had such dreams since I was a child."

"Harpies!" Timóteo's eyes grew wide with wonder.

Thomas smiled. "Perhaps the Padre was right to discourage you from studying the classic tales. You might find yourself having dreams such as mine."

"No, these dreams you have, they are important! They must be." He looked as though he was about to say something more but held his tongue.

"They visit me so often, I cannot but think they have some importance. Perhaps you can tell me what Christian allegory they represent."

Timóteo looked away. "I . . . I do not know if these are Christian dreams."

Does he begin to doubt his beliefs? He who seemed so unshakable in his faith in the Santa Casa? Or does he believe I have fallen away from mine? Thomas thought it might be wise to change the subject before Timóteo could deliver a sermon. "Did you enjoy your ride on the elephant today, Timóteo?"

"Oh, yes, Tomás! Thank you for convincing the Padre to let me ride it."

"No thanks are necessary. Did the Mirza treat you well?"

"He did. Very well. I do not think these *muçulmanos* can be as evil as the Padre says."

"No doubt the good Padre meant only their beliefs, not the men themselves. Did the Mirza discuss his faith with you?"

"No. We agreed not to while riding the elephant. I tried to tell the Mirza of the glory of Our Lord, but . . . I think I annoyed him. Perhaps I am not yet ready to be a missionary. Or perhaps he is not yet ready to receive the word of God."

Thomas stifled a laugh. "It is good that both of you are patient."

From outside the tent, Thomas heard Padre Gonsção say, "Timóteo? *Es ali?*"

"*Sim*, Padre." The boy stood and went to the tent flap, then turned and said, "Perhaps . . . perhaps the next time you dream, you should ask the harpies . . . ask them about snakes."

"Snakes? Why?"

Timóteo opened his mouth as the Padre called, "Timóteo?"

"*Venho*, Padre! I will tell you later, Tomás. Sleep well."

"Good night." As the boy left, Thomas lay back on his pallet, wondering at the notion of asking his dreams a question, and why it should be about serpents.

"Khabardar!"

"Ya!"

What foolishness, thought Thomas, sourly, as he threw off his blanket and stood. *I will surely get no further slumber this night with such wardsmen to keep it at bay.*

He pulled aside the flap of his tent and a chill wind, armed with dust, smote him across the face. Now that the shouters were silent, Thomas could hear the wind whistling through tent-ropes and clefts of nearby boulders. *'Tis no wonder these heathen believe in restless spirits that haunt the wilderness—the very air of this Deccan is constant in movement.*

The air of dread engendered by the nightmare had not left him, and Thomas felt a need to do something useful. By the light of the camp torches, and a bright crescent moon, he made his way to the entertainer's wagon. *I must not do this often, lest watchful eyes make note. If luck is with me, those who would be watching have had better luck at sleep.*

The entertainer's wagon was a gaudy, gilded, painted ox-carriage provided by the Sultan. It had been furnished with musicians and dancing girls, who entertained in other ways as well. And although the wagon was forced to stay at the edge or rear of the Mughul army column due to Muslim sensibilities, at night it often received many visitors. Thomas was thankful he would not seem unusual by going there at such an hour.

In fact, there were giggles and happy cries, male and female, from inside the gilded wagon as Thomas walked up to it. *How fortunate are they, who can take joy in simple pleasures.* Then he remembered that Aditi lay in her coffin in that wagon, and wondered if she would be offended. *Nay, she was froward enow with me. Belike, she'd be amused, if she knew.*

Thomas hoped he would not have to disturb anyone at their revels, but again fortune was in his favor. The man he sought was sitting outside the wagon, near a campfire whose flames were wind-whipped into frenzied dancing demons among the burning brands. He sat playing softly on a stringed instrument that was mainly a fretboard with a large gourd at each end.

"Gandharva?"

The blind Hindu musician turned his head in Thomas' direction. "*Kawn heh?*"

"It is I, whom you call Tamaschinri," he replied in Greek.

"Ah, the young, mourning lover returns. Your lady is still constant to you, not that she has a choice in her current state."

Thomas wasn't sure how he felt about Gandharva joking in this manner, but decided it meant all was well. He sat down on the dirt beside the musician. "I was restless and could not sleep. My dreams were full of omens of the impending arrival of something mysterious and terrible."

"Were they? Interesting. Do you often have prophetic dreams?"

"I do not know if my nightmares speak of things to come or not. If so, the dire fate they herald is yet ahead of me. I wondered if you had any news of the *rasa mahadevi.*"

"Oh, impatient one. We have been on the road only two days. Depending upon the haste with which the Mahadevi dispatches her gift . . . it is possible it might intercept us two days from now. But more likely three."

"Ah. Will Aditi survive after so long a . . . sleep?"

"She has been well preserved, my friend, swathed in honey and wrapped in bandages steeped in myrrh. She lies in a box sealed from the consuming air. Her revival may take time, but she will be whole, never fear."

"Honey and myrrh," said Thomas. "There was much expense in her preserving."

"Indeed. I spent all that I am worth to the Sultan for her. But I do not mind. She has been a friend in a life where I have had many acquaintances but few friends. And I expect the Mahadevi will repay me, one way or another."

"I owe you as well, though I have nothing with which to repay you."

"No, no, Tamas, you owe me nothing. You arranged for this cart to be here, nai? You are saving Aditi's life—how could I ask more?"

The back door of the entertainer's wagon burst open and three women leaped from the brightly-lit doorway, laughing. With their veils floating behind them like diaphanous wings, Thomas felt a moment of shock, as if seeing the three pursuers of his nightmares become real. But they ran to Gandharva and tugged on his arms, cajoling him in their lilting, musical language.

"If you will excuse me, despotas," said Gandharva with an embarrassed but pleased smile, "it would seem my entertainments are desired elsewhere."

"I would not think of detaining you," said Thomas. He watched as Gandharva was guided, pushed and pulled into the wagon just as Joaquim staggered out.

"Ai, Maria, I picked a good time to leave," said the Goan *soldado*. He stopped, comically open-mouthed upon seeing Thomas.

"Tomás! So you, the holy miracle worker, are here too! Do the angels decline your bed so that you must seek more earthly sport?"

Thomas wondered what the Padre would say to such blasphemy. "You are drunk, Joaquim."

"Of course! The most blessed state of man, to be drunk. Feel free to step inside. I have finished with the lovely Aziza, but I am sure she would not mind more company."

Lie atop a whore beside the corpse of Aditi? I think not. "No, not this night, Joaquim."

"Ah, you still miss your vanished dancing lady from Bijapur, wherever she may be. She has found another, Tomás. You will only forget her if you do the same. There must be one of the lovelies in the wagon who will teach you this."

"Not for me." But Aditi had made him forget his former sweetheart, the daughter of his Master in London. Thomas could now scarce recall what Anna Coulter looked like. *God forbid that I should take another while there is hope that Aditi may yet live again.* Thomas did not wish to be tempted to forget her—he did not wish to learn if he was the sort of churl who could.

"Have you truly chosen the life of a saint, then? I have seen that men who lose a love will renounce the world and all pleasures in it. But such vows are soon enough broken and sin is again allowed to enter their door. Me, I hope to be a fabulous host to sin. Just tonight, I have tasted of drink, and of opium, and of the sweet perfume of women. Let's see . . . how many sins is that?"

"I am skilled at neither mathematics nor theology, Joaquim."

"Well, I am sure it is many, though not nearly enough. If I am to be doomed to Hell, Tomás, I want to enter the flaming portal with great fanfare." The thin, wiry *soldado* stood close to the campfire, the flames casting a strange, ruddy light on his face. He threw his arms out in a dramatic gesture. "Make way for Joaquim

Alvalanca! Sinner of sinners, whose decadence in life knew no bounds! Make way, and be ashamed of your puny attempts at evil!"

Thomas did not know how serious the Goan was, but he still found the speech disturbing. "Joaquim, you have far to go before you achieve such notoriety. You were only a thief."

Joaquim lowered his arms with a heavy sigh. "Ai, even in sinning, I lack the will to greatness. Ah, well." The *soldado* staggered back from the fire. "I have aspired only to be Satan's lapdog. To beg for the burnt crumbs from his sulfurous table. Do you think I reach above myself?"

"I think you reach in the wrong direction. But, surely it is the *arrak* speaking, not you."

Joaquim sat heavily on the ground beside him. "Now you are talking like the good Padre. I will not stay to be preached to, Tomás. Even by a saint-in-training."

"I apologize. I am hardly one to preach."

"Apologize you should, Tomás. My plight is all your fault, you know. It was for this mad expedition that I was pulled from the safety of the Aljouvar and sent to work for the Santa Casa. It is because you worked a miracle on the Padre that I could not return to Goa."

Thomas snorted. "The safety of being hanged, you mean. And is that not what would have happened if you had returned to Goa?"

"Who can say, Tomás? Perhaps another miracle would have happened and the governador would have spared me. Perhaps even now, I would be returning to Lisboa to find that some rich uncle I never knew had died and that I could go back to university and continue my studies."

"Perhaps cows will climb cathedrals and ring their bells."

"Ai, now you are being cynical, and that is not a good way for a saint-to-be to think."

Thomas found himself deeply annoyed at the *soldado*'s words. "I am no saint, nor will I ever be. It was no miracle that the Padre regained his health—"

"And now you are lying, which is even worse, Tomás. Still, I cannot blame you. The saintly are taken into the Kingdom of Heaven early—I have seen it. While the devil, at least, gives his followers some time on earth to enjoy themselves."

"I will hear no more of this," Thomas said, standing. "The morose philosophy of drunken men brings no joy to sober ears."

"Then you should get drunk too, Tomás. Perhaps my babble would sound better then."

"Some other time, Joaquim. Rest you well." Thomas wrapped his arms around himself and walked back toward his tent. The wind had turned colder and he felt within a storm approaching, although there were no clouds and the stars burned terribly bright.

The Mirza Ali Akbarshah, Omrah of ten thousand men and trusted general of the Padshah Emperor Akbar, had been unable to sleep, and so he walked among his men, trying to gauge their mood. Although his Mughul horsemen, those still awake, greeted him with praise and blessings, many of the foot soldiers spared him only a terse nod.

He came to the tent of his lieutenant, Jaimal, and to his surprise, a lamp was still lit within.

"Jaimal? May I enter and speak with you?"

"My lord?" came the startled reply. "Yes, of course."

The Mirza pulled the flap aside and stepped in. Jaimal and another man, whom the Mirza recognized as a lesser officer but whose name he could not remember, both stood and bowed.

"Thank you for your service," Jaimal said to the other man, "and remember all I have instructed. Now leave us."

"My lords," said the officer, and, with a nervous glance at the Mirza, he swiftly departed.

"Many are awake tonight," said the Mirza.

"So they are, my lord. Our expedition flows in a new direction, like a newly changed watercourse. With the unknown obstacles we face, is it any wonder the waters are troubled?"

"It is to be expected, of course," said the Mirza, seating himself cross-legged on the carpeted floor of the tent.

"Would my lord care for some refreshment? I have water and spiced tea."

"I thank you, no." The Mirza noticed, as always, that his lieutenant's *jama* and turban were spotless and quite correct and that his beard was well trimmed. Jaimal had served him well for five years now, but the lieutenant was Shi'ah and the Mirza was Sunni, and this difference in sect had always been an unseen, unmentioned barrier between them. The Mirza's trust had to always be modified with tact.

"That fellow who was just here—is he an example of these troubled waters?"

"In fact, he is, my lord," said Jaimal, seating himself. "His men are camped near the foreigners and he wished advice on how to deal with them."

"What advice did you give?"

"Only that he and his men should keep a respectful distance from the heretics. But observe them carefully. For now."

The Mirza rubbed his beard. "That is advice wise in its caution, and yet I cannot but think that there might be use in becoming better acquainted with these foreigners. Under the guise of friendship, they might be more willing to share their knowledge with us."

"That is assuming," growled Jaimal, "that they have any knowledge of value to us."

"You think they do not?"

"If I may speak freely, my lord, is it not clear to you that the Sultan Ibrahim forced these heretics upon us in order to distract us and lead us astray? If the tales we follow be true, the Sultan would have no wish for our Empire to make alliance with this powerful Queen of Life and Death. These westerners are at best deluded and at worst evil. If you would learn what they know, then, when we are sufficient distance from Bijapur, let us torture it out of them and then kill them."

The Mirza paused. He knew his answer must be cautious for

it is deadly to a commander to appear weak, heedless, or indecisive. "Your thoughts have merit, Jaimal, surely. But consider this—the foreigners were as surprised, and displeased, as we were when we met them at Ibrahim's court. They have no great wish to be with us. The Christian priest who leads them seemed quite sure of himself and his knowledge, and they had no hesitation on choosing the direction to go. I believe they do know things, and ill treatment might only cause them to lie to us. If we are hospitable, as we are taught to be with strangers, they may prove of greater use."

"Surely the All-Knowing has blessed you with wisdom and thoughts of peace, my lord," said Jaimal, "But consider this: what if we are successful and find this immortal Begum Shah? Will the Christian priest not try immediately to sway her to their heresy and win her favor for the west with all manner of silver-tongued lies? You have seen the same yourself when Christians come to the court of Akbar."

The Mirza chuckled. "Yes, but perhaps you do not know the result of such visits. The Jesuit Christians of Goa so bickered and argued amongst each other, in the very presence of the Emperor, that he lost all respect for their faith. It seems the way of these westerners to make fools of themselves. No, I am not concerned that they will impress the immortal Begum Shah."

"Then consider this," Jaimal persisted in a softer, yet more urgent voice, "the strange powder that your Sufi Masum got from that yellow-haired westerner—the one who asked you to let the boy ride on your elephant—it is apparently a poison."

"That does not surprise me. The yellow-hair, Tamas is his name I believe, is an herbalist, as is Masum, and they know many poisons as well as healing herbs. I do not give much credit to their art, but I do not think they intend harm."

"My lord," Jaimal said, leaning toward him, "one of my men has said that one of the whores in the entertainer's cart sent by the Sultan told him a frightening thing. That there is a body of a young woman in the cart, and that the yellow-hair requested that the corpse be brought along so that some infernal ritual of sorcery may be done upon it when the Begum Shah is found."

The Mirza could not restrain his laughter. "Jaimal, Jaimal. You have been a soldier nearly as long as I. Surely you know that gossip and stories spread and grow among men who have nothing to do but march and eat all day? The fact that this tale is traced to the words of a whore shows that it cannot be trusted." The Mirza stood, fearing that to stay would only encourage his lieutenant to tell more gossip.

Jaimal stood also, frowning. "My lord, you would do well to consider what I have said. Many of the men will not long tolerate the presence of these heretics among us."

"They will tolerate it so long as I order it," said the Mirza firmly. "You must see to it that the men understand that we have more to gain, in this instance, from cooperation than from combat. If the foreigners prove themselves to be a hazard or too great a nuisance, then I will reconsider what is to be done with them."

Jaimal bowed. "I will tell them that is your will."

"Good. Now get some rest. More than ever, I will need your vigilance in the days to come."

"I will, my lord. May sleep come to you as well."

The Mirza Akbarshah left Jaimal's tent more troubled than when he had entered. He walked a little farther and saw his Sufi advisor, Masum al-Wadud, sitting alone before a small fire, whittling on what might eventually become a flute. The Sufi's hair stuck out from under his turban and his beard was somewhat unkempt, but the Mirza had learned that Masum was not a thoughtless man. Merely, that his thoughts were on things other than himself.

The Mirza was a good man of the Faith, follower of the Law and keeper of the Five Pillars, but he was not a philosopher by nature. Yet since traveling from Lahore in search of a folktale, he had seen, in a shrine, a human hand made of stone—so detailed that he knew it could only have been made by a miracle, or great sorcery. Either possibility filled the Mirza with dread, and so he kept Masum with him, despite his endless Sufi tales and his odd viewpoint that sometimes seemed to approach madness. Should the tales prove true, the Mirza knew he would need someone who could see what he could not.

"So, you, too, cannot sleep, Masum."

The Sufi looked up with a smile. "Since becoming a *murid,* my lord, I have had little need for sleep. But what brings you wandering this way?"

The Mirza sat on a rock beside him. "I do not know. An . . . unsettled feeling. A commander learns to know when all is not well with his army. I felt it after we left Ahmadnagar. It is even stronger now."

Masum nodded. "They are far from home in unfamiliar lands."

"And without a clear goal," sighed the Mirza, "and with strangers among them. Does it not bother you to have these heretics traveling with us, Masum?"

"The presence of a flawed gemstone only makes the wonder of the perfect gemstone more apparent."

"Yes, of course. But many of these men are not so observant."

Masum nodded again. "They do not see the light within the dark."

The Mirza shifted uncomfortably. "Er, yes. Already they spread rumors amongst each other that the foreigners are sorcerers who lead us to our doom. That yellow-haired one you have spoken with—do you think he is a sorcerer?"

Masum took a deep breath and closed his eyes. "He is a seeker of knowledge, and one who has come to know suffering and has himself suffered. He has touched Power, yet, I do not see in him one who wields power for its own ends."

"But if he is a seeker of knowledge, might he not be striving for sorcerous power? If we seek a Queen of Life and Death, might he not attempt necromantic rites to find her?"

Masum chuckled. "My lord has been listening to stories born of ignorance and fear. The Great Sophia will not be found in such a manner. Besides, I think the young westerner does not know what he seeks."

The Mirza looked up at the black vault of the night sky, bright stars visible despite the smoke and light from the little fire. "If only I could have something tangible to inspire the men, and distract them from their fears—a sign."

"What of the hand in the tomb of the nameless *shahid?*"

"Remember Jaimal thought it a fake and the work of a faithless rogue. No, I need something even he will accept. If he believes, the other men will as well."

"The Age of Miracles is past, my lord. But we shall see wonders, I have no doubt of that. Can you not smell it in the wind, my lord? Our destiny approaches."

The Mirza breathed in, but smelled only woodsmoke, and dust, and the offal of animals. "I must trust that your senses are keener than mine, Masum."

Porphredo waited in the dim tunnel, her horse shifting uneasily beneath her. Her saddle was well padded to soothe her old bones, but still she was aware it had been a long while since she had ridden. She did not want to remember how many years precisely . . . the answer too often arrived in terms of decades, or worse.

At last there appeared a greater darkness in the shadows with the scent of sandalwood and rosewater. "Why was I kept waiting?"

"People had to be moved from the tunnel, for their safety, despoina."

"There were people in the tunnel? Why?"

Porphredo waited as the despoina, swathed in black from head to toe, rode up beside her on a pale grey horse. "Because they live here, despoina."

"Living here? These tunnels are for Bhagavati's defense. Who has permitted such a thing?"

As they proceeded down the tunnel, the horse hooves softly

clopping in the dust, Porphredo noted by the dim rush light a discarded doll beside the rocky wall, a copper bracelet, and other items showing the denizens' panicked departure. "I think no one permitted it, but perhaps the new young mayor looked the other way."

"Then he shall not be mayor long. Foolishness! Who would want to live here, in such darkness, in any event?"

"I would ask that you not judge the mayor so soon, despoina. These people moved in here from necessity, not desire. Our city has been prosperous and your people have thrived. All too well."

"What do you mean? Were these tunnel-dwellers driven out by their families?"

"Only by their numbers. They moved here because there was no space elsewhere."

"Could they not build another story on their houses?"

"They have done so, despoina, until the houses are unsafe. And they dare not encroach further on what little farmland there is in the mountain bowl."

"Why did you not tell me of this, Porphredo?"

"You may recall I did, despoina. Was it . . . two years ago? You were studying Tantric philosophy at the time and didn't wish to be bothered."

"Do not take that disapproving tone with me, Porphredo. My sister proved that if a mortal can look upon her or me with pure love and without fear, he will not die. Is not the search for such a love worth the study of centuries?"

"But was it worth so many teachers' lives?"

"They are not dead."

"They might as well be, adorning your cellars as they currently do. You know you will never revive them all."

"Shush. In an immortal life, who can say what I might do?"

"Who, indeed? Do you still hate Euryale after all these years for finding what you have not?"

"What nonsense. How can I hate her, when it was she and her lover who gave me hope?" She clicked her tongue. "What a stink there is in here. And look how they have dug into these walls! An army could come through here! This cannot be permitted. These people must be moved back into the city."

"We cannot, despoina. There is no room."

"What?"

"I had tried to suggest that you allow some families to move to the village beside the river at the foot of the mountain."

"That cannot be allowed, Porphredo. The growth of the village would be noticed, bringing others snooping into the area."

"It seems to me that this very journey we are taking is because some are coming 'snooping.' We have not kept ourselves hidden very well. Particularly when you insist upon meddling in foreign affairs."

"Why did I ever choose such a nagging old crone as you for my travelling companion?"

"Because we have been together since childhood?"

"A curse of the gods worse than Athena's."

"You forget I am cursed also, despoina."

"At least mortals can look at you. Not that they would wish to see your leathery, lizard-like face."

"My lady is too kind, as always," Porphredo said, dryly.

"Since you pride yourself on being wise, you may come up with some other solution to where these people can go."

"I have one simple one."

"Well?"

"You will not like it."

"I like little of what you say. What will it matter?"

"Very well. Your palace takes up one quarter of the mountain's bowl—"

"Our palace! You would move these . . . unwashed, overbreeding creatures into my home?"

"One wing of the palace alone would house twenty families in great comfort, despoina."

"Ah, yes, but how long would they stay there, eh? Would they not have more and more children, and bring in their animals and their relatives until I am squeezed into a tiny area, afraid to move?"

Porphredo sighed. "You need not give up such freedom—"

"I will not discuss it any further. I knew I should not have asked you. Sometimes I think you live only to discomfort me."

There came a rumble ahead of them as the outer door was rolled aside, revealing a sky filled with stars and a breeze that smelled of the desert.

I believe I live, despoina, thought Porphredo, *in order to save you from yourself.*

IV

SAGE: This herb has wrinkled, green leaves and brings forth violet blooms in late summer. This plant is thought a great safeguard to health, that some have said to have sage in one's garden will keep away all illness, and do much to prolong life. Sage tea will strengthen the liver and cure the headache. Mixed in a tincture with vinegar, it will ward off the plague. As with the rosemary, it is said sage will thrive only where a woman rules the house. Others say the herb will reflect a man's fortunes, thriving at his success or withering with his fall....

Enyo wrapped her *shal* tighter around her ancient shoulders against the predawn chill as she padded toward the despoina's quarters. The palace seemed silent and empty.

Only three days has it been since Porphredo and the despoina have gone Outside, and already this place feels like a mausoleum. Porphredo said she was going to suggest to the despoina that some families be allowed to live here. I hope the despoina agrees—then these corridors might be filled with laughter and pleasant chatter instead of this deadening silence. Even the bleating of animals, such as the goats she despises, would be a relief.

Enyo walked quickly through Stheno's chamber, not wishing to see the carelessly strewn clothing and coins and trinkets. *She is like those birds who collect bright baubles in their nests, though they have no understanding or care of what they gather.* She paused a moment at the back of the chamber, thinking she heard a rustle amongst the debris. But in the dim light cast by a nearby rush wick, she could see nothing. *One of her pets, no doubt,* Enyo thought. She was tempted to scare it away for none of Stheno's pets, animal or human, ever lived long, at least in the flesh.

Enyo took the rush wick down from the wall and moved a carved-ivory screen aside. Behind it was a simple wooden door, now rarely used. Enyo turned the wood latch and pushed it open.

The small, dark, windowless room beyond held only a plaster statue of the Hindu warrior goddess, Durga, sitting astride a tiger, each of her many hands holding a bloodstained weapon. The statue was old and the plaster was cracked, the faded paint flaking. It was also hollow, and Enyo easily moved it aside.

Behind the statue, dusty stone stairs led down into darkness. Holding the rush wick high in one hand, and the skirt of her sari in the other, Enyo descended. This was the ancient heart of the palace, the center of the original temple that had been old when Stheno and Enyo and Porphredo had arrived so many centuries before. Enyo could not remember to which deity the original temple had been dedicated. The local priests had not minded when Stheno arrived and took the temple for her own, and swallowed it up with her sprawling palace. The place had a sacredness in and of itself, the priests believed. It did not matter to them which avatar of the Great Goddess dwelled there.

Enyo, however, had always felt somewhat disturbed by that sacrilege. All too well, she remembered what invaders had done to the temple of her home village, and the sorrows to which that had led.

The stone stairs curved gently, following the rounded wall of the deep subterranean room. At the bottom lay a circular dirt-floored chamber, preternaturally cool and more silent than the palace above. Across the chamber from the end of the stairs stood another statue—but this one was made of weathered stone, and was even older than Enyo, or the despoina herself.

It had been part of the temple of their village, back when Enyo, Porphredo, and Stheno had been mere mortals, living simple lives. When the curses had fallen and they had fled, only this was brought with them, a reminder of their past.

It was not a graceful image. The female figure depicted was squat, large-hipped, and full-breasted. Her tunic was short and plain. To either side of her were crudely carved leopards. Her plump face was split with a grin, and her tongue protruded from between wide lips. Her belt was two intertwined serpents and she had snakes for hair.

Enyo crouched and placed the rush wick in a post hole off to one side. Then she slid forward on her knees and held out her hands, palms upward, toward the statue.

"O Medusa, Lady Of Beasts, for whom the sister of my despoina was named, and for whom she died; You, for whom my youth and that of my sisters, was stolen, hear me. Spare my despoina from the madness that again threatens her. Whisper wisdom to her, that she will not destroy as she has in the past. Guide her—"

"Ah, the heart of the earth," whispered a voice in Sanskrit. It echoed through the room such that Enyo at first thought it came from the statue itself. She turned swiftly and saw Prabaratma standing at the bottom of the stairs, his hand lightly touching the wall.

"You startled me, holy one!" said Enyo. "How did you get in here?"

"I saw your light," said the old priest. "I followed the sound of your footsteps. I felt drawn here." His sightless gaze was turned to peer at the stone wall as if he could see through it.

"I do not think Stheno would want you here. This is a very private place."

The Brahmin tilted his head another way, considering this. "Ah. It is offensive for a mortal such as I to be here?"

"It is not that. Only, Stheno has secrets she does not wish everyone to know." *But why do I bother to protect her? He is blind and cannot see the statue, and Stheno has not been here herself in centuries.*

The priest tilted his head again. "There is another presence here."

Enyo rose to her feet, startled, and looked around. "We are alone, holy one."

"No. Someone is there." He pointed at the statue.

"Oh. It is only a stone likeness, holy one. Perhaps the light from the rush wick made you think it was alive."

"She speaks," said the priest. Rolling his eyes heavenward, he began to softly chant, "She, the Earth, whose golden breast is the forest and meadow of all living creatures, who brings forth fire and mates with the Bull—"

"What is this you are saying, holy one?" Enyo's hands trembled.

"It is from an ancient *veda* I learned as a young man. Is it not appropriate?"

"It is very appropriate, holy one. This statue is of the Lady of Beasts. She was worshipped by my people a very long time ago."

"Ah. I have not heard of this avatar. Should I make *puja* to her?"

"No, I . . . that is, you will have to ask *Stheno* when she returns."

"This likeness resembles She whom we serve, does it not?"

How can he know this if he does not see? "Um, yes, holy one, in a few ways."

But the priest had closed his eyes once more and was swaying, humming to himself. The echoes of his voice in the chamber circled back upon themselves in random discord and harmony, building a sound that made Enyo's hair stand on end.

"Holy one, please stop!"

Prabaratma sighed. "She has heard you. She is bringing about the renewal you seek. In time, in time."

Enyo had often heard the despoina wonder aloud if Prabaratma were mad. Porphredo had no doubt of it. *But what if he can hear the voices of gods?* Enyo found this thought terrifying. "Please, holy one, let us ascend."

"In thought or in spirit? Show me the way, immortal one, and I will follow."

"In the flesh, holy one, if you please." Enyo scooped up the rush wick and gently grasped Prabaratma's arm, tugging him toward the stairs.

The priest meekly allowed himself to be moved, but his mind seemed to be elsewhere again. "Like the graceful deer, She charms the tiger into approaching Her."

"Who does?" said Enyo.

"She whom we serve."

As Enyo guided the Brahmin up the stairs, she grumbled, "Tigers eat deer."

"Yes, and in such sacrifice, the deer nourishes the beauty of the tiger. Our Lady shows her beauty in such courage."

Enyo shut the wood door at the top of the stairs behind them and latched it. "Stheno does not seek death. She seeks love. She has spent the last several centuries at it."

"In Kali, they are both sides of the same whole."

"Do not speak that name! Stheno is not such a monster!"

"Not now. But she has been. And will be again. The cycle is turning."

"Not if I can do anything to stop it." Sickened, Enyo brushed by the old priest and hurried on her way.

Padre Antonio Gonsção entered the tent of the Mirza Akbarshah, followed by the three Goan soldiers, Brother Timóteo, Brother Andrew, and Tomás Chinnery. They had been summoned to share a midday meal with the Mughuls, and while the Padre was pleased to be out of the sunlight, he did not anticipate this meeting with joy.

They were now four days out of Bijapur—four days of dust and barren wilderness in the midst of foreign heathens. Gonsção was beginning to understand certain Biblical stories better and wondered if this time of trial would have been bearable if he did not have a profound sense of purpose. And while the Mirza seemed a just and reasonable man, he was of a people whose ways Gonsção had little understanding of, and of a faith he had been taught from childhood to distrust.

The Mirza was seated in the dim recesses of the tent, along with his second-in-command and, the Padre was dismayed to see, the unkempt Sufi mystic. There were other Mughul soldiers toward the back of the tent, but the Padre could not determine how many.

"*Al salam alekum,*" said the Mirza, inclining his head.

"*Walekum al salam,*" replied Brother Andrew.

"What does his greeting mean?" Gonsção said softly to the Scots monk.

"He says peace be on you, and I replied the same to him."

"Ah. I notice he does not stand to receive us."

"Perhaps his men would be offended by such courtesy to heretics. I advise that you overlook the slight, Padre."

"As you say. I am too sapped by the heat to make argument."

The Mirza extended his hand and swept his arm in an arc to indicate the pillows set beside a low table in front of him. Gonsção understood the gesture and, inclining his head just as little as the Mirza had, he went to one of the pillows and slowly, awkwardly, eased himself into a cross-legged position. *What I would not give to sit in a good, plain, sturdy chair again.*

The Goan soldiers, Joaquim, Carlos, and Estevão, all sat to Gonsção's right, plopping themselves beside the pillows with clumsy ease. Andrew, Timóteo, and Tomás sat to his left, with greater grace and caution. Gonsção noted that a glance of recognition passed from the Mirza to Tomás, bringing new suspicions to Gonsção's awareness. *It is as if they have encountered one another somewhere other than the audience with the Sultan. But when would they have had the chance? While I was trying to interrogate the dancing woman? And why should they have reason to talk? I should ask Tomás . . . but would it do any good? Would he not simply lie, as he has so often?*

The Mirza clapped his hands twice and women entered,

bearing platters with refreshments. The women were decorously covered from head to foot in veils, but the cloth was the flimsiest, sheerest stuff and might as well not have been there at all. Carlos and Joaquim called out the girls' names, speaking lewd comments that made Gonsção glad their hosts did not comprehend Portuguese. The Mirza and his advisers showed no sign of noticing. *How can there be any hope for Christendom in this land, when men allow themselves to be such poor examples?*

He felt a tap on his knee. "Padre," said Brother Andrew softly, "if you please, cover your bare feet within your robe. The sight of them is offending to our hosts."

"What can they expect, when we must remove our shoes upon entering?" But Gonsção observed that the Mughuls had, indeed, artfully arranged their clothes, or sat or knelt in such a way that their feet were not visible. *And how difficult it is to set a good example, when local custom is so perplexing.*

The women set before the Goan party ewers of water that had been flavored with lemon and cloves, and trays of dried fruit and flat bread that had onion and garlic baked into it. The women then picked up large fans of palm leaves on long poles and stood at the sides of the tent, wafting the air. Gonsção could not decide whether such warm, close artificial breezes, redolent with the scents of their perfumes, made it cooler or even warmer than before.

"Padre, the Mirza asks if we have been comfortable in our travel."

"Hmm? Oh, please tell the Mirza that the tents, bedrolls, and horses supplied by Sultan Ibrahim are serving us very well. The food provided by the Mirza's cooks has been satisfying and healthful although, I must say, it has been a bit too heavily spiced for my taste."

Brother Andrew grinned and spoke to the Mirza. The Mughuls chuckled politely, and the Sufi babbled for a moment.

"Our friend Masum says that spice in food makes it more healthful, for it stimulates the blood and brings the body into balance with the influences of earth, air, fire and water."

Timóteo sat up and said, "My grandfather taught much the same thing! That is why garlic is so good for you, and peppers."

"Yes, but my master has cautioned," chimed in Tomás, "that ill use of spice can disturb the stomach and overheat the blood, and therefore care must be taken in how much is used, and in what combinations."

As Brother Andrew translated these for the Mughuls' sake, Gonsção let his mind wander, as it seemed more wont to do since his revival. It was as if his spirit had been poorly rejoined with his body and his intellect, and he was less willing to focus upon the unimportant.

Therefore he was not aware how much time had passed before he heard Brother Andrew again speaking in his ear. "Padre, did you hear me? The Mirza is asking a most important question."

"Eh? Pardon me, I was distracted by other matters. Please say again."

Brother Andrew sighed with overtried patience. "He points out that we have been on the road for three and a half days and that he is ready to send his scouts forward. But he needs to know what signs they should be looking for, in what direction. He hopes that we have some information to supply on this."

"Oh." Gonsção did all he could not to look in Tomás's direction. He slowly set down the porcelain cup in his hand, knowing he must not divulge how much, or how little, they truly knew. "Has our source revealed to you any signs that I may pass on to our hosts?"

"Our source," said Brother Andrew, his gaze straight ahead, "has been no more forthcoming to me than to you."

"Then I fear we must tell the Mirza that we have nothing to offer him at this time."

"Padre," Brother Andrew said in low but forceful tones, "I pray you, let this not be our answer! Let us lie if we must, but do not snub the Mirza's request in this way. It will only add to their distrust of us."

Gonsção noted a scowl was already beginning to form on the

Mirza's thin, handsome face, to match that already in full bloom on his lieutenant's.

"Hmmm. Yes, I have learned how silence or evasion leads to mistrust. Very well, let me think." Gonsção closed his eyes and tried to visualize the map that had been drawn by the sorcerer De Cartago. Gonsção regretted that he had not taken the time to study it more while it had been in his possession. *But how could I have known the* inglês *would steal it from me on my deathbed?*

The map had been too simple, consisting of only three dots, some wavering lines, and symbols in each of the corners. When one held it a certain way, it became clear that one line was the coast of India, and therefore one dot represented Goa. The *inglês* had supplied the information that the middle dot was Bijapur. By that orientation, the third dot was to the south and west, beneath another waving line. Another coast? Gonsção had no idea and did not wish to seem an utter fool or liar in the Mughul's eyes. And he could not consult Tomás at this moment, which would give away exactly who was the important, unexpendable, member of the expedition.

As he heard restless shifting around him, Gonsção considered the symbols on the map. The one in the lower right corner was a crown with four blue lines radiating from it. Brother Timóteo had said it reminded him of some Hindu deity. . . . "Timóteo, do you recall that symbol I showed you on De Cartago's map, the crown with the four blue lines? What it meant to you?"

"Oh, yes, Padre. That would be a symbol of Krishna, the God of love. My mother told me about such things, although she is a good Christian."

"Krishna!" said the Sufi, and he babbled excitedly to the Mirza.

"Well," said Brother Andrew, "I must congratulate you, Padre. Apparently there is a river by that name, flowing south of here, west to east."

Out of the corner of his eye, Gonsção noticed the *inglês* Tomás staring at Timóteo. *What does it mean? Are we wrong, or all too right?*

"The Mirza asks what to do in regard to this river."

"Tell him we must continue south and east until we reach it."

"And then?"

"More will be divulged when we reach it."

"Padre . . ."

Gonsção sighed. "Let him know that our party is in . . . disagreement as to how much we can reveal and when. Tell him I must have time to consult with all of you and convince you that full cooperation is best."

"A good strategy, Padre. Shall I argue with you to make it more plausible?"

"I think you have argued enough. Just say it."

The Scotsman nodded and began translating, hesitating here and there with dark glances at Gonsção. The Mirza waited and stroked his beard pensively before replying in firm, grave tones.

"The Mirza understands. But he reminds us that Sultan Ibrahim enjoined us to have fair dealings, for our mutual survival. With so many men as his responsibility, the Mirza's patience is limited. He will not take kindly to being tricked or misled. They have no wish to come so far only to become lost in the wilderness."

Gonsção bowed. "Tell His Highness we, also, have no wish to have traveled so many miles for nothing, and our quest is quite serious. I will give him all the assistance I can, when I am permitted to do so."

"He suggests, then, that we begin our deliberations at once, so that he may sooner have the information he needs. He says we may have until tonight after evening prayers to resolve our differences."

"Padre, a word, if you please," the *inglês* Tomás hissed toward him.

The Scotsman growled at Tomás in what Gonsção presumed to be English.

Gonsção caught Brother Andrew's arm. "No, let him speak."

"Padre," the young man was clenching and unclenching his fists, "let it be tomorrow before we give answer."

"Why?"

"Because . . . because the sign we are waiting for may not come before then. You must trust me on this."

Gonsção raised his brows. *What is he planning for tomorrow, I wonder?*

"Shall I tell the Mirza that, Padre?" said Brother Andrew.

"Very well. Let us see if he is at all agreeable to it."

Before Brother Andrew was finished, there began an uproar among the Mughuls, which the Mirza cut short with a shout. When he spoke again, the Mirza's countenance was dark as thunder.

"The Mirza says such a delay is unacceptable. His men are already impatient, and he will not add to their discomfort. We may have until after the prayers at sundown tonight. If we have nothing more to offer at that time, then he will be forced to reconsider our usefulness to them."

"So. He makes himself very clear." Gonsção looked at the young *inglês* who seemed even paler than before. "Let us depart his company now so that we may begin our deliberations at once."

"He gives us leave to go."

Gonsção stood and bowed, grateful to no longer be kneeling. The Goan *soldados*, hands on their swords, stood around him. Brother Andrew offered lengthy, mellifluous words of either thanks or propitiation. Gonsção noted Tomás exiting the tent with haste. Gonsção caught up with him quickly.

"So, Tomás. You now see how being secretive can cause difficulties."

The young man turned and faced Gonsção. "Is that something you have learned in the Santa Casa, with its Rule of Silence?"

Gonsção felt anger flare in him. "Let us leave that office of the Holy Mother Church out of this. You may care little for me or those whom I serve, but have a thought for Timóteo and the other Goans who have been swept up in affairs you have set in motion. All our lives lay in the trust you ask us to give you. Perhaps even your own. So. What is this sign that you are awaiting?"

The young man ran his hands through his straw-colored hair. "I would tell you if I could, Padre, but I cannot. I do not know what it will be, what form it will take."

"Then how will you know this sign when it appears?"

"I will know." He strode off quickly into the midst of the army camp.

Gonsção turned to the *soldado* Joaquim. "Follow him. Watch him. Find out if he is getting or giving information from any other source. If we can learn nothing by this evening, we shall have to come up with a plausible lie."

"*Sim*, Padre," said the wiry *soldado*, scratching his beard. "You know, I have often seen him at the entertainer's wagon, yet he takes none of the women there. He just chats with the blind musician and asks him for some of his horrible music."

"Interesting," said the Padre. "Take note of his trips to the wagon then, and this blind musician."

Thomas walked swiftly back toward his tent, trying not to look toward Gandharva's wagon. He wrapped his arms tightly around his chest as though it were cold, even though the sun was scorching his head and shoulders. *What a wretched tangle I have made, more useless than the web of a drunken spider. What if the messenger Gandharva awaits does not come tonight? What lies shall I concoct to stay the Mughul knives from all our throats? I never read De Cartago's map and do not know the clues he laid thereon. In truth, the Padre knows more than I. I would pray for guidance, yet I know not Whom to ask, nor Who should answer.*

He heard heavy footsteps behind him and Lockheart said, "Whither goest, Tom?"

"Where no trouble may be seen, if there be such a place."

"None I know of," grumbled Lockheart. "Thomas . . ." the Scotsman put a hand on each of Thomas's shoulders and gently spun him around. "Tom, I will gladly be of aid to thee. My tongue is practiced at dissembling, as you have noticed. Only give me some small crumb of truth and I shall bake thee a cake from it. But I cannot build upon nothing."

Thomas sighed, "Alas, Andrew, I've nought to tell you. We await a messenger from Aditi's home, but I know not whom that will be or when he will arrive, or by what means the *rasa mahadevi* will be delivered."

"But that *vina* player knows, does he not? Mayhap I should go and force him to sing us a tune—"

"No! We must not give sign that he is our hope, else the Padre and Mughuls alike will be down on him like hounds on a fox. No, if the messenger is not timely, then we must concoct a story on our own, with what little we know."

"Very well," said Lockheart, releasing Thomas's shoulders. "I'll set myself to this impossible task. I pray you think on it as well. We must make our tongues and wits sharp as swords to beat back the Mohammedan blades."

Thomas nodded. "Aye. I shall think hard upon it."

"Do so." With a glance of baleful warning, Lockheart turned and strode away.

Thomas returned to his tent to ponder and wait out the long, hot hours.

Porphredo picked her way down the rock-strewn gully toward the camp of the Mirza Akbarshah. She had left her horse behind with Stheno, as the sight of an old woman on horseback might confuse the Mughuls as to her status and wealth. In truth, she found it a relief to again be on foot, even on uncertain ground. Her bones ached in unaccustomed places and her back was weary. *Alas that one might have eternal life, but not eternal strength.* Stheno had insisted upon riding as long and as fast as the health of the horses would permit. *My health, of course, did not concern her in the slightest.*

The turbanned watchman at the periphery of the Mughul camp stood suddenly at Porphredo's approach. "Who are you?"

No doubt he was astonished to see a tall, elegant, elderly woman wearing a glittering sari of lapis blue silk, and a *shal* of woven silver studded with small sapphires, and a heavy bag slung at her hip. Porphredo bowed and addressed the guard in High Court Persian. "Forgive this lowly woman for disturbing your watch, O He With The Eyes Of a Hawk."

He looked wildly around, as if trying to see where she came from, and if there were others like her. "What . . . what is it you want, honored grandmother?"

"I am here to redress a shame, O watchful one. My grandniece has run away to join an entertainer's wagon which follows this army, in the company of a known scoundrel, a blind *vina* player named Gandharva. You see I come alone, on foot, in penance, praying to Allah the Merciful, for forgiveness for the shame she has brought upon our family. I would be grateful if you would tell me where to find this wagon, so that I may properly chastise this grandniece and the scurrilous musician who brought her here."

The watchman chuckled. "He Who Watches was merciful indeed, that you were not set upon by Thuggee, dressed as you are. But I know the very scoundrel you mean, honored grandmother, and the wagon he rides in. It is not far. I will guide you to it myself."

Porphredo bowed again. "That would be a great kindness, sir. I thank you."

It was clear the watchman was happy to have a respite from boredom and gleefully told her tales he had heard about the heathen scoundrel Gandharva as he led her to the wagon. Porphredo noticed that Gandharva had managed to get the wagon positioned at the southern edge of the camp, beside a stand of tamarind trees. *Good. Stheno will be able to hide herself.*

"Here we are, honored grandmother. Tell me the name of your wayward grandniece and I will bring her out to you."

Porphredo put on her sternest expression. "I will not speak that name, lest I bring more shame upon our family. Bring me the musician, if you please, and I will deal with him."

Laughing, the watchman said, "As you will, grandmother." He flung open the doors to the gaudy ox-carriage, and in a moment was dragging out Gandharva by the collar of his *jama*. "Hey-o, you wretch, here is an ancient one you have dishonored! You had better plead your case well." He flung the poor, bewildered musician to his knees before Porphredo. "Here he is, grandmother."

"I thank you, and now please go. What I have to say to him no woman should be heard saying."

With loud chortles, the watchman bowed and strode back to his position.

"Wh-who do I have the honor of addressing?" asked Gandharva.

"The very scoundrel I was seeking," said Porphredo in Persian. Then, in Greek, she added, "It is I, Porphredo. I see your reputation has not faltered since you last graced our palace."

Gandharva sat up and bowed, smiling. "Despoina Porphredo. It is a great honor that the Mahadevi sends you, her very handmaid, to bring us the *rasa mahadevi.*"

"Oh, better than that, Gandharva. Stheno has come herself to administer her gift."

Gandharva's mouth dropped open and he turned his head this way and that. "The Mahadevi? She is here?"

"She is in hiding at the moment, fear not. She wanted Aditi to have the surest chance of recovery. And she wanted to see what army this is that approaches Bhagavati. And I think she was eager to get Outside for a while."

"She . . . she does not intend to stop the Mirza's army with her powers, does She?"

"I expect that will not be necessary. We have a plan to confuse and mislead them so they become lost on their own."

The musician sighed with relief. "That is wise. Oh . . . there is one you must meet. The one who helped me arrange that Aditi come with this expedition. He is a foreigner, who comes seeking the Mahadevi, and I believe he has been Aditi's lover. We owe him our gratitude."

"Very well. So long as it is only one man."

"Yes. He has learned the power of the *rasa mahadevi,* though he does not know its source. He has even used it."

Porphredo frowned. "Did you teach him this?"

"No. Apparently he learned it from a Goan named De Cartago. Your arrival is timely, Porphredo. This foreigner is in need of a sign. The Mughuls, believing that the Goans know more than they do, are demanding that the Goans tell them where the kingdom of the Queen of Life and Death lies. They need to know by sunset tonight."

"I see. Timely indeed. This may give me a very good chance to speak to the Mirza and turn him from his path."

"An excellent thought! I will send you to this foreigner at once, and he can take you to the Mirza."

Thomas was awakened out of a leaden nap by the voice of a girl chattering outside his tent. It sounded as though she were trying to speak Greek. "Despotas!" she began, then trailed off into nonsense.

Apparently Brother Timóteo had been nearby, for his voice joined hers. "Tomás! Your messenger has arrived, she says."

Thomas leaped from his bedroll and flung open the tent flap. He saw the wagon girl standing beside a most extraordinary elderly woman, dressed in native garb of blue and silver. She was taller than Thomas, and thin, but with an almost regal bearing. Thomas could believe that the dark eyes in her tanned, deeply seamed face might have witnessed the passage of centuries.

Thomas bowed to her in the Hindu fashion, and said in Greek, "Greetings, despoina. Are you . . . the messenger from the Queen of Life and Death?"

The old woman inclined her head and said, "I am Porphredo, handmaid of the one called the Mahadevi." Her smooth Greek was that of a native speaker, although she had an unusual accent.

"Your arrival is most timely. Are you . . . a relative of Aditi?"

An ironic smile quirked the edges of the woman's thin lips. "No, although I helped to raise her."

"Ah." He found himself momentarily at a loss for words, so impressive was her countenance.

She looked Thomas up and down as if taking his measure. "You are from the north, nai?"

"I am, despoina. From a place the Romans called Londinium."

She raised her brows. "You are far from home."

"Indeed, despoina. Very far."

"I understand we have you to thank for saving Aditi."

"I did what I could to make her revival possible."

The old woman nodded. "You will be rewarded."

Joaquim came up to stare at the visitor. "Who is this old witch?" he said in his scholar's Latin. "She looks like a lizard transformed to a human."

Porphredo's dark eyes glittered and she responded in Roman Latin, "You are partly correct, centurion, for I have, indeed, been transformed."

"Ai . . ." Joaquim stepped back, startled.

"This is the messenger I have been awaiting, Joaquim," said Thomas, "and you will speak to her with respect. She is the one who will help us find the Queen of Life and Death."

Joaquim removed his morion helmet and bowed in flamboyant Goan fashion. "Pardon me, Domina. My mouth often moves before my thoughts."

"Fear not, centurion. I have been called worse."

"If the despoina would be so kind," said Thomas switching back to Greek, "the reward I ask is only this. The Mirza who leads this army demands from our party knowledge of the location of your hidden city. It matters not to me if you tell him the truth or not, but he must hear something and it must be convincing, else I fear for our lives. If you would do this, I would be most grateful."

The old woman nodded once. "I have been apprised of your

situation, and I will be pleased to speak with the Mughul commander."

Thomas sighed, silently blessing Gandharva and all the Fates. *Now the Mirza will have his information and we will no longer be in danger. Once again my fortune is better than I deserve, but at least no man will die for my mis-steps.*

Thomas turned and saw Timóteo standing open-mouthed beside him. "Don't you be rude as well. Bow to Domina Porphredo. She is going to save our lives."

Timóteo pointed at her and said, "You are the one with the tooth!"

The old woman stood very still a moment, then smiled a grim smile. "Then you'd best beware my bite, little *flamine.*"

Thomas gently cuffed Timóteo's arm. "Stop this childishness. Now, if you would be useful, go and fetch the Padre and Brother Andrew and tell them to meet us by the Mirza's tent."

"But Tomás!"

"Go."

With a last glance of terrified awe at the old woman, Timóteo took off like a rabbit.

Thomas shook his head and turned back to the visitor. "The Mirza's tent is this way, Despoina Porphredo. If you will please follow."

Porphredo inclined her head and stepped up to walk beside Thomas. Softly she said, "Aditi's revival will be done tonight, after dark. Gandharva says you are an herbalist and have used the *rasa mahadevi* before. We could use your assistance."

"I will happily do whatever I can to help," said Thomas. "Allow me to apologize for the boy's outburst just now. I do not know what he meant."

"You do not?" said the woman with another judging gaze.

"No. He is an imaginative boy, the grandson of a great herbalist himself. He is intelligent and helpful, but I cannot countenance all the things he believes."

Porphredo nodded, saying, "It is wise, not to believe everything one hears."

V

FERN: This plant bears long, green fronds, with golden seeds beneath. It grows best in damp and shadowed places. It is also called Hart's Horn, Rock Brake and St. Christopher's Herb. It is said that on Midsummer's Eve, fern brings forth one golden blossom that can lead one to treasure. Tea made from fern root will cure ailments of the head and chest. A poultice of the leaves will soothe burns and bruises. Sorcerers will not bide in a room where fern root is hidden, though northmen believe fern in the home brings bad fortune. Welshmen believe that to wear fern leaves makes one lose one's way, and to be followed by serpents....

The Mirza Ali Akbarshah walked swiftly back toward his tent.

"It is as I told you, my lord," said Jaimal at his side. "These infidels have no more courage than puppies. Bark at them loud enough and they will roll over and show their neck."

"That or my ultimatum helped them to resolve their differences," said the Mirza. "They have caught us off guard, though. I expected they would delay as long as possible, waiting until after our sunset prayers."

"My lord, we are prepared for treachery. I have taken the liberty of having swords hidden in your tent, should we need them."

The Mirza stopped a moment, about to chastise his lieutenant, when he thought better of it. "Thank you, Jaimal. Although I think even the Goans would not be so foolish."

"Who can say what desperate men will do, my lord?"

"Who, indeed?" said the Mirza, regarding Jaimal a moment before walking on.

He nodded at the guards who opened the tent flaps at his approach and entered. The entire Goan party was standing inside, surrounding someone dressed in blue.

Masum was there already as well, and the Sufi stood at the Mirza's entrance. "My lord," he said, eyes shining. "A most wondrous messenger has come."

"A messenger? What has this to do with the westerners' cooperation?"

"Everything, my lord. Behold."

The Mirza sat upon his cushion in the center of the tent and turned to face the Goans.

The woman in their midst nearly took his breath away. Not for her beauty, for her long, deeply lined face was no handsomer than a camel's. Not for her garments, though her sari was the blue of Kashmiri mountain lakes and her *orhni* was shimmering silver cloth studded with gemstones. But her eyes and her carriage showed much wisdom and assurance. The Mirza knew he was in the presence of someone extraordinary.

With smooth grace unexpected in one so aged as she, the woman knelt and bowed until her forehead nearly touched the rug beneath her. "To the Great Shah of the North, who serves the Kalifah Emperor Akbar, on whom may all blessings of Allah the Praiseworthy fall, my sovereign lady, the immortal Queen Stheno who is known as the Mahadevi, Guardian of the Secrets of Life and Death, sends greeting."

"She speaks like a begum," whispered Jaimal.

"She does," admitted the Mirza. The old woman's voice had some of the husk of age but no tremor. She had spoken in the quaint court Persian of his grandfather's time, and the Mirza fancied for a moment that she might be some lost princess of Babur's palace, mad and wandering in the wilderness. "You are welcome, lady, to my humble dwelling in the desert. If your queen is who you say, then your arrival is a miracle, for my emperor has sent us in search of a begum of that description. Please tell us your name, and where you have come from."

The woman sat back on the heels of her sandalled feet and regarded him with her calm, dark eyes. "My name is Porphredo, Great Mirza Al-Ghazi, and I come from Bhagavati, the Kingdom Hidden in The Mountain. It is there that my lady, Queen of Destruction and Resurrection, holds her court. She has watched your approach from afar, and like the shy maiden pursued by an ardent lover, her heart is warmed by the many hardships you have endured for her sake. Thus, like the maiden won, she wishes to welcome you into her company, and allow you a glimpse of what you have so bravely earned."

The Mirza replied, "Her messenger is sweetly spoken. We are flattered and honored by the greetings of your queen."

"Great Mirza," whispered Masum in his left ear, "do you recall the story told by the keeper of the tomb of the nameless *shahid?* How his ancestor was visited by just such a woman, who brought back the remnant of the saint?"

"You cannot possibly be suggesting she is the same one?" asked the Mirza.

"I cannot know, but she does remind me of it."

"My lord," whispered Jaimal in his right ear. "Notice how the yellow-haired one beams upon her proudly, as if he conjured her himself. And the boy stares at her as if she were a djinn. The priest and the one called Lakart look upon her dubiously. They are not in agreement about this woman. They may have found her in the entertainer's cart and dressed her up to trick us."

"I am aware of that possibility, Jaimal." Aloud to the woman, the Mirza said, "I have no wish to seem uncourteous, Wise Elder, but my lieutenant has pointed out to me that you come alone, with no royal retinue, and in the company of men who might have reason to deceive us. We have, at times, encountered tricksters in our travels, who would have us believe false stories. Again, please forgive my mistrustful nature, but it would be helpful if you could show some proof that you are whom you claim to be."

The old woman inclined her head. "There is no dishonor in your request, mighty prince. My queen herself has sown lies throughout the land to keep secret the whereabouts of her kingdom. She would not have sent me to you without some proof of her powers."

The ancient lady removed the sack of raw silk that hung at her hip. She laid it before her and spread the cloth open to reveal a young mongoose. Its eyes were shut, its paws tucked against its chest. The creature appeared to be dead.

The woman sat back and said, "This poor animal perished but a few hours ago from the bite of a serpent. But through the power of my queen, it shall once again be given life. Do you wish to examine it closely, noble lords? You may convince yourselves that it is truly dead." She gently picked up the brown furry carcass and held it out to Jaimal.

The lieutenant frowned and poked at the mongoose with his finger. Then he pulled a dagger from his belt.

The Goan boy, Timóteo, leaned forward, mouth open in a mute cry of protest.

"Carefully," counseled the woman. "The animal will heal more quickly if you do less damage."

Jaimal lightly stuck the point of the dagger into the haunch of the mongoose. The animal did not bleed and showed no movement. "Yes," he said. "It appears to be dead."

The Mirza declined when the woman offered the mongoose to him to examine. "I shall accept the word of my lieutenant."

But Masum held out his hands to accept the small corpse. He placed his ear against the creature's belly and listened for a time. Gently, he pulled back one eyelid and then the other. With a sigh, he handed the mongoose back to the old woman, his face sad. "Yes. She is dead."

The woman placed the mongoose back on the silk cloth. Then she pulled from her waistband a tiny stoppered vial.

The Goan boy leaned over to the yellow-haired one and

whispered something that included the words *rasa mahadevi.* Masum looked up sharply at them with a pensive frown.

Porphredo carefully pried open the jaws of the mongoose and unstoppered the vial. She poured from it what seemed to be a dark liquid into the animal's mouth. Then she closed the jaws once more and placed the vial back in her waistband, sat back on her heels and waited.

For long, silent moments, nothing happened. Then the body of the mongoose jerked once. The little jaws moved back and forth and a tiny pink tongue worked in and out of the mouth. The creature squinched its eyelids and wrinkled its nose, as if it had just eaten something distasteful. Slowly it rolled over onto all fours and shook its head once, then twice. It opened its eyes and blinked. Dazed, the mongoose looked around at all the people. It sat up on its hind legs and sniffed the air. Suddenly the mongoose leaped up, turned tail, and scampered fast as it could out the door of the tent.

The tent was filled with sighs and laughter and the clapping of hands. Jaimal stared at the woman, open mouthed. Masum rocked back and forth, smiling. The Mirza let out a long breath, unaware that he had been holding it. "That is most amazing, lady."

A flicker of a smile crossed Porphredo's face. "It is but a small example of my queen's powers. Have you any other questions of me?"

Jaimal rubbed his beard and asked, "Are those truly sapphires on your dashal, madam?"

"Why, yes, they are. These stones are common in the mountain where I dwell. Do you admire this garment? It is but silver silk, some old coins and baubles; merely an old woman's trinket. Here." She removed the cloth from her head and shoulders and held it out to Jaimal.

His eyes opened wide. "I . . . I could not accept such a valuable gift, Lady."

"But I have said it is only a trifle to me. I regret that my visitor's gift is so poor, for I have many better ones at home. If you feel this wretched garment would please your wife or beloved, please take it and give it to her with my blessings."

Jaimal should have refused at least twice more for courtesy's sake, the Mirza thought. But the gleam of greed was in the lieutenant's eyes as he gratefully accepted the heavy fabric in his arms and caressed it.

Masum leaned across the Mirza to examine one of the coins sewn onto the hem of the dashal, under Jaimal's watchful glare. "Iskandr!" the Sufi said.

"Yes," said the old woman, a wistful tone to her voice. "The coins are very old. Quite useless now. Is there anything else you would ask?"

"Yes, I have a question, Wise Lady of the Wise Queen," said Masum. "What are the Three through which all things have come, and are the processes through which all must pass?"

The Mirza frowned at the Sufi mystic. *He asks her a Sufi riddle? Why should he believe she is of that sect?*

Porphredo tilted her head, her brows creased. Then she closed her eyes and sat silent a moment. When she opened her eyes again, she smiled, amused, and said, "Why my learned *faylasuf,* they are the One, the Intellect, and the World Soul."

Masum sat back with an admiring sigh. "You truly are learned in the ancient wisdom, Lady."

Porphredo nodded. "My queen prides herself on her knowledge. She keeps a library filled with all manner of scrolls and books from lands throughout the world."

"She has a library?" breathed Masum with nearly worshipful awe.

The Mirza regarded the old woman with more wary respect. *She has skillfully charmed them both with what they both most desire. Let us see if she can satisfy my question as skillfully.* The Mirza cleared his throat and said, "I have a question, Generous Lady. We, indeed, come in search of your queen in hopes of establishing relations between your kingdom and that of my Emperor Akbar. But, alas, until we reached Bijapur, we traveled with only stories to guide us. The good Sultan Ibrahim joined our expedition with that of the westerners beside you in hopes that they could offer better guidance, and they have led us this far, south and east of Bijapur. Can you tell us how to find your Hidden City? Are we proceeding in the right direction?"

Porphredo bowed and said, "I come before you, Noble Mirza, because you are no longer on the correct path. Bhagavati is south of Bijapur, yes, but south and west. Many days to the south—where the Ghats turn east and reach heavenward. That is where the high mountains lie. That is where you must go. I advise you to go no further in your current direction, for ahead lies a great wilderness—the Plain of Stones, whose sharp edges will tear the pads of your elephants and break the hooves of your horses.

"The infidels," hissed Jaimal, "have lied to us."

"Patience, Jaimal." The Mirza noted that Lakart was translating her words to the Goans. The yellow-hair looked shocked and the Christian priest was glaring at him. The old woman was somewhat perturbed by their reaction. "They would seem to be as surprised as we are."

"It may be pretense, my lord."

"I think not. Let us wait and see what they do."

The one called Lakart was busily talking to the priest and to the yellow-hair. At last he turned to face the Mirza and said, "Great Lord, we beg you not to think we have betrayed you, or in any way misled you. If what Lady Porphredo says is true, there may be a simple explanation for our error. East and west have very similar sounding words in English, as well as Portuguese. It may be that we misheard. The other source of our knowledge was a sorcerer's map that may have been drawn to deceive any who found it."

"One moment," interjected Masum. "What of the river Krishna which you said was depicted on this map? For there is indeed such a river to the south and west of us. Madam messenger, what do you say to this?"

The old woman sighed and tilted one shoulder. "If this sorcerer chose to deceive, he did all too well. The Krishna River flows from the very western edge of the Deccan to the Bay of

Bengal. Anyone searching its banks would spend many long, fruitless months in bleak and dangerous country. It is possible, if you heard a description of the map, that he meant the Shimsha River, for that winds to the south and east of the Hidden City."

The Christian priest was now regarding the woman with open suspicion. The Goan soldiers were arguing among each other. The yellow-haired foreigner was ashen-faced.

Both Jaimal and Masum began speaking to the Mirza at once: "My lord—"

"Silence!" The Mirza held up his hands and glared sternly at all in the tent. "There is no need for this chaos. Honored Lady, I assume since you know the path we must take, and bring words of welcome from your queen, that you will be willing to guide us there yourself."

"Certainly I will guide you much of the way, and give you complete directions on how to find the city from there. But my queen has given me many tasks, of which this is merely one."

"Indeed?" The Mirza stroked his beard and watched her a moment. Was there a trace of uncertainty in her austere gaze? "Jaimal," he said softly, "I want you to select four horsemen and send them south and east immediately. I want to know if this Plain of Stones exists by tomorrow morning."

"My lord, is it not rudeness to doubt the lady's word?"

You want to believe her because of the riches she promises, don't you? "Merely practical, Jaimal. If the lady is wise, she will understand."

"But it is clearly the westerners who are lying! We must do something to show our displeasure."

"No, Jaimal, not without proof. But for now, take their horses from them. Any of our riders can run down a man on foot, should they decide to flee."

Jaimal ducked his head in assent, though he was clearly not appeased. "As you will, my lord."

"It is my hope," said the old woman, "that my words will not cause you to do harm to these men whom you think may have misguided you. I notice they are of many nations, and my queen would be pleased to hear of such distant and disparate lands. They would be welcomed in her court, and she would be displeased to learn that they had come to grief because of her own attempts to sow confusion."

"But, lady," said Jaimal, "these men are of a false faith, and may have meant to do *us* harm."

"From what they are saying to me," said Porphredo, "I do not think that is so, most valiant lord."

"Enough," said the Mirza, feeling a need for clear air and clear thought. "Our evening prayer approaches, and we need time to prepare. Jaimal, you will do as I have ordered. Masum, see that comfortable quarters are prepared for our new guide. We will have another discussion later tonight, if need be. Or tomorrow. Now begone from my tent."

Ai, what have I done? thought Porphredo as she stood, knees aching. *I should have realized that Stheno's game might bring harm to Aditi's rescuer. I must see that he, at least, is spared, even if I cannot help the rest of his party. What puzzles my despoina builds for me to solve. My far-away sister Deino would have no qualms about sacrificing the Europeans. Enyo would more likely sacrifice herself, silly thing. But I, how will I untie this Gordian knot?*

The Goan priest was scowling at her and restraining the wide-eyed young boy by the collar. "God have mercy upon you," he said in Latin. It was spoken as a curse, not a benediction. The priest left, dragging the protesting boy with him.

Tamaschinri approached her with a sad face. "Despoina, I thank you for your attempt to speak us fair, but I fear your words may have doomed us."

"Please forgive me," Porphredo said, "I do only what I must. I will do what I can to see you do not come to harm. Tell Gandharva what has happened. Now speak to me no more, lest more suspicions are aroused."

"Nai, despoina." The young man bowed and left the tent.

The burly, dark-haired northerner approached and stared

silently at her. *What a mixture of emotion lies behind those eyes,* thought Porphredo. *Hunger and fear. Hope and hate.* Perhaps, like the priest, he speaks Latin. "*Inimica tua non sum.*" I am not your enemy.

"*Videbimus,*" he replied. We will see.

The Sufi came up to her, but his face was full only of wonder and joy. He bowed and said, in the Persian of Sufi poetics, "O wise and generous Lady, it is my honor to guide you to a place of comfort, and to offer what humble hospitality we may. If there is anything you require, or that would be pleasant to you, you need only ask and I will do all I can to provide it."

Porphredo could not suppress a smile. "You are most kind, good *faylasuf,* to one who is but a humble messenger."

"We of the Faithful," said the Sufi with a mischievous twinkle in his eye, "put great store by messengers. If you will come this way, Lady."

"But Padre, I know who she is! She is one of the Grey Ones!"

"Hush, Timóteo!" said Gonsção, more roughly than he intended. They were a few yards away from the Mirza's tent and Gonsção looked around to make sure they were not overheard. "Yes, I have no doubt the witch is from the place we seek, but that does not mean we should trust her, or listen to her lies."

"Senhor De Cartago was a liar, too."

"But he had less to protect, my son. No, that creature is here because we are all too close to her Queen's sacred city and she means to turn us away from it. What I would like to know is where Tomás found her and why he believed she would save us."

The three Goan *soldados* came up and surrounded Gonsção and Timóteo nervously. "Padre," said Carlos, "What are we to do?"

"They are taking our horses, Padre," said Estevão. "I could not stop them. I had hoped we might be able to run back to Bijapur, but now we cannot."

"We are your men, truly, Padre," said Joaquim. "But we are only three and we will not last long, even fighting for our lives."

"Calm yourselves and pray for strength," said Gonsção. "Despite his misguided faith, the prince-general is clearly a man of peace and no fool. I do not think he has entirely swallowed the old witch's story, or else we would have been slain then and there. Let us hope he can expose her lies for what they are before his other men decide we are worthless."

"She tried to help us," said Timóteo, sullenly.

"Which only shows that she is no fool herself, as that kept us from killing her. Really, Timóteo, you have much to learn about the outside world. Joaquim, have you been watching Tomás? Do you know where he might have dredged up that creature?"

Joaquim shrugged. "He has never left the camp, Padre. The only interesting place he goes is to the entertainer's wagon. And as I have said, it is not for the women. He talks to that blind gourd-player and listens to his horrible noise, that's all."

"Hmmm. In Lisboa, there were beggars who could make great show of being blind or lame or diseased, when in fact they were no less healthy than you or I. This musician may be more than he seems. The next time Tomás goes to the wagon, follow him closely, Joaquim. Pay attention to all he does and whom he speaks to. The answer must be there."

Evening turned to dusk as the Mohammedans bowed toward the setting sun, and the Padre and Timóteo held vespers in their tent. Thomas paced anxiously through the small area set aside for the Goans' tents, awaiting the fall of darkness.

Finally in the hour of twilight when shadows blended seamlessly into the shapes that cast them, Thomas set out for the entertainer's wagon.

No sooner had he stepped beyond the circle of Goan tents when Joaquim fell in step beside him. "Tomás. *Quo vadis?*"

Thomas sighed. "Ah, Joaquim. Ever my faithful watchdog. I

am going down to the entertainer's wagon. I thought I would finally take your advice and meet a woman there."

"Excellent! I am glad to hear it, Tomás, for you know we were quite worried about you, the way you keep company with Timóteo so much. Which fine lady of veils will be graced with your company?"

"I do not know yet."

"Ah. Well, I suppose it is best to see first who is available. That way one is not disappointed. But I will come with you, Tomás, to ensure that you get a girl who is suitable."

"Oh, and here I thought you were following me because you did not trust me."

"But of course I trust you, Tomás. It is the Padre—he does not trust you."

"So you will tell him whether I find a girl who is . . . suitable?"

"Fear not, Tomás, I will tell him nothing of your love tryst. The Padre does not like to hear such things. He frowns upon my frequent visits to the wagon, and accuses me of fraternizing, though my interest is anything but brotherly."

'Sblood, how will I rid myself of this pest? He may ruin all . . . or will he? Would he try to stop my resurrection of Aditi? By the time he could raise an alarum, it would be too late and the deed would be done. I do not think Joaquim would be so callous as to slay her again. "But what if the lady I am to see is shy, Joaquim? I do not want you scaring her away."

The soldier waved a thin arm as if swatting flies. "Do not worry, *amigo meu.* All the girls know me—hey, I can put a good word in for you, eh?"

"You are too kind, Joaquim."

"Nonsense! Were we not brothers in the Aljouvar? Nothing is too good for you. Even if you have been leading us the wrong way."

Thomas whirled to face him. "I have *not*—oh, what is the use? Believe the old woman if you want to." He turned and continued walking.

To his dismay, Joaquim still followed. "But it is no matter,

Tomás. I forgive you. I have always known this expedition is doomed. Such are the best sort. Is it not so in all of the stories?"

Thomas sighed again. "Why didn't you stay in Bijapur, Joaquim? You could have joined the Sultan's forces. And you were a scholar—surely you would have had something to offer Ibrahim's court."

"There is something to be said, Tomás, for following one's duty. Even if it leads to Hell. What do you follow now, Tomás?"

"At the moment, instinct. And duty of my own sort. Well. Here we are, but the place would seem deserted."

A single torch had been placed on a pole in a narrow clearing between the entertainer's cart and a thick grove of tamarind and palmyra. The torchlight glimmered off the paintings of dancing elephants and peacocks on the side of the cart. But there was no laughter or singing of girls from within. "Hellooo?" Thomas called. "Gandharva?"

The blind musician scuttled out from under the tamarinds, stopping at the torchpole. "Tamaschinri? Is that you?"

"Good evening, Gandharva," Thomas said in Greek. "I was told it is time to bring a blossom from cold winter into summer."

"O, Despotas Tamas, we have been accorded a great honor! A great honor!"

"He is trembling like a bridesmaid," said Joaquim, in Latin. "What is he babbling about?"

"Who else is there?" said Gandharva tilting his head.

"It is that idiot soldier Joaquim," said Thomas in Greek. "He insisted upon following me and I could not shake him. I do not think he will do harm to our plans. I told him I was meeting a woman here and he insists upon seeing her as well."

"Ah," said Gandharva. "Then I suppose he must. But come forward, Tamas, into the light so I may introduce you."

Thomas stepped, puzzled, into the small pool of light around the torchpole. "To whom? I see no one."

"This is he, despoina. The one who saved your daughter."

"Ai . . ." there came a sigh from the trees and a susurrance like leaves in the wind, although the air was perfectly still. "Kallikouros. What a beauty he is. It is no wonder my Aditi loved him." The voice was low, melodious, and Thomas felt his hair begin to stand on end though he could not think why.

"Is that the lady you are to meet, Tomás?" said Joaquim. "She has a voice to make a man's loins glow like sunrise."

Thomas ignored him. "Is this . . . Aditi's mother?"

"She is," said Gandharva. "The Mahadevi herself."

Thomas stared into the trees but could see no one there. He could not believe that a Hindu goddess actually stood somewhere before him, but he was aware of being in the presence of someone remarkable. "I greet you, great despoina," he said, his voice wavering more than he liked. "I am pleased to have been able to rescue your daughter and bring her to you." He wondered if he should bow, or in what manner.

"How his hair shines like the sun, Gandharva," the beguiling voice went on. "He must be the one Pra foresaw. My Savitr. My Krishna."

Gandharva sucked in his breath. "Despoina, let us hurry in what we must do."

"Ah. Nai. One moment."

Joaquim was nearly dancing from foot to foot. "Ey, Tomás, it sounds as though your pandering musician friend has captured you quite a prize. She is not one of the usual wagon girls. But remember our agreement—I must have a look at her first!"

"Please, Joaquim, you now know I have not lied to you. Please be a gentleman and—"

"Good centurion," said the honeyed voice, now speaking the same ancient Latin that Aditi spoke. "I would gladly give you what you ask, but it is my way to be veiled—not just any man may look at me. But if it will content you, come and hold me here in the shadows and I will grant you a kiss. Will that suit you?"

Joaquim grinned. "I will accept that coin of payment gladly, Domina."

"Excellent. But first I have a love token to give Tamas, and then you may have your kiss."

"Go among the trees," said Gandharva urgently as he tugged on Thomas's arm, "and get the *rasa mahadevi.*"

"Ah. Yes. At once."

Thomas walked forward between the nearest trees, seeing only firelight glimmering on leaves and shadows within shadows.

"Close your eyes, my beauteous one." The voice was so near, Thomas jumped. "And hold out your hands."

Thomas did so, but not before seeing a woman's arm snake out of the shadows. He felt something smooth and warm slide into his cupped palms. "May I know what to call you, despoina?"

"My name is strength. Now go and awaken poor Aditi, while I distract your inquisitive friend."

"Nai, despoina." Thomas backed out of the trees as fast as he could. *Strength. Yes, "stheno" is the word she used. So De Cartago was not muttering prayers. He was stating her name. Unless she plays a jest with me.* "The lady says you may approach her now," Thomas called to Joaquim.

"Then I go with great joy. What is it you have there, Tomás?"

Thomas looked into his hand and saw a tubular bottle of the same iridescent glass as the bottle he had gotten from De Cartago, the first time he had seen the resurrection powder. "It is . . . perfume, I think."

"Come, my handsome centurion. I eagerly await the touch of your lips."

"Very well, but I warn you, sweet lady," said Joaquim as he swaggered into the trees, "I am a master at kissing. You may forget my friend once you have tried me."

"We must hurry," Gandharva whispered to Thomas. "We must finish before the girls return."

"Where are they?" asked Thomas as he ran to the rear door of the wagon, Gandharva holding his arm for guidance.

"Far on the other side of the camp, dancing for one of the Hindu officers for his birthday. It will be a surprise for him, since his birthday is not for some months yet. But I have never known a Hindu lordling to turn away festivities."

Thomas thought he heard a loud gasp from the trees behind him, and he paused at the carriage door. But there was no further sound other than the susurrance he had heard before. *Mayhap she offered more distraction than a kiss to the fortunate Joaquim.*

"What are you waiting for? Get inside, quickly!" said Gandharva.

Thomas clambered into the cart, pulling the musician in after him, and then closed the rear doors.

The inside of the entertainer's wagon was a mess of strewn silk garments of every hue, though rose and scarlet were more common. Pillows and cushions and small, plush carpets were piled in the corners. There were scents of patchouli and sandalwood, all overlain with the heavy, sweet smell of honey. Little oil lamps had been set on each flat surface. The myriad little flames gave the wagon the aspect of a chapel, although Thomas wondered about the threat of fire.

At the other end of the wagon lay a long, open box. Thomas crawled to it and peered in. *Ah, Aditi, how changed you seem. Death becomes you not.* Her entire body was wrapped in linen strips, save for the face where Gandharva had cut the cloth away. Her lovely face still glistened with its sticky coat of honey.

"Hurry," urged Gandharva. "The *rasa mahadevi* works best when fresh."

"Pray help me by opening her mouth, good Gandharva, so that my aim is true."

"If I can." The blind musician joined Thomas beside the box and reached in. He gently felt along Aditi's face until his hands found the right position and he pressed against the angle of her jaws until her mouth opened slightly.

Thomas unstoppered the iridescent bottle and tipped it over the parted lips, expecting a brown powder to flow out. Instead, drops of a deep red liquid spattered onto Aditi's teeth and tongue. Thomas's hand shook and some drops fell onto her chin. "This is fresh blood!"

"Yes, what did you expect?" hissed Gandharva. "Be careful and do not waste it!"

Thomas willed his hand to stay steady as the last drops poured out and then he quickly restoppered the bottle. He sat back on his heels. "So . . . Aditi's mother . . . a woman . . . is the source of this miraculous substance," he breathed.

"No mere woman," said Gandharva. "Why do you think it is called the blood of the goddess?"

"Do not fault me, Gandharva, but as a Christian I find it difficult to believe in pagan deities."

The blind man chuckled. "It does not matter to me what you believe. My own thoughts about the world change daily."

"Why does she not wake? The Padre revived in seconds from the powder."

"How long had the Padre been dead?"

"I . . . don't know. Minutes only, I think."

"And our Aditi has been gone for days, Tamas. The blood has much work to do."

So, it shall be more like the resurrection of De Cartago in the Santa Casa. Thomas did a quick calculation in his head and realized Aditi had been dead two days longer than the unfortunate Goan sorcerer, but she had seemingly decayed far less.

The body suddenly shook violently.

"Ah, she returns," said Gandharva.

Aditi's brows knit together in a frown and her lips moved in an effort to speak.

Thomas, noting how her lashes were stuck together, gently pried her eyelids open. Her grey-blue eyes stared up at him but did not seem to comprehend what they saw. "Welcome back, my love," Thomas said. "You are back in the world of the living."

"Ba . . . ma . . . ha . . . hala . . . hasa . . ." Aditi whispered.

"What is she saying?" Thomas asked Gandharva.

"It is nonsense, I think. It will take some time for her to regain her senses. Now you must lift her out of the box, so that we may send her home."

"Now? Shouldn't we wait until she has regained more of herself?"

"And give others a chance to find her while she is still weak?

What if your Goan priest, whom you fear was her murderer, finds her thus?"

"Ah. True. I cannot say what the Padre would do."

"Come. We must take her to her mother."

Thomas reached into the box and put his arms under her armpits. His shoulders still ached, but they had healed considerably over the past week, and he found himself capable, with some pain, of lifting her. He draped her awkward form over his right shoulder and clumsily made his way to the wagon doors.

"Ba . . . maha . . . ras . . . ras . . ." Aditi whispered.

"Shhhh," said Thomas. "Peace, my love. You are going home." He pushed open the doors of the wagon and peered out. The clearing was still deserted and there was no sign of Joaquim. He jumped down from the wagon and, shifting Aditi into a more secure position on his shoulder, he ran across the clearing into the shadows beneath the tamarind trees. "Despoina Stheno, I have brought her."

"Ah, my poor Aditi. Bring her this way, my beauty."

"Where is the soldier I asked you to distract?"

"He has departed."

A hand grasped Thomas's sleeve and pulled him through the trees to the other side of the grove. There, in the light of the waxing moon, stood three horses, saddled and ready for riding.

Gandharva also came crashing through the grove right behind him. "You must hurry. I heard someone else near the wagons."

"You will ride behind her, my beauty, and hold her so she does not fall."

"I, despoina?"

"She cannot very well ride by herself, can she? Besides, we have promised to reward you and I am told you are in danger if you remain here among the Mughuls. You will be one of the few outsiders accorded the honor of entrance into Bhagavati."

Thomas looked back toward the camp, though he could not see it through the trees. *All she says is true, and I would be a fool not to take this chance to free myself. Has my goal not always been to escape this mad expedition? Save that now I know it is not mad, for there is a source to the miraculous powder and she stands before me. And yet, it seems the core of cowardice to leave them . . . Andrew and Joaquim and Timóteo. But what could I have done for them, I who am no soldier or diplomat? And the Padre has sworn to destroy the source . . . this woman, so I dare not reveal her presence to them. Farewell all of you, my companions on the road to Hell, as Joaquim once said. Farewell, little Brother Timóteo. May the Mughuls spare you for your youth. Would that you, at least, could come with me. May God send you better work than the Santa Casa. May you become a great herbalist like your grandfather. You I shall miss most of all.*

"Someone comes," said Gandharva.

Wincing with the ache in his shoulders, Thomas lifted Aditi to lay her across the saddle of the nearest horse.

There came a crashing of leaves at the edge of the trees. "Tomás! Where are you going?"

"My God! Timóteo, why are you here?" *So 'tis true one should be careful what one wishes.*

"I followed you. Are you leaving us? You aren't deserting us, are you?"

"Who is this child?" hissed the Despoina Stheno. Thomas could see her now, a human form swathed in black, a deeper shadow in the night.

"He is from the Orlem Gor in Goa," said Gandharva.

Timóteo suddenly saw Stheno and cried, "Tomás! *Cuidado!* She is—"

Thomas released Aditi and clasped a hand tight over Timóteo's mouth. "Fool! Do you want to get us all killed?" he whispered harshly in the boy's ear.

"What will we do with him?" said Gandharva, sadly.

"He must not return to the others," said Stheno.

Thomas's blood chilled at the veiled threat in her words. "Then he must come with us," said Thomas desperately. "He is but a boy. You cannot think of harming him."

"Hmmm." Then there came low laughter that made Thomas's skin crawl. "Perhaps I have not only regained a daughter but gained a son as well. Very well, since my beauty asks it, the boy will come too. He shall take Porphredo's horse."

"And what of your servant Porphredo?" asked Gandharva.

"She is resourceful. I have no doubt she can steal a horse and find her own way home."

"Are you not coming along, Gandharva?" said Thomas, relieved that no harm would come to Timóteo.

"A blind man like me? I would only slow you down. Now please be on your way before others find us."

"Come on," Thomas released Timóteo's mouth and grabbed him by the arm.

"You must not look at her," Timóteo whispered.

"I cannot. It is dark and she is veiled." Thomas growled back.

"Good."

Thomas led Timóteo to the last remaining horse and boosted him aboard. The boy had a bulky bag draped over his shoulder. "You've brought something?"

"I brought your herb notebook and other things, Tomás. I could tell you were leaving us when I saw you walk away toward the wagon."

You knew before even I. Thomas felt angry, yet also pleased that the boy would not face the vengeance of the Mughuls. "I was supposed to protect you. Whatever will the Padre think?"

"You are protecting me, Tomás. And I will protect you. What is that?" The boy pointed at Aditi.

"That is the dancing girl, Aditi, whom I lost in Bijapur. She was dead, but I have revived her."

"She was dead, Tomás?"

"When she has revived enough, she will tell us who killed her." *A truth that shall no doubt break your heart.* Thomas carefully mounted his horse and pulled Aditi up to sit astride before him. She dangled in his arms like a lifesize rag doll.

"Are you ready?" said Stheno from the darkness ahead.

"We are ready," said Thomas.

VI

PARSLEY: This plant has divided green leaves and brings forth sprays of white flowers in summer. A powder of the root mixed with wine enhances memory and heals the brain. However, this humble garden herb is more than it seems, for ancient peoples have long held it sacred to the dead. The Romans and Greeks bedecked graves with it. Those who witness the Wild Hunt, it is said, will come to no harm if they ask the passing shades for parsley. To cut parsley brings ill fortune in love. And one must not move the herb from one garden to another, for it will bring a death in the family. . . .

Porphredo rose early and dressed as the Mughuls cried out the pre-dawn prayers. She had not slept well, it having been so long since she had lain in an unfamiliar bed, in foreign territory. *I have been spoiled by peace and prosperity. Too long a life in one place makes one unready for anything else.* She did not miss the very old days, however, when she, her sisters and the Despoinas Stheno and Euryale had been hounded from place to place as monsters and forced to live as thieves.

As Porphredo wound the last loop of the sari around her thin body and draped the remaining cloth over her head, she peered out through the tent flap at the dawn. *I wonder if Aditi again lives to see this morning. I hope all went well. I wish I had been able to do more than send Gandharva a message via one of his girls, about the danger the westerners are in. But I cannot bring too much attention to him . . . he is more vulnerable than I.*

She heard movement and voices around her tent as the prayers finished and the Mughul soldiers began their morning routines. Porphredo sat on one of the many large cushions in the tent, and began to wonder when she might expect a meal, when footsteps came to the front of her tent.

"May the glories of the morning shine upon you, o messenger dove of the Great Begum." It was the Sufi, Masum.

Porphredo smiled. "I thank you and wish the same for you, o master of poetics. What would you at the door of my home in the wilderness?"

"I bring you refreshment in the name of Lord Mirza Ali Akbarshah, who bids you break your fast and partake of his hospitality. May I enter?"

"Please do. I had just been hoping for such hospitality."

"He Who Provides answers all wishes," said the Sufi as he entered. Two young turbanned men came in behind him.

"True, good *faylasuf*, but the answers may be more than one wished for."

One of the young men placed a steaming tureen at Porphredo's side. "This contains towels steamed in hot rose water," said Masum, "to refresh your hands and feet."

The other young man set down a brass tray, incised with geometrical patterns and a verse from the Qu'ran. On it sat a silver ewer. Beside the ewer were porcelain plates on which lay sliced plantains, melon, and coconut, dried and salted mango, and slivered sweet cane that had been soaked in gingered honey.

Masum lifted the ewer and poured a milky juice into a glazed pottery cup. "Allow me to serve you this drink, Lady. It is from the juice of coconuts and mangoes, spiced with cinnamon and cloves. The more impious Hindu among us call it *soma*, the drink of the gods."

Porphredo gratefully accepted the cup from his hands, noting how warm his fingers were. She sipped the cool, refreshing juice and said, "Where I come from, this would be called nectar."

Masum signaled to the two men, who bowed and departed. "Kindly forgive the modest repast, Lady. This is but a rough army bivouac and not the Mirza's palace. For much of this, you may thank in your prayers the Sultan Ibrahim, who sent these provisions with us. My lord Mirza confesses he, himself, has little imagination for such impracticalities."

"Your lord Mirza seems to me a most wise and foresightful man."

"So he is, Lady, and it is my great honor to serve him. Nonetheless, he is like the mountain climber who watches the path ahead for stones, yet does not pause to admire the beauty of the mountain he is climbing."

"Is that why you are in his retinue? To show him the mountain?"

Masum smiled through his fly-away beard. "It is my hope that I can help him catch a glimpse of it. But he did not call me into his service. You see, I—but forgive me. I do not wish to be tiresome company, and some lose patience with my tales."

"I have never found Sufi poets to be tiresome, good *faylasuf*. Please sit with me and tell me your story." *Have I suddenly become flirtatious? At my age? For shame, Porphredo.*

Masum chose a cushion not far from her, though not too near, and sat. "It is this. For seven years, I have studied with a Chisti *pir*, at Shahpur Hillock, which lies just outside Bijapur. Some weeks ago, I began to dream—much the same dream every night. That I must seek a great prince in the north who would lead me to the Great Sophia. My *pir* was so overwhelmed with my recounting this dream day after day, that at last he said, "Go! Clearly this is a sign from the Awakener that you must undertake a journey. Go seek this prince, that your troubling dreams may cease." And so, eating and sleeping little, I wandered north from Bijapur and, lo and behold, just south of Ahmadnagar I encountered the Mirza Akbarshah. My Lord Mirza doubtless thinks of me as a cat who appeared from nowhere and, on a whim, has chosen to follow him."

Porphredo thoughtfully chewed on a piece of melon. "Cats are practical. They chase and kill vermin."

"Once I was a soldier," said Masum, "and that might have been my purpose. But since becoming a *murid,* I have studied other things. You could say I am on this journey in the name of love."

"Love?" said Porphredo, raising a brow. "Love of war or love of women? I did not think that was the Sufi way."

Masum shook his head. "It is often misunderstood, the Sufi meaning of love. It is not desire for any earthly thing. It is the luminous knowledge of the Divine, which can only rest in the heart, not the mind. To the Suf', love is the very nature of the Divine Power."

"This is a curious thing, good *faylasuf,* for my queen also, for these many years, has pursued the study of love." *Albeit of a more earthly form.*

Masum sat back and clapped his hands, eyes shining. "Then I am truly on the right path. I have great hope that your queen, who balances life and death in her hands, can teach me to know such love."

Porphredo sighed. "I cannot say what she would teach you. She is . . . selective in her pupils." *O poor* faylasuf. *How fortunate you are that you will not meet my despoina. She would surely disappoint you.*

Masum bowed. "Forgive me, I speak above myself. But allow me to dream that I might someday sit at her feet and learn from her great wisdom."

"I think, Masum, that it is she who could learn much from you."

The Sufi blushed and laughed. "Oh, no. Now you flatter me too much, noble lady."

A pity. Of all the members of this expedition, this is the one who would most appreciate the knowledge gathered in Bhagavati. Stheno would do well to learn from his humility and gentleness. Alas, it is not to be. "Nonsense, good *faylasuf.* I never flatter. It debases the recipient as well as the speaker."

"Only when it contains no truth," said the Sufi. Then he sighed, "but I prattle too much—a fault the Mirza kindly suffers for my sake, but I will not ask that of you. It will be a little while before my Lord needs to speak with you again. Would you like some other form of entertainment? Would music please you?"

"Music is one of the few pleasures I can still appreciate at my age," said Porphredo.

"Ah. I understand there is a *vina* player among us who is quite skillful. I also have modest talent in music. I have just finished making a flute and I have not yet tested its worth. Would you be so kind as to allow me to play on it for you?"

Porphredo reclined on the cushions, basking in the rare pleasure of the company of an attentive and interesting man. "That would please me greatly, good *faylasuf.*"

Padre Antonio Gonsção awoke late, squinting in the sunlight that slashed through the tent entrance. His wool robe stuck to his skin, and his head swam in the heat. *Why did Timóteo not wake me for matins?* "Timóteo?"

There was no sound save for the bellows of animals and the distant chatter and shouts of men that was constant in the Mughul army. Gonsção rose with a groan. He saw that Timóteo's bedroll was tidy. Either the Padre had slept through the boy's rising or Timóteo had not returned to the tent the night before.

Gonsção rinsed his face and hands in a bowl of tepid water. He decided to forego the heavy black cape, and stepped outside the tent in his once-white robe, now almost a tawny red from the dust of the Deccan.

Two *soldados,* Carlos and Estevão, still lay sleeping beside the tent. Gonsção nudged one of them with his foot. "Estevão."

"Mmm? Oh, Padre. Madre do Deus, what hour is it?"

"Too late an hour for men who are supposed to be vigilant to be sleeping."

"Padre, we were up late worrying about the *muçulmanos,* but there is only so long a man can go without sleep."

"Never mind, Estevão. We are, as yet, still alive. Have you seen Brother Timóteo?"

"No, Padre. Ey, Carlos. Wake up." Estevão slapped the other *soldado* on the shoulder.

"Mmmm? What do you want, pig face? Ai!" At Estevão's second, harder slap, Carlos sat up. "Jesu e Maria, what is it?"

"We slept too long. And the Padre wants to know if you've seen the little brother."

"Oh! Forgive me, Padre." Carlos struggled out of his bedroll, fully dressed—even his sword still strapped to his side. "No, I have not seen him."

"You are forgiven," sighed Gonsção. "And where is your confederate Joaquim?"

Estevão scratched his head. "He went to follow the *inglês,* as you ordered, Padre. I saw them heading to the entertainer's wagon last night."

"And did you see them come back?"

"No, Padre. They probably are still there sleeping off their drinking and whoring."

"And the little brother," said Carlos, "likes tagging after the *inglês,* so maybe he is there too."

Gonsção scowled in the direction of the entertainer's wagon. *If Tomás has debauched Timóteo* . . . But something else was preying on his mind. Gonsção turned and looked back inside the tent. Timóteo's burlap sack, which contained the few belongings the boy had brought, as well as the herbs he gathered along the way, was missing. *Could he be out herbing now? Without telling me?* Anxiety began to creep over Gonsção like lice. He threw the tent flap shut. To the soldiers he said, "Come with me."

He was aware that several of the Mughuls were watching them as Gonsção and the soldiers walked swiftly toward the entertainer's wagon. *Let them watch. If there is treachery or ill behavior, let them see that not all of us approve.*

When he reached the gaudily painted wagon, Gonsção

pounded on its sides. "Come out!" he cried in Latin. "Timóteo! Tomás! Joaquim!"

There was stirring inside, and the back doors swung open. Dancing girls scarcely dressed emerged sleepily, wiping their eyes. "*Kitne hai?*" they murmured.

"Where are the *inglês*, Tomás, and the boy Timóteo?" Gonsção demanded. Though he knew they would not understand all he said, they might recognize the names.

The girls shook their heads and chattered back at him like a flock of discomfited songbirds. Gonsção tried to peer into the wagon, but the girls blocked his view. "Tomás! Timóteo! Joaquim!" he called again.

"Qui es?" said a man's voice and the head of the blind musician poked out from between two of the girls.

"You!" said Gonsção. Surprising himself, he grabbed the collar of the blind man's *jama* and dragged him out of the cart. Slamming the small musician up against the wall of the wagon, Gonsção growled in Latin, "I know you speak a western tongue. I know Tomás Chinnery has been here. Tell me what you know. Where are they?"

"P-please, *sacerdos*, do not harm me! The three you name did come here last night, but they left soon after. I have not seen them. I do not know where they are!"

Gonsção slowly released the blind man, wondering at his own rage. *Once I thought myself a man of reason. Has this land of madness so infected me that I am overpowered? Do I fear the retribution of the Mughuls so? Why should I, whose soul has passed the gates of death before, fear it? Or do I fear that I will not complete the task I have come so far to do?*

"Ai! Padre!" Carlos called from the grove of tamarind trees. Gonsção left off his musings and ran toward him.

He found Carlos leaning, horror-stricken, against a tree. The *soldado* pointed a shaking finger at the body lying before him. "I have found Joaquim, Padre."

Gonsção crouched down to examine the body. Had it not been for the cuirass and the shirt of Goan make, Joaquim would have been unrecognizable. His face and neck were covered with dozens of tiny, swollen puncture wounds. His skin was purple and white near the holes, grey and flaking on his nose and lips. His eyes were milky and discolored. "It is as though he had fallen into a nest of vipers," Gonsção murmured.

"Snakes are plentiful in this country, I am told," said Carlos, tremors in his voice.

Gonsção quickly glanced at the ground around him but saw no serpents and heard no slitherings amongst the bushes. "Possibly." *Could it be murder? Might the Mughuls seek to reduce our number? Or perhaps it is the work of the old witch who claims to come from the Immortal Queen. I cannot think Tomás capable of this, but I have been wrong about him before.* Gonsção stood. "Go and find Brother Andrew, if you can. And have Estevão continue searching for Tomás and Timóteo. It appears I shall have to conduct a funeral this morning, instead of a mass."

The Mirza looked up from his writing table as Masum entered his tent. "I trust our visitor from the Hidden Mountain is comfortable?"

"She is, Highness," said Masum with a wide smile.

"You have spent much of the morning with her, I notice." *How the Sufi's countenance glows like that of a new bridegroom. Surely an elderly matron such as she would not . . .* The Mirza had heard of Tantric Sufis who achieved their religious ecstasy in ways more earthly than spinning in circles. "May I ask, Masum, how you and the noble lady passed the time?"

"I am yours to question, most noble lord. Lady Porphredo and I had much intimate conversation."

"Indeed? What did you speak of?"

"My lord, we spoke of love."

"Love?" The Mirza wondered if his imaginings neared the truth. "What sort of love?"

"All sorts, my lord. She is very knowledgeable."

"I see. And did you find her . . . agreeable?"

"Most agreeable, my lord. I found great pleasure in her companionship." Masum sat next to him and said softly, "She even admired my flute."

"Your flute?"

"She praised it highly, and said she was amazed I could create such great scope of feeling with so small an instrument."

"Ah."

The Mirza's bemusement was interrupted by one of the guards outside his tent. "Lord General! Your scouts have returned."

"Excellent. Send them in."

Seven young men entered, looking ill-rested but otherwise fit, and bowed to him.

"Please, sit, all of you, and be refreshed," said the Mirza. "Who is it who shall speak for you?"

"I will, Lord Mirza," said one toward the center. "My name is Sabur."

"I am eager to hear your tale, Sabur, of what all of you have found."

"My lord, we have searched in every direction. And we have seen no Plain of Stones, such as Lord Jaimal described to us. To the east, there is a wide desert plain, and a river called Bhima. To the north and west, it is the same, but a high cliff overlooks the desert. To the south, there is a river named Krishna, and some stony hills. To the south and west, the river Dan flows down a canyon until it reaches the Krishna. There are ancient roads there, but I was told they lead to the ruined city of Vijayanagar, and they were much decayed."

One of the scouts seemed ill at ease and kept watching the tent entrance as if expecting someone. "What is the matter with your companion?" asked the Mirza.

Sabur glanced at the uncomfortable scout and replied, "My lord, that is Rafi. His brother, Mumit, has not yet returned from his ride and he worries for him."

"What direction was Mumit to ride in?"

"The south and east, my lord."

"I see." The Mirza felt a growing disquiet. "Well, most likely Mumit was merely delayed and will return soon."

"Sometimes silence speaks louder than a shout," said Masum, softly.

The Mirza paused, and then said, "If you have nothing more to report, I give you leave to search for the missing Mumit. It is his tale that I have most interest in hearing."

Sabur bowed again and stood. "We shall bring him as soon as we find him, Lord Mirza." All the scouts seemed relieved and eager to go.

As they departed, the Mirza turned to Masum. "Is it possible our honored visitor is less honorable than we have believed?"

Masum's normally cheerful face was troubled. "My lord, I have no doubts that the Lady Porphredo is whom she says she is."

"That may be. But such an emissary may have as much reason to keep our army from discovering her hidden city, as to guide us to it."

Masum lowered his gaze. "That is possible, my lord."

"Please send word to Lady Porphredo that I will want to speak with her again, after the noon prayers."

"I will, my lord."

Enyo carried her water jug through the oak and cypress trees, grateful that their shade shielded her from the harsh midday sun. It had been lonely in the palace, with Porphredo and the despoina gone, but here in the grove, Enyo never felt totally alone. The cool earth beneath her bare feet soothed her, and the water that fell upon her toes as she splashed it among the tree roots felt pleasant. And then she noticed she was watering the feet of another . . .

"Prabaratma! What are you doing here? Are you following me?"

The old Brahmin priest smiled as he sat fingering his rosary of sapphire beads. "I did not follow you, immortal one, but She whom you follow."

Enyo sighed. *Why does the despoina keep him? He spouts such disturbing nonsense. Surely the goddess of my homeland would not speak to this Hindu who worships such horrid, animal-faced creatures, or a monster like Kali.* "What are you talking about?"

"She guided me here. She said here is where it would happen. Here in the Grove of the Moon."

"Where what would happen?"

Prabaratma sighed ecstatically. "The Reawakening."

The only awakening Enyo hoped for was that the priest would come back to sanity. If he had ever had any. "And who is going to wake up?"

"She will. The World. Many roads lead to knowledge of the Durga, and many souls' paths lead to this place."

"It sounds as though I should prepare for guests."

"Yes."

Enyo tapped her foot in annoyance. "Why here? This is our private garden."

"Here is where the Devidurga rests. This is a place apart, a land elsewhere. This soil, these plants are foreign, are they not? What strange beauty of scent they bring . . . a piece of Indra's Paradise come to earth."

"I am pleased that you like this place, but I assure you it is just a garden with a little lake and some nice trees."

"You test me, as the Mahadevi does," said Prabaratma with a sly smile.

"I would never be so cruel," protested Enyo.

"Or so kind? She has blessed this small soul with much vision." Prabaratma tapped his forehead.

Such an odd thing for a blind man to say, thought Enyo.

"Ah. She is pleased," said Prabaratma, and he pointed toward the sky.

Despite herself, Enyo looked to where he was pointing. Between the crowns of two cypress trees, a pale sliver of moon floated in the blue sky, curved like a smile. Enyo picked up the water jug and hugged it to her chest as she walked away, wondering if she shouldn't prepare some guest rooms, just in case.

VII

IVY: This evergreen vine has long entwined itself in legend. It was sacred to the Greeks, and their god of debauchery. Ivy brings luck to the house on which it grows, but woe betide the household when it withers and dies. If given away, it breaks friendships asunder, and ivy will not grow on the grave of a troubled spirit. The leaves are good as dressings for wounds, swellings and burns, and a tea made from them is good antidote for snake venom....

The horizon shimmered with liquid air. As the sun rose higher in the morning sky, the heat sapped what strength remained in Thomas's limbs. He tried not to let his head droop onto Aditi's honeyed shoulder and nod off in the saddle.

They had ridden nearly continuously since leaving the Mughul camp, with only a few stops to rest the horses. Thomas had been surprised that no sentry had interfered with their departure. To their good fortune, the mysterious despoina who led them seemed to find her way easily in the dark. Aditi had spasmed violently at times for the first couple of hours, nearly knocking both herself and Thomas off the horse. As time passed, however, she seemed to gain more control of herself and now was actively holding on by her own power, for which Thomas's aching arms were grateful. She still did not speak, other than occasional nonsense syllables, but there seemed to be more presence behind her eyes.

Beside them, Timóteo rode, looking small on the large horse. He, too, was nodding off, jerking himself awake whenever he fell too far forward.

Their horses walked briskly across a flat, treeless flood plain that seemed to stretch for miles around them. *Where can our guide be leading us in this desert?* Thomas watched the woman riding ahead of them on her pale grey horse, the slight, hot breeze billowing her black *shal* and sari. *All she needs is a scythe,* Thomas thought sleepily. He shook his head to avoid the direction his thoughts were taking. "Despoina," he called softly, "How much further do we ride?"

The woman turned slightly in her saddle. The breeze fluttered her veiled cowl and Thomas glimpsed the silhouette of a face of striking beauty. "Further to where, my golden one? To my hidden city?"

"To where we might rest and refresh ourselves, despoina. The boy, as you see, is in danger of tumbling from his mount. We are all in need of food and shade."

"There will be a village ahead where we will change horses. There you may rest, but only for a little while."

Thomas peered at the horizon, trying to discern such a village. He thought he saw a grey-green smudge in the distance, but it was hard to discern amid the wavering air. "Is there a need for hurry, despoina?"

"Surely. My handmaid has informed me the Mirza Akbarshah is no fool. Men will be following before long."

Thomas turned to look behind him but saw nothing in the land they had ridden through. "I see no one pursuing us." He wondered if Padre Gonsção himself would come after them once discovering Timóteo had gone. *Would the Mughuls permit it? Or will they insist upon it?*

"Nor should you. Tell me, my beauty, how is it you have come in search of me?"

Thomas wondered how much he should explain, and whether the truth might make him suspect in her eyes. *What might Aditi tell her when she is well enough to speak. I cannot tell if Aditi is awake enough to notice if I lie.* "From a Goan alchemist, De Cartago by name, I had gotten a bottle of . . . the *rasa mahadevi*, as it is called in Goa. He also had a map that hinted at where your hidden city lay."

"Ber . . . nar . . . do . . ." sighed Aditi, so softly that Thomas doubted that Stheno heard it. He squeezed Aditi's shoulder to reassure her.

"And you wished to find the fountain from which this substance flowed, did you?" said Stheno, dark humor in her voice.

"It was not my choice, despoina. I would not have sought it myself. But the Santa Casa of Goa, which Aditi calls the Orlem Gor, captured me and De Cartago. They tormented us, and only by claiming I would lead one of their number to the source would they release me." Thomas was glad to be speaking Greek, for he feared Timóteo would have contradicted him.

"I see," said Stheno. "I have heard of this Orlem Gor, and they have much to answer for. There were priests of that place, then, riding with you among the Mughul army?"

"One priest, despoina."

"Only one? Did he kill my daughter?"

How perceptive she is in her surmise. What powers does this creature have that I know nothing of? "I . . . I do not know, despoina, though I believe it is possible. You will have to ask Aditi herself when she can answer."

"I wish I had known this sooner. Did this boy who rides with us serve that priest and the Orlem Gor?"

Thomas felt as though a pebble of ice had dropped into his stomach. "He is just a boy, despoina."

Her laughter was brittle. "Do you think I will take vengeance on a child? Give it no thought, my beauty. In taking him from the priest, we have rescued the boy from a worse fate, nai?"

"Perhaps," said Thomas.

Carlos and Estevão carried the shrouded body of Joaquim into Padre Gonsção's tent. *He will have to be buried soon,* thought Gonsção. *A pity he will not be able to lie in blessed soil. For all his minor sins and irritating ways, Joaquim deserved better than this.*

Just as Gonsção was about to enter the tent himself, he heard heavy running steps come up behind him.

"Padre, who is it? Who is hurt?" said Brother Andrew.

Controlling his anger, Gonsção turned slowly to face him. The "brother" no longer in any way resembled the Jesuit monk Gonsção had met in the Plaça do Catedral in Goa. Brother Andrew Lockheart now wore only native dress over his portly form, and his dark hair and beard were fully regrown. He even wore a turban.

"Had you been more willing to suffer our company," said Gonsção, "you might have known as soon as I. Brother."

Lockheart scowled. "By suffering the company of our hosts I may be prolonging our lives, Padre. I have been learning much that we may put to use. Now who is it who was borne into your tent?"

"It was Joaquim Alvalanca, God rest his soul."

"Joaquim is dead?" Lockheart shoved his way into the tent and stood over the body. "What has happened?"

Gonsção followed and stood behind the Scotsman. "It appears to be the work of serpents."

"Many serpents," said Carlos.

"Serpents?" Lockheart crouched beside the body. "Did he step into a nest of vipers?"

"Only if he walked upside down," said Estevão. "The bites are on his face."

Lockheart pulled the cloth back from Joaquim's head and

sucked in his breath. "I have never seen anything like this. You should call in Thomas. He knows some things about snake venom."

"I was just going to ask you," said Gonsção, "if you had seen the young *inglês*, or Brother Timóteo, or if you know where they are."

Lockheart looked up sharply. "I have not nor do not. Why?"

"They have gone missing, brother. No one has seen them since last night. And Timóteo's effects are gone as well."

"Why did you not tell me this earlier?"

"We have been occupied with the unfortunate Joaquim, and you have been difficult to find yourself," said Gonsção. "You know, for one who had pledged to Tomás's father that you would watch over him, it would seem you have done a poor job."

The Scotsman's countenance darkened. "No worse than that you have done in guarding the little brother, it would seem." He looked back down at Joaquim's corpse. "A pity there is no more of the *pulvis mirificus,*" he murmured. "Perhaps Joaquim could tell us where they are—" Lockheart suddenly blinked and stared out the tent doorway. "The old woman! She used the powder on the mongoose! She very likely has more. Perhaps we might beg her to part with some."

"No." said Gonsção. "I forbid it."

The Scotsman slowly stood. "You . . . forbid . . . What hypocrisy is this?"

"Had you any true faith, you would understand. It is precisely because of my own experience that I forbid it. Joaquim has gone to whatever reward he has earned. I shall not interfere with the will of God in this."

"Even if we might learn the fate of Thomas and the boy?"

"That is a poor reason to tear a man's soul from heaven, brother. It is up to us to find our lost sheep."

"Please, Padre," said Carlos, "think on what Ermão Andrew says. If Joaquim might have a chance at another life, the same chance that you had—"

"No! You see the terrible temptation this powder has become," said Gonsção. "I will hear no more about it. I do intend to question the old woman, to see what she might know of this."

"The Mirza should be informed," said Lockheart coldly. "Perhaps he can send a detail of men searching for Thomas and Timóteo."

Gonsção nodded, although he had begun to fear the worst. He did not wish to hear that the Mughuls might have killed Tomás and Timóteo. *Better that the* inglês *had fled, fearing the Mirza's retribution for his lies. But why, oh why, Lord, did he take Timóteo with him?*

A wailing cry split the air. Not the joyous warble of the Muslim prayer-caller, but the scream of a heart torn by pain. Without a single word, the four men shared a fearful glance. Gonsção tore the tent flap aside and ran out, followed closely by the others.

The Mirza Akbarshah also heard the fearful cry and emerged from his tent into the hot sunlight. Men were running past, swords drawn. "What is it?" he called to them.

"We do not know," said one of the soldiers, "but we will find out."

The Mirza turned and began to walk swiftly in the direction they were running. One man was coming toward him; one of the scouts he had sent. The man ran up to the Mirza, dusty tears streaming down his face. "My lord . . ." he gasped.

"What is it, Sabur?"

"My lord, it is Mumit. We have found him. He is . . . you must come see."

"Very well, take me to him. Is he dead?"

"Alas, Allah have mercy. You must come see."

"Lead me."

The Mirza followed Sabur for some distance past the edge of the Mughul camp, to the south and east, where he had to climb over a natural wall of boulders that lined a deep gully in which a trickle of a stream flowed. On the far side of the gully, a cluster of men stared into a narrow side canyon.

The Mirza and Sabur jumped down into the gully. "Let His Highness the Mirza through," said Sabur, pressing through the knot of silent men.

What has happened here? thought the Mirza. *Did the scout fall into this gully to his death? That would be most unfortunate but not cause such a stir—* And then the Mirza saw.

The scout Rafi knelt in the cleft, weeping. "Mumit, my brother, my brother." Before him was . . . a statue. A grey stone likeness of a man leaning back against the rocky wall, arms flung out for purchase. The expression on his face was terror, as if he had just discovered some great monstrosity.

With caution, the Mirza edged his way over to the sorrowful Rafi. He crouched down and gave the scout an embrace of sympathy. Then he stood again and approached the statue. *How like the stone hand at the tomb of the nameless* shahid. Just as with the relic in the tomb, where the clothing was far from the body, it was cloth, but where it came near, it blended seamlessly into stone. The face showed every pore, every hair, much finer than any sculptor's craft. The eyes had turned the white of pearls. *The keeper of the tomb had said the* shahid *was transformed by Allah to spare him from the temptations of the immortal queen's beauty. But from his expression, it does not seem that Mumit saw anything beautiful.*

Out of curiosity, the Mirza turned and faced the same direction as the transformed Mumit. On the opposite side of the cleft was a small hollow. He stepped over to it and examined the dirt and rocks. There was charcoal on the ground and streaks of soot on the cleft wall. *Someone was encamped here, briefly. Someone who was displeased, perhaps, at being found.*

The Mirza heard fearful murmuring among the men behind him, talk of curses and sorcery. *I must prevent their panic.* He stood and called back, "Sabur, someone else has been here. Take two others and search this area for foot or hoofprints."

"I will, my lord."

Turning to the mourning scout, he said, "Rafi, come from there. We must see to the proper burial of your brother."

Rafi closed his eyes in a spasm of grief and leapt up. Crying, "Mumit, Mumit!" he embraced the statue his brother had become.

But, to the Mirza's horror, the statue crumbled at the brother's embrace, the arms breaking off at the shoulders, the legs shearing at the knees. The stone man toppled beside the Mirza, shattering into rubble at his feet.

Whimpering, Rafi knelt at the pile of stones, touching them gently. "What have I done? What have I done?"

If the Mirza had had any doubt that the statue was formerly a living man, he lost it now. For though some of the stone man had crumbled to dust, other parts held their distinct form. Here was a reddish stone in the shape of a liver, there one much like a human heart. White bits of marble retained the form of bones. The Mirza had seen many wounded and dead men in battle, men who had been torn to pieces, some whose wounds he had delivered himself. Yet the sight of the demolished Mumit sickened him worse than had any battlefield casualty of flesh and blood.

Porphredo paused, lowering the washing cloth from her face when she heard the terrible cry. *What could have happened? Stheno and Aditi should be long gone by now. I hope it has nothing to do with us.*

But soon she heard running feet approaching her tent and knew her hopes were in vain.

"Begum Porphredo!" called Masum from outside her tent.

"Yes, good *faylasuf*, I am here. What has happened?"

"Lady, you are bid come with me. There is something the Mirza asks you to see."

Porphredo draped the long end of her blue sari decorously over her head and emerged into the hot sun. "I heard a scream a short while ago. Is it related to that?"

The mystic was hopping from foot to foot, hands flapping in

half-gestures, eyebrows turning up and down on his face like bowing caterpillars. "It is an amazing thing, lady. A miracle! Or terrible wizardry! I cannot explain. Come, the Mirza hopes you can enlighten us."

Fearing she knew what she would see, Porphredo said, "Of course, good *faylasuf.* I will come and see this wonder."

She became more certain in her fear as the Sufi led her to the southwest edge of the Mughul camp, and then to the gully where Stheno had taken refuge to wait for nightfall. Down in the cleft beside the gully, a turbanned man knelt, wailing over a pile of rubble. Among the stones, Porphredo could discern a forearm, half a face, a foot. *Ai, despoina, what have you done? Have your years not taught you caution?*

"Ah, Sri Porphredo," said the Mirza, stepping beside her. "Might this be another example of your immortal queen's magic?"

Porphredo drew herself up into her most imposing posture. "I cannot say, Highness, for I do not know what has happened here. I see a man weeping over a broken statue. Was it a treasure you were transporting? I had thought graven images were forbidden in Islamic law."

The Mirza did not reply for long moments, regarding her with narrowed, measuring eyes. "My man Rafi believes that the statue was once his living brother. Though I am normally skeptical of magic and miracles, examining the stone, even after it fell and was broken, has led me to agree. I thought that you, who have shown us potent magic of your own, might understand how this has occurred."

Does he think I have done this? "My queen's magic is that of life and wisdom. But the Deccan is a vast wilderness, Highness, and many demons and sorcerers are said to dwell here. Creatures who do not wish trespassers in their land. Surely you can see the importance of leaving this place, and soon."

Again, the Mirza did not reply at once, instead stroking his beard and regarding her. The discomfort of the long silence was broken when four of the westerners, two Goan soldiers, the priest, and the burly northerner came running up to them. All scowled at her with suspicion.

"My lord," said the northerner who had translated for the Goans the previous night, "we heard someone cry out and have come to see what has happened."

"It is not a matter that need concern you," said the Mirza coolly.

"Ah, but it may, Highness, for we have also come to tell you of our own troubles. One of our number is dead and two are missing."

Porphredo felt the knot in her stomach grow tighter. *No, not more.*

The Mirza raised his brows and lowered his hand from his face. "Indeed? In what manner did the dead man die, and which of you was he?"

"One of our soldiers, my lord. It seems he died from many snake bites on his face. We found him by the entertainer's wagon."

Porphredo was unable to mask her shock. *Ai, despoina, was such a horror necessary?* "What a terrible thing. You have my sympathy."

"That is strange, indeed," said the Mirza, "On the face, you say?"

"Just so." A crafty expression came into the northerner's eyes and he glanced sidelong at the Goan priest before asking, "Lady Porphredo. Your queen's magic revived a mongoose and I have seen it revive a man. If you have more of the amazing powder, you would do us a great service by restoring the soldier to us."

It was clear the Goan priest did not understand Persian, for he demanded of the northerner in Latin, "What are you saying to her? Ask her about Timóteo and Tomás!"

The northerner hushed him, and said to Porphredo, "Well?"

Which ones are Timóteo and Tomás? Let me see, there were seven in the Mirza's tent last night. Who is missing? Ah, the golden-haired one who was Aditi's rescuer. I assume Stheno took him with her, but who is the other? The boy monk? What would the despoina want with him?

The Goan soldier must have tried to stop them from leaving. Alas, revival for him is out of the question. "Good sir, while it would be within my queen's power to revive your fallen comrade, alas I have no more of the substance with me. It is very precious, you understand, and I am given only a small amount."

"How . . . unfortunate," said the northerner.

"Wise begum," said Masum, who had stood by silently all this while, "If your queen has the power of life over death, is it possible there is something that can be done for the one whose remains lie shattered below?"

Porphredo glanced down into the gully. This she could answer truthfully. "If it is as you say and the statue was once a living man, she could have revived him if he were still whole. But as he is, too much as been lost."

"Even if he were . . ." Masum searched for words, "put back together again?"

Porphredo shook her head. "It would be very doubtful. You would have to find every piece, for if a part of his heart or brain were missing . . . he would not survive his revival long."

"For a queen with great powers of Life and Death," said the burly northerner sardonically, "Your queen would seem to have severe limits on her abilities."

Porphredo was spared delivering a sharp retort as a man on horseback rode up to them. "My Lord Mirza, we have found hoofprints leading away from here toward the entertainer's wagon. Three horses, we think."

Three? thought Porphredo. *So she took mine as well. I serve her for centuries, and still she thinks nothing for my safety. I am but a slave to be tossed aside.*

"Can you tell how long ago these horses left?" asked the Mirza.

"There is some horse dung that is hours old, my lord. The horses must have left during the night."

"So," the Mirza turned back to the northerner, "you have my apologies. It may be that our tragedies are linked after all. Is the yellow-haired one a sorcerer? Might he have been responsible for this," the Mirza waved a hand at the pile of stone human debris in the gully, "as well as the death of your soldier?"

"Thomas is a simple herbalist, my lord, and he shunned doing harm to anyone."

"Yet he is gone and two men are strangely dead. Tell me," said the Mirza to the rider, "did you see hoofprints departing from the area of the wagon? Could you tell what direction they were headed?"

"It was difficult, my lord, but we seemed to find prints heading to the south and east."

Again, Porphredo fought to display no reaction.

"My lord," said the northerner, urgently, "I beg you give me leave to follow those tracks. Send several of your own men with me if you wish. But lend me a horse, and let me find my countryman."

The Mirza stared at him and then nodded. "Better than that, I will come with you myself."

Porphredo turned. "Highness, surely you see the danger. I ask that you reconsider."

"She is right," said the northerner. "There is no need for you to abandon your men—"

"I have decided it!" Turning to the rider, the Mirza said, "Find us two swift horses and two more men to ride with us."

The sudden cacophony of shouting voices around her made Porphredo feel alone in the center of a human whirlwind. The Mirza strode away delivering orders, the northerner and the Goan priest argued with one another, Mughuls trying to dissuade their general or volunteering to go along.

Then Masum spoke quietly beside her. "Begum Porphredo, I am ordered to accompany you back to your tent."

Where I am to be made prisoner, no doubt. It must be I am grown too old for this game to have failed so. It will take all my remaining wit to plan how I will escape. "I understand, good *faylasuf*. I obey."

* * *

The Mirza Akbarshah strode back toward his tent, ignoring the shouting behind him. He remembered well the advice he had learned at his father's side, on long hunting trips in the forests of Kashmir—*"Good planning and foresight serves a leader well. But most important is the instinct of the heart. Thought will put you in the proper position, but sensing the moment of movement and seizing it, that will win you the battle, or the hunt."*

The Mirza's heart told him the yellow-haired Tamas was the one who knew the way to the hidden mountain, and now that the old woman had lied to distract the Mirza, Tamas had fled to seek the hidden city himself. Whether the young man had anything to do with the two dead men, it was clear he would lead the way to the immortal Queen, or whatever she was. And the Mirza knew he had to follow close behind, to prevent an alliance and to speak for the Emperor Akbar. Or to stop the westerners from learning her powers, if it was not already too late.

"My Lord!" shouted his lieutenant Jaimal, running up to him. "My Lord, can it be true what I hear? That you are abandoning us?"

The Mirza turned and laid his hand on Jaimal's shoulder. "Two westerners have escaped, Jaimal, and one of them has killed one of our men. For the sake of justice, I must track them down."

"But you yourself need not—"

"I must, or I am a poor leader of men. But I hope to return very soon. I place you in command of my forces while I am gone. I know you have longed to prove your qualities of leadership. Now Allah the All-Seeing has provided you the chance."

Jaimal's mouth fell open and great wonder filled his eyes as though he were witness to a miracle. He sank to one knee and clasped the Mirza's hand. "My lord, you do me a great honor to show me this trust. I swear by all that is sacred, I will prove worthy of this command."

"I trust your true qualities will shine forth, Jaimal. Lead the men well, and if I do not return in five days send more men after me, for there may be treachery ahead." The Mirza went inside his tent to retrieve his long *talwar* sabre and tie it onto his belt sash. When he again stepped outside, Rafi had ridden up on a tawny mare.

"My lord, I have learned you will chase the sorcerer who has killed my brother. I entreat you to let me come with you so that I might see justice done."

"Although we may not find the one who killed Mumit," said the Mirza, "I cannot deny your request, Rafi. Ride with me, and let us solve this mystery together."

"I thank you, wise lord."

On a small, black pony sat the westerner Lakart, who was listening to all with an anxious expression. *So. You had better hope your friend Tamas is innocent and not the evildoer I fear him to be.*

Sabur rode up then on a bay horse, holding the reins of a spirited grey. A water skin and bags with provisions were tied to its saddle. "Great Mirza, Lord Shahbad offers his steed to you and hopes that you find him suitable."

"It seems a fine beast," said the Mirza, accepting the reins. "What does Lord Shahbad call it?"

"He is called Albaki, my lord."

"The Enduring. An auspicious name." The Mirza quickly mounted the horse, and noted how pleasing it was to be astride a saddle once more, instead of sitting upon a lumbering elephant. By now, the tale of Mumit and the fled westerners had spread through the camp and a crowd of soldiers and horsemen had gathered. Many volunteered to come with him, of whom the Mirza chose only two more.

Then he raised his arm and called out to them, "Hear me, all of you. I now depart to serve justice and right a great wrong. Be it known that I have placed my trusted officer, Jaimal, in command while I am gone. Be as attentive to his orders as you would be to mine. I expect to return in a couple of days. Until then, stay vigilant, and may Allah the Merciful be with you all."

The Mirza nudged his horse forward and the crowd of men

parted before him. The rest of the riders followed closely behind, and Lakart brought his horse up very close.

"Lord Mirza," the westerner said, "Are you not taking a great risk by leaving your troops? I have been hearing rumors about Jaimal—"

The Mirza gestured for silence. "It shall be as God wills."

VIII

TURMERIC: This spice comes from the ground root of a plant which grows in the East which bears yellow flowers. In Latin, it is called *terra merita*, or "meritorious earth". A tisane of turmeric eases the colic. A tincture of saffron and turmeric in ale will cure jaundice in a horse. Some say turmeric will flourish only where blood is spilled. It is said Hindus believe it has powers to bring good fortune, and it is proper as a gift to show respect for the elderly. Evil spirits are banished by the scent of burning turmeric and this is ofttimes used as a test to learn whether someone is mortal or a demon....

Thomas opened his eyes and peered over Aditi's linen-wrapped head. His cheek was sticky from resting on her honeyed bandages. Ahead of them was a broad, brown river. On the other side of it was a village shaded by many trees. *How long I have been dozing? 'Tis a wonder I have not tumbled from the saddle.*

He turned his head and saw Timóteo now riding behind him, blinking in the noontime sun. "How fare you, little brother?"

"I am well," the boy called back, "but I am sleepy and hungry."

"As am I. Despoina, will we rest in this village?"

"Yes, yes, we will rest. But, remember, not for very long." She appeared to be searching for something along the river's edge. At the bank, she walked her horse back and forth until they came upon a rock to which a rope had been tied. "Aha. Here it is. This way." Stheno kicked her horse and walked it across the river, the water appearing to only be hoof-deep.

Thomas guided his horse to follow and found they were on a wooden structure that lay just below the water's surface. *A submerged bridge. Is the river ordinarily lower or was this deliberate?*

Once across, the horses stepped more lively, clearly also looking forward to the shade and rest the village promised. Thomas could smell the odor of cattle dung that characterized every Hindu village he had seen.

Three men dressed only in the diaper loincloths he had heard called *dhoti* came running out of the village to greet them. They were shorter and darker-skinned than the people Thomas had seen in Bijapur. The villagers stopped a few yards from Stheno's horse and suddenly flung themselves to the ground in extreme prostration.

As Stheno spoke to them, Thomas turned to Timóteo. "Do you understand what she is saying?"

The boy listened a moment, then shook his head. "My Papa once said there are more languages in India than God could understand, and that is why the Hindus have so many gods."

"An interesting philosophy."

"Devidur . . . ga," said Aditi.

"She says 'Great Goddess,' " Timóteo said.

"Poor thing. We must get her to some shade."

Two of the villagers ran past them to where they had crossed the river. They grasped the rope attached to a rock on this side and pulled very hard, then let go of the rope, which slithered into the water like a snake.

So, I am answered. thought Thomas. *Unless I miss my guess, that route can no longer be used by any who pursue us.*

The third villager ran back to the squat thatched huts, shouting something. Whatever he said had immediate effect for there was suddenly a flurry of activity as natives ran chasing after livestock and children and carrying them into the huts. By the time

Stheno's horse stepped into the outermost shade of the trees, the village seemed to be deserted.

There was an open area under the trees beside the nearest hut, and there Stheno stopped her horse and gestured for Thomas and Timóteo to do so as well. "Here is where you may rest."

As Thomas gratefully slid out of his saddle, he said, "Is it possible we may bathe Aditi in the river? Her swaddlings are discomfiting her and the honey is beginning to attract flies."

"I do not think it wise. How strong is she?"

Thomas reached up his arms to help Aditi dismount. She was able to reach down to him and lean against his chest. But as he set her on her feet, she slid further down him, her legs unable to hold her weight. "Alas, her strength has not fully returned, despoina."

"Then the current might sweep her away. We must wait until we reach Bhagavati."

She was right beside him, and Thomas could smell Stheno's sweat and perfume. For a moment, he looked at her veiled face, surprised that she was as tall as he. Through the black silk, he thought he glimpsed the outline of a strong pointed chin, and full, sensuous lips. He could almost see her eyes. . . .

She swiftly turned her face away. "I will have food and drink sent to you. Have a pleasant rest. I will return when we are to depart." Stheno walked away, a graceful, elegant roll to her gait that made it hard for Thomas to tear his gaze away.

"But, despoina, aren't you going to join us in our meal?" called Thomas after her, but she did not reply. He felt a stinging slap on his shoulder. "Hey!"

"I warned you!" said Timóteo. "Do not look at her!"

Thomas sighed with exasperation, the heat and weariness sapping his patience. "Have you become as judgmental as the Padre, now?"

An old man from the village came up to them and bowed, and took the reins of their horses. He led them away down the one road through the village, the way that Stheno had gone.

Thomas said, "Help me with Aditi here, Timóteo. My arms ache so I can scarce hold her."

Timóteo picked up her bandaged feet and together they carried Aditi to where a large mat of woven leaves had been spread upon the ground. Aditi sighed as they set her gently on the mat. A faint smile crossed her lips and she stroked Thomas' cheek with her fingers. She murmured something Thomas did not understand.

"What is she saying, Timóteo?"

"I think she called you her camel."

Thomas laughed, awkwardly. "Did she? Perhaps because I have bourne her for so far across the wilderness."

Aditi closed her eyes, and for a moment Thomas feared the revival had failed. But the pulse on the wrist was strong and her breathing remained regular. She was merely sleeping.

Timóteo knelt beside her and began to pray.

"She is not a Christian, Timóteo."

The boy looked up, surprised. "What does that matter? Surely since she has returned from the dead, she has seen the Truth."

"But she might not . . . oh, never mind." Thomas remembered that the carpenter's boy he had revived on the *Whelp* had described dreams quite unlike any heaven or hell Thomas had heard of. And the Padre had refused to describe his experience. Who knew what Aditi had seen?

Two native girls came running into the clearing, each carrying a wooden box. They dropped these on the ground about a yard away from Thomas, turned and ran back into the nearest hut.

Thomas retrieved the boxes and looked inside them. "They have left us food and drink, but did not tarry in serving them. These people are much afraid of strangers." Thomas pulled out from one box a hollow gourd with a hole at the narrow end. He poured some liquid out of it into one hand and tasted it. The liquid was water flavored with the juice of some unknown fruit.

"It is the lady they fear," said Timóteo.

"Who, Aditi?"

"No. The other one."

"How can that be? Stheno clearly knows this place and has been here before."

Timóteo looked toward the nearest doorway. Some children were spying on them from behind the plain doorcurtain. Timóteo put his hands up behind his head and waggled his fingers at them. The children's faces disappeared, accompanied by keening and stifled whimpers of fear.

"Stop that, Timóteo," said Thomas. "You are frightening them."

"They fear the lady will turn them to stone."

Thomas wondered for a moment if the heat had severely addled Timóteo. He had seen few cases of such summer fevers in Master Coulter's shop, but Master Coulter had told him of farmers who had worked so long in the sun that they became delirious and if not given shade and water immediately, would drop down dead. But there was a calm seriousness to the boy that Thomas had to doubt himself.

"Timóteo, do you feel well?"

The boy did not answer, but instead picked up the burlap sack he had brought with him from Goa. Looking around as if fearing to be watched he came closer to Thomas. "I must give you something, Tomás."

"That can wait. You must eat and drink something."

"No! It must be now. I may not get another chance. Here." Timóteo pulled out of the sack a small, silver-backed mirror. It had a wide brass frame, embossed with crosses, roses, and lilies. He handed it to Thomas.

Thomas glimpsed his own reflection and was surprised at how like bleached straw his hair had become, and how thin and tanned his face was. "It's very pretty, Timóteo, but I do not understand. Why did you want me to have this?"

"It is for protection," Timóteo whispered loudly. "Do not look at the lady, except in the mirror."

Thomas regarded the boy's earnest brown face with confusion. "If this is some jest, Timóteo, it has missed its mark."

"No! It is—I read it in the ledgers. In the Santa Casa."

"What did you read?"

"I . . . I cannot tell you."

"Ah. Yes. The Rule of Silence."

Timóteo nodded.

"But we are nowhere near the Santa Casa, nor the Padre."

"That does not matter. I swore an oath to God."

"Oh. But you can tell me I must use a mirror to look at Stheno. Yet I have beheld her for these many miles and no harm has come to me."

"If she is not veiled. You must use the mirror. Like Perseus."

"Like . . ." Thomas had been well read enough in the classics to recognize the name of the ancient Greek hero. "Timóteo, you cannot mean . . . that Stheno is . . ." his voice dropped to a whisper, "a medusa? A gorgon?"

But Timóteo stared into his food box and rummaged among the wrapped leaves and fruit, refusing to say more.

Porphredo sat in her tent, allowing her old bones to absorb the stifling heat, trying to think how escape might be possible. Or, if not possible, whether she could bear the pain and damage they might inflict upon her. And how much suffering she owed to the despoina Stheno.

The few men who chased after Stheno were not a worry. *If they catch up with her, the despoina can easily deal with them. It would be a pity about the Mirza, however. He seems a wise and capable man—the very qualities that might lead him to his death.*

Masum spoke from outside the tent. "Begum Porphredo, someone is here who, I think, wishes to speak with you."

"Who is it?"

"The priest from Goa. I do not understand what he wants as I do not know his language."

I should send him away. Yet now, more than ever, I must allay suspicion. "Let him enter, good *faylasuf.* I am pleased to speak with any who wish."

Masum entered first. *Perhaps to protect me? At least I have not lost his trust.* The thought was more pleasing than Porphredo expected. The priest entered next, in his dusty, once-white wool robe. In this smaller tent, it was clearly apparent the rumors that westerners of this day and age did not bathe often were true.

The Goan priest bowed slightly, his hazel eyes staring at her with admixed distaste and desire to know her secrets.

I have heard these priests of the Orlem Gor are merciless in their persecutions. But what can he expect to do to me here?

As he sat, the priest said, in his oddly accented Latin, "Good day to you, Domina Porphredo. I regret that we must meet again under such unfortunate circumstances."

Porphredo bowed her head and said, "Again, I share your sorrow for your loss and hope the lost ones of your party are found safe and well."

"And not fallen prey to demons or sorcerers."

He looks at me as though I were one. "Just so, *sacerdos.*"

After a pause, the priest said, "Your Latin is strange."

"As is yours to me, *sacerdos.* But I learned my Latin long ago."

"You may call me Padre Gonzao."

Porphredo tilted her head. "Padre? But you are not my father, nor could you be, given my age."

The priest closed his eyes. "It is . . . never mind. I would like to show you something." He pulled from a pouch at a rope belt a string of wooden beads tied into a circle with a small silver cross among them. He handed this to Porphredo.

Reluctantly, Porphredo took it. She murmured to Masum in Persian, "What does he expect me to do with this? Is it a gift?"

"I do not know, lady," said Masum. "I am unfamiliar with the ways of Christians. But I have seen such beads before . . . the Hindus use them for counting *vedas* as they chant them. Perhaps it is a similar thing."

"I see." Porphredo closely examined the silver cross. As she feared, it showed a man clearly in pain, nailed onto the crossbar.

"That is their holy symbol," said Masum.

"I know," Porphredo said with distaste. She handed it back to the priest. "I thought your symbol was once a stylized fish."

"That was very long ago, Domina," said Gonzao studying her thoughtfully. "The cross signifies sacrifice, and God's love for mankind."

"What does he say?" asked Masum.

"He says it is a symbol of sacrifice and love."

"Ah. Of course. It is the sacrifice of the material self to unite with the Divine."

"I am not sure that is what he means." To the priest, Porphredo said, "I find it an odd way to demonstrate love, *sacerdos.*"

The priest sighed. "It is a difficult philosophy to explain to the ignorant."

Coolly, Porphredo said, "Among my people, sacrifices are made to the gods to show one's devotion and to instill in them love and mercy for mortals. I assume that is not the same as what your symbol means."

"You are correct," said Gonzao. "It is not. If I may beg your patience a little further, I would like to read something to you." He placed the string of beads back in his pouch and pulled out a small, leatherbound codex.

"What does he say?" asked Masum.

"Now he wants to read to me. Do you think I am being tested?"

"It is possible, lady, though I could not say for certain."

Gonzao opened the codex and Porphredo caught a glimpse of one of the pages. "How regular the letters are!" she said. "A very fine scribe must have made that."

The priest looked up, brows furrowed in puzzlement. "It was not the work of a scribe, Domina. This book was created on a printing press."

"Masum," said Porphredo in a soft aside to the Sufi, "have you heard of a device that prints books?"

"Yes, lady, I have heard of such a machine. You can make many copies of a text with it, all exactly the same. My *pir* believes such devices are foolish, and will only spread confusion among the unlearned."

"But what a wondrous thing," said Porphredo. "Much information could be disseminated without error." Turning back to the priest, Porphredo said in Latin, "My queen will be most interested in your book and how it was made, and learning more about this marvelous device, the press." *Actually, she wouldn't, but I and my sister would and we would force the usefulness of it down our self-centered Stheno's throat.*

"So, there is something we know your wise queen does not. I am gratified to find I have something worthwhile to offer, but I am more interested in your thoughts on the content of the book than the means of its making." The priest cleared his throat and read a short Latin poem. It sounded as though it were a prayer, but it was about a helpful, generous royal shepherd. When the priest was finished, he seemed to be watching her.

He wants some reaction. Politely inclining her head, Porphredo said, "That was very pleasant. I believe my queen would like it, for she herself once tended animals long ago. Although, in her case, it was goats."

The priest closed his eyes as he closed the book. "I thank you for proving my foolishness to me."

Porphredo thought she heard irony in his tone. *But what have I proven? That I am not a demon to be banished by his holy symbols and spells?* Before she could think further on what he might mean, there came more shouts at her tent entrance.

"Make way! The commander approaches!"

Without any polite preamble, two Mughul soldiers entered, followed by the man called Jaimal, to whom Porphredo had given her silver *shal. Ah, the Mirza's second-in-command. What will this one do with me now that his master is gone?*

Porphredo stood and bowed low to him. "Good Commander, I wish you well at this trying time, and I hope I may be of as good service to you as to your Lord Mirza. Please make yourself comfortable, for all here is made possible by your gracious generosity."

"Well spoken, as always, honored ancient one," said Jaimal. "I came to see for myself that you are still comfortable, and to discuss how we might best serve one another."

Noting his correctness and cleanliness of dress, the thin line of his mouth, the intensity of his dark eyes, Porphredo thought, *This one is precise in his demands and desires. I must be careful if I am to make use of him.*

The commander glared at the Goan priest. "I hope you were not being disturbed."

"Not at all," said Porphredo. "We were having an interesting discussion about books."

"I see." Jaimal sat down near Porphredo, carefully positioning himself between her and Gonzao. The Goan priest, however, made no move to depart. "And this one," Jaimal said, indicating Masum, "has doubtless been pouring Sufi tales into your ear."

"Actually, he has been most helpful, Lord Commander, and I hope he may remain my advisor and host while I am among you."

"Hmpf," said Jaimal. "As you wish. I have come to beg your patience, lady. I am greatly worried for my general and hope that he does not come to harm on the Plain of Stones, of which you have warned us."

Not certain where he was leading, Porphredo said, "I trust your Mirza will soon encounter those who have fled before they come to harm. Then we may turn and make our way to the hidden mountain."

"Yes," said Jaimal, regarding her sidelong. "But until he returns, we are placed in a difficult position. Even an army so small as ours will quickly use up the resources available in this area, and if we are forced to wait several days here, our supplies may run very low. The local traders and caravans which pass through here are not all friendly to the Empire of Akbar and will not trade with us without sufficient encouragement."

Ai, is he testing me too? What does he want? Ah! Of course, what an old fool I am. "Please forgive me, Lord Commander," said Porphredo bowing until her forehead touched the floor of the tent. "I have been so thoughtless. Accept every apology imaginable that I have brought this hardship upon you and your men." Turning, Porphredo fished under the cushions for the wide, blue silk waist sash she had worn when she first entered the Mughul camp. She lay it before him and unfolded the cloth. Inside were seven flat silver bars, each about three fingers wide and one finger thick.

"I realize this is only a small token, Lord Commander, and I am embarrassed to be offering such a pittance in recompense for your troubles. I hope this will help in some way to provide food for your troops."

"I . . . indeed. Yes," said the commander, wide-eyed and staring. "This will be . . . helpful."

"I only wish I had more to give," said Porphredo. "But this is only a little travelling currency. I promise that when we reach Bhagavati, you will be recompensed in full."

"Just as was given to Ali Ahbad, when the stone hand of the nameless *shahid* was brought to him," breathed Masum, who now stared at Porphredo with eyes full of wonder.

Porphredo looked up sharply at the Sufi. *How does he know about that?*

Commander Jaimal took up the seven silver bars reverently. "Your humble gift, lady, is most acceptable. I, myself, have never doubted your good will. And yet, my Lord Mirza still persists in giving some credence to the insistence of the Goans," Jaimal quickly glared at the priest, "that your hidden mountain lies to the south and east. The fact that his scouts did not find your Plain of Stones only has made him more uncertain. Here you are, one lone elderly woman come into our camp to tell him we are ill-directed. Admittedly, you display great learning and . . . wealth. I cannot think what will convince my Lord Mirza that you speak the truth."

Or will convince you? "Was he not convinced by my demonstration of my queen's magic?"

"Ah, yes. The mongoose. Well, you know, in this land, animals are trained to do many wondrous things. Elephants do great feats of heavy labor. Cobras are taught to dance out of baskets. Birds are taught to speak. Who knows what a mongoose can do?"

He wants to believe, I can see that, but he needs another sign. For what? Another bribe? I have nothing more to give him. Ai, there is one more thing I can do, though it will weaken me, and endanger me if I fail to convince him. In her coldest, most austere voice, Porphredo said, "You doubt my queen's magic?"

"It is not I who doubt you," said Jaimal, holding up his hands. "I, myself, would follow your guidance in a heartbeat. It is only that I must explain to the Mirza and his men why it must be so."

Something is amiss here. I do not think the Mirza is in his thoughts. Perhaps he wants to lead the army away on his own. That could be to my advantage. But if I do not offer proof now, his own doubts may grow. Porphredo fixed her gaze on the ornate handle of a dagger that protruded from Jaimal's belt. "I understand. May I borrow your dagger, good commander?"

The two Mughul guards stepped forward in alarm. Masum sat up, eyes wide. Jaimal placed his hand on the hilt, frowning mistrustfully.

"Fear not, my hosts. I do not mean to commit murder, nor harm any of you. You wish a further demonstration of the magic that protects me. I will grant your desire."

After a pause, Jaimal nodded to the two guards and they backed away. He drew the long, recurving blade from its sheath and handed it to Porphredo, ivory hilt first.

Porphredo accepted it in both hands. The knife was a *khanjarli*, wickedly double-curved and, fortunately, quite narrow at the point. Porphredo held the dagger with the point to the side, so as not to arouse suspicions before she was ready. She forced her attention to focus to each passing moment in time, as Prabaratma had taught her, and other Brahmin mystics before him. She eased herself into a calm, but rigid, posture. She sought with her mind a certain spot within the body, a place between the heart and lung. Remembered pains found it for her.

Swiftly she let go of the knife with her right hand, and swept aside the upper drape of her sari. With a quick exhalation of breath, she plunged the dagger into her withered chest.

Coldness. And then pain. She scarcely heard the shocked cries of the astonished men around her. Porphredo waited one agonized heartbeat. Two. Three. Dark spots formed before her eyes. The floor of the tent blurred. Now. While she could still feel her arm, Porphredo pulled the *khanjarli* out of her chest, feeling the warm flow of blood down her underblouse.

"Honored lady, are you all right?" Masum's arms reached toward her.

Porphredo's lungs ached, yet she held her breath a moment more. Already she could feel the intense itch that meant the wound was healing. The flow of blood slowed. At last she took a ragged breath. "Yes, good *faylasuf,*" she said, softly. "I am well." She sensed, with relief, that there had been no damage to heart or lungs. Harm to those organs would have made her useless for at least a day or two.

Wiping the blade of the *khanjarli* on her underblouse, Porphredo handed it back to Jaimal. "You see, commander. My queen's magic protects me."

Jaimal stared in astonishment from the knife to her chest and back. The Goan priest appeared stunned and touched himself on head and shoulders in a ritual gesture. Masum lowered his arms and smiled with sad sympathy.

"T-truly, great lady," said Jaimal as he took back the dagger, "there can be no further doubt."

"I thank you." Porphredo even managed a smile. "I hope our alliance may continue now on a basis of trust."

"By all means," breathed Jaimal.

"Lady Porphredo, is there anything I can bring you?" asked Masum. "Any . . . medicine?"

"No, good *faylasuf.*" Porphredo pulled open the tear in her underblouse. The wound was now only a white scar. "As you can see, I have no need of any."

Jaimal was tossing the dagger between his hands unsure what

to do with it. Finally he handed it to one of the Mughul guards and said, "Clean this!"

The guard took it as though it had been dipped in poison and ran out of the tent.

Jaimal stood and bowed to her, lower this time. "I thank you and beg your forgiveness for troubling you, great lady. You have shown me all I need to see. Now I must go and make preparations that we may follow your guidance and advice as swiftly as we may." He left, pushing the remaining Mughul guard out of the tent ahead of him.

Masum watched him depart with a concerned frown.

The Goan priest stood, then, and said, "I do not know what I have seen here, Domina, whether sorcery or miracle. I cannot help but admire your courage. But I fear what you may bring upon us."

"Padre Gonzao, as I have told your fellow travelers, I wish no harm to any of your party. I will do what I can to see that no misfortune falls upon you."

"As it fell upon poor Joaquim? Somehow, Domina, I think, despite your impressive show, there are things beyond your power, whether your intentions are good or ill." He bowed and departed.

"Truly, lady," said Masum, "you have been touched by the hand of a Divine Power."

"Or cursed by it," Porphredo said, finally allowing herself to slump down onto the pillows.

"That cannot be," said Masum. "Experience of the Divine is the very goal of the Path. It is what we are taught to seek with all our hearts."

"There is a saying, good *faylasuf*, that one should take care what one wishes for, for the gods might grant it. If you please, I would like to rest for a while."

"Forgive me," said Masum, "I will disturb you no longer. Rest well, honored lady. May angels send you dreams of Paradise." There was sorrow and longing in his gaze—yet Porphredo sensed that whatever he longed for, it was nothing she could comprehend.

As the tent flap fell closed behind him, Porphredo curled around the cushions, allowing herself a quiet moan for the aching throb in her chest. *As long as I live, I swear by She of the Forest and the Moon, I will never, ever, do that trick again.*

Breath puffing, leg bones aching, Enyo at last reached the top of the stone stairs that encircled the Dove Tower. Though a breeze cooled her face, the sun seemed to beat down ever hotter. *Why do I forget my age so? But here I am, so hungry for news that I must come fetch it myself. I am so unused to Porphredo being gone that worries swarm around me like flies.*

Ahead of her was a carved basalt cupola, whose walls were an intricate lattice-work of stone. On the domed roof, stone doves perched, their tails fanned behind them. From within the cupola came the cooing of live birds who served as messengers to spies and allies of the despoina.

An old man in a dhoti stood in the shade of the cupola. "Your pardon," Enyo called out to him, "but have you seen Vayu, the bird keeper?"

The old man smiled. "I am he, Sri Enyo. I am pleased to see you once again." He brought his palms together before him and bowed deeply.

"But you cannot be. Vayu was . . . was . . ."

"Was much younger when you last saw him, Sri Enyo. It is usually your sister who comes. I understand time is not the same for you as for us lowly mortals."

Enyo cast her gaze downward, embarrassed. She remembered clearly the last time she had climbed the Dove Tower. It was to receive word that Vijayanagar had fallen. Then, Vayu had been a vigorous, handsome man. Enyo wished she had watched time pass gently across his face, not taken one great leap to age. "Forgive me, Vayu. I had forgotten."

"The gods never need forgiveness, Sri Enyo. Sattva has

brought a message." He pointed to a very white dove perched behind the stone lattice-work. "It is from Devidurga." Vayu smiled. "Both Devidurgas." He held out to Enyo a plantain leaf.

"They are nearly returned, then." Enyo smiled with relief. She unfolded the plantain leaf and read what was inscribed upon it:

Enyo,
I am returning.
I bring two guests.
Make rooms ready.
Me.

"Is that all?" said Enyo, frowning.

"It is the only message I have received in days, Sri Enyo."

There is no word of Porphredo. Is Aditi one of the "guests"? Did she revive? What sort of guests? So few strangers are allowed into Bhagavati. Probably male, the few strays the despoina brings in usually are. Ah, well, who can predict her whims?

Enyo handed the plantain leaf back to Vayu. "I thank you. Please do with this as you do to all others."

The bird keeper took it, bowing once more. "It is ever my honor to serve you and your house. Perhaps I will have the joy of seeing you again in my lifetime, Sri Enyo."

Enyo turned to hide her wince of guilt. "I hope so too." Not knowing what else to say, she gathered her sari around her and hurried to the steps to begin the long descent. *How sad. Well. It will be good to have Porphredo back again.*

IX

EMERALD: This green beryl hath great beauty and virtue. Drunk powdered in a tincture, or worn over a wound, the emerald will cure pestilence, poisoning, snakebite, and flux. It can prevent fits, or ease leprosy. The Hindoos believe an offering of emerald to their gods would confer knowledge of the soul and eternal life. Worn in a ring, it is said an emerald will warn of the approach of poison, and destroy the sight of serpents. It is oft placed on the limbs of corpses as a memento of eternal life. Emeralds are said to help men recover what they have lost, and will bring good fortune to travellers....

The long shadows and golden light cast by the setting sun made the boulders through which Thomas rode appear like fantastic behemoths turned to stone. *Damn the boy, for firing up my imaginings so. Everything I see will be thought a gorgon's work.* He watched Stheno riding ahead of him, her horse picking its way surely through the maze of rock and thorn bush. Thomas could not take his gaze from her, despite Timóteo's warnings. The more so because of them, in fact; Thomas studied the back of Stheno's head, seeking any sign of hair straying from her *shal*—and saw none.

But Andrew once said the Mohammedans do not allow strangers to view any strand of their women's hair, thinking it immodest. But Stheno is no Muslim. Round and round his speculations went. *I have not seen her eyes, and yet that too may be a matter of her people's traditions.* He could think of no polite way to ask her without hinting that he knew her nature, if gorgon she was. *And if she is no monster, what offense might she take? I dare not lose her good will. And if she is, what might she do upon learning her secret was known? She bears the blood that brought Aditi, and others, back to life. Is't not proof enough?* Thomas tried to recall what he had learned long ago of the ancient myths, but could not remember what was said about gorgon's blood.

Other than his thoughts whirling like dust devils in the desert, the ride was pleasant. The rest and repast had revived Thomas's spirits. A change of horses had given them more energetic steeds. Now that they were in the hills beyond the village, and the sun had lowered, the air was cooler. Aditi now had regained the strength to sit behind him on the saddle, her arms wrapped around his waist. He would have found the sensation of her pressing her body against him pleasanter still, were it not for the stickiness of her honey-soaked bandages oozing onto his shirt.

Timóteo was blessedly silent, riding last in the file, gaze firmly fixed on his horse's neck.

As they passed through a crack in an enormous boulder, Thomas thought, *'Tis well I have such a guide—had I come seeking her city on my own, I would never have had success. From afar, this cleft seemed too narrow for passage. And whatever signs guide her way are invisible to me.*

As they rode out of the cleft, on the other side of the enormous boulder, they came into a bare clearing. The far side was faced with a cliff in which a deep hollow, nearly a cave, had been scoured by wind and sand. Stheno stopped her horse and dismounted. "Here is where we will rest for the night."

Thomas slid off his horse, grateful for the chance to stop, yet dismayed by the roughness of the bivouac. As he helped Aditi dismount, he asked, "Should Timóteo and I gather firewood, despoina?"

"No. No fires. The smoke might be seen."

"Ah." *It will be a cold night, then.* "What shall we do for food, despoina?"

"In the bags on your saddles you will find rice loaves the villagers made. Forgive me, my beauty, for such poor fare, but I assure you there will be a feast for you when we reach Bhagavati. The floor of the grotto is filled with a fine sand, treated with a mineral that insects avoid, so you may sleep on it, or in it, comfortably."

"What mineral might that be?" asked Thomas. "Such a mineral might prove a valuable commodity to keep vermin from houses."

Stheno shook her head and laughed. "You are thinking like a lowly shopkeeper, herbalist. What I will reveal to you when we are home will be secrets beyond the deepest desires of alchemists and philosophers."

Thomas felt a tap on his arm. Aditi was handing to him a square bundle wrapped in a sort of leaf he found familiar. "Grape leaves? In India?"

"I grow them in my gardens," said Stheno. "But this climate is not good for grapes, and the wine they produce has been abysmal. Still, the attempt has been interesting. Now if you will excuse me, I must go and see that our trail is erased and the path hidden."

"I will gladly help, despoina," said Thomas. But Stheno had already vanished among the thorn bushes without a reply. "She surely cannot be a queen, she does so much of her own labor."

Aditi smiled and shook her head. "She . . . hunts for flies. For her little ones."

"Little ones?" Thomas wondered if Aditi's wits were not returning quite as fast as her health. He took her arm and guided her over to the sandy grotto where Timóteo already sat. Thomas crouched beside the boy and eased Aditi onto the sand.

"You have not said much this evening, Timóteo."

The boy shrugged and bit into his rice loaf.

"Are they good?" asked Thomas, undaunted by his silence. Thomas unwrapped the grape leaf and found a block of pressed rice with bits of onion, garlic, and lentils mixed in. He took a small bite. It had been spiced with cardamom, ginger, and cinnamon. He quickly downed the rest, thinking it the best meal he had had in quite a while.

He watched Aditi, to see if she were eating. She delicately nibbled on the rice loaf, but did not seem to be consuming much. "Aditi, have you ever . . . seen your stepmother?"

She looked at him, startled, her mind returning from some distance. "To gaze upon the Mahadevi is death."

"So you have said. But, what sort of death?"

Aditi blinked her grey-blue eyes, her face solemn. "Death" was all she replied. Her gaze shifted to the thorn bushes, or it may have been a distant boulder. In any case, Thomas suspected her mind was not on the immediate environs, but on matters beyond.

Someday I must ask her where she has been those long days her body lay in the wagon. Surely a Hindoo will be more free to speak of Indra's Paradise than a Christian will of Heaven.

But satisfied that no answers would be forthcoming from Aditi for now, Thomas threw his full attention on his dinner.

Padre Antonio Gonsção rose from kneeling, his legs aching. He glanced around and noticed that Estevão and Carlos were no longer praying behind him. For a moment, he panicked until he spied the *soldados* sitting and drinking outside his tent. *Much time must have passed while I was lost in supplication.* The sun had nearly fully set and the *muçulmanos* were no longer crouched upon their prayer rugs. In fact, the Mughul soldiers were bustling about with great activity; tearing up stakes, folding down tents, moving and grooming the animals—

Madre Maria! They are preparing to march! And Tomás and Timóteo have not yet returned. Gonsção strode over to Carlos and Estevão. "How can you sit here when this is happening all around you?" he shouted at them. "Go at once and find out why we are departing, and if the Mirza has returned."

"But Padre," said Carlos, "we do not speak the Mughul's languages. How can we ask?"

"*Sim,* Padre," said Estevão. "Usually it is Brother Andrew or the little brother who speaks for us, and they are both gone."

Gonsção balled his fists until his hands hurt, and then caught himself. *Peace, peace. There must be some solution. Who else present can I communicate with? That wastrel, the blind lute player spoke some Latin, but I would not trust anything he says.* Then his heart sank like a cold stone as he remembered another . . . the witch Porphredo. *If I must deal with allies of dark powers to complete the task for which I was permitted to return to this world, then so be it.* "Wait here," he said to the *soldados,* and turned in the direction of the witch's tent.

Her doorway was guarded by two sturdy Mughuls who regarded Gonsçâo suspiciously as he approached. As Gonsção came up to them, they blocked his way with drawn swords and growled questions at him.

Unable to understand them, Gonsção called out, "Domina Porphredo, are you in?" in Latin. "Please do me the favor of coming forth and speaking with me, if you are. A matter has arisen that is most urgent and I . . . I need your help."

"Indeed, *sacerdos,* I am present," was said within the tent. The doorflap of the tent moved aside and the tall, austere old woman emerged. The Mughul guardsmen looked uncertain but did not lower their swords. "What would you have of me?"

I am not intimidated by you, witch. "I find myself at a loss, Domina. I see around me, this camp preparing to depart. And yet I have heard no word of the two of our party who are lost, nor have I seen the Mirza return. I have no wish to leave this place until the boy and the *inglês* are accounted for. Yet neither I nor my soldiers can speak the Mughul tongue and—"

"You would like me to translate for you," said the old woman.

"I would," admitted Gonsção. He wondered if there was truly the hint of an ironic smile on her lips or if he were imagining it.

"I would be happy to give you assistance, *sacerdos*, but I have been informed by Lord Jaimal that, according to his people's custom, it would be unseemly for a respectable woman to wander an army camp at will."

How tiresome these foreign customs can be. But perhaps she might ask her guardsmen what is occurring. Before Gonsção could make the request, the heretic mystic Masum poked his head out through the tent opening and made questioning noises at Porphredo. *And she dares to speak of seemliness when she entertains a man in her tent. Such hypocrisy.*

After murmuring to the mystic some moments, the old woman turned to Gonsção and said, "Masum will do you the favor of seeking out Commander Jaimal and learning what matters are."

"I am grateful to him and will await his news," said Gonsção, not pleased that his source of information would be the odd unkempt Sufi.

The mystic flashed him a friendly smile and ducked underneath the guardsmen's swords. Gonsção stepped back as Masum took off at a run.

Madre Maria, Gonsção thought as he fidgeted, not wanting to meet the old woman's gaze any longer than he had to. *What strange path do you lead me down?*

Porphredo kept her gaze upon Masum's departing back, aware of the priest's discomfort beside her. *I am as curious as you,* sacerdos, *as to what is in the wind. Alas, I fear I know what has become of the two you have lost, but that information would not please you. You could have asked Gandharva, of course, but it is a good thing that you did not consider that.*

Long minutes passed before Masum returned, closely followed by the Mughul commander Jaimal striding proudly, closely followed by several armed and watchful men.

It cannot be fear of me that leads him to protect himself with escorts. No, they watch the camp around them. He fears other Mughul soldiers. I smell treachery.

"Good Lady Porphredo," said Masum, who was the first to reach her, "I have brought the commander, who says he will gladly answer all your questions."

"You have exceeded my expectations, good *faylasuf.* I am most grateful."

Jaimal and his cohort walked up, not hiding their dislike and distrust of the Goan priest. The priest seemed wary but held his ground. The Mughul commander smiled and bowed deeper than he needed to Porphredo. "Great and Wise Begum, messenger of the Immortal Queen of Life and Death, I am told you are troubled. Please tell me your concerns and I will, with great gladness, do all I can to allay them."

So. It would seem my little knife trick has won him over. Or he wishes me to think it has. I wonder if this bodes good or ill. "Good commander, it is not me who wishes reassurance, but the poor priest here, who has lost two beloved members of his party."

Jaimal scowled at him. "What does he want?"

"He is perplexed by the activity he sees around him, which appears greatly as though we are preparing to move again. Yet he has heard no word of his comrades, nor seen the return of the Mirza, whom he wishes were here to advise him."

"Tell the heretic priest that his lost lambs are not our concern. This army was given its mission by the Shahinshah Emperor Akbar, and we shall not stray from our purpose. You have convinced me, wise lady, that yours is the path we should take. Let the Mirza go chasing sorcerers in the wilderness. He will catch up to us when he has had enough of his futile hunt. We will wait no longer while our men come closer to starvation in this desert. We turn around tonight and head in the direction you advise."

My, my, I have succeeded all too well. The advantage here is that your vainglory and greed will help you make foolish mistakes, commander. The disadvantage is that I will be nearby when you make them. Porphredo sighed and turned to the Goan priest. "The noble commander offers sympathy in the disappearance of your fellow travellers. He reminds you that no less a personage than the Mirza himself has gone in search of them, and he hopes they are found well and unharmed. However, the Mirza left orders with the commander to move the expedition to a safer campsite, as it is clear from the loss of your man to snakebite and his to sorcery, that this place is ill-omened and dangerous. The Mirza will easily catch up to us once your companions are found."

The priest shifted from foot to foot and regarded her with an uncertain frown. "I see. I can understand that the Mirza would be concerned for the safety of his men. We will not go far then? It is the boy I am most concerned about. He may have simply wandered off seeking herbs and gotten lost. If anything untoward happens to Timóteo, those responsible shall answer to God for it." He looked pointedly at the commander.

Porphredo smiled sympathetically and turned to Jaimal. "The heretic priest offers sincere gratitude and apologizes for not before acknowledging the magnanimity of your Great Mirza in searching himself for the lost westerners. The priest will gladly cooperate fully with your wishes, hoping only that he might soon see his lost companions again. He offers the blessings of his god upon you."

Jaimal raised his brows and lightly rested his hand on the hilt of the sword at his side. "That is well. Tell him he and his pointy-hatted soldiers had better behave like civilized men, and not give us any trouble. If they cause any disturbance, it will go hard on them."

"I will tell him," said Porphredo. "Padre Gonsção, the commander thanks you and swears by his sword that you and your men need not fear. He has every hope that the boy and the other will be returned safely. In the meantime, you will be treated with all respect and courtesy and if you have any wishes or concerns, you need only make them known to him. He wishes only harmony between your people and his."

The priest sighed, his face relaxing almost into an awkward smile. "It is clear how different our cultures are, for I nearly thought his words more belligerent from his tone of voice. I am glad my impression was in error and that the commander appears to be a man as honorable as his general. Thank him and tell him we will follow to this new campsite to await the return of our friends, may God preserve and watch over them." The priest bowed and walked back toward the two remaining Goans.

Porphredo translated this last speech nearly verbatim.

"So," said Jaimal, "these heretics are capable of reason. Although I suspect, lady, that you have honeyed my words a bit."

Porphredo smiled ruefully. "It must be my womanish nature, commander."

"Of course," said Jaimal. "Masum tells me that it brings you discomfort to be closeted in your tent. If you like, you may do me the honor of joining me in my howdah on my elephant tonight when we depart."

So it is your elephant now, eh? "It would be my honor to ride with you, commander, and share stories of the wondrous things you will soon see."

"Excellent! I will send for you when we are ready. Until then, you may feel free to walk where you will."

"Your kindness to a lowly messenger is great indeed, noble commander." Porphredo bowed. "May your fame grow ever greater."

Jaimal drew himself up a little. "So it shall, Lady Porphredo. And soon."

As he and his bodyguards strode away, Porphredo noticed Masum regarding her pensively. *So you caught the lies I was telling, did you, good* faylasuf? *Can you ever forgive the sweet discord I must sow in order to protect my despoina and her people?* Despite her newly offered freedom of movement, Porphredo returned to the enclosed darkness of her tent.

The Mirza Ali Akbarshah squinted in the dim twilight at the cracked and broken ground before his horse's hooves.

"My lord!" called Sabur from ahead of him, "We must stop for the night before it is too dark. I am no longer able to find the track and my horse nearly stumbled into a ditch."

"No," said the Mirza. "They already have too many hours' advantage. If they stop for the dark we may have a chance to catch up to them."

"But we cannot see! The moon will not be bright enough tonight."

The Mirza dismounted. "Then we will gather firewood and make torches." He tied his horse to a boulder nearby and began to pluck branches from the few scrubby, dead bushes around him. His men and the westerner Lakart did the same, choosing larger branches to be the brands and smaller ones to fuel a fire. When enough twigs were set in a pile on the ground, Lakart proved to be skilled with firemaking, first coaxing a spark from his flints onto the twigs, then gently breathing life into the flames by blowing on them.

"You have done this often," the Mirza observed.

"I have wandered the world, Highness, and many a night have I found the spirits of fire to be my only warm companions. They have saved my life a time or two. Like your fine horses, treat them well and they give you good service. Mistreat them and they can do you grave harm."

The Mirza was disturbed by this personification of a simple, if useful, element. *Fire may be a gift from God, but it is not divine in its own right. Perhaps this man is a Parsi after all, for it is said they worship fire. What a puzzle he is.*

"For what have you wandered the world, Lakart?"

The westerner stood and dipped his brand into the leaping flames. "In service of a demanding mistress, my lord."

"A queen? A lover?"

"A great lady, Highness, but although she rules my heart and owns my life, my affections are but chaste and distant." He raised his torch and gazed toward the heavens.

The Mirza turned his head to follow and saw only a thin crescent moon. "Does the moon remind you of her?"

"So she does, my lord." Lakart went to retrieve his horse. "Shall we ride on?"

"Let us stay on foot so that we might better see the track in the firelight. It is fortunate that the trail runs so straight to the south and east. Whoever is the guide of those horses knows exactly where he is going."

"So it would seem, Highness."

"You believe it is your yellow-haired friend, the one whom you gave an oath to his father to protect, that we follow."

Lakart paused, then said, "That is both my hope and fear, Highness."

"Do you believe he truly knew the way to the hidden mountain, and these tracks may lead us there as well?"

More softly, Lakart said, "That is also my hope and fear."

"Why should you fear? Perhaps this queen will be like the one whom you serve, and thus seem familiar."

"That, my lord, is my greatest hope and greatest fear."

The Mirza sighed. *He persists in speaking in riddles.*

"Lord Mirza," said Sabur, "We should hurry on."

The Mirza paused, wondering if he should return to the camp to convince Jaimal and all the rest of his men to come this way, despite what the mysterious old woman had told them. *But winds may come and obliterate the trail. And a queen who stays hidden may welcome fewer men than an army.* "Very well, Sabur. Let us continue."

X

CYPRESS: This venerable tree bears small needles which are evergreen, and grows in nearer Asia and the Holy Lands. It is a plant of cooling, ruled by Saturn, and therefore good for fevers and for burns. The fruit eases pains of the bowels, and chewing the seeds brings health and strength. To the ancients, the cypress is sacred, and it is said the cross of our Lord was hewn from it. The ancients believed the pillars of Solomon's temple were made from cypress, as were the bow and arrows of Eros. It is a tree of the Fates and the Furies, as well as the rulers of Hell. The coffins of heroes were made of cypress wood, for it was thought a symbol of the immortal soul and woe....

Porphredo awoke before sunrise, her back and limbs aching from lying upon rocks and uneven ground. As the morning prayers of the Muslims filled her ears, she fished among the pillows and brought out a small oil lamp. In her sack of few belongings, she brought out a flint and lit the wick of the lamp, balancing it precariously on the nearest large rock.

The little light it cast showed her that the central tent pole canted at a dangerous angle and the corner poles each leaned in a different direction. The tent had no floor, only rugs and pillows thrown over stony ground. The flickering shadows cast by the lamp flame made the tent seem in the midst of continuous collapse.

Jaimal had marched the army through much of the night, down one of the abandoned roads that lead southwest to Vijayanagar. The sight of hundreds of torchbearers had been magnificent from Jaimal's *howdah,* but Porphredo could not make herself comfortable with the commander's open, solicitous greed. *A good thing I am so ancient. Surely his hand would have been upon my knee, or worse, were I of younger form.*

The army had finally camped late in the night, without consideration for the lay of the land. So tents had been set up hodgepodge around a narrow, stone-filled gully. It was dry now, though clearly in earlier months, it carried monsoonal torrents down to the Krishna river.

"Lady messenger?"

The whispering voice at her tent flap made Porphredo jump. "Yes? Who is it?"

Without waiting for permission, Masum entered. He hesitated just inside the tent, his expression anxious and sad.

"Good *faylasuf.* Why are you not praying with the others?"

"Allah the Merciful forgives when there is reason." His hands were shaking and he could not seem to stand still.

"There is reason you must visit me before dawn?" For a moment, Porphredo wondered if he had come to do violence upon her, yet she could not imagine that being in his nature. *And surely my knife-in-the-chest trick convinced him of the futility of such an act.*

"Indeed." He rubbed his eyes and ran his fingers through his wild beard. "I come to you, lady, for I do not know whom else to trust."

"I am . . . honored that you still trust me, Masum."

He looked at her. "I trust what you are doing can only be for good reason. My heart tells me, whatever else, you cannot be evil. What sins you commit, you do in the name of peace."

Porphredo felt an inner ache that she had not experienced in a long time. "I am pleased you think so, for I have cause for what I do. But it seems, good *faylasuf,* that what your heart tells you brings you sorrow."

Masum shook his head and sat on the dirt as though a chair

had been kicked out from under him. "It concerns matters other than you. Last night, before we departed, I remained at our old camp to gather the last things left behind. Jaimal thinks little of me so he gives me the lowest tasks. But while I was there, hidden from sight, I suppose, by some bushes, Jaimal rode up with four bowmen. I heard him order them to remain among the rocks beside the road, to wait for the Mirza's return."

"In order to ambush and kill him," Porphredo surmised.

"Just so," Masum whispered, staring at his hands.

Porphredo sighed. *Why is there this ache in my soul? Is this divisiveness not what the despoina wanted? It will destroy the expedition utterly. But . . . the Mirza is an honorable, intelligent man. And I have no wish to bring victory to the likes of Jaimal. As for Masum, who seeks only peace and joy and knowledge . . .* "Good *faylasuf*, have you come to me hoping for my aid?"

The Sufi looked up, tears in his eyes. "It is much to ask, I know. But dear lady, if there is any part of your queen's magic that might save the Mirza, I beg you to use it on his behalf. I, myself, am not skilled in subterfuge, or I would seek out those loyal to the Mirza and raise a revolt against Jaimal. But I do not know who is loyal and who is not. Jaimal has promised great wealth to all the men once we find your hidden city. Those who loved the Mirza may have been corrupted by the promise of gold. I never was a good soldier. Perhaps that is why I was called to The Path. I hid and prayed so often on the battlefield for protection that prayer became my natural vocation."

Porphredo laid her hand on Masum's arm. "I do not know what manner of magic would save your Mirza. But perhaps, between the two of us, cleverness can."

His eyes opened wide. "You will help us?"

"My task for my queen is done. My message is delivered. Now I may do as I choose. You understand, however, that in helping you I must tell you secrets that no one else may hear."

"Dear lady, I swear upon the light of my soul, that your words shall be known only to me and to God."

"Very well. I think help for your Mirza is possible, for I know where the trail he follows leads. And where he will, by necessity, stop. If he has been unfortunate, then our efforts will already be in vain. But if he still lives, I know where we can find him, and warn him."

"But great lady, to do so we would need the wings of angels. He has travelled opposite our direction and, if he is not yet returning, he is many miles away. We cannot steal horses—they are guarded more jealously than men guard their wives."

"We will not need horses, good *faylasuf.* Now, I must reveal to you that there is one other among us who serves the queen as I do. It is the blind *vina* player, Gandharva, whom perhaps you may have seen among the dancers in the entertainer's wagon."

"Indeed, I have spoken with him—at Ibrahim's palace as well as on our journey. He speaks like a most clever fellow."

"I assure you, he is. We will need his assistance. You must be the go-between for him and me, for I wish no suspicion cast upon him. You must go and ask him if he has any doves left. If he does, our plan becomes simple. If he does not, then our task becomes more difficult and dangerous."

"Speak on, Lady Porphredo. I am as attentive as the monkey to the breadfruit merchant."

"If Gandharva has no doves, then we must carry the message ourselves. To that end, we must consider the Hindu god of love, and speak of wine."

The coolness of the grave seeped into Thomas's bones. The earth was close around him. Overhead there were cries of women mourning. *Have the harpies had their will of me at last? But I yet live, or have the semblance of quickened thought.* With great effort, he managed to raise his right arm a little. He began to dig at the dirt around him, faster and faster, hoping to claw his way out before he suffocated. . . .

And woke to find himself sprawled in the sandy dirt beneath the rock overhang, on the trail to Stheno's hidden city.

"Tomás?" said a rumpled and dirty Timóteo, sitting up out of the sand beside him like another corpse rising from its grave. "Is everything all right?"

Thomas sighed. "I think so."

"You had another dream, yes?"

"Yes. I dreamt I was dead."

Timóteo shook the dirt out of his black, bowl-cut hair. "That is not a good omen, Tomás. It warns you to be careful."

"Perhaps." He heard a rustling to his left. Two doves were sitting on a bush just outside the grotto. They burbled, sounding for a moment like two weeping women. Then, disturbed by something unseen, they flew away.

He heard a sound between a whine and a moan behind him. Aditi was sitting with her back to the grotto wall, plucking dolefully at her linen wrappings.

Yet here is one who is truly risen again. Thomas went to her and gently grasped her shoulders. "Aditi?" She was no longer sticky for the fine coat of dust that covered her.

"These . . . off," she said.

"No, no, Aditi. Your mother says you will be fully bathed when you get home."

She looked up at him sharply, her steel-blue eyes wide. "Mother?"

"Nai, Aditi. She is here and she is guiding us to your hidden city."

"That . . . cannot be."

"It is true. It was her blood that revived you."

"So," said Stheno, coming around the face of the grotto, "have all the souls returned from the banks of Lethe?" Her voice was low, musical, and slightly mocking. Again, she was swathed completely in black silk, resembling a dark ghost or its shadow.

How my thoughts do dwell on death this morn, when I might be rejoicing at my freedom.

"Mahadevi!" cried Aditi. She flung herself prone on the ground and crawled to Stheno's feet. "Forgive . . . me."

"There now, dear Aditi." Stheno bent down a little, but did not touch her. "Do not trouble yourself."

"But . . . I failed you."

"We can discuss that later, when you are better. Tell me only this. Who was it who slew you?"

"I . . . neck. Sword blade."

"Yes, we have seen the wound but who dealt it?"

Aditi shook her head. "The priest . . ."

"The priest of the Orlem Gor?"

"He . . . tried . . . threatened . . ."

"There, now, you have said enough."

"He . . . would have hurt Tamas!"

Thomas felt a pang in his heart. *She gave her life to spare me. How can I ever repay such sacrifice? Or have I done enough to return the life she lost?*

"Peace, now, child. We will talk more on it later."

A good thing Timóteo does not speak Greek, or he would be shouting denials to the skies. It may be that the Santa Casa does not kill, as he has claimed before, but Padre Gonsção is far from the Santa Casa and may no longer feel bound by its strictures.

Stheno turned her head toward him. "You seem pale, golden one. Did you sleep well?"

"I dreamt that I slept all too well, despoina."

"You speak in riddles, my sphinx. Come. You must eat and then we must be on our way."

The spiced rice loaves had become dry, and were not as appetizing as they had been the night before. Stheno did not eat with them, as before, and Thomas wondered, *Do immortals have no need of earthly sustenance? Or is she like the Hindu whom Joaquim once threatened to torment . . . one who thinks eating a distasteful thing to be done in private? Or is what she eats so foul that she must hide it from us?* Fearing he might anger her, Thomas chose not to ask.

Stheno led into the clearing three horses—fresh horses, not the ones they had ridden from the village. *From whence come these, I wonder.* But Thomas helped Aditi onto the saddle of one and mounted up behind her.

As Stheno took the reins of her horse, the animal balked and shied away. The black-swathed woman cursed it beneath her breath in some language unknown to Thomas. The horse backed up, ears flat, eyes wide and Thomas feared it might rear and lash out with its hooves at her. A gust of wind whipped through the clearing, causing the cloth over Stheno's head to flutter and ripple.

As Thomas watched in horror, Timóteo had already slipped out of his saddle and was beside Stheno's mount, stroking her horse's neck and speaking softly to it. *Dear God, he will be trampled!* But the beast calmed and at last, with an uncertain whinny, stood still.

"So," said Stheno in Latin, "there is some use to you, child of the Orlem Gor. I thank you and shall remember this."

Timóteo murmured something Thomas could not hear, staring fixedly at the horse. He held the bridle as Stheno remounted, speaking to it and stroking its cheek. Then the boy turned away from her and walked back to the horse he had been given.

As he passed, Thomas sighed and said, "You still dare the intercession of angels, do you? Remember what the Padre warned you about that."

Timóteo shrugged. "I worked in the stables in the Santa Casa when I first came there. I learned a lot about horses. They are like the lost sinners who came to us. They are fearful, but they need only gentleness and to know the love of God to ease their spirit."

"Ah." *There is something uncanny about the boy. Perhaps he does not need the mirror for protection. Perhaps the angels will intercede for him, even if he faces a deadly visage out of legend.*

Leading the way through a rocky cleft that Thomas was sure hadn't been there the night before, Stheno guided them through a labyrinth of thorn and stone. If there were signs to show the way, Thomas could not spot them. *I wonder if De Cartago had known of this, and gave hint in the map he drew? If so, the Padre knows more than I who never saw it.* The slope grew gradually steeper. The trail was cunningly laid, however, so that Thomas could only see the hilly ridge behind them and the ridge before, but not know if there were higher mounts beyond.

But of course. A great mountain that overshadowed the desert below would be clear to see and a beacon for any seeking a fabulous city. This way, one is not certain there is a mountain at all.

After a couple of hours of tedious riding, they came to a high cliff face with large boulders at its base. Thomas glanced around but could see no trail leading left or right from there. Stheno slid from her horse and walked up to the cliff, examining the rocks that towered over her.

Does she mayhap seek a sign that points the way from here?

Stheno picked up a stone and approached one of the boulders. As Thomas wondered what in Heaven's name she might be doing, she rapped on the boulder with the stone. The sound it produced was not the clacking of rocks, but a hollow knocking as if upon a door.

There came a deep rumbling from within the cliff and Thomas looked quickly up to see if a rockslide might be cascading down the cliff. But the only rock that moved was that which Stheno had rapped upon, which rolled impossibly by itself to the side.

"Tomás, look!" said Timóteo. "It is like the stone the angels rolled away from our Lord's tomb!"

Though amazed, Thomas suspected there was more artifice than miracle at work. An enormous, iron-banded door was revealed behind the rock, which slowly opened inward.

"Come," ordered Stheno as she remounted her horse. "Quickly."

Thomas nudged his horse with his heels to follow her. The beast went willingly toward the dark entrance as if it knew the way. As they reached the door, Thomas turned his head and saw the boulder that rolled was, in fact, painted wood on a frame. He thought he perceived a small man in turban and *dhoti* hiding within it. "There, you see, Timóteo. It is no mystery. Her people are very clever, and would do any theatre master proud."

"I have never been to a theatre," said Timóteo.

"Then you have been spared from many sins," said Thomas, chuckling.

The enormous door led into a tunnel, lit very dimly with rushlights. As Timóteo's horse passed through, the door shut behind them with another rumble, leaving them entirely shut off from the world.

The air was very close and smelled of damp earth. But there were also the familiar smells of a Hindu village. As they stood in silence, Thomas could barely discern the sounds of people around them—the rustle of clothing, the clink of jewelry, whispers to hush frightened children. *Do people live here in this darkness? If this be the hidden city, it is more Hades than Olympus.* "Is this your home, Aditi?" he said softly in her bandaged ear.

"Home," she said in a tone so tentative, Thomas could not tell if it were affirmation or question.

Somewhere ahead of them, Stheno called out, her voice like the crack of a whip. Footsteps pounded far ahead of them, running away. A man cried out the same words over and over.

"Can you tell what he is saying, Timóteo?"

"No, Tomás. But I think he is saying the queen is coming."

"Are you still there, my golden one?"

"Nai, despoina. Is this your hidden city?"

Her laughter echoed off the rock walls and ceiling. "Why, what must you think of me? This is only an entrance. We have a ways to go yet. Come along now."

Thomas nudged his horse, aware now of an occasional human-shaped shadow lurking in side tunnels that branched off here and there. Their horses' hooves plopped softly on the dirt floor. Timóteo whispered a continuous litany of prayers behind him. On and on they went, the tunnel sloping upward. Thomas became uncertain as to how much time was passing. The world narrowed to this tunnel of echoing whispers and faint islands of torchlight amid the darkness.

At last, after what may have been hours, there came a rumble ahead of them. Thomas flung his arm up before his eyes as sunlight seared the tunnel to brilliant white.

"Welcome to my city, golden one," said Stheno. "Welcome to Bhagavati."

* * *

The Mirza walked his horse for the twentieth time along the river's edge. He gazed across the brown, swift-flowing water, at the village on the far side, frustratingly near. "There must be a way."

"My lord," said Sabur, who was soaking wet from the waist down, "we have searched all morning. I tell you, the tracks end at the water and they do not turn left or right."

"Then they must have crossed at that point."

"I have searched the water, my lord. One horse-length from these reeds, the water drops off and becomes too deep. The current would sweep any horses downriver."

"And I have tried to shout across the river," said Lakart, "but the villagers either ignore me or run out of sight."

"The ones we chase," said the Mirza, "would not have simply walked their horses into the river to drown." He studied the brown, bouldered hills that rose, each ridge rising slightly higher than the one before it, beyond the village. On such ridges everywhere in the Deccan, the Mirza had seen ruined fortresses from ancient, fallen kingdoms. But there were no fortresses on these hills. *A sign that a greater city lies that way, or that one never has?*

"My lord," persisted Lakart, "if we return to your main force and lead them here, we have rope and men enough to build a makeshift bridge. It would take but three to four days, at most, and the weather may stay calm for that long."

"No!" said Rafi. "Do not listen to the unbeliever, my lord. If we leave the chase now, Mumit's murderer will too easily slip away."

The Mirza sighed. "There is much in what each of you say." He turned in his saddle to look back the way they had come. It was many hours' ride back to the main camp, and he did not wish to return empty-handed. Jaimal would, no doubt, fight all the more against continuing in this direction. But what more could he do here at the riverside?

"Highness," said Lakart, "can you or any of your men swim?"

Reluctantly, the Mirza shook his head. "I cannot." Sabur, Rafi, and the others as well said no.

"I grew up on the cold, rocky shores of Scotland," said Lakart, "and I know some things about swimming against the pull of water. I could cross the river alone, and see if I could learn from the villagers where a ford might be."

"My lord," said Rafi, "this unbeliever could leave us behind while he goes and finds the city of the Sorceress by himself."

The Mirza raised his brows and asked the Scotsman, "So. Can we trust you?"

Lakart gave him a self-deprecating smile. "I swear by all that is holy that you will see me again before sunset."

"But you and I do not consider the same things holy," said the Mirza. "Will you swear by the moon?"

Lakart's smile fell. "As you will have it, then, Highness. I swear by the moon."

The Mirza nodded. "Go, then. And may you have success. We will look for you by the sunset prayer."

Lakart kicked his horse and rode some ways up river along the bank.

"He will never return," muttered Sabur. "What sort of oath is that, to the moon? What sort of idolater is he?"

"I believe he is a man who chooses his oaths carefully," said the Mirza. "And he rides with us because of an oath he made unwisely, or against his will, long ago. He will return."

If Bijapur had been a city out of fairy tale, Bhagavati was surely an apparition out of legend. Once Thomas's eyes became adjusted once again to the bright sunlight, he could not help but blink in awe and wonder.

Bijapur had been ornamented with elegant calligraphy and delicate lattice-work; its austere mosques embellished with hints of lotus and other botanical imagery in its columns and walls, teasing the gaze to seek out detail. Bhagavati, however, assaulted the eyes with sculpture everywhere; every pillar, post, lintel, and wall was covered with carvings in stone. Horses, camels, elephants, tigers, bulls wearing heavy necklaces, from small to life-size and greater, pranced, crouched, and reared in relief or stood almost fully rendered as if being born from the rock. Human figures were carved as well; nude female dancers, hunters shooting arrows at fleeing deer, priests making devotions, warriors in fierce battle, musicians with flute and drum, nobles in grand procession. More disturbing were the figures of what Thomas presumed were Hindu deities—half-human, half-animal; fat ones with elephant heads, women with many arms and great bulging eyes and lolling tongues, and the graceful creatures who were serpents from the waist down—some of whom had snakes on their heads as well.

One could scarce determine the shape of the houses, or tell dwelling from temple for the profusion of creatures adorning the walls. From the blocks of entry stairs to the top of the stepped, pyramidal roofs, all was covered with the incredible carvings. The city seemed in constant, writhing movement, an unending dance frozen in stone. It was dazzling, dizzying to the sight, and Thomas saw that Timóteo as well could not keep his gaze fixed in any one place but constantly turned his head this way and that, eyes and mouth opened wide.

In strange contrast to the liveliness of the architecture, Thomas noted the streets were silent, save for the distant tolling of deep, clear-toned bells. As in the village below and the tunnels they had just emerged from, there was sign of habitation but no sight of it. Thomas sensed there were people all around them, hidden within the buildings, but saw no one. It was as if the city had instantly become deserted the moment he had set foot in it.

"Aditi, where are all the people?"

"They . . . hide. Out of respect for the Devidurga."

"Respect or fear?"

"Is . . . not the same thing?"

"In my country, when the queen passes, the ways are made clear for her, but the people crowd the windows, doorways, and walks, even to the very gutters and rooftops, in hopes of catching a glimpse of her."

"Here . . . that is forbidden."

For respect of her or because she may be a danger to them? pondered Thomas. *Though oft with many monarchs, it is much the same thing. Their fear alone does not prove she is more than mortal.*

The road wound about in circular, spiralling fashion, bringing them ever nearer to a mount in the center of the city. Other buildings obscured what was on the mount until a plaza opened before the riders. In the center of the plaza was an elephant, one foot and trunk raised in fear and challenge. As they rode by, Thomas could not help but wonder if the elephant had ever been real. At the far end of the plaza, a series of broad steps rose to a wall of black stone, in which had been set two huge bronze doors.

Behind the wall, the central mount rose, covered with monumental porticoes, pillars, domed cupolas, octagonal towers, and arrays of colonnaded buildings which resembled drawings of Greek temples that Thomas had seen. The mount was an architectural monstrosity, nothing fitting in a unified design, no attempt to blend one portion to another—bits and pieces from different eras and civilizations all tossed together. "A jackdaw's palace," Thomas murmured.

The bronze doors opened, and a line of men in long saffron robes emerged and arrayed themselves on the steps. At some unseen signal, they began to chant in low tones that boomed and echoed across the plaza and made Thomas's skin prickle.

"They sing . . . to welcome us," said Aditi.

"You understand them?"

"It . . . is one of the *vedas*, but I do not know it."

"Why are these men blessed with the privilege of being in their queen's presence?"

"They . . . are priests. Therefore they are all blind."

"Ah." Sickened, Thomas scanned their faces, noting what Aditi said was true.

Through the opening between the bronze doors, a small old

woman, wearing a plain beige shift gathered at the waist and shoulders, emerged. This one was clearly not blind, for her eyes were intact and bright with hope as she hurried down the steps and up to Stheno's horse. "Welcome back, despoina!" she said, in Greek. Is . . . ah, Aditi!" She ran to Thomas's horse and held up her arms to Aditi. "What have they done to you? You look like a dead queen of Egypt!"

Thomas helped Aditi slide down into the old woman's arms. "Is . . . Gandharva's fault. To preserve me. This one," Aditi pointed up at Thomas, "saved me."

The old woman looked up at Thomas. "How amazing! I have not seen one with his color hair in many ages. Will he understand me?" At Aditi's nod, she continued, "I thank you, shining lord, for returning our Aditi to us."

"It was my honor and pleasure to do so, good woman."

"Ah! Ah! He speaks our tongue," cried the old woman. "It has not faded from the world after all."

"It is one of the tongues of scholars, madam, and thus remains preserved."

"That is pleasing. But . . . where is Porphredo? Is she not with you?"

Thomas was momentarily taken aback by the mention of the crone who had entered the Mughul camp. *But of course, servants of the Mahadevi would know one another.*

"If you have finished prattling, Enyo," said Stheno, "You may take Aditi and bathe her and make her comfortable. You may also see that our guests are shown to their quarters and given refreshment."

The little old woman was not to be deterred. She walked right up to the black-clad Stheno and demanded, "Did you leave her behind? By herself? How could you?"

Stheno sighed, "Your sister is quite capable of handling matters, unlike you, and I have no doubt that she will return when she pleases. Besides, she has Gandharva to help her. Now will you see to my daughter and our guests or must I send you to do inventory in the crypt?"

The old woman sighed and then noticed Timóteo who was staring at her. "Who is the boy?"

"A tag-along," said Stheno, "but an important one. Treat him as an honored guest."

"Tomás, I know what she is!" Timóteo exclaimed in Latin. "She is another one of the Grey Ones. Perhaps she is the one with the Eye!"

The old woman's eyes went wide and she put a hand to her throat. "Despoina . . ."

"Pay the child no mind, Enyo. Take Aditi and go."

The old woman put her arm around Aditi and, with fearful glances back at Timóteo, led her up the stairs.

"It appears I must see to your lodging myself. Leave your horses where they are and follow me."

Thomas slid off his horse, feeling ill at ease. "You should not have been rude to the old woman, Timóteo," he said softly to the boy.

"But it is true, don't you see?"

"Hush. We will discuss this later." *If this Queen Stheno is merely a monarch with unlikely habits, it will not do to offend her. But if she is as Timóteo fears, his knowledge may endanger us, and then we are no safer than we were in the midst of the Mughuls. Mayhap, e'en less so.* Thomas followed Queen Stheno, a walking sliver of night, up the stairs and through the great bronze doors, doing all he could to shut his ears against the eerie chanting of the sightless priests.

XI

COLUMBINE: *This plant is named for the petals of its blue or white flowers which hath the shape of five doves, for columbus is the word for dove in Latin. It is also called Lion's Herb, for it is said that to rub the leaves upon the skin brings courage. A decoction of the root will ease the gullysuffe, and a salve from it eases the rheumatics. Tea of columbine leaves soothes all aches of the mouth and throat. Although an herb of Venus, it is a symbol of love deserted, and some think it an herb of folly. . . .*

Gandharva patiently turned his *vina* as he rode on the roof of the entertainer's wagon. The string he plucked at was old and he could tell it would soon be breaking. Suddenly, there was a jingling from the dove basket.

"Gandharva!" said the girl Pramlocha, "A dove has flown down and walked into your cage! I did not believe you when you said the ones you sent would be replaced."

"Excellent. Well, now you see the value of faith, my sweet. What color is the dove?"

"It is white."

"Ah. It is from Devidurga, then."

"You are sent doves from the gods?"

Gandharva smiled. "You might say so. If you please, look closely at the bird and see if there is some paper or leaf wrapped around its leg."

"Yes, there is."

"Do me the favor of removing it, gently mind you, and giving it to me."

"The dove is very tame, Gandharva. Is it someone's pet?"

"No, it merely knows its job and does it well. Do you have the paper?"

"It is a frangipani leaf. But it is all scarred up."

"Do not mar it further, girl, just hand it to me."

"As you wish."

Gandharva held out his hand and felt her press the leaf onto his palm. He let his *vina* fall to one side of his lap and placed all his attention on the leaf in his hands. The "scars" of course were letters incised onto the leaf so he could read it by feel. The letters were Greek, therefore the message was from Stheno.

The priest killed her.
Bring him to me. Alive.
Stheno

"Why do you fondle the leaf so, Gandharva?"

"It speaks to me, dear girl."

"I heard nothing. Do the gods send a message of good fortune?"

"It speaks of justice to be done."

"Ah. The gods are so stingy with their gifts sometimes. They can be very cold."

"So they can, my dear. Very cold indeed."

Padre Antonio Gonsção still seethed as the Mughul army halted to make camp for the evening. His brows ached from scowling all day through the dust and the heat. *They lied. The witch or the commander or both of them. They do not care if Timóteo and Tomás are found. They even leave their general behind, allowing that withered sorceress to lead them through the wilderness with stories of great treasure.*

Gonsção dismounted from the bony nag the Mughuls had given him to ride. Carlos and Estevão, who had ridden beside him, did likewise. A silent Mughul came and took the horses from them.

"Padre, I fear that we are no longer considered welcome here," said Carlos.

"I fear," said Estevão, "that tomorrow they will give us no horses at all and we will have to walk behind the elephants."

"Brother Andrew, before he left us," replied Gonsção, "assured me that these *muçulmanos* take great pride in their hospitality and fairness. This commander Jaimal owes us much, if this is true."

Carlos shook his head. "I would believe it of the Mirza, Padre, but not of this other fellow. This Jaimal has never regarded us with courtesy. He always looks at us as if we were thieves."

"I would be careful in approaching him, Padre," said Estevão.

"Fear not. I will not risk all our lives so easily. Let us find the witch woman and have her translate for us again."

But as the Goans wandered among the men who were setting up tents and penning the camels and the horses, they got no helpful reply to their question, "Begum Porphredo?"

At last, Gonsção said, "This is foolishness. These Mughuls probably do not want us speaking with her. Ah. There is that entertainer's wagon. Perhaps we can convince that craven heathen of a lute player to tell us something."

Gonsção led the soldiers to the gaudy, gilded wagon as the Mughuls were laying out their mats for prayer. The blind Hindu musician was sitting beside the wagon, intent upon tuning a string.

"You, there. Musician. Gandharva, is it?" Gonsção said to him in Latin.

Gandharva tilted his head. "Ah, the priest of the Orlem Gor. Gonzao, is it?"

Gonsção held his irritation in check. "Yes. We are searching for the woman Porphredo. Have you seen . . . Do you know where she is?"

"Yes, yes! She was here not long ago. I think she will be back soon. You may sit here and wait for her. I will entertain you to help pass the time."

"That will not be necessary," said Gonsção. He gestured to Carlos and Estevão to search around the immediate vicinity.

"Ah, but the good priest misunderstands. I have many stories to tell. Secrets and advice to offer. I can be helpful to the westerners, if they only ask."

"Secrets," scoffed Gonsção, "what secrets would I care to know from you?"

As the prayer-songs of the Muslims echoed around them, Gandharva said, "You know that the path we now take is a false one."

Gonsção blinked in surprise. "You know that the old woman lies?"

"Of course she does," said Gandharva. "She protects her Mahadevi's hidden city. Why should she want an army appearing on her doorstep?"

Gonsção folded his arms across his chest. "Now you will tell me that you, alone, know the way to this hidden city?"

"The priest of the Orlem Gor is very wise."

"The priest of the Orlem Gor is no fool. How much did you think we would pay you to lead us there?"

"Nothing."

"Hah! You would lead us astray, then, so that others could rob us."

Gandharva shook his head. "It does not bring good *karma* to live in suspicion of those around you."

"I have found it brought me much good to be cautious in dealings with others."

"The priest of the Orlem Gor does not understand."

Gonsção heard a shout from one of the soldiers some ways behind him. He did not reply to the musician, but turned and called, "Carlos? Where are you?"

"Down here!"

Down? Gonsção pressed his way through a dense line of bushes and found himself at the top of a steep, rocky embankment, that sloped down to a rushing brown river. Carlos and Estevão stood at the river's edge, examining a piece of blue cloth.

Estevão motioned for Gonsção to join them. "Come look at this, Padre!"

Gonsção skittered clumsily down the embankment. "What is it?"

"Was this not a part of the old woman's dress?"

Gonsção examined the torn piece of blue silk shot with silver thread. "Yes, that appears very similar."

"And look here, Padre. These look like spots of blood. And they are still damp."

Gonsção gazed out at the river. *Did someone else recognize her lies and do violence to her here?* "Have you found any other signs of her?"

"There were footprints, Padre. And over there it seems some wine has been spilled onto the sand. But nothing else."

"If she has been drowned," said Gonsção, "it is possible her body has already washed downriver where none of us would find it."

"But I thought the old woman was invulnerable, Padre. Protected by her queen's magic. Did you not tell us you saw her stab herself and not die?"

"Perhaps," said Gonsção, "her queen's magic only protects her when the damage is expected. Perhaps she was not immortal after all."

"The commander will be very angry," said Estevão. "He was counting on her to lead us."

"Yes," said Gonsção. "We must inform him of this. Perhaps it will put us in his good graces again if we bring this to his attention. He may finally listen to us and return to where we last saw Timóteo and Tomás. Come."

They clambered back up the embankment and Gonsção looked around for the blind musician. He was no longer beside the wagon.

"What will we do without him to translate for us?" asked Carlos.

"We will make Commander Jaimal understand. There are ways." Gonsção gazed across the backs of Muslims crouched in prayer and saw the commander's large, striped tent.

The Hindu sentries at Jaimal's tent lowered their lances toward Gonsção and the soldiers at the Goans' approach. Gonsção held up the torn blue cloth and said only "Begum Porphredo."

The sentries exchanged dismayed glances and one of them ducked inside the tent. A loud argument ensued, of which Gonsção understood nothing. When the Hindu soldier re-emerged, he motioned angrily with his lance for the Goans to enter.

"I suppose the commander was angry with him for disturbing the prayer," said Carlos, as they passed into the tent.

Indeed, Jaimal stood frowning beside his prayer rug. Gonsção bowed to him, in European fashion, and held out the scrap of bloodied blue silk.

Jaimal snatched it from his hand and stared at the swatch.

"We found it," Gonsção said slowly, carefully and a bit loudly in Latin, "by the river. You understand? River?" Gonsção undulated his hands in the motion of the water. "We fear she has been harmed."

Jaimal barked out a sentence and the sentries re-entered and grabbed Gonsção's arms.

"What are you doing?" Gonsção shouted. "Surely we would not have brought you this evidence if we were the ones who harmed her!"

Carlos and Estevão each stepped back and drew their swords.

"No!" said Gonsção. "Drop your weapons, both of you. This is merely a misunderstanding. It is not worth our deaths."

With great reluctance, the soldiers did so.

Looking back at Jaimal, Gonsção said, "Search for Gandharva. The blind musician. Gandharva can translate for us. Find Gandharva."

Jaimal spoke to the sentries again and Gonsção was led away, the two soldiers following.

The gods must delight in imperfection, thought Porphredo as she clung to the bundle of inflated wineskins, *for nothing has happened as I would wish it.*

She had hoped to leave after dark, but Jaimal had let her know he expected her company after evening prayers. She and Masum had had barely enough time to hurry to Gandharva's wagon to fetch the wineskin floats that he had prepared and get to the river's edge before sentries were posted at the camp's perimeter. In her hurry, she had scratched herself on a thornbush and torn off part of her sari. *But I am an old worrier. No one would find that unless looking for it.*

And she had more immediate things to worry about. The water of the Krishna River was fast at this point, and there were boulders to avoid or flow over with caution. To her surprise, Masum was handling his float well, slipping through the rapids with ease. When the river widened and its water calmed, and they were clearly far from the Mughul camp, Porphredo shouted out to him, "Good *faylasuf,* I did not know you could swim!"

"Neither did I!" he replied with a grin.

"Then you take to the water remarkably well."

"Water is a necessity to all life. How can I not feel at home in it?"

Porphredo, feeling only cold and wet, shifted her grip on her float and clutched the wineskins tighter. "I fear I cannot agree, Masum." *From all this soaking, I wonder if I can become any more wrinkled than I already am.*

Somehow the Sufi swam closer to her and extended his arm. "Take my hand."

Porphredo did so, though uncertain of the wisdom of it.

"Listen to the rhythm of the water and let it soothe your spirit. Watch the play of light on its surface and let it beguile you. Let its smoothness draw away your fears. Breathe deeply and let the water bear you up, for surely it is in water that the soul of the Divine resides."

Whether it was the touch of his hand or the sound of his voice that caused it, Porphredo began to feel calmer and let herself drift with the river current. She reflected that were she still a young girl this would all seem a grand adventure. She cast a sidelong glance at Masum's soggy-bearded, happy face and found herself very much wishing she were younger.

The Mirza frowned toward the setting sun. Its light, glinting off the ripples of the Krishna River, stabbed at his eyes like tiny, bright daggers. Noting the lateness of the hour he resumed his vigil, watching the Hindu village across the river.

"He will not return," said Rafi, sitting beside the Mirza under a stunted tamarind tree. "We should have gone back to the main force long ago."

"We will wait a little longer," said the Mirza.

No sooner had the words left his lips when a commotion was heard from across the water. A figure burst from between two thatched huts in the village and came running up the far bank, pursued by villagers throwing rocks and sticks. The Mirza stood. "It is Lakart. It seems he returns after all, though, perhaps, not willingly."

As his pursuers drew nearer, the stocky westerner dashed into the river and began to swim toward the Mirza. But the current was strong and Lakart was still carried downstream.

"Let us go see where the river takes him," said the Mirza, mounting his horse. "He may need our assistance." Not waiting to find out which of the other men followed, the Mirza rode along the river until he found Lakart clinging to an overhanging branch. The Mirza dismounted and extended a branch to him, pulling the soggy, gasping Scotsman onto the bank.

"I am glad to see," said the Mirza, "that you are a man of your word."

"Kindly forgive my delay in returning, Lord Mirza," puffed Lakart, "but, as you can see, I had little cooperation from the natives in my search."

"You are forgiven, but only if you tell me all you have seen."

Lakart sat heavily on the riverbank and paused, catching his breath. "I was unable to find any tongue I had in common with these blackamoors. Nor did they pretend to comprehend my gestures. I must have capered like a madman to try to make them understand. Eventually, they simply ignored me and went about their business. I find it interesting however, that these primitive folk seem well fed and healthy despite living in such an isolated collection of hovels.

"I looked for hoofprints, but any tracks there might have been were obscured by the passage of the villagers' feet. I sat in a clearing under a tree and wondered what to do. But after sitting quietly a little while, I heard the snorting of horses, and, following the sound, I discovered a hutch where three horses were tethered—horses that were still sweaty from having been ridden a fair distance."

The Mirza stared at the village. "So. Your friends may yet be hiding somewhere near."

"No. I suspect they have ridden on, using fresh horses—the hutch showed sign of much use as a stable. But there is more. While examining the horses, I heard the burble of doves."

The Scotsman paused as if this were significant information, and for a moment the Mirza wondered if Lakart perceived it as an omen. "Doves, eh? What of that?"

"Again I followed the sound and discovered several doves. In cages."

The Mirza began to understand. "The sort of doves used for sending messages?"

"Just so," Lakart said with a knowing nod. "I set one of the birds free and watched as it flew quite directly to the south and west, into the hills. Then the villagers found me and gave chase."

"Perhaps they thought you were trying to steal the birds."

"Or thought I had already learned too much."

"Mmm."

Rafi then rode up. He did not seem pleased that the westerner had returned. "My lord, shall we return now to the camp?"

The Mirza gazed back the way they had come, across the barren wilderness. Bringing the army back this way would mean greater resources to cross the river and perhaps get answers from the villagers, or the Begum Porphredo. But it would also mean several days delay, while the trail of those they pursued would become covered with dust. Jaimal would not be pleased to take the westerner's word and would require some convincing to agree to turn the army this way. What had the Sufi said about his dream, long ago? The Mirza could not quite remember. A cup that held water or dust or gold or blood. This cup, it seemed to him, had a hole in its bottom and the contents were running out before he could determine if it were dust or gold.

"My lord?" Rafi pressed.

"Let us consider how we might cross the river," said the Mirza. "If we cannot find a way by sunrise, then we will return."

Thomas had not known what he expected to see in Stheno's palace. The Gagan Mahal, the Sultan Ibrahim's palace in Bijapur, had been filled with treasures and designed so that everywhere one looked the eye was delighted or dazzled with architectural decoration or graceful gardens. Master Coulter had once been to Whitehall, where Queen Elizabeth lodged in winter, and had described it as full of people, constantly coming and going on some business or other.

Stheno's palace was like neither of these. The stone corridors they had been led down were dark and bare, and though recently swept, they smelled of dust and mold and age. At times, a sliver of daylight on a wall revealed a fresco that had long ago faded. If there were royal treasures, they were hidden or in some other part of the palace. Of people, the only other denizens Thomas saw were the occasional blind priest. The corridors were silent, save for the mournful cry of a peacock from some distant garden.

It has more the semblance of a tomb than of a palace, Thomas thought. *A palace of the dead. Or one who should be.*

At last, Stheno stopped before a wooden door. "Here is where you will be lodged, my golden one. And there," she gestured toward another, smaller door, to the left, "the boy may stay."

"We thank you, despoina," said Thomas, "but may I ask—"

Stheno had put her hands to her head as though it ached. "You must excuse me," she interrupted. "I . . . must leave you for now. I will send Enyo to see to your needs. Do not wander the palace without her escort, for it is . . . old and parts of it are dangerous. I will see you again this evening." She turned and hurried down a side corridor.

"Despoina, are you well?" Thomas called after her. But she did not reply and quickly vanished amid the shadows of the dark passageway.

"Perhaps her serpents bite her," said Timóteo.

"Hush! Speak no more of that. Not where she or her servants can hear you."

"I do not think she cares that I know, Tomás."

Thomas found this more chilling than reassuring. "Let us not risk insult, at least, by speaking of it openly. We do not yet know the dangers in this new place. Come, let us see what lodgings we have been given."

Thomas pulled open the wood door, noting with some concern that it could be barred from the outside, and stepped in.

Here was the sumptuous opulence he had been expecting to see: the narrow bedframe was polished gold, with stylized cobra heads on the posts. The counterpane was linen with many gold threads woven in. Crossed swords with golden hilts hung high on the wall. A chair and table were carved ebony. The plush rug on the floor was similar to those in Ibrahim's palace. Large brass lamps hung from the ceiling, each suspended by three chains. The lamps were necessary because, Thomas noted, the room had no windows.

"Tomás! I think these are Roman swords!" said Timóteo. He rushed over to look at them, but they were out of his reach. "My grandfather once told me about the gladiators and centurions."

"Did he?" said Thomas. He sat on the bed and noticed that the counterpane was frayed at the edges and slightly stained. And clearly quite old. He also observed the small piles of dust and cobwebs near the walls. "It would seem the Domina Stheno does not have guests very often."

"We are very lucky, Tomás."

"Somehow I suspect luck does not enter into it," said Thomas, thinking over all the decisions and events that had led to his arrival.

"You are right, Tomás. It is not luck. It is God's will."

"Or someone's." Not knowing which deity was now guardian of his soul, whether the Protestant God, or the Catholic, or the pagan goddess his father had worshipped, Thomas was loth to ascribe his fate to any one of them.

Thomas heard movement and the clicking of crockery by the door and he waited for a servant to enter. When, after a while, no one did, Thomas got up and opened the door.

A wild-eyed monk wearing only a *dhoti* and saffron string jumped back, shaking and bewildered. He fell to his knees and bowed several times. Several bowls were lined up beside the door.

"Er, your pardon. Timóteo, can you come speak to this fellow?"

Timóteo walked up. "He is doing *puja.*"

"What is this? Some form of ceremony? A welcoming rite, perhaps?"

Timóteo shrugged. "I do not know. It is Hindu worship and I know little about such things."

"Worship?"

"I have seen people in Goa doing such things on the steps of temples, before their idols."

"As if I were . . . a god?"

"I do not know, Tomás."

The small old woman with bright eyes came around a nearby corner and gasped when she saw the monk. She shouted at him and fluttered at him with her hands, shooing him as if he were a stray dog pissing on the doorstep. With much mumbling and bobbing of the head, the monk acquiesced and went shambling away down the corridor.

"Forgive us," said the old woman in Greek as she gathered up the bowls and set them aside. "That was just Prabaratma. One of the despoina's pets. He is harmless, though sometimes I believe he is mad."

"No need for apology. I was merely startled. What was he doing here?"

"Who knows? Pay him no mind, he is mad." She straightened up with a sigh. "Are you finding your quarters comfortable?"

"Yes, they seem quite . . . adequate. How is Aditi?"

The old woman's face broke into a glorious smile. "She is well and will recover fully. I thank you again, despotas, for rescuing her."

"You and she are most welcome. Although I had help from one known as Gandharva."

"Ah! Gandharva! We miss him too. He was such a pleasure to have nearby. Will he be returning soon?"

"I fear I do not know, madam."

She took a step closer. "If you please, can you tell me if Porphredo is all right?"

"The Despoina Porphredo is . . . your sister?"

The woman nodded. "I am Enyo. And it is not truly right to call us despoinas for we have been servants all our lives. Please, is she well?"

"The last I saw of her, she was quite well and preparing to guide an army of Mughuls in a direction well away from here."

"Ah." The trace of a worried frown remained in Enyo's brows. "So she may not be returning soon."

"As to that, I cannot say."

"I see. I thank you. Is there anything I may get or do for you to refresh you?"

"I do not know about Timóteo, but I should like to bathe, if I may."

Timóteo came out from behind Thomas and Enyo stepped back, clearly wary of him.

"What has she been saying, Tomás?"

"Merely asking if we are happy with our quarters, and asking after her sister, who was the grand sorceress who revived the mongoose." To Enyo, Thomas added quickly in Greek, "The boy means no harm, he is merely curious."

Hand to her throat, Enyo nodded, uncertain. "I am glad to hear it, despos. If the young magister wishes, I can speak Latin."

"That might be better." To Timóteo, he said, "Is there any request you have for your comfort? I have requested a bath."

"A bath!" Timóteo echoed, earnest wishing in his eyes.

"Alas," said Enyo, now speaking her oddly accented Latin, "if my sister were here, we could bring a tub to you and hot water. But she is not, so I must guide you to our hot-spring pool, if that will please you."

"That would please us," said Thomas. "May I ask why there are so few servants here? This seems a very large palace—it surely must require a great deal of care."

Enyo fidgeted and looked aside. "The Domina Stheno is . . . selective about whom she keeps near her. For her safety and theirs. She prefers to live simply, and have only a few servants."

"But she must have a kitchen with cooks, mustn't she?"

"The people of Bhagavati provide us with food. And the monks have their own cook, and they eat very little."

"I see. And gardeners?"

"My sister and I groom the gardens."

"Ah."

"The monks sweep the corridors and clean the . . . latrines as part of their devotions. Really, I cannot see how our common daily habits would interest you. Let me guide you to the hot spring. But you must please follow me and do not stray from the way that I lead you."

"Yes, the Domina Stheno has already warned us. Parts of this palace are old and dangerous."

"Precisely. This way, if you please."

They passed by the door Stheno had indicated as Timóteo's quarters and Thomas briefly opened that door and glanced in. The room beyond was small, strewn with what appeared to be soft cushions, and one low, round table. But it was open on one side, a graceful colonnade separating it from a balcony that overlooked a garden.

"Hm," said Thomas, "your room is in some ways pleasanter than mine, Timóteo."

"Is it? We could switch if you want, Tomás."

"No!" said Enyo. "You must not do that. The Domina Stheno was very specific that you, Domine Tamas, have the . . . grander room. She would be very upset to learn you had lodged somewhere else."

"Well. We mustn't upset the Domina Stheno, must we?"

"That would be unwise," said Enyo.

Thomas and Timóteo looked at one another and continued following the old woman.

She led them on a circuitous route, but Thomas sensed they were again spiralling inward toward the center of the palace. Timóteo would dash from wall to wall, peering down side corridors, behaving far more boyishly than he had in Stheno's presence. It was clear his curiosity was unsettling to the servant Enyo, but she did not chide him until he pressed his face to a narrow opening between walls at the juncture of two corridors.

"Tomás! Come look! I have never seen trees like this before."

Thomas walked over and likewise pressed his face to the opening. "Those are cypress, Timóteo. They grow in Europe.

And there are oaks, too! I never thought to see such trees in this far land. It is near enough to make me homesick. What a lovely arboretum."

"And look," Timóteo said, "there is a pond or lake in the middle."

"If you please, magisters!" called Enyo from behind them. "You are not to look there."

Timóteo left the opening and ran up to Enyo. "Please show us the way down to that garden. I would like to see more of those trees."

"No," said Enyo, firmly.

"But I am an herbalist! So is Tomás! We study plants so we can heal people."

"I am most sorry, young magister," said Enyo, tension in her voice, "but that is a holy place. A sacred garden. You are not permitted to enter."

"No doubt," said Thomas, going over to them, "the Domina Stheno would be most upset if we were to enter it, even accidentally?"

"Yes," said Enyo. "She would."

Something in the old woman's manner led Thomas to believe that Enyo would object even more than Stheno. *I doubt I could convince her to slip us in without the Domina's knowledge.*

"Please, is there no way we could just peek at it?" persisted Timóteo.

"Pray leave off pestering our guide," Thomas said to the boy. "We must be respectful of our hosts and their strictures. This includes places they regard as holy. You wouldn't have visitors blundering into the sacristy in the Santa Casa, would you? Even if they begged and pleaded."

Timóteo subsided somewhat. "You are right. I am sorry."

The little old woman's shoulders fell and she sighed. "That is all right. You are new here and do not know our customs. If you will, the hot-spring pool is nearby. Kindly follow closely."

She turned and entered a staircase that led down into a dark grotto, lit only by openings in the rock dome overhead. It struck Thomas as being similar to the Aljouvar in Goa, the grotto prison where men awaited the judgment of the governor. But instead of being filled with hopeless men, this grotto contained a large pool, steaming with warm water. The steam carried a faint mineral scent, far more pleasant than the stink of the Aljouvar. Still, the spring was nothing like the airy, dazzling pools of the Gagan Mahal. This pool felt more ancient, hidden, secret, primal. Though its facing stones were clearly hand-shaped, it was more a thing of nature than of man.

"Enter and be comfortable," said Enyo. "I will go and fetch you towels and fresh clothing. I must insist that you do not leave this place until I return to guide you. Will you promise me this?"

"Yes, of course," said Thomas, wondering just what dangers lurk to prey on the unwary in such a deserted palace.

Enyo left them and Timóteo flung off his robe and jumped into the water. Thomas did the same and felt the mineral waters instantly soothe his skin.

"It is like Cupid and Psyche," said Timóteo as he sputtered and splashed around.

"Who? What?"

"One of the old stories my grandpapa told me. A beautiful girl, named Psyche, has to go off to this big, mysterious palace, where she can only live in one part and mustn't see the rest. And Cupid, the god you know, he comes visit her at night and . . . kisses her, I guess. Only, she can't look at him, ever, and she doesn't know who he is. Finally, one night she lights a candle and sees him and . . . something bad happens. I forget what."

Thomas remembered the compliments Stheno had plied him with and shivered. "Your story is not reassuring, Timóteo. But all palaces have forbidden places. Besides, there is already one tale our hostess belongs to. We should not mix our myths, should we?"

Timóteo did not answer but ducked his head underwater, then came up and shook his bowl-cut locks like a dog.

Besides, thought Thomas, *my part in this story should be nearing its end. I have brought Aditi safely to her home and found the source of the* rasa mahadevi. *Here I might discover ancient knowledge that I can take back home to England. Knowledge that will allow me to be welcomed home as a great travelling scholar and not a failed apprentice. That should be my story, and not some sad and faded legend.*

XII

SAINT JOHNSWORT: This small herb has long, narrow leaves, and the scent of turpentyne. It brings forth yellow flowers in midsummer. It is thought to be particularly efficacious on St. John's Day, from whence it has its name, and some will place the herb in an amulet for children to wear so that it may protect them from all ills. St. Johnswort oil will help heal and clean deep wounds, and a poultice of the leaves will draw venom from a snake bite. Crusaders who brought the herb from the East called it "demonsbane" and it is said to protect a home from demons and disease. Some say the leaves show scarlet blotches upon the day of the year when Salome, it is said, demanded St. John's beheadment. If a man treads upon the wild herb, some say a fairy horse will appear beneath him and bear him away....

Aditi dressed herself slowly, gazing at the moon. Though only half full, its light was bright on the balcony outside her room. Her arms and hands were slow to obey her will. Her thoughts moved slowly as well, as if the honey in which she had been embalmed had seeped into her mind. But one thought was ever present since returning to consciousness in Gandharva's wagon: *I have been given another chance.*

Her door opened and Enyo came in. Aditi smiled at the old woman, who hadn't changed at all since Aditi was a child and a foundling. Seeing Enyo again reinforced Aditi's gladness. *At last, I am home.*

"How are you feeling?" Enyo asked.

"Much . . . better," Aditi managed to say. "But everything is . . . slow."

"That is all right. You have all the time you need now. Although the despoina would like to speak to you when you are ready."

The reminder of her adoptive mother, Stheno, made Aditi's hands tremble and brought doubt like a gust of cold wind to disturb her serenity. "I am . . . ready. Almost." As Aditi buttoned up her *peshwaz* jacket, she asked softly, "Does she . . . forgive me?"

"Forgive you for what, dear? Truly, the despoina rants and blathers about so many things it is hard to tell what upsets her these days, or pleases her. Except that I do not. I never have, and she never lets me forget it. Her loathing of me is the only emotion of hers one can rely on."

"Oh, Enyo," sighed Aditi with a smile. The *aya*'s complaints were old ones, as familiar as a favorite pillow from childhood. "You know the despoina relies on your good humor and gentle nature."

"Takes advantage of it, you mean. Ai, I will be so happy when Porphredo returns. Her skin is so much tougher than mine. She can turn aside the despoina's barbs like chain mail turns away swords."

Aditi only answered with another smile.

"Oh here, dear, you have missed a button." Enyo came up to her and fussed over her clothing and combed and braided her hair. Aditi bore it with the delicious feeling of being a child again. *As if I had, indeed, been reborn.*

Finally Enyo stepped back. "There—now you look presentable. She can't chide me too much. Are you ready to go?"

Aditi nodded and took Enyo's arm, for her steps were still unsteady. She had not walked in days, and her legs had to relearn the motion, it seemed.

Slowly they proceeded down one of the many palace corridors. Aditi was glad they needed to go slowly, for her eyes wanted to drink in the precious, familiar sight of the dimly lit passage and remember those years of childhood when the palace was a playground, and every twist and turn of passageways held mysteries, ancient stories in the faded frescos, strange inscriptions, broken statues, and wild, half-tended gardens.

It was odd, she now knew, that she had never missed the company of other children. She had had the monks and her *ayas*, Enyo and Porphredo, to be her friends and playmates. And with an entire palace full of wonders to roam in, she had rarely been bored. Now she had Tamas to share it with. Aditi wondered what he thought of it.

Enyo led her out into a garden with a raised platform—The Garden of the Monsoon, Aditi remembered it was called, for it faced the direction from which storms approached and often bore the brunt of the first heavy rains. It could be used now, for it was the dry season.

On the platform stood several columns supporting nothing, as if it were a ruined temple. Aditi paused, for the moonlight on the columns reminded her of some image from visions she could no longer recall—visions she had had after her death. Screens of black cloth were placed here and there amid the columns, for a purpose. Somewhere in the shadows they cast sat the Mahadevi, the Devidurga, the Despoina Stheno.

"We are here, despoina," Enyo called out.

"Good. Leave us, mouse. I would converse with my daughter alone."

Ah, Aditi's skin tingled to hear that voice again. So rich with wisdom and power.

Enyo bowed and swiftly departed. Aditi stared at the darkness at the heart of the platform but could not speak.

"Welcome home, Aditi."

Aditi opened her mouth, but her lips trembled and no words emerged. And she suddenly found herself falling to the flagstones, lying prone with arms flung forward. "Please . . . Great Mother," she whispered at last. "Forgive . . . me."

"Forgive you . . ." There came a long pause. "For which transgression do you ask forgiveness?"

"For Goa," Aditi said. "For so many . . . lost to the Orlem Gor." And Aditi, who had so rarely cried her entire life, felt tears on her face.

"Ah. The priests of the Orlem Gor are monsters. There will be vengeance, Aditi, I assure you. It is a pity you could not prevail against them but you are only a mortal, though one with skills and knowledge few mortals possess. It is true you did not succeed as well as I had hoped, particularly after you had started so well, with the governor and the viceroy. A pity."

"Forgive me!" Aditi said again.

"Aditi. Did I not bring to you my own blood of life, entering the heart of the Mughul army so that you might live again? Does that not speak of forgiveness? Did I not, myself, guide you and your savior back here to my sacred city of Bhagavati? Does that not speak of forgiveness?"

Aditi was not certain how to answer. "Yes?"

"Had I been furious with you, my child, I would have left you dead. But if you wish to make an offering, a gesture, to make amends to me, then here it is: give me Tamas."

Aditi slowly rose up to sit back on her heels, wondering if she understood what she heard. "Great Mother?"

"Surely your wits have returned enough by now. I said, give me Tamas. His aspect pleases me. Such golden hair. I have had no man to give me pleasure other than those mindless, blind monks for so many years. You cannot imagine—no, of course you cannot. He is fond of you, clearly, but that can be changed. Men are so changeable once you find the fulcrum on which their souls are balanced. Give Tamas to me and all is forgiven."

Aditi blinked, her sluggish thoughts churning on whether she owned Tamas sufficiently to give him away and whether . . . so strange to think it, whether this was fair. She was a goddess. The Mahadevi could have any sort of mortal man she wished, couldn't she? *Why does she demand the one I love?* thought Aditi. *Was it Prabaratma who once said, the gods are most pleased when we sacrifice those things dearest to us?* What sort of cruel justice is there in this?

A tiny part of her heart, which since adulthood had respected no sultan or governor or nobleman or authority other than the Mahadevi, suddenly found itself contemplating rebellion.

"Why do you not speak?" demanded the Mahadevi.

"I . . . my thoughts . . . are slow," said Aditi. "I . . . please let me speak with him. Once more. To tell him."

"Ah. Of course. He will accept your rejection better from your own lips, I am sure. Speak well of me to him. I would like him to be eager. Seductions can be so tedious when men are uncertain. Do it soon. Do it tonight, if you can."

"If . . . that is what the Great Mother wishes."

"It is. Go now. Get your rest. We will discuss what new purpose we will find for you when you are more fully recovered."

"Yes, Great Mother." With some difficulty, Aditi stood and walked with uncertain steps away from the platform. *She has changed, or I have in the years since I have been home. Can a god become as petty as a mortal woman? Has my pride grown so that I can conceive of defying her, even after she has returned my life to me? In the ancient stories, sometimes mortals do defy the gods. If they are clever, sometimes they win, though at great price. Gandharva says I am clever, but my thoughts drift like clouds in a windless sky now. What can I possibly do?*

Her foot caught on a paving stone and Aditi stumbled but did not fall. *Careful. I must be more slow and cautious.* Watching her step, Aditi felt her way back toward the dim light of the corridor.

The Mirza Akbarshah looked up from the campfire at the moon. He did not like that moon, for it seemed to be staring down at him like a half-lidded eye, narrowed in disapproval. *Have I made some terrible error?* he wondered. *Should I have returned long ago to the main force rather than pursue this flight of fools? Rafi's hunger for vengeance has abated and I begin to doubt my wisdom. Perhaps Lakart is in collusion with the sorcerer who turned Mumit to stone, or plots with the woman Porphredo to tear apart my expedition. Perhaps he has already been successful and there is no longer a main force to return to.*

The Mirza turned his gaze from the moon to Lakart's sleeping form. The man was exhausted from the day's exertions and now snored with the gruntings of a wild pig. *What dreams do you have, you who hold your thoughts closed like the doors of a khalwat? What enlightenment does your spirit seek within yourself? Allah have mercy, I am beginning to think like Masum.*

The other men slept also, but more fitfully. They seemed troubled by their dreams. *What injustice have I done these men by bringing them here into the wilderness?* The Mirza felt very alone, beneath the scrutiny of the moon and stars.

Out of the corner of his eye, he noted a change in the quality of the moonlight on the Krishna River. A dark shape floating, drawing near the bank. Alerted, the Mirza stood and reached for his dagger.

"Allah akbar!" cried a voice from the river. "Is that the Great Mirza Ali Akbarshah I see?"

The Mirza strode toward the water's edge but stopped well back from it. The bushes on the bank were dark shapes casting shadows, making it impossible to discern who, or what was speaking. For a moment, the Mirza wondered if some djinn of the river was summoning him to his doom. Perhaps it was the sorcerer who had transformed Mumit, or a Son of Shaitan trying to ensnare his soul. "I am the Mirza Akbarshah, emissary of the mighty Emperor Akbar!" he called out, to banish the fearful thoughts in his mind. "Who speaks?"

"Allah be praised!" cried the voice, very near to the riverbank. "It is I, Masum Al-Wadud, and I bring the Begum Porphredo. We have come seeking you." Two dripping figures rose from the water to step out onto the sand.

"Masum?" the Mirza said in astonishment.

"What is it? What is happening?" shouted Rafi from the campfire.

"Bring a brand from the fire here," commanded the Mirza. "Hurry!"

In moments, all four of his men rushed up, brands and daggers in hand. By the light of their torches, the Mirza now saw it was indeed the Sufi Masum standing on the riverbank, more bedraggled than ever, and leaning heavily on him was the old woman Porphredo.

The Mirza went to her side and took her arm. "How can this be? What—" he could think of no better word "—miracle has brought you out of the river in this place?"

"We bring a message of great importance," Porphredo began, and then she collapsed in a fit of coughing. The Mirza picked her up, finding her surprisingly light for such a tall woman, and carried her to the fire.

"My lord," said Masum following behind, his wet clothes squelching, "we have come to warn you."

"Warn me?" The Mirza laid the old woman carefully down on the soft dirt beside the fire. By now, Lakart was sitting up, blinking and frowning. "Warn me of what?"

"You must not return to your army," said Masum, breathless. "Commander Jaimal has turned against you and means to lead your expedition. He has set archers in ambush along the route by which you would return."

The Mirza and his men stared at the Sufi in astonished silence some moments.

"My lord," Sabur said at last, "how do we know this one has not been sent by Jaimal, or come for purposes of his own, to keep us separate from the army so that we may die out here alone?"

"I swear on my soul!" said Masum. "I swear by all that is holy, may Allah judge that which I say, I speak the truth."

The Mirza studied the Sufi's earnest face. "I believe him, Sabur. I have known Jaimal might do such a thing. I now see that I should not have left with him in command."

"Forgive me, Lord Mirza," said Rafi. "It was for the sake of justice to my brother Mumit that we came this way. It is my fault."

"Or mine," said Lakart, standing. "We came chasing my fellow traveller, who may or may not be headed for the hidden city."

The Mirza held up his hand. "Enough. Let us say we all share blame equally and let Allah be the judge when all is finished. Now we must think on what to do next."

"We could return by a different way," said Sabur, "and thereby ambush those who would ambush us."

The Mirza rubbed his beard and nodded. "A possibility."

"I would remind my lord," said Lakart, "that we are only five men, unless the good Suf' chooses to abandon his vows and take up the sword in which case we are six. Not many for a counterinsurgency against five hundred."

"Surely there are men still loyal to the Mirza!" said Rafi. "When we return they will rise up with us against the traitors."

"But who can say what lies Jaimal has told them?" said the Mirza. "If he has promised them treasure, sometimes gold can buy a man's honor."

"Such men deserve to die," said Rafi.

"If you please, my lord," rasped Porphredo below him, "I have a different suggestion to make."

"What is it?" asked the Mirza.

"You have come all this way seeking the Rani of Life and Death. I will tell you that you were right to come this way, for her hidden city lies beyond those hills across the river. I will guide you there myself."

Her suggestion was greeted with silence for some moments. "You mean to say," the Mirza said at last, "that you have lied to us before, but now you are telling the truth and will help us find what we seek?"

The old woman sat up, the impressiveness of her gaze returning to her eyes. "I had no wish to bring an army to the walls of our hidden city. I must protect my queen and her people that much. But you are now few, and I believe the Great Rani should receive the emissary of the mighty Emperor Akbar, whether she wishes to or not."

The Mirza raised his brows. "So you, a servant, would disobey your queen for us?"

Masum eagerly said, "Remember the story we heard at the tomb of the nameless *shahid,* my Lord? Of the old woman who brought the remnant of the *sheykh* back from the hidden city because she was shamed by the queen's behavior?"

The Mirza did not reply, but stared wonderingly at Porphredo. *Could it be . . .*

"Yes," said Porphredo, dryly, "I am very much like that one. As a good servant, I must sometimes save my queen from herself. I believe she has been too long isolated from the world, and this has not been healthy for her. I believe it is time she learned again that there are others worthy of note in the world around her, and that there are other ways to govern, to live, than the existence she has chosen."

"All well and good," said Lakart, softly, "but how can we be led to any city beyond the river when we cannot even cross it?"

"An important point," agreed the Mirza. "How can we believe you, woman?"

"Will it be proof enough," said Porphredo, "if I provide you with a crossing?"

"Very well," said the Mirza, getting to his feet, "show us your crossing and we will decide."

The old woman extended her arm to Masum who helped her stand. Again the Mirza paused to wonder, *What is between them? What bond do they share? Has she somehow beguiled the Sufi to treachery?*

Porphredo took a burning stick from the campfire and, with Masum's help, walked along the river until they were directly across from the village on the other side. The old woman waved the branch and began to shout words that the Mirza did not understand.

In moments, a dark figure appeared on the opposite shore, also waving a torch and shouting. Their conversation went on for some time until the villager returned back among the huts. The old woman fell back against Masum, who caught her and steadied her, helping her walk back to where the Mirza waited.

"Soon," she said in a hoarse voice, "you will have your proof and your crossing."

The Mirza and his men waited. He could tell there was some activity in the village across the river, but the moonlight did not reveal what was happening. After a while, he heard a faint rumbling and beneath his feet he felt a subtle vibration in the ground. Earthquake? he wondered.

"Look there," said Porphredo, pointing out over the river.

Moonlight trembled on the water, the current disturbed by some movement beneath the surface. A wide, dark band appeared, stretching from one shore to the other.

The Mirza took a burning brand from Rafi and walked down to the water's edge. A flat bridge of wooden planks was rising above the river.

"What sorcery is this?" asked Sabur.

"The only reliable sorcery," said Porphredo. "Engineering."

When the bridge had risen two hands-breadths above the water's surface, it stopped, as did the vibration in the ground and the distant rumble.

"So, Lord Mirza," Porphredo went on, "do you accept my proof? Shall we cross? I will go before you or after or however you may desire it."

"My lord," counseled Sabur, "it may be a trap. She might collapse the bridge while we are on it, even if it means losing her own life."

"She will not!" said Masum. "I swear this on my soul as well."

The Mirza sighed. "Your soul is taking on quite a burden, Masum. But very well. There is a time for suspicion, Sabur, and a time for trust. You and the others gather our horses and pack up our camp. We will cross." The Mirza noticed the westerner Lakart staring speculatively at the bridge. "Are you wondering how it was done? Perhaps the Begum Porphredo will part with that secret as well."

"Actually, Highness, I was considering more philosophic meanings of the bridge and the river."

"Ah, yes, of course," said Masum. "The river's flood brings nurturance and death—most suitable, given our goal. And more fortunate yet that the river is named Krishna, for the Hindu god of love, for is it not for the sake of love of the divine that we make this journey?"

"Er, perhaps," said Lakart, "but my thoughts were more

upon borders and boundaries. Beyond lies a foreign country, both of land and of spirit. The river is a tangible sign of a decision made, a step taken, perhaps with no turning back."

"Oh, I see," said Masum. "Crossing the river indicates a change in the state of spirit, a step further on the holy Path."

The Mirza sighed. "Perhaps it is merely my weariness, but I see only an obstacle overcome, with doubtless many more to follow between here and our goal."

"Yes, indeed," said Masum. "There is worthiness in what you say as well."

Sabur returned to where they stood. "My lord, we are ready."

"Well, then," said the Mirza, "let us cross."

Thomas sat with Timóteo in the boy's room, looking out over the balcony at the moonlit, half-wild garden below. It was far pleasanter here, with the cool night breeze, than in his own close, gaudy chamber. "Such neglect," he mused, "amid such wealth. Does the despoina not know what she has, or not care?"

Timóteo shrugged but said nothing. After the bath, he had not been inclined to much conversation.

"What is the matter? Ah, it has been a long day and you are doubtless weary from our travels."

Timóteo sighed. "I think about the Padre. I wonder if he is all right."

Thomas almost felt a pang of guilt. Almost, until he reminded himself that the Padre had had Aditi killed. "Padre Gonsção is stronger and . . . more resourceful than you might realize, Timóteo. I am sure he will manage somehow."

"But now I will have to tell the story of God to the Queen Stheno all by myself, without his help. It . . . it is a heavy burden, this thing I must do."

"You intend to proselytize the Despoina Stheno? Even though she is a . . . if she is what you think she is?"

"Especially if she is a gorgon. For then she will know the

glory of our Lord and she may pray to save her soul and He will take the serpents from her head."

Thomas shook his head, amazed at Timóteo's faith, as well as his imagination. "Then perhaps it is just as well the Padre has not come. You know, do you not, that it was his intention to destroy the source of the *pulvis mirificus?* That means he would want to kill the Despoina Stheno."

Timóteo glared at him. "He would never do that. The Santa Casa does not kill."

Alas for your faith, thought Thomas, *but there is one among us, newly brought back from death, who knows otherwise.* "We are no longer in the Santa Casa, Timóteo. And who knows what a man may do if he is angry or frightened enough?"

"The Padre is a brave and wise man."

"Yes. But he is a man, for all that."

A knock at the door made them both start. "Who is there?" asked Thomas, in Greek.

The door opened. "It is me," said Aditi.

Thomas leapt to his feet and went to her. "Aditi! How lovely you look! So much better. How do you feel?"

"I am . . . recovering. Slowly."

"What a miracle." He began to take her into his arms and then remembered the boy behind him. "Timóteo, would you be so kind as to go into my quarters for a while?"

"Why, Tomás? Is there something you want me to find there?"

"I would like to speak with the Lady Aditi in private. If you please."

"Oh." Timóteo hurried out, bowing to Aditi, a dubious expression on his face. Thomas took Aditi by the hand and led her into the room, shutting the door behind her.

"Your companion . . . disapproves?" asked Aditi.

"He is yet innocent of many things. I think he is confused and does not know what he is disapproving of."

Aditi laughed and Thomas thought it the most wondrous

sound he had heard in days. Suddenly needing the comfort of her touch he brought her close and kissed her. He did not let go until she gently pulled away.

"Ah, Aditi," he whispered, "your lips are still as sweet as the honey that surrounded you."

"I am glad the kiss . . . pleased you," she said, taking another step back. "For it may be our last."

"What?" Thomas felt as if he'd been struck.

Aditi went to the wall and leaned against it, as if her legs still had difficulty bearing her up. "The Mahadevi . . . has asked that I relinquish you. As penance for failing her in Goa. You are no longer to be mine . . . but hers."

Thomas blinked. "What?" he said again. He felt a bizarre mixture of dismay and disgust, yet gilded with flattery. "Does your Despoina Stheno think I am like a . . . a . . . prize sheep to be bargained and traded for?"

Aditi shrugged. "She is the Mahadevi. She can demand whatever she wants."

"You truly believe she is a goddess, don't you?"

"I no longer know . . . what I believe. I talked with Enyo about it. Enyo says that the Mahadevi is changing. She has been too long alone and now falls into madness. It is a cycle with her, Enyo says. Like the seasons, but centuries long. Enyo says there is a greater goddess whom the Mahadevi should be honoring, but she is not. Enyo says perhaps that is why the Mahadevi is being punished with madness."

"Whom the gods would destroy . . ." as some ancient has writ. Divine help I will need indeed if my hostess is disordered in her wits. "A greater goddess, you say? Well, if my father and the Scotsman who travelled with me are correct, I was pledged to a goddess as a child, one who owns me body and soul, no matter what other creeds or gods should make claim to me."

"Were you?" said Aditi, wonderingly. "Which goddess is this?"

Thomas took Aditi by the hand and led her out onto the balcony. He pointed up at the moon. "That one. Artemis. Diana. The Divine Huntress. The Lady of Beasts."

Aditi looked at him. "I have heard Enyo use that name for the greater goddess as well, the Lady of Beasts."

Despite his doubts about matters pagan, Thomas felt a small, internal shiver. "Indeed?"

"If this is true," said Aditi, "and you are pledged to the Greater Goddess, then the Mahadevi cannot have you after all." A hint of a smile appeared on her lips. "You need not be my sacrifice to her."

That word stirred fears and memories in Thomas. "Aditi, while you were . . . that is, after you had . . . died, I had a dream. Of you. You had led me to a cave where you sat like a sibyl and gave me a prophesy."

Aditi blinked. "I did? I . . . remember very little of what I saw after death. It has all faded now, like dreams. What did I tell you . . . in the cave?"

"That I should treasure life, and prepare for death."

"Ah. Well, that is wisdom for all mortals, nai?"

"I had the feeling you were telling me my death might be more imminent than a man's normal span of years."

"Ah." Aditi looked down at her feet. "Forgive me, Tamas, but I do not remember this."

Thomas squeezed her shoulder. "No matter. Perhaps just as well. But can you tell me if I and Timóteo are in danger of being harmed by the Mahadevi?"

Aditi looked up again, with a steady, stern gaze. "The Mahadevi can be vengeful when displeased. I have heard stories . . . she has killed some even for little things. You must be careful, Tamas. Give her no cause for anger."

"But denying myself to her might surely cause such anger, nai? And your servant suggests that madness is descending upon the Mahadevi. I wonder how her anger might be avoided. It might help if you could tell me what sort of danger I face. How does she destroy those who displease her? Perhaps I can devise some defense."

"If you would know," said Aditi in a low, soft voice, "I can show you what is done. Follow me." She opened the door and walked out into the passageway, taking a torch from a sconce on the wall.

Thomas followed her, wondering for a moment if he should have alerted Timóteo. *No, let the boy rest where he is and wonder. I should not lead him into trouble.* Through dim passageways they walked, the only sounds the whisper of their footsteps, and the distant chirp of crickets. Thomas became convinced that the palace was laid out as a deliberate labyrinth. *How easily one may be lost here. I must remember and use caution, should I go exploring alone.* He tried to keep count of left and right turns, and what few landmarks he could note . . . a faded fresco of bare-breasted women holding lotus blossoms, a frieze of cavorting monkeys over an archway, a broken amphora in a corner. The passageways became narrower and the walls became naked of plasterwork, showing only bare stone. *We must be entering the more ancient part of the palace, that which Enyo said I should not enter.*

Aditi stopped at a wooden door set in an alcove with a niche beside it. A small bronze statue sat in the niche with a candle burning before it. One arm of the figure reached out, as if beckoning, the other was held high, a cup in its hand. On either side of the figure was a bronze spotted dog with four eyes. Thomas stared at it, reminded of the medallion Lockheart wore that depicted the woman flanked by hunting hounds. "Is this . . . the goddess who is greater than Stheno?"

Aditi laughed. "No, that is Yama. He was one of the first mortals, the first man to die. Now he is Guardian of the Dead and welcomes souls to his underworld." Aditi put her hand on the door and hesitated. Faint voices could be heard down the corridor to their right.

Aditi turned and handed the torch to Thomas. "Go in alone. I will go distract whoever is coming, for you should not be found here."

Thomas took the torch. "But—"

"Go. Quickly. I will be waiting for you here when you come out." Aditi hurried away down the passage.

Thomas sighed and pushed against the door. It opened with

a slight squeak and he slipped through the opening, trying not to scorch the wood with the torchflame. He shut the door behind him and turned—he faced another niche with another idol.

This one was of a man bound in cloth from the waist down, a bulbous crown on his head. His arms were crossed on his chest, one holding a shepherd's crook, the other a flail.

Are you a deity of death as well? thought Thomas. Do you also welcome me into your underworld? He held the torch up high and saw stone stairs to his left, leading down. Thomas descended two curving flights of steps, seeing a niche with an idol at each bend. Thomas did not examine those, wishing no more reminders that he was clearly entering a crypt. The walls of the stairway smelled of damp and mold, although they had once been limewashed.

Thomas came around the final bend and jumped in startlement, nearly dropping the torch as he avoided collision with the two men in front of him. "Your pardon, I beg—" he began. And then stopped. The two men before him had not moved.

He held the torch higher. They stood to either side of an archway, two men in Arabic robes and turbans. Both men held their arms before their faces as if shielding their eyes from the light. Their mouths were open in soundless cries, their faces frozen in expressions of horror. Both glistened, being made of stone.

"Dear God," whispered Thomas. "Is't true?" He reached out with one hand, but did not quite touch one of the statues—for fear of damaging it. The garments seemed formed of translucent pale onyx, the faces and hands formed of marble of a darker hue. Every feature was perfect, the details the same as in life, except that the eyes were plain milk-white orbs.

This is finer carving than I have ever seen. What sculptor has such skill in the drape of cloth or the pores of skin? Thomas had regarded Timóteo's warnings as a curious possibility, worthy of philosophic musings. Their enormity had not struck him until now. His stomach began to turn and the torch shook in his trembling hand.

Over the archway, someone had written Greek letters in charcoal. Thomas automatically translated. "Panta proeteon . . . elipda . . . oh. All hope abandon you who herein enter." *What cruel wag would write such a cold jest?* With horrified fascination, Thomas went through the archway.

And wished he had not. For instead of sedate tombs, more statues filled the crypt as if a crowded marketplace had been frozen in stone. Some stood, some leaned stiffly against the wall, some lay on their side on the floor, some lay . . . only in pieces. There were men and women in all manner of dress—Hindu, Persian, Arabic, and other garments Thomas could not identify, and some with no clothing at all. There were children and adults and even long-bearded old men. All wore expressions of fear, save one. An ancient wearing an ankle-length fringed robe and a curly beard cut square at the end, had a face etched with deep sorrow.

She has spared no one, not even the children or the aged. How many has the Despoina Stheno murdered thus? Some of the statues, including the sad long-beard, had votive candles set before them whose faint illumination almost brought some semblance of life to their faces. *I wonder who has left these offerings for the dead? Do the monks or Enyo grieve these deaths? Do the souls of these people remain trapped within their stone bodies, awaiting some magic to be released? I must ask Aditi.*

Thomas walked a little ways further, peering at the glistening, blank-eyed faces that seemed to recoil from him in open-mouthed horror, or shouting some silent reproach or warning. His hair began to stand on end and his skin prickled as if wishing to slither off his body and crawl away on its own. He came to the back of the chamber, where figures had stood so long that plaster and minerals had seeped down off the wall and ceiling, covering them in a frozen waterfall. In some places only outstretched arms and silently screaming faces could be seen, as if they were trying to escape a wall that was devouring them.

Something crunched beneath Thomas's foot and he looked down. He had stepped on what had once been a hand, but now perfect stone knucklebones protruded from finger shards. His gorge rising, Thomas lost all heart for his exploration. He staggered back, bumping into another statue, which began to wobble. Thomas dropped his torch and ran to the archway and the stairs, as the unfortunate fell to the floor and crumbled.

Thomas raced to the door at the top of the stairs and pressed his ear against it. He heard no sounds other than the pounding of his heart. He pushed open the door, grateful to step into the dry, empty corridor. Except that Aditi was not there. She had not returned to wait for him.

Thomas took deep breaths as he considered whether he should wait. But every part of him longed to be far away from the horrible crypt. *She said I should not be found here. I'd best go.* Thankful that he had memorized the landmarks, Thomas ran, swiftly as he dared, back to his quarters.

XIII

MANDRAKE: This plant has purple, bell-like flowers, and brings forth fleshy yellow berries in Midsummer. Its root grows in the shape of a mannikin. The juice of the root has been known since ancient times as a means to deaden pain, but great care must be taken in its use, for it can be a most dangerous poison. A tincture of the root will ease ailments of the lungs and throat and flesh of the raw root makes an excellent purgative. Some ascribe to the Mandrake the power to incite lust, while others would wear it as a charm to bring wealth and good fortune. Witches are said to use it in their most potent spells, and it is ofttimes known as the Plant of Circe for it is with mandrake, the legends say, that the sorceress enchanted and transformed her victims....

In the hour of cool stillness just before dawn, Prabaratma felt his way down the stairs. The stone beneath his feet felt curiously soft and alive, and the wall beneath his hand felt responsive, like a lover's skin. *The Earth herself welcomes me.* The demon Enyo had been right to chase him away from the Golden One's door. That had not been the proper place for *puja,* nor the proper time. Here and now was best.

Prabaratma had just finished placing new offerings in the crypt, as he did every morning, with prayers that the Mahadevi would show mercy and bring again to life those entombed in stone. But one of the petrified ones had fallen—the messenger from Madras whose name had been Chambuta—and now he would never live again. Prabaratma did not know by whose hand Chambuta had died the final death, but it was surely a Sign, part of the change signified by the arrival of the Golden One.

At the bottom of the stairs, Prabaratma stopped, his dim, partial sight of no use in the darkness of the underground chamber. Instead, he reached out with his spirit, to find the Presence, the "likeness" as the demon Enyo had called it. In moments he knew where he should walk and he went forward until he touched the stone idol of the Goddess. Prabaratma knelt before it, opening a satchel he wore at his side.

Bowing his head, Prabaratma reverently took the saffron thread that lay across his right shoulder and transferred it to his left shoulder. He took from the satchel a tiny covered bowl that was filled with raw white rice. He placed this on the stone floor before the Presence. Prabaratma reached again into the satchel and took out a hibiscus flower and a cake of sandalwood incense and he placed these also at the feet of the Presence.

Finally he brought forth from the satchel a small stoppered ewer that contained *rajas,* the milky, sacred liquid that flowed from between the loins of the temple dancing girls. He poured this onto his left hand, savoring its scent. He then smeared it upon the protruding tongue of the Likeness. Setting the ewer down carefully, Prabaratma embraced the stone idol, laying his head upon its shoulder.

Visions came to him then; not the vibrant, flickering images he saw in flame, but distinct, pale figures emerging out of darkness like fish rising to the surface of a murky pond. He saw the many-armed demoness Durga riding astride a tiger. She saluted him with her many swords and then faded back again into the darkness. The ancient crone Uma came forth and nodded to him and stretched out her hand to touch his brow before also sinking out of sight. *You appear but yet you do not speak with me, Great Mothers,* thought Prabaratma. *Have none of you words for me?*

At last a young woman with many pendulous breasts emerged, bearing palm and tamarind branches in her hands. "Do you know who I am?" the indescribable voice sung in his mind.

"Yes!" Prabaratma sighed, his heart pounding with joy. "You are Sita, Mother of the Earth and all the world's creatures. She who brings forth life."

"You see clearly. Soon there is to be a Renewing."

"I know."

"Already the wheels are in motion. I must set you to spinning as well, for you are part of the sutra whose words must spin another. Listen and I will tell you how this will be done."

"I am listening, Mother Illusion," said Prabaratma.

Padre Antonio Gonsção sighed and tried not to wish for more air in his lungs. He could sense the slow crawling of the sun up the dome of the sky. For every hour that the sun beat down upon him, the asses' skins in which he and the *soldados* had been bound shrank and tightened, until squeezing the very breath out of their bodies. Perhaps, if the skins shrank further, thought Gonsção, they might eventually break his bones. Impossible to say whether he would succumb to heat or internal bleeding or suffocation first. It was an unfortunate advantage to his profession that he knew how much damage could be done to a man without killing him.

The Padre again murmured a prayer, wondering if there had been anything he could have done differently the night before to avoid this fate. Apparently a search of the camp had been conducted and when it was found that the witch Porphredo had left clothing and other items behind, the Commander Jaimal had assumed that the Padre and his soldiers had killed her.

Did he think I was boasting about the deed, wondered Gonsção, *when I brought the bloodstained cloth to him? What sad irony there were no trustworthy translators present. Or perhaps these infidels are as untrustworthy as their reputation makes them, and the Commander wanted an excuse to murder us.*

Whatever the reason, three asses were slain and skinned and the Padre and the *soldados* had been bound tightly within them and carried to the top of a nearby ridge to die. As Gonsção had lain awake and prayerful through the night, his body bound and his cheek resting on sharp, cold stones, his only consolation had been that he had at least been warm.

Gonsção breathed in, trying to be content with the small amount of air he could obtain. He heard the creaking of the skin surrounding Carlos beside him and Gonsção winced with guilt.

Not for me, oh Lord, show your mercy, for I have seen the world beyond death and do not fear it. But for them. I have led them to this wilderness where they suffer for my sake. And though my cause is great, they had no choice in it. Save them. Watch over Timóteo, wherever he may be, for I have known none more devoted to You. And allow me to pass in peace again to that Distant Shore, if that is Your will.

Carlos gasped beside him, "Tell me again, Padre. Tell me again about the voyage of Death. I am . . . so afraid, Padre."

"You have nothing to fear," Gonsção whispered, conserving his air. "There is a world beyond, in which God will show you wonders." It did not matter that the wonders Gonsção had seen confused and disturbed him. There was no need for the suffering *soldados* to know what lay beyond might not be what they expect.

To his other side, Estevão grunted, "Why did they not just kill us with snakes, Padre, like they did Joaquim? That would at least have been swift. Why this?"

"We do not know who killed Joaquim, my son," said Gonsção, although he had his suspicions about the *inglês* Tomás. "Or why. Do not waste these precious few hours with speculation. Pray and absolve yourselves, so that you may be certain to be received in Heaven."

"Is there no hope for us, Padre?"

"There is always hope for the eternal soul, my son."

"I . . . I meant for our lives."

"I am sorry. I can think of none." Save for one puzzle that nagged at Gonsção. *Why was I returned to this world only to die in this manner? I had thought I had a mission to accomplish, a duty to see done, one that surely would have favor in the eyes of Heaven. Was that not why I was brought back? Dear Lord, help me to understand Your will.* He became aware of Estevão's quiet weeping.

"No. No, my son, do not waste precious breath and tears so. Think on the glory that is to come, and that you are leaving the sorrows of this world behind."

"Padre," said Carlos, "I hear horses coming."

For a moment, Gonsção wondered if Carlos was only attempting to give hope to Estevão, and then he heard them—horses walking up the ridge. "You are right, Carlos. I wonder what this means."

A minute later, they appeared: a Mughul on one horse leading another, on which sat the blind musician Gandharva.

Gonsção would have laughed had he the breath. He wondered if the cruel Jaimal had ordered this as an additional torment—for the Goans to be sung to their final sleep to the tune of horrible foreign music. Or was the musician to be punished also? But Gandharva's hands and arms were free.

The Mughul stopped the horses in front of the bound men and dismounted, drawing his long, curved sword.

Gandharva spoke then, in Latin. "Commander Jaimal and I wish you all a good morning."

Gonsção eyed the Mughul's sword and wondered if the commander had chosen to be merciful and give them a swift death by beheadment. "If I am to be seeing Heaven soon, then it is a good morning indeed."

"Perhaps not so soon as you think," said Gandharva with a smile. The Mughul came around behind them and pulled Gonsção up to a kneeling position. Gonsção closed his eyes awaiting the blow to his neck, a prayer on his lips.

Instead, he felt the sword blade slip beneath the leather bindings on his back and pull on them. In a few moments, the ass's skin fell free and Gonsção's chest felt as though it could expand to the horizons. In silence, the Mughul left him and did the same for Carlos and Estevão.

Gonsção lay on the ground, taking joy in being able to gasp in lungfuls of air. "Thanks be to God. And to Commander Jaimal for this mercy."

Estevão and Carlos fell forward gasping also, Estevão's tears turning from despair into joy. The Mughul threw down a water-skin before them and Estevão snatched it up eagerly. He brought it toward his mouth, then glanced guiltily at Gonsção, and held it out to him. "Pardon my disrespect, Padre."

"No, no, drink your fill, my son," said Gonsção. "You need your strength as much as I. Perhaps more."

Estevão managed a sad, grateful smile. "Thank you, Padre." He squeezed a great stream of water into his mouth and then handed the bag to Carlos who did the same.

"I managed," said Gandharva, "to convince the commander to give me audience, unfortunately too late to save you from your torment. But I brought forth witnesses who had watched you all yesterday and had not seen you near Porphredo. As it happens, the Sufi who had been advising the Mirza has also disappeared. It was a simple thing to transfer blame from you to the missing Suf', whom Jaimal never trusted."

"You have given false witness?" said Gonsção, amazed at the continuing list of sins committed for his sake.

"Let us say that I did not contradict a false impression already made. The commander is an ambitious but God-fearing man. He would rather risk false justice against a heretic than a Christian."

"I see. Then I must owe you thanks for our deliverance."

"What is he saying, Padre?" gasped Carlos as he attempted to stand. "Are we free to go? Are we pardoned?"

"It would seem we are pardoned, my son, but I do not know to what extent we are free." To Gandharva, Gonsção said, "What is to become of us?"

The Mughul growled some words at the musician who spoke back at him in some length. After the Mughul's reply, Gandharva slid off his mount and let the Mughul take both horses back down the ridge. The blind man took a few tentative steps toward Gonsção.

"As for your question, Magister, I do not know what the commander has in mind for you. I think currently his thoughts are on other matters. But I have an offer, which I think it would do you well to hear."

Gonsção sat back against a short, scrubby tree and rubbed his arms and shoulders which ached from their hours of constriction. "An offer? You?"

A wry smile appeared on the musician's face. "Humble I may seem, but are there not plain birds that make wondrous song, or humbly bound books that contain great knowledge?"

"There are also rogues," said Gonsção, "who seek to disguise themselves in humble dress. If I am not mistaken, your Latin has suddenly become much better, though your pronunciation is strange."

Gandharva bowed. "You are not mistaken, Magister. But now communication is more important than appearances. I assume it is still your wish to find the source of the *rasa mahadevi*, as well as to learn the fate of your charge, the little monk."

Gonsção went very still. "Do you know where Timóteo is?"

The blind musician nodded once. "I know where he has very likely been taken, along with the golden-haired one."

"Tell me," Gonsção rasped. "At once."

"Do not fear. I believe he is safe, for now. He has gone where you wish to be—to the hidden city of the immortal queen."

"So," whispered Gonsção, "Tomás did betray us."

"Let us say he had compelling reason to depart."

"Did he kill the other of our party, the *soldado* named Joaquim?"

Gandharva tilted his head with a puzzled frown. "Why, no. I can assure you the golden-haired did not do that. Your companion was killed by snakes. They are common in this region, you know."

"What is he saying, Padre, please?" insisted Estevão.

"That he knows where Timóteo and Tomás went, and that

Joaquim was slain by serpents." To the musician, Gonsção said, "What is your offer?"

"To grant you your wish. To take you to the hidden city. I have informed my queen of your approach and she wishes me to bring you."

"Is that where the Sufi and Porphredo have gone as well?"

"You are perceptive, Magister. They have indeed. My queen has no wish for an army to appear at her gates, but she does welcome visitors from other lands. In the name of . . . justice, she has asked that I guide you, also, to her."

"What does he say, Padre?"

"He offers to be our guide to the hidden city, Carlos."

"Our guide? But he is blind, Padre."

"Gandharva, how can you be a guide to us if you cannot see? Or is that a ruse as well?"

"No ruse, alas, but I have not always been blind. I was born in the hidden city of Bhagavati and know the surrounding land well. I can tell you the landmarks to look for as we go."

"That offer is sadly like the one Tomás made to us. Why not simply tell us the way we must go? Help us draw a map we might use."

"First, because a map can be stolen from you and read by others. Second, because one of you can be caught and tormented by others until you say what you know. And third, I wish to leave these Mughuls and return home, and I need your help for that. Are these not reasons enough?"

"Will the Mughuls permit us to leave?"

"I think it unwise to depart with their knowledge, particularly if they suspect where we might be going. No, we must be cautious and leave in secret. May I assume, then, that you accept my offer?"

So this is why I have remained alive, thought Gonsção. *Before my death, I was never one to believe in fate; why else would God have given Man free will. But can I demur when the hand of God points so clearly?* He turned to the *soldados*. "Estevão, Carlos, I believe that I must trust this man, for I see no other choice that will allow me to find

Timóteo and accomplish my mission. But there is no need for you to follow me in this dangerous venture. Perhaps you can ask the Mughuls to allow you to return to Bijapur."

"Never, Padre," said Carlos. "Death awaits us back in Goa, and we would have no place in the Mughul city. We will not abandon you." Estevão nodded his agreement.

"Very well. I am grateful for your loyalty and courage," said Gonsção. To Gandharva, he said, "Let our paths be joined, then. Let us make our plans."

Enyo hurried down the corridor as fast as she could with the heavy tray in her hands. She had complained again this morning to the despoina that more servants were needed in the palace, particularly if the despoina was going to insist upon having guests. But Enyo suspected that, as always, her words had fallen on adamantine ears. Having Aditi home again was of some help, but not enough to offset the distressing absence of Porphredo, and Enyo had not wished to tax Aditi's strength too heavily, so newly returned to life was she.

The morning had brought another unsettling portent. Vayu had come down from the Dove Tower to report that all of the messenger birds from the village of Devidurga had arrived during the night without messages. It could be nothing—perhaps the village children had been clumsy or mischievous and set the birds free without purpose. But Enyo had been unable to banish a growing anxiety from her mind.

She placed the tray beside the door and knocked before entering. "Despotas Chinnery?" She heard inarticulate moaning and decided to open the door. "Despotas, are you all right?"

The young man was seated on the edge of his bed, wearing only trousers, his head in his hands. Blearily, he looked up at her. "What is it?" he asked.

"I have brought you breakfast, despotas. May I serve it to you?"

At his grunt and nod, Enyo brought in the tray and set it on the ebony table. The young man did not move. *Ai, he does not look well. Is he ill?* "Despotas, are you well?" she asked again. "Do you need medicine or a doctor?"

"No! No . . ." He stood and rubbed his face with his hands. "I merely . . . did not sleep well."

"Was your bed uncomfortable, despotas? I could have the mattress or the coverlet changed, or give you a new bed entirely."

"No, it was not that." The young man sighed. "My sleep was disturbed by dreams. Nightmares. I have suffered them from childhood."

"Oh. I am very sorry to hear so." Enyo set out the bowl with yogurt and cucumber, and another with rice and a third with *dhal*, and a plate with fried flatbread. Not knowing the young man's customs, she did not know whether it would be polite to inquire as to the nature of his dreams, or offer to send a monk to interpret them.

The young man began to pace the room. "No matter. I am used to them. Every nightmare has the same three women—Furies, I think you would call them—who torment me. They did so again last night. I dreamt I was bound naked, hand and foot to the bed. They stood over me and gloated and placed serpents to crawl over my body and . . . I would prefer not to say what else they did."

As Enyo poured out tea, she said, "I am most sorry your sleep was troubled, despotas."

"And then this morning," he went on, his voice rising with an anxious edge to it, "I woke and lit the lamp beside the bed. And there was a woman's footprints in the dust, and drips of tallow wax from a candle. If you look . . . they are still there."

Enyo glanced at the stone floor, a sad suspicion creeping into her mind. "I am most sorry, despotas. Your room should have been cleaned better. I shall see to it at once."

"They weren't there yesterday," the young man said, his hands balling into fists.

Enyo wondered what might have happened to bring the young man so close to the edge of hysteria. "Is there anything I can do, despotas, to bring you comfort?"

The young man turned to her, pleading in his eyes. "You seem a good woman, Enyo. Please tell me . . . surely you would not welcome a guest into the house you serve knowing he might meet his doom there. Would you?"

"What can you mean, despotas?" said Enyo, fearing she knew very well what he meant. "You are favored in the despoina's sight. Very few are granted the privilege of living in her palace. You are fortunate to be so chosen, despotas. You are her guest, not her enemy."

"And if, some day, I no longer meet with her favor?"

Enyo opened her mouth, but found she had no reply.

"Timóteo and I . . . are we safe here, Enyo?"

"Wh-what a question to ask, despotas!" *Alas, what a weak fool I am. Somehow he has learned of the despoina's nature. And yet I protect her, for what little thanks she gives me.*

"What I meant, Enyo, is that . . . if you were to learn of a threat to a guest in this house, would you not do what you could to warn, and perhaps assist, that guest?"

What could she do to me, thought Enyo, *if I were ever to rescue someone she chose to enstone? She cannot kill me. I who am as immortal as she is. Send me into exile? Call down the wrath of the Lady of Beasts against me? Stheno is no goddess, much as she poses as one, so if I were to disobey her, it could not be hubris. Surely it is she who has stepped beyond* moira *and broken the Order of Nature. Surely it is she who is deserving of* nemesis.

Enyo sighed and said, "Although I serve my despoina in all things, I swear I will never value her whims above your lives. By the Lady of Beasts and her priestess whom I once served, I swear this."

Porphredo awakened in the small dark hut and remembered that she was now in the village of Devidurga. From the heat and the sunlight coming in through the doorway, she could tell it was late morning. The Sufi Masum's face hovered into view above her.

"Begum Porphredo. You are awake? You are well?"

"Masum. Why did you let me sleep so late?" Porphredo sat up, her back and muscles complaining.

"Your pardon. I did not know how much rest you needed. You were so tired last night. I told the Mirza that we needed you to be strong and rested if you are to guide us."

Porphredo got up off the reed mat pallet and rearranged her sari, which she had slept in. *I must surely be a dishevelled sight.* The Mirza's men had insisted upon seeing the underground mechanism that allowed the villagers, pushing on a huge wheel, to raise the bridge over the Krishna. Porphredo was exhausted by the time the tour was done. Though grateful for the rest, Porphredo had hoped for an earlier start. The order she gave—that the Despoina Stheno not be informed of her arrival—was so counter to the villagers' prior instructions and training over the generations, that Porphredo had little hope of it being obeyed.

She stepped out of the hut and blinked in the bright sunlight. Villagers approached, bowing humbly, with bowls of rice in their hands. Porphredo squinted at them, wondering if she should recognize any of them. She came into Devidurga so rarely that she might have last seen these individuals when they were infants. The men and women touched her arms, asking gentle questions about her health. But their eyes held fear. *They wonder if the despoina has turned against them. What can I, in honesty, say?*

"All is well, all is well," Porphredo murmured and waved them away. She declined their offered food, as she did not feel hungry. She strode down the central dirt path of the village, stretching her muscles and letting the sun warm her old bones. *Perhaps I am like a lizard,* she thought, *as the despoina is fond of telling me.*

She followed the path out to the river, hoping to find the Mirza. Instead, she came across the burly northerner, Lakart, standing at the water's edge, staring to the north and east, back the way he and the Mirza had come.

Porphredo peered in the direction of his gaze, wondering if he saw something of concern. She saw nothing but shimmering on the red-brown horizon.

"What do you see?" she asked him at last. "It cannot be that Commander Jaimal's army is approaching."

Lakart started a little and glanced her way with a rueful smile. "Ah, Begum Porphredo. No, it is no army I see bearing down upon me, but my future."

"If you plan to accompany me to the hidden city," said Porphredo, "your future lies in another direction entirely."

"Perhaps," murmured Lakart, "for some say, do they not, that man's fate is woven on the divine loom, his deeds cast by the weaver's shuttle until his thread of life is cut."

"So they say," Porphredo replied.

"But what if a man should declare he dislikes the pattern being woven for him? What if he should, by an act of choice, cause his shuttle to fall between the warp strings and thus disentangle himself from Fate's loom?"

Porphredo frowned, wondering what this strange man intended. "I am not familiar with your faith, sir. But among my people, that would be considered impossible, for the soul and the thread are one. How can you know whether, in questioning the pattern of your life, you are not in fact following the pattern set for you?

"Oh, the pattern of my life has been set in stone and bound with oaths that sing in the very blood. I know the way prescribed for me. Impossible to change, is it? How tantalizing the illusion of choice is, then. Merely by recrossing this river, or letting its current carry me wherever it will, away from those I have been bound to, it seems the pattern of my life could be diverted, shattered. Look, how simple it would be—" Lakart dramatically held out his arms toward the river and took one step into the shallow, muddy water. And then he took another. And yet a third.

Does he mean to drown himself? wondered Porphredo. *How shall I stop him?* She heard a crashing through the low, dry hedge off to her right. And then bleating and a child yelling. A black blur came tearing out from behind the nearest hut, dragging a rope tether behind it. A young girl chased after it with a stick, crying in her Telugu dialect, "Stop! Stop! You stupid beast!"

But the animal charged right into the river, plowing into Lakart and knocking him over backwards onto the bank. When it stopped moving Porphredo could see it was a little black goat. It glared for a moment down at the wet Lakart splayed on his back and elbows. Then with a disgusted "blehhhhhh," it took off again, its young mistress yelling and splashing after it.

Porphredo chuckled and said, "So, good philosopher, it would seem Nature is intent on enforcing her Order, and keeping your shuttle within her strings after all."

"Yes," said Lakart solemnly, staring after the goat, his face pale. "I am well rebuked."

"Ah, we have found her," said the Mirza behind her, and Porphredo turned. The Mirza was staring at Lakart with a peculiar expression.

"Yes, Highness, here I am. Are you and your men ready to depart?"

"We have been ready since dawn, lady. Only Masum told us you were in need of recovery. And apparently Sri Lakart was in need of a bath."

The northerner shook his head and clumsily stood, water cascading from his arms and tunic. "In need of correction, rather," he said, "which I have received."

The Mirza raised his brows at Porphredo who decided to leave matters a mystery, so as not to unduly embarrass the northerner. She drew herself up to seem more energetic than she actually felt. "And I have received the recovery I required. If you will gather your men, Highness, we may be on our way."

XIV

RUE: This ever-green herb has leaves that bring forth an essential oil, and yellow flowers that bloom in late summer. It has long been a symbol of sorrow and repentance, and is therefore also called Herb-Of-Grace. An ointment of the oil will ease gout and the rheumatics, while an infusion of the leaves will drive out worms and cure ailments of the stomach. Yet rue is a bitter herb and a poison and will bring sickness and fearsome visions if ill used. The ancients have writ that weasels eat rue as proof against snakebite, and craftsmen partake of it to make their sight keen. Sprigs of rue have been used for the casting out of demons, and strewn in courts of law to keep out vermin. Eating rue can be an aid to chastity, for to taste it when tempted will remove the desire. . . .

Aditi hugged tightly the stoppered pottery jar she had gotten from the flykeeper as she entered the Mahadevi's inner sanctum. The faint hum and vibration from inside the jar made it seem almost alive. The memory of doing this very task as a girl, bringing flies to the Mahadevi, was heartwarming but also now tinged with disquiet. Aditi had never known what the Mahadevi did with the flies, exactly—as a girl she had imagined the Mahadevi set them free in a great black, buzzing chaotic cloud. Now Aditi suspected the poor creatures did not leave the Mahadevi's presence alive.

Aditi paused at the first door to the Mahadevi's quarters. She saw on the wall beside the door one of the frescos of Kali that Enyo had warned her were appearing all over the palace . . . this one was nearly done except for the face. Shifting the jar to rest in the crook of her right arm, Aditi scratched the stone tiger between the ears as she used to when a girl, and then opened the door.

Aditi stepped into the next room and stopped. There were voices beyond the beaded curtain ahead of her—the Mahadevi and someone else. Slowly and silently Aditi lowered the jar to the stone floor, listening. Ah, it was Prabaratma she was with.

"All is becoming as it must be," the blind Brahmin was saying. "Krṣna is brought upon the back of Ganesha. Love rides with Wisdom. Kali and Shiva shall soon become one."

"Yes," the Mahadevi sighed. "He is quite extraordinary, Pra. I have not seen a man with such beautiful hair and features, such a delightfully large *lingam* in a very long time. I have visited him while he slept and enjoyed looking upon him and touching him. In his dreams, I am sure, he has enjoyed my attentions."

They are discussing Tamas, Aditi realized and she froze, kneeling on the floor. She did not wish to hear what Stheno and Prabaratma were saying, and yet she could not stop herself from hearing it.

"Garuda circles," Prabaratma went on, "his wings uplifted by the Lord of Storms. The cojoinment of powers will be amazing to behold."

What can he be talking about? thought Aditi. She remembered when Prabaratma had come to the palace, he had been a wise scholar and a good teacher. Now, apparently he had gone mad. But that was often what the Mahadevi did to men, Aditi had noticed. She wondered if that would happen to Tamas—that someday he might gouge out his blue eyes and sing songs of mad joy to the Mahadevi. The thought sickened her.

"You should have seen how he responded to me, Pra," the Mahadevi said, her voice low and breathy. "Even in his sleep. He will come to love me and when he does . . . ah!"

"The sword of the king shall penetrate the divine power," Prabaratma chanted, "and the flow that surges forth shall renew and quicken the world."

"Yes!" cried the Mahadevi, and suddenly Aditi realized what She must be doing, with Prabaratma or to Herself. Aditi knew she ought to flee, but her legs would not obey her.

There came soft, shuddering sighs from beyond the bead curtain, and then a long moan. Aditi still could not move. She could not understand why this proof of the Mahadevi's desires of the flesh astonished and dismayed her. Was it not often said how the gods desired extraordinary mortals? *And I am no innocent myself* . . .

She heard a rustling and jingling and without thinking glanced up at the bead curtain. A nude woman was approaching the curtain, tall and slender with a nimbus of brown writhing shapes around her head. Her hands parted the curtain and . . . Aditi swiftly twisted around to turn her gaze away. But not before she had seen . . .

"Aditi!"

"Forgive me, Great Mother. I did not wish to . . . disturb you."

"You have not, but what are you doing here?"

"I have brought you flies from the flykeeper."

"Where is Enyo? Why didn't she bring them?"

"She is tending to T—your guests, Great Mother. As you said I should relinquish the golden-haired one, this is what we felt would be proper."

"Ah. Yes. Very good. It is a pleasure having you home again, Aditi. I brought you up well, I can see."

"If you would be so kind as to consider having more servants in the Palace, Great Mother, there would be less danger of this occurring, and it would be of great help to Enyo and me."

"Oh, no, has that wrinkled little mouse been filling your ears with complaints too? Very well, I will give it thought. Now you had better leave. I would not wish to have to revive you yet again. And, as you know, reviving those who have looked upon me is more . . . costly and uncertain."

"Yes, Great Mother."

"Do you happen to know where Tamas is? I have a desire to speak with him and ask him if his dreams were pleasant."

Does She deliberately taunt me? Or is this a test? Carefully keeping her voice neutral, Aditi replied, "How would I know where he is, Great Mother, when you have asked me to have nothing more to do with him? You must ask Enyo."

"Ah. Of course. I will do so."

Aditi stood, careful not to look back, but before she could run out, the Mahadevi went on, "Aditi, do you think Tamas would prefer to see me in a red sari or a blue one? I must dress and cannot decide."

She is being cruel. "Tamas has never expressed to me a preference in color, Great Mother. I fear I cannot advise you."

"Hmmm. Perhaps the red one, then. It is a color that excites the senses, I am told. It is a bit more sheer and immodest a garment, but perhaps he will not mind that, nai?"

"Few mortal men mind such a garment, Great Mother."

"Being out in the world has taught you much wisdom, Aditi. So, go, go! Why do you stay and endanger yourself? Begone. We will speak again later."

"Thank you, Great Mother." At last, warm with simmering fury, Aditi hurried from the Mahadevi's chambers. *Poor flies, you have no hope. Poor Tamas. May what you have seen in the crypt keep you from loving a creature such as that!*

Thomas followed Enyo down more dusty, ancient corridors, relieved that they seemed to be going nowhere near the entrance to the horrid crypt of statues. Timóteo plodded along silently beside him, still sulking over Thomas's disappearance the night before, and the fact that Thomas wouldn't tell him where he had gone, or what he had seen.

But what good would it do him? At worst, he might seek the place out himself, putting himself in danger. Or he might blurt out that I had seen it with who knows what consequence? Better that he despise me for a little while, if it keeps us safe.

For the day's diversion, Enyo had offered to show them the palace library. Timóteo had agreed to this with such eagerness that Thomas thought it best to go at once, in hopes of cajoling the boy out of his doldrums and giving himself a means to forget his nightmares.

Enyo led them to a door at the end of a dusty passageway that seemed even more forgotten and neglected than the others. In a niche above the door sat the statue of a woman seated on an open lotus blossom. In one hand she held a book and in the other a stringed instrument that Thomas had seen before.

"Gandharva would like this deity," Thomas said.

Enyo turned with an unexpected smile. "Yes, he does. This is Sarasvati, the goddess of learning and the arts. We thought her an appropriate guardian for the library. Were I Hindu, she is one I could consider worthy of worship." Enyo worked at the latch several moments before she finally was able to coax the door open.

The first room they entered was tiny, and each wall, floor to ceiling, was lined with deep shelves filled with tightly wound scrolls. "This is where the monks keep the vedas," Enyo said, "So I must ask that you not disturb these works, for the monks hold them sacred. Besides, unless you read Sanskrit, they would have no meaning for you."

Thomas looked at Timóteo who was frowning abstractly at the scrolls. "We will respect them, Enyo, even though they are not of our faith."

Timóteo shot Thomas a guilty glance as though he had read his mind.

"Very good," said Enyo. "If you will please continue to follow me." She pushed aside a curtain of faded vermillion and white and a small cloud of dust rose from the cloth.

With a cough, Thomas followed her into the next room. It was much larger, lit with narrow windows high in the wall. But here, too, the tables and benches that filled the room were coated with dust and cobwebs. The shelves were untidily crammed with books, scrolls, codices, folios, and loose pages of vellum, parchment, paper, linen, and papyrus. At the far end of the room was another archway, curtained by a blue cloth that was clearly rotting off its hooks.

"Please pardon the disarray," said Enyo, clearly embarrassed. "No one has been here to care for it in a long time. There is only so much my sister and I can do, and the monks . . . well, they are mostly blind, you know."

Thomas gazed about him with growing wonder and dismay. At random, he chose a golden cylinder from the shelf nearest him. Carefully, he removed one end and slid out the rolled-up papyrus within. He held his breath, noting that the words upon it were Greek, and the lines seemed to be of a poem or play. The edge of the papyrus began to crumble in his trembling hand, and Thomas quickly slid it back into the cylinder and closed it up again. "Do you know what wonders you may have here?"

"Most certainly there must be wonders, despotas. Scholars from the world over have brought things to us. And some of these are from the despoina's travels before she came here. The despoina has herself boasted that she . . . rescued items from the Great Library of Alexandria before it was burned."

"And yet, there is no order to this? No way to find particular works on herbal knowledge, say, or medicines?"

Enyo sighed sadly. "None. I am most sorry, despotas. You will have to search for such things yourself."

"What is this?" cried Timóteo, holding up a length of papyrus decorated with blue and gold paint, with pictograms on it in black.

"That would be Egyptian," said Enyo. "Please be very careful. I am sure that is quite old."

Timóteo quickly dropped it back into the carved box he had pulled it from as if the papyrus scorched his skin. "And what is this?" He said, holding up a thin board of wood upon which were vertical lines of painted black characters Thomas could not identify.

"That is from a place called Chang'an, far to the east."

"Cathay," Thomas murmured. "China." He felt a strange ache, for that had been the destination of the ill-fated expedition he had set out upon from England.

Timóteo tossed the board back onto the shelf and wandered further along, completely absorbed in all he saw.

"If you will please excuse me," Enyo said, "I have many other duties I must perform. You may stay here as long as the light permits. There is another room with more such works through there, though it is in no better order than this one. But I am glad that this library may be seen again by those who appreciate what is kept here. Until later, despotas, and you, little master." She bowed to them both and departed through the vermilion curtain.

"Is this not wonderful, Tomás!" said Timóteo, his sulk apparently quite forgotten. "I wish I could read them all. What stories might be here!"

"What stories indeed," Thomas said, wandering beside the shelves, not knowing what he dared touch. He saw a wooden scroll tube on which was inscribed, in Greek, *Phaethon's Trees*. He gently teased the scroll out, hoping it might be an herbalist's work, but upon quick examination found it was a play about three mourning women. Respectfully, Thomas returned the scroll to its casing and continued browsing through the shelves.

His gaze fell on a leather-bound tome that seemed less ancient and he picked it up. Inside were crisp parchment pages of tightly penned Latin, surrounding beautiful illuminations of plants and fantastic beasts

"This would seem to be the work of some traveller noting down his discoveries," Thomas murmured. He sat on the nearest bench and peered at the writing to see if he could translate it. "Timóteo, come here. You might find this interesting. There seems to be lore of plants in this work, although whether they are mythical or actual, I cannot yet tell. Timóteo?" Thomas looked up and saw the boy standing, frozen, staring at something past Thomas's right shoulder.

Thomas turned. It was Stheno, dressed now all in red diaphanous silk that covered her from head to toe. But "cover" was only a relative term, for although her head was thickly wrapped and her face veiled, from the neck down her shapely form was quite revealed, every curve of waist and breast and thigh. "Good morning, Tamas," she said, her voice melodious yet with a timbre of hidden power.

Thomas swallowed, his throat suddenly dry. He tried to still the violent shaking of his hands. "And you . . . despoina. Good morning."

To Timóteo, she said in Latin, "Little monk. Good morning to you too."

Timóteo gasped, then hastily crossed himself and ran out of the room through the rotting blue curtain. Thomas envied him and wished he could flee as well.

Stheno laughed, her laughter sounding like flat stones falling against one another. "I regret I am so intimidating to your young friend. I am glad you are not so shy as he. Are you enjoying my library? I must have Enyo and Porphredo clean this someday . . . it is not fit for guests."

"Truly, this library is full of wonders, despoina. Could you, perhaps, show me which tomes might contain knowledge of medicines?"

"No, I truly do not know what is here anymore. I long ago lost interest. Much of what man has chosen to apply stylus or pen to is, I have found, foolishness." Stheno reached idly toward one shelf and pulled off a large, square object wrapped in purple silk. She blew the dust off the cloth and unwrapped it. Two square wooden boards were held together by a knotted cord, between which were pages of thick, rough paper. Stheno peered at the top board and read, "*The Veda Of The Seven Illuminated Ones*. Pfui. A fanciful Hindu story. Whyever do we preserve such nonsense?" She tossed the book back onto the shelf. "So. I trust you have slept well, my Tamas?"

Dear God, what do I say? If she be mad, she may take the truth ill and I may join those other sad souls in the crypt. If I lie, she may think

I wish to encourage her to visit more. "I . . . slept, despoina, although my dreams were . . . not as I would wish them."

"Not as you would wish them," Stheno echoed as she walked behind him. "That is a very cautious description." She ran her fingertips lightly across Thomas's shoulders.

Thomas had to muster immense control to keep from shuddering at her touch. Her sari was heavily scented with patchouli, cinnamon, and rosewater. He began to feel ill. And yet the dark honey of her voice was conjuring a warm swelling between his loins. *What ensorcelment is this? That part of my body will rise to her calling whilst my will reviles her?* "Have you never thought so, despoina? Never dreamed of one thing or person and wished it were another?"

"I rarely dream," she said. "But whom did you see in your dream that you wished was not there?"

Fortunately, this Thomas could answer truthfully. "Furies with great black wings and voices that cry for vengeance. They often haunt my dreams."

"Ah. And whom did you wish to see?"

"That would be . . . too forward of me to say . . . despoina." He hoped she might mistake the breathiness of his voice for desire instead of fear, and then realized he felt both and immediately hoped she would not know it. "Besides, the . . . feelings brought forth in my dreams of last night are those my people more properly confine within the bonds of marriage."

She laughed again and twirled a lock of his hair between her fingers. Thomas sat very still so that he would not flinch away. "You are a polite, restrained sort. I am glad to see it. It suits me well. Men who are fawning or vulgar do not please me. These people of Bhagavati, these Hindu, also make much of the bonds of marriage. Ah, I see you have found the chronicle of François Aphasius. Now there was a scholarly sort. He stayed here a long time, only a couple of centuries ago. He found me quite fascinating. But, alas, for the wrong reasons."

Stheno leaned over him, her breast brushing Thomas's shoulder. "Would you like to meet him? Perhaps he could translate his book for you."

God help me, she is mad. "H-how would that be possible, despoina, if he lived two centuries ago?"

"Such are my powers, Tamas," she said, stepping away from him. "I can work all manner of miracles. That is why my people know me as the Mahadevi. By my will, life can be restored, or suspended . . . or ended."

Does she mean to threaten me? "I . . . I hope I never give the despoina cause to wish my life to end."

"But why should you—you who have rescued my daughter? I wish to honor and reward you. You need only ask for anything and I—it will be yours."

She is nigh as froward as a strumpet. But is that not the way among the gods and demons of the ancient tales? How may I keep her from flinging herself upon me? "What if, despoina, the things I desire are things I dare not ask for, improper . . . dangerous things?"

"Ah. You have heard, no doubt, that to gaze upon my face brings death. But my sister Euryale discovered, long ago, that if one gazes upon us without fear, with love, that one is not harmed."

But the riddle is, how could one gaze upon you without fear? "Indeed?" was his reply.

"You doubt me? I could introduce you to the one who succeeded. But he was so old when he finally—well, and much as he loved my sister, he never approved of me. But have no fear, my golden Tamas, your desires may not be as unreachable as you think. Be patient. Do they not say that the gods reward those who are patient?"

"This . . . brings another matter to mind, despoina. Something I was told I should inform you of. When I was a child, I was dedicated, body and soul, to a goddess. One whom you apparently know as the Lady of Beasts."

Stheno stood very still a moment. And then she laughed again, but her laughter this time was colder and more harsh.

"Someone has been giving you poor advice. Enyo? Or was it Aditi? Well, I would think less of her if she had not tried. But understand, Tamas, that it does not matter to me what idol or name you have been promised to, if your words are true. The Lady of Beasts is a powerless hag," Stheno's voice rose with bitter anger. "She did not protect my sisters and me from Athena's curse, and she will not protect you for Aditi's sake. Unless the moon spits her forth and she rides down to claim you herself, I shall not believe in her, nor respect your consecration to her!"

The wrappings on her head began to writhe and Thomas turned his gaze away, wondering if he had already doomed himself.

But Stheno paused, and then returned to her flirtatious tone, her voice a little sadder. "Forgive me, Tamas. You have found an old wound which, I fear, will never heal."

"If you please, despoina, it is I who should beg forgiveness. I had no intention of upsetting you."

"I know. I forgive you. It is . . . unwise of me to lose my temper. I will leave you to your studies, but please remember. Your wishes are not impossible. Be hopeful and brave. You are meant for great things, Tamas. Even my priests have advised me so. All a mortal man could wish for shall be yours."

Thomas heard her footsteps depart. He glanced carefully over his shoulder to be sure she had gone before he let out his breath with a great, groaning sigh.

Gandharva sat in the sun, idly plucking a complex *raga* pattern on his *vina*, as he worked upon a troubling conundrum in his mind. The Goan priest of the Orlem Gor was being difficult. He would hear no talk of falsehoods or disguises, and seemed to have little aptitude for guile. *Now that Aditi is safely home, the Mahadevi sees fit to set bewildering tasks for me instead.*

Gandharva heard soft footsteps approaching and the faint, hot breeze brought the scent of sweat and delicate rosewater.

"Ah, Pramlocha. Have you come to bring joy to my dreary afternoon?"

The girl laughed and asked, "How do you do that, tell us girls apart, even before we speak to you?"

"Your charming scent, my dear, announces you from afar."

"But we girls all live crammed in that wagon together. Surely, by now we must all smell the same."

Gandharva smiled and shook his head. "Just as every lotus blossom has its own distinct perfume, though it floats in a pond with many others, so you have yours. In truth, I was also hoping that it would be you."

"Were you?" She sat beside him and leaned against him, putting her arm around his.

Gandharva thought this very pleasant and rubbed his cheek against her hair.

"Were you hoping it was me," Pramlocha went on, "because you like me, or because you hope I bring you news?"

"Yes to both, if you must know, my blossom. I am fond of the doves I keep, but doubly so because they carry messages for me."

"Well. I do have some news for you." She plucked at the sleeve of his *kamiz* and twisted her fingers in the cloth.

When her pause became too long, Gandharva said, "News, my pet, should not be delivered in the manner of a dancer slowly removing her veils. More, it should be delivered with the urgency of young love in spring, or a meal to a man who has fasted. To do otherwise is cruel."

"Forgive me. I . . . there is much to say. Lord Jaimal dithers, and some say he is worried because the Mirza has not yet returned. But then some are spreading the rumor that the Mirza has abandoned us, so that he can have the fabulous treasure of the immortal queen all to himself. And some say that Jaimal has had the Mirza killed and is only pretending to worry. With the old woman gone, no one seems to be sure which way to go."

"Ah." Gandharva had wondered if Porphredo and the Sufi had managed to find the Mirza and warn him, as had been their plan. *It would seem Porphredo has succeeded in her task of sowing discord and confusion within the Mughul army, though it would have been better if we were farther from Devidurga. Then, that would have made my task of delivering the Goan priest more difficult. Strange how matters weigh one against another.*

"Is that all you can say?" wheedled Pramlocha. "Ah? Is that all? The other girls and I, we are all very worried. What will happen to us if the men fall to fighting one another? I have heard of what happens when men decide there are no laws to bind them."

Ah. She does not sit so close because she feels affectionate but because she is afraid. Gandharva let go of his *vina* and patted her hand. "My dear, my dear," he said in what he hoped was soothing tones.

"I have seen you talking to the Goans, Gandharva. You . . . you wouldn't have brought me with you out to this wilderness just to abandon me, would you? I was the one who told you about the dead dancing girl, the one whose body we preserved and brought back to life? The one whose mother is a goddess? Surely I deserve some better reward for that, don't I?"

"Yes, yes, of course you do," Gandharva said quickly. "I will pray to the Mahadevi for you, for she is often known to be merciful. And you are quite right, you are owed something for rescuing Aditi."

Pramlocha rested her head on his shoulder and he could feel her tears soaking onto his skin. "Please, Gandharva. Do not leave me."

He stroked her face gently with his fingertips and sighed, as the conundrum in his mind grew, twisting like a snake surrounded by a myriad newborn little snakelets.

After there had been silence in the library for some time, and Timóteo had prayed long and urgently enough that the distressing swelling in his loins had gone away, he went back through the blue curtain. Tomás was still sitting at the table, face in his hands. "Tomás?"

The *inglês* jumped and then stared at Timóteo. "Oh. You startled me. It is all right, Timóteo. She is gone."

Timóteo walked over to the table, head hung down. "Forgive me, Tomás. I was a coward. I should not have run away."

Tomás smiled sadly. "There are times, little brother, when running away is the wisest course. I confess, I wished I could have joined you."

"But I . . . I did not want to insult the Domina."

"I think she was more amused than insulted, Timóteo."

Timóteo sat heavily on the nearest bench and drew aimless circles in the dust on the table. "She . . . she made me think about things I should not think about."

"She seems to excel in that," said Tomás.

"But you could have been in danger. How can I do what I was sent here to do if I am a coward? I should not have run. I didn't run from the tiger. Why do I run from her?"

"Tigers cannot turn you to stone."

Timóteo looked up. "You believe me now?"

Tomás nodded solemnly. "I believe you."

"What did she tell you, Tomás? What did you talk about? Did she tell you about Mount Olympus?"

"No, no, nothing like that. She prefers to talk about herself. I fear she has . . . designs upon me. She said that if she is gazed upon with . . . love, and without fear, that one can look at her without harm."

Suddenly Timóteo felt hope filling him again. "But that is wonderful news, Tomás! That means . . . that means if I can look at her through the love of God, and that way not fear her, then I can look at her face and prove to her the Truth of Our Lord, and save her soul."

"I do not think that is the sort of love she meant."

"But it must be! It is the greatest love there is!"

"Please, Timóteo," Tomás said sternly, reaching across the table to grasp his arm, "you *must* be careful. Your faith is strong, there is no doubt, but you must bear in mind that there may be some things stronger than your faith."

Anger flashed through Timóteo and he snatched his arm away. For a moment he thought Tomás was treating him like a child again. Then he saw how pale and serious Tomás was, and felt ashamed. "You are right, Tomás. It is the sin of pride, that the Padre warned me against. I will remember. You be careful too, yes? You still have the mirror I gave you?"

"Mirror? Oh. Yes. It is among my things. Yes, I should still have it."

"Good. Then we can use it when we feel our faith is not strong enough, yes? For protection."

"Yes, I suppose so." The *inglês* sounded doubtful. "Timóteo, I must ask you—may I sleep in your quarters from now on?"

"You want to switch rooms, Tomás?"

"No! I think—" he looked at the vermillion curtain as if making sure no one was standing there. Leaning closer, Tomás went on, "I think we should both stay there. My room is . . . too close. I believe it holds foul vapors which . . . which gave me nightmares and which would be bad for our health."

"My room is small, Tomás."

"I can sleep out on the balcony. It is the dry season and the nights are pleasantly warm. I will be comfortable there."

"The Domina will not mind?"

"I do not care if she minds."

"Oh. As you wish, Tomás." A little angel within warned Timóteo that there was something important that Tomás was not telling him. However, Timóteo also had the feeling that whatever it was, he did not want to know.

XV

ASTER: This small flower is very like a daisy, yet it is in its colors more varied, white, rose, and blue. Its shape has long allied it with the stars of the sky, and astrologers count it as an herb of Venus. In the East, wine fermented from the stems and leaves is said to prolong life and stave off bad fortune. Its blossom is oft used for determining who one's love shall be, and one's lover's constancy. The ancients would adorn their pagan altars with aster wreaths, and it is said the Greeks would burn the flower so that its smoke would drive away serpents....

May we light a fire, Begum Porphredo?" asked the Mirza Ali Akbarshah. The cool evening breeze which had at first felt so pleasant had begun to chill his skin.

"No. No fires." The old woman peered around the clearing in which they had stopped for the evening. "We do not know who watches and might see the light or smoke."

"They have been here!" called Lakart from beneath a rocky overhang. "The little Brother from Goa has left a sign."

The Mirza went over to him and gazed past the Scotsman's shoulder. Even in the dim light of sunset, he could make out a cross and roman letters and numerals beside it. "What does it say?"

"Merely his name and the date. But at least we now know we are not misled."

"Or that we have been misled the same way they were."

"A point, Highness. But my search is for my charge, Thomas Chinnery, and this sign shows I, at least, am on the correct path for my goal."

"Ah." The Mirza turned as he heard Rafi, Sabur, and Masum returning.

"My lord," said Sabur, "We have tied the horses over there, but there is little forage for them, other than thorny bushes." He glared at Porphredo as if the old woman had deliberately planned it so.

"We should be entering Bhagavati tomorrow," Porphredo said, mildly, "and there will be plenty for your horses there."

Rafi was constantly glancing over his shoulder around the ring of boulders that surrounded the clearing. The Mirza understood that he feared ambush—the site was perfect for it. And yet, the whole day their path through these hills was close set with brush and rock, their line of sight no farther than a few feet ahead and to either side. The ridges of the hills themselves lay hidden in such a way that the Mirza had been unable to determine their progress, and had it not been for the sun, he would have had no idea of the direction in which his party had ridden. It was a veritable labyrinth. Apparently Porphredo had known signs or landmarks by which she found the trail, but the Mirza had been unable to see what guided her.

The Mirza sat on the sand beneath the rocky ledge, his back to its curving wall. The position afforded some possible protection from attack, as well as sheltered him from the cool breezes.

Should I be branded a coward, he asked himself, *for so readily deserting my army to follow this woman in hopes she leads me to the Queen of Life and Death? As Jaimal himself so often reminded me, a good commander always considers the well-being of his men. And now I have abandoned them to whatever errors Jaimal will commit. Yet my orders from the Shahinshah were clear—that I must find this queen and, in finding her, secure for him her friendship and knowledge. That order is paramount above all else. May Allah who judges all determine if I am behaving dishonorably.*

The others joined him under the rocky ledge, setting out their blankets and unwrapping the rice and plantains they had been given in Devidurga. The Mirza noted how anxious and grim Rafi and Sabur looked. The westerner Lakart was merely curious of all around him. But the Sufi Masum, more than ever, seemed suffused with joy. The Mirza envied him his madness, if such it was. *How light the world must weigh on Masum's shoulders.*

The Mirza turned toward Porphredo, who had sat a short distance away, though not amid their circle. *Is it a sense of a proper woman's place, or fear, or some other feeling that causes her to set herself apart from us?* He motioned for her to join them and as she did, the Mirza marveled again at how she moved with such stately grace, given her age and how weary she must be from travelling.

"Lady Porphredo, since you have graciously decided we are worthy of meeting your queen, it would be of help to us if we might know more of her nature and how we should approach her."

"It is hard to know where to begin, Lord Mirza. First, I should give you warning. You must not gaze upon her bare face, nor meet her eyes, for the legends are true—that will bring death."

"Was it she who killed Mumit?" demanded Rafi.

"I fear it was," said Porphredo. "Although I suspect his death was not intended. Perhaps he came upon her hiding place and startled her."

"That makes no difference," growled Rafi.

"If she is a queen of life as well as death," the Mirza asked, "could she not restore Mumit's life to him?"

"Had he remained in one piece, it is possible, though it would be costly to her and I doubt she would have been willing to do so. However, since Mumit has crumbled, that is now impossible."

"What if we were to put him back together?" insisted Rafi. "We have all the pieces."

"Are you certain?" asked Porphredo. "How do you know some vital artery or other necessary organ did not turn to dust, uncollectable? Were he to be revived without it, a possibly agonized death would soon follow. No, you must resign yourself that your brother's loss is absolute."

"Then she must pay!"

"Rafi," cautioned the Mirza, "we will try to ensure some justice for you, but we must not antagonize this queen. The Emperor Akbar is vitally interested in establishing relations with her, and it would bring greater danger to your family if you become an obstacle in this."

Rafi subsided but the Mirza knew he had not been mollified. In sudden realization, the Mirza asked Porphredo, "If the death of Mumit was your queen's work, does that mean she herself visited our camp that night?"

"She and I arrived together," said Porphredo. "I, to mislead your army, she to rescue her daughter."

"Her daughter! Who is this daughter and how came she among us?"

"I am not certain of the details," Porphredo said, "but she was smuggled among you in the entertainer's wagon."

"And it was you," said the Mirza turning to Lakart, "who requested that wagon. Clearly you and your golden-haired friend knew more than we suspected."

Lakart held up one hand. "Peace. I know less than you think. My charge, Thomas, said I must request the wagon, for his ladylove Aditi had been killed by the Goan priest and he hoped that by finding the source of the *rasa mahadevi* she might be revived. I did not expect the source of the life-giving blood to come to us. Nor that she would not only take her daughter, but Thomas and Timóteo as well."

The Mirza stroked his beard. "Yet you did not see fit to inform me that this was the purpose of the wagon. I find this lack of trust discomforting."

"Please forgive me, Highness. Not being in all ways familiar with your faith, we did not know how you would feel about a woman's corpse being transported in your midst. And, truly, we wished to be certain that the Goan priest Gonsção, whom we think was her murderer, did not know of it."

"I see. You had no care that transporting this dead woman would bring danger to my men."

"We foresaw no danger, Highness. Our fault was a lack of imagination upon our parts, not wishing harm upon you and yours."

"Ah." The Mirza sighed and leaned his head back against the cold stone. "So. Begum Porphredo, why did your queen not make herself known to us, if she was near? Why the subterfuge?"

"Is it not apparent from Mumit's death the danger in such a visit?" replied Porphredo. "My queen has learned some caution over the centuries. But I must advise you that she has little interest in formal relations with your emperor. It is my hope that you can convince her otherwise. She has been too long shut up in her palace and forgets there is a wider world. She dallies in foreign intrigue but has little understanding of its consequences. My sister and I fear she has become . . . unbalanced. I am hoping your arrival will bring her to her senses once more."

"You may expect more of me than I am capable of," said the Mirza, "but for the sake of my emperor, I will do what I can. What do you suggest I offer her, since I am unable to bring her gifts?"

"Influence. Recognition. Knowledge. All these she values. Appeal to her vanity and her curiosity and you should succeed."

"You do not, then," said Lakart, "think of your queen as a goddess?"

Porphredo stared at the westerner, amusement in her deeply lined face. "No. She is a woman accursed, as I am. We have adapted to our afflictions, but they are no less a trial for that."

"She cannot be the Divine," mused Masum, "she can only be the image of the Divine, come forth to elicit our love for the eternal Bilqis, the wise Sophia."

"Love?" snorted Sabur. "How can one love a woman whose face would strike you dead?"

"To look upon the face of the Divine itself is more glory than naked mortal can withstand." Masum replied. "But the image of the Divine, like a mirror, reflects that glory only. And therefore the mortal soul, if clothed in love of the Divine, can gaze upon that reflection without fear, without harm."

"The image of the goddess," murmured Lakart. The Mirza looked at him sharply, but the westerner seemed lost in thought.

"Good *faylasuf*," said Porphredo, "your words speak closer to the truth than you may know. My queen has made a study of love for these many years, for she believes if she can find one who will gaze upon her without fear and with love that man will not die. But the sort of love she has in mind is not the same as yours. I would advise you to take care."

"I do not intend to take care but to give it freely," said Masum.

The Mirza grew uncomfortable, again sensing there were matters of spiritual importance that his practical nature would not let him recognize, as if he were one of those who are blind to certain colors, or unable to read script. "We have important work tomorrow, it would seem. Let us all sleep so that we may be well rested." *And, by the Merciful, may I not dream, for I fear I would not have the wisdom to comprehend its meaning.*

Thomas lay on the balcony, staring up at the moon. It was not so full as it had been, it seemed. *If thou art my protectress,* he thought, *then pray watch over me this night, and save me from she who would challenge thy sovereignty over my soul.*

He felt foolish, like a child wishing upon a star, yet he was of a mind to welcome any precaution. Thomas had set the mirror Timóteo had given him propped up against one of the carved posts of the balcony railing, near his head and pointed toward the door. He doubted Stheno would be so bold as to visit him in the bright moonlight, with Timóteo near, but the presence of the mirror gave him some ease.

He could hear Timóteo's soft snoring behind him, and he envied the boy. *Is it his faith or his youth that permits him such carefree slumber? Did I sleep so well when I was his age?* Thomas found he could not remember. His life in England seemed so long ago.

Thomas rolled over onto his stomach and sighed, hoping he at least would have no nightmares. He tried to set his mind to practical thoughts. *With the knowledge contained in Stheno's library, there is much I could bring back to England, could I stand to sojourn here awhile. If I can but keep her ardors at bay, turn her gently aside with kind words and feigning modesty, I might in time escape with the wisdom of the ages in my grasp. Is this not worth some small discomfort, some slight dissembling and flattery, though she be a monster? Mayhap I might learn from her the secret of her life-giving blood and become the greatest physician in all Christendom. Might this not be the purpose of my journey intended by whatever divine power guides me? Courage, Tom, for all things come to he who waits.*

Sleep came to him at last, light and fitful. Thomas did not know what time it was when he was brought awake by the tick of the latch at the door. He did not move, but opened one eye. The moon had set, leaving only the faint light of the stars to illuminate the balcony. *Oh, inconstant moon, hast thou deserted me?* he thought. *But surely it is only Timóteo at the door returning from using the garderobe.* Thomas glanced at the mirror and saw he was mistaken.

First he saw the candle, illuminated by a small, dancing flame. Then the slender hand that held that candle. And then he saw two large, round breasts above a slim waist. And above those, a strikingly beautiful face with full lips, aristocratic nose and large, dark eyes. And surrounding that face . . . the serpents; numerous, languidly writhing, with glistening skins and tiny eyes that glimmered with a faint incarnadine glow.

Thomas shut his own eyes firmly and fought against the rebellion of his stomach. *Dear God, dear God it is true.* Though the statues in the crypt had convinced his intellect, now no part of him could deny what sort of creature Stheno was. He dared not move and hoped the gorgon would accept his immobility for sleep.

He felt her lift the cotton coverlet off him and he now regretted that all he wore beneath was a Persian shirt. He felt her hand caress his calf, his thigh, his buttocks, her admiring sighs echoed by the hissing of her snakes.

Then he felt her lips pressing against his legs, each gentle kiss surrounded by the slithering of smooth serpent scales against his skin, their little, probing tongues tickling him.

Thomas slowly clenched his fists and gritted his teeth, steeling his will to not cry out in horror. *I must not. If I awaken Timóteo, I may doom him, as well as doom myself.*

"Despoina!" came a harsh whisper from the doorway.

"Hush!" rasped Stheno and the hissing of her serpents was like a storm wind through dry leaves.

"Despoina—"

"What *is* it, Enyo?"

"You must come. At once!"

"Gods take you," Stheno growled, but Thomas heard her stand and step away from him. He did not breathe again until he heard the door latch shut.

"Gods bless you, Enyo," he sighed in deep relief.

Enyo stood in the corridor awaiting the first blasts of the despoina's stormy temper. She did not have to wait long.

"How *dare* you disturb me when I am with a guest!" hissed Stheno in the darkness, as soon as the door was shut. "Do you know what harm you could have caused?"

Your unveiled face would be my fault, would it? "I dare when there is an urgent matter you should be aware of, despoina."

"What could be so urgent?"

"There are rioters at the palace gates, despoina, demanding your attention."

"Rioters? Impossible. My people do not riot."

"Perhaps you should come and see for yourself."

Angrily muttering, Stheno stormed ahead of Enyo who had to hobble along as best she could to keep up. "You are fortunate I know you are not clever, Mouse, or I would claim you were deliberately interfering with my love-making."

It is fortunate you do not think me clever, Enyo thought, *because we did intend to interfere, Aditi and I. She gathered the townspeople, assuring them of your attention. I waited until I saw you enter where Tamas slept. Between us both perhaps there is a clever enough mind to steer you towards better deeds.*

By the light of the few torches and the myriad stars, Enyo picked her way up the stairs that led to the top of the Palace wall. Like so much of the structure, the wall was crumbling in places, long unrepaired, and Enyo had to watch her footing. She reached the watchtower above the palace gate long after Stheno had gotten there.

Impatiently, Stheno demanded, "Give me your *shal.*"

Enyo took the cloth from around her shoulders and handed it to Stheno who swiftly draped it over her serpents and pulled it low over her face. Then Stheno peered out through the narrow slit in the wall. "This is what you call rioting, mouse?"

Men and women of all castes stood with arms upraised or knelt or lay prostrate on the palace steps. Some wailed for the Mahadevi to hear them, some chanted *vedas,* some shook their fists at the palace gates demanding that the Goddess hear their pleas. They were surrounded by bowls with floating candles or oil and rush lamps. Many held flowers or bowls of offerings, and the steps resembled a temple during the festival of Diwali.

"They arrived in anger, in a rush, despoina. Who could say what they were capable of? I felt you ought to know right away. See how they call out for you?"

"What do they want?"

"Just listen to them. One family says the tunnel they live in nearly collapsed upon them. Another says their house has fallen because of the extra story they built to house their family."

"What have I to do with their poor construction skills?"

"They need room, despoina. More land. So little of this palace is used—"

"You are just like your sister! You want me to provide my

beautiful palace as a hutch for these human rabbits to breed in until I am driven out! Why can't they control their numbers?"

"Many children are considered a gift of Lakshmi, despoina. They make the work of the family lighter and bring prosperity."

"So I have been too generous, and they have prospered too much. Why do they complain to me?"

In her sternest voice, Enyo replied. "You are their Goddess! You are the Mahadevi, their Great Mother, who provides all things. They rely upon your power and wisdom to protect them. You have proven your greatness and goodness to them, by the very prosperity you now disparage. Who else would they show such trust to? Who can better answer their cries for help?"

Stheno was silent for some long moments, staring down at the wailing people. "Very well," she said at last. "Tell them I, their Goddess, have heard them and that they will be answered. Have the mayor and the town Brahmins come for audience with me tomorrow at midday. Send Aditi to me and we will make arrangements."

"Nai, despoina." Enyo bowed, sighing with relief.

"Do not trouble me again tonight. I have much thinking and planning to do." Stheno walked away, her bearing a bit more regal than before.

Enyo sagged against the cold watchtower wall. *How much easier to bear this would be if Porphredo were here. What has become of her? Why have we not heard from her? Hurry home soon, dear sister. Before the despoina becomes impossible to handle and all comes undone.*

Padre Antonio Gonsção sat atop the entertainer's wagon, swaying with its movement and enduring its bumps and jars. Commander Jaimal had refused the Goans horses or even mules, forcing Gonsção and the *soldados* to ride in the wagon with the musicians and the dancers and the whores. The main body of the Mughul army walked ahead of them, each man bearing a torch for this unusual night-time march. *I wonder if that is what Hell looks like,* Gonsção thought, *souls proceeding to their doom amid smoke and fire. I wonder if I will find out if I fail in the task set before me.*

It was strange for Gonsção to have to rely so much upon others whose powers and skills were alien to him. He had tried without success to explain to the blind lute player, Gandharva, why it was unthinkable that Gonsção should, for example, wear women's clothing as a disguise for escape. The lute player seemed to have no concept of sin. Even now, sitting across from him on the wagon top, Gandharva had one of the little whores clinging to his arm and he did nothing to send her away or even request she sit aside from them, although he and Gonsção were supposed to be having a serious discussion of their escape plans.

And yet my life and those of Carlos and Estevão now depend upon this man. Clearly great proof of the saying that the Lord works in manners mysterious.

"I notice, Gandharva, that the army has again reversed direction and that we now go south and east once more."

"You are correct," said the blind lute player. "My little spy here," he went on, patting the hand of the girl beside him, "tells me that Jaimal has become suspicious of the absence of the Mirza. He now believes the Mirza has discovered a route to the fabled hidden city and goes alone to keep the treasure for himself. So we follow the route taken by the departed Mirza."

"Our commander does not accept the possibility that the Mirza may have fallen prey to calamity or mishap?"

"None that Jaimal had intended."

Gonsção raised his brows. "I see. Is there advantage for us in this treachery and change of direction?"

"There is good luck and bad luck in all events, Magister. Going this way, the river widens, but we are brought closer to our goal, yet also we run the risk of guiding Jaimal to the hidden city."

At the moment, his limbs and back still aching from his night in the ass's skin, Gonsção wondered if it wouldn't be more expedient to simply tell the Mughul commander how to find the hidden city and ride all the way there with army escort. He quickly chided himself, however. *What is my comfort compared with the horrors that will follow if the* muçulmanos *gain control of the source of the* rasa mahadevi? *I should be willing to suffer far worse, even die once more, in order to prevent this.*

XVI

LILAC: This shrub bears plumes of white or pale purple flowers. It is said the first lilac grew when the seeds were dropped by a falcon into an old woman's garden. A passing prince left a plume from his cap on the plants, which then brought forth similar blossoms. Some believe that bathing in lilac dew upon the first of May will give one beauty for the rest of the year. One should not bring lilac into the house, particularly the white, for it assures there will be a death soon in the household. Nor should one wear the flowers any day other than May Day, for that means one will never marry and to give lilac to one's betrothed shows that one is ending the engagement....

Thomas gazed out through the balcony rail at the garden below. The morning sun revealed it to be just as neglected as the rest of the palace. Yet the untrimmed trees and overgrown bushes bore bright flowers of red and orange, and were filled with riotous birdsong which had woken him up earlier. Now and then, he thought he heard the clamor of a distant crowd of people, but he could not be certain. *It might well be the din of some exotic bird I know nothing of.*

He pushed away the silver tray that he and Timóteo had found just inside the door. Some thoughtful person had left them a breakfast of flatbread filled with spiced chopped egg and onions, and mangos. Thomas tried not to speculate on who might have left it. Had it been Aditi, he would have felt guilty at not being awake to greet her. Had it been Enyo, he would have wished to be able to thank her for her intervention the previous night. Had it been Queen Stheno, he did not wish to know at all.

Timóteo had been quieter than usual, murmuring prayers upon rising, but otherwise not saying much. Thomas wondered if this was merely a sign the boy was caught up in his thoughts, or that he may have witnessed some of what had happened in the night and dared not speak of it. In case it was the latter, Thomas did not press him, nor demand the boy reveal a reason for his silence.

Someone rapped on the door and Thomas started. *Let it only be Enyo.* "Qui est?" he said, at last.

There came babbling in a high-pitched male voice from the other side of the door.

"It is one of the Brahmins," Timóteo said and he leaped up. The boy opened the door and babbled with whoever was beyond for a few moments and then turned toward Thomas. "We are lucky, he speaks Kannadan. He says we are to come with him right away. The Mahadevi invites us to her audience with Bhagavati's mayor. She says it is important that you come."

"Well, I suppose she will not cause me too much embarrassment in public." Thomas stood and stretched. "If the queen commands us, then we had better obey."

The Brahmin was a man of about forty, who wore a long cream-colored coat and loose trousers. He was blind, as all the palace priests seemed to be, and now Thomas understood the necessity of such a condition. *At least it is not the old, mad one who had offered sacrifices at my door when we first arrived.*

The priest led them by feeling along the walls with his fingertips. He was so sure of the way that the lack of sight seemed hardly a handicap to him.

Thomas kept careful note of which way they turned, noting that they did not go near either the older section of the palace, nor near the sacred garden, nor the library. "This Palace is so huge," he murmured to Timóteo, "I do not think I could learn it all even were I to live here my entire mortal span."

"I could," said Timóteo. Thomas wondered if the boy meant that he had wit enough or that he wanted to spend the rest of his life there.

The priest led them to a set of double doors made of dark, polished wood, banded with iron. The Brahmin pulled on one of the great iron rings and slowly pulled one of the doors part-way open. Before Thomas and Timóteo could enter, however, Enyo came out.

"Ah, there you are, despotas, monachulum," said the old woman, bowing to them both. "The despoina was anxious that you might not come or would be delayed."

"Surely, if she can command our attendance," said Thomas, "she has no cause for such concern."

The old woman winced. "Sometimes, despotas, even she prefers her subjects willing. If you will follow me, please. I am to be your translator."

Thomas began to translate for Timóteo what Enyo had said as they entered the doors. And then he stopped as he gazed at the great hall before them. The floor was an expanse of black marble. Enormous pillars, painted the color of blood, flanked the walls. There were no windows—the only illumination being the flames from bronze braziers, one in each corner and two flanking the high, tiered dais to their left that dominated the hall. Atop the dais was a tall screen of pale silk that stretched from one side to the other.

'Tis is more like a pagan temple than a queen's court, thought Thomas. *But, then, I suppose that is suitable for a queen who claims to be a goddess.*

Enyo led them to the far side of the hall to a lower dais on which sat three ornate chairs. She indicated that Thomas was to sit in the middle chair, with Timóteo to his left. She sat in the chair to his right. As soon as they were seated, Enyo called out in Greek, "We are here!"

Thomas heard the jingling of bangles and saw Aditi come

out from behind the screen and step down to the middle step of the dais. She wore a sari of scarlet and gold thread and wore a circlet of gold over her dark, braided hair. "Aditi!" Thomas called to her, but Enyo grasped his arm.

"You must not speak to her, despotas. I am sorry, but the despoina has ordered it."

Aditi glanced toward him and then swiftly looked away. Thomas slumped back in his chair with a frustrated sigh. *Strange how the more desired are those things which are denied us.* He tried to find something else on which to focus his attention. To his left, in the wall directly opposite the great dais, stood a pair of bronze doors even larger than the ones through which he and Timóteo had entered. Each door was divided into panels, in which animals and semi-naked human figures embraced or fought or danced. *There must surely be a story in every one of them, just as every cathedral bears the history of saints in its stones.*

He thought he heard the muffled rumble of many voices just beyond the doors. "Enyo, are there many people gathered here?"

"Yes. The people of Bhagavati have asked the despoina to ease their overcrowding. She is to give them answer at this audience, and I hope her decision is a wise one."

"If they do not like her answer, would the townsfolk revolt against her?"

"Oh, by the heavens, no. Or if they tried they would soon be stopped by her . . . magic." Enyo frowned at the doors. "I hope it will not come to that," she added, softly.

"As do I, good Enyo, as do I."

"What is she talking about, Tomás?" asked Timóteo.

"I beg your pardon, young one," said Enyo, switching to Latin. "This is the language I should use so that you may understand too, is it not? I was telling your young magister that Queen Stheno has gathered us to announce how she will give the people of Bhagavati more room for their houses and families. I, myself, am hoping she will give up some of her palace, for there is far more room here than she needs."

Timóteo nodded, and then said, "But would that not be dangerous?"

Before Enyo could reply, Aditi spoke in a clear, commanding voice and the far doors slowly began to open.

Aditi herself seems far more a queen this day than Stheno, thought Thomas.

About twenty to thirty men in long jackets and trousers like those the Brahmin had worn, filed in through the door and knelt in rows before the great dais.

"They sort themselves according to caste," Enyo said. "The first row is the *gamabhojaka,* the mayor, and his two brothers. Behind them are representatives of the other Brahmin clans. Behind them are those of warrior castes, and behind them the merchants. Behind them, the rest—musicians and weavers and so forth."

So Nature's Order reflects herself e'en here in this strange land, mused Thomas, *with man arrayed from high to low, each in his station.* The similarity should have been reassuring to Thomas but instead it felt oppressive. *Is there no man who ne'er wishes he were born to another state? The king's son wishing to be a merchant or the peasant wishing to be king? Is there no place upon the Earth where a man might not inherit burdens at his birth? I would give much to not be my father's son. But they say blood will out and Dame Nature will have her Order, when all's done.*

As the last men knelt, the great doors were shut by palace priests. A sound . . . a deep, lowing blast as if the Hunting Horn of God were being blown, reverberated through the hall. And then another began over the first, their tones alternately blending and colliding. And then a third joined in, until the sound—one could not call it music—hummed in Thomas's very bones. He clasped his hands over his ears and looked around wildly for the source. At last he noticed in the dim light a gallery high on the wall across from them, behind the pillars. Monks stood in the gallery holding impossibly long brass horns which must have been hung from the ceiling.

The horns droned on and on, the sound they produced seeming to circle about the room like a hawk gyring to strike. It was an amazingly complex sound, containing a texture that made his skin prickle and his mind imagine that, at the edges, he could hear the alleluias of angels or the gibbering of demons. Then, just as suddenly, the horns stopped. And the silence that followed rang like a bell of pure crystal.

"Tibetan horns," said Enyo, conversationally. "From the mountains far to the north. Impressive, are they not?"

"Indeed," breathed Thomas, "for their sound did press itself upon me most surely."

Timóteo took his hands from his ears and crossed himself. "Madre Maria. I had thought it was Gabriel and this was the Last of Days."

"No doubt the Final Trump must sound much like that when the Day comes," agreed Thomas. "Or if it be worse, I hope my spirit will no longer have ears to hear it."

Aditi clapped her hands and spoke to the assembled men in a lovely, fluid language. "She is welcoming them, in the Mahadevi's name," Enyo translated. "She tells them that, in the person of the Mahadevi, the heavenly light of the Divine has come to rest upon the lowly Earth, to inform it and transform it as husband and wife do upon their wedding night one to the other."

Thomas frowned at Enyo. "Is this a thing to speak of at an august assemblage?"

"It is meaningful to these people," said Enyo. "The joining of opposites has great power in their beliefs."

Aditi stopped and seemed to be waiting for something. Then she went on, gesturing gracefully as if her upper half were dancing.

Enyo clicked her tongue and shook her head. "Ai, Stheno must be late. This is the speech we give, full of praises to the Mahadevi, when she hasn't shown up yet. She can be so disrespectful of her subjects. This can sometimes go on for hours. I hope she has not been so unkind as to call us all together for nothing."

"It has not been for nothing," Thomas murmured as he watched Aditi speak.

Thomas heard a faint rustle and jingling from behind the screen and Aditi seemed to pull her speech to a conclusion. There came a sudden flash of light behind the screen—clearly two more braziers had been ignited there—and a shadow was cast upon the silk. The shadow figure had many undulating arms, several legs, and serpents waving languidly about the head.

Timóteo grabbed Thomas's arm. "You see? You see?"

When Thomas found his voice, he said, "Yes, little brother, I know. I did not doubt you. Though I wonder how she sprouted the extra limbs."

Stheno seemed to be artfully allowing different parts of herself to be shadowed with clarity upon the screen; now the silhouette of a heavy, jewelled necklace adorning a round-bosomed, small-waisted torso; now several pairs of gesturing arms; now a strong profile framed with snakes.

Were I a simple Hindu, thought Thomas, *I would well believe this was a pagan idol come to life.*

Then Stheno spoke, and her voice contained some of the quality of the Tibetan horns. Thomas wondered what mechanism she might be using to cause the effect.

"She welcomes the citizens of Bhagavati," Enyo duly translated, "and says that she has heard their cries for help and comes, in her mercy, to give them answer. But because they have been foolish in squandering the prosperity and increase that she has brought them, her assistance comes with a heavy price. Ai, I do not like the sound of this."

The man who was pointed out as the mayor spoke then, and Enyo translated, "He says the grateful people of Bhagavati will pay whatever price the Mahadevi asks, for she has sustained and protected them for generation after generation.

"Too many generations, Stheno answers. And now she says, that she has been advised that much of her palace is little used and might be better served giving homes to some of her people.

Ah, yes, despoina! Now you are showing wisdom. Now she says that as she recently had to sacrifice her daughter in order to gain a greater gift, so the people of Bhagavati must also make a similar sacrifice. Ai, no! She wouldn't!" Then Enyo fell silent and chewed on a knuckle as Stheno spoke further. At one point, the men of Bhagavati sat up, astonished, and protested, only to be shouted down by the creature behind the screen.

At last, Thomas had to gently shake Enyo's shoulder. "Enyo? What is it? What is she saying?"

"It is better and worse than I feared," the old woman muttered. "She has asked that every family in Bhagavati give up their unmarried daughters, any virgin girl of eight years or older. They must bring them to the palace, where the girls will serve out the rest of their lives without husbands or children. Ai, I hope she does not intend to blind them all. She says the girls must be brought to the palace by sunset tomorrow. She says in three days time, there is to be a great wedding—the girls will be married to . . . her, in her aspect as the god Shiva, so that they may have no other husbands."

Thomas stared aghast at the screen. "*She* is going to marry the girls? That is . . . that is abominable!"

"But in keeping with the faith of these people, alas. They are quite strict and ordinary in their own family lives, but they think the strangest things of their deities."

Several of the Bhagavati men turned and looked at Thomas.

"What now?" Thomas asked.

Enyo lowered her gaze apologetically. "Young Magister, she says that, in her aspect as Kali, the despoina will also take a husband. You are to be that husband."

Thomas felt his jaw drop and he stammered, "I . . . I will not . . ." he started to rise out of his chair.

"Forebear, Magister!" cried Enyo. "Do not embarrass and anger the despoina before her people, or else innocents will be harmed by her wrath. Calm yourself, please. Later we may have time to beg her to reconsider."

Thomas sat back down, seething. He met Aditi's gaze and

saw sad sympathy in her eyes. "Stheno did not even ask me if I would marry her."

"The Mahadevi never asks anyone's permission," sighed Enyo. "Ai, what a mess all this will be. How I wish Porphredo were here."

Porphredo dismounted, grateful to be off the horse's bony back, and approached the cliff. She noticed the Mughuls behind her watching warily, as they doubtless thought this clearing another fine place for ambush. *I'd best get them inside the mountain quickly,* she thought, *before they panic and flee.*

Moving the false ivy strands aside, Porphredo found the latch for the false boulder and, even with her old woman's strength, easily rolled it aside. She heard the Mughul called Rafi exclaim behind her and call her a witch.

"It is merely a false front," Porphredo said, "A simple trick."

"What other trickery might she pull, my lord?" Rafi defensively asked the Mirza.

"It will be an education to discover it," said the Mirza with an admiring half-smile.

Porphredo turned to the great round door and pulled upon a particular ivy-rope. Then she waited.

And waited.

And waited.

The door did not open. Porphredo leaned close to the door and shouted in the local dialect of Telagu, "I am Sri Porphredo, bringing guests to the Mahadevi! Open the tunnel at once, or you will suffer the punishment of Queen Stheno!"

Again she waited, but the door did not move and there was no sound of voice or footstep beyond it.

"It appears," said Lakart dryly behind her, "that one of her tricks isn't working."

"Alas for us," said the Mirza, "it would seem to be an important one."

"Something has happened," said Porphredo, not hiding the

concern in her voice. "This tunnel had people living in it not a week ago."

"Perhaps," said Sabur, "we have been seen after all, and your people have been forbidden to let us enter."

"Perhaps," agreed Porphredo, "but I feel it is some other cause. I fear I must call upon you of greater strength to help me. Let us see if we can push this door inward. If it was not barred inside, it might be pushed open."

"I will try it," said Lakart and he dismounted and walked up to the door. As he pushed on it, he was joined by the Mirza, and then by the Sufi Masum. But the three men could not make the door budge.

"Shall we help as well?" asked Rafi, holding their horses' reins.

"No," said Porphredo. "I fear it would be pointless."

"Well then, wise begum," said Lakart, rubbing his hands, "what shall we do now?"

"There is another entrance," said Porphredo, *Bless Stheno and her devious ways*, "but it is a distance, and you will have to do without your horses when we get there."

"Give up our horses!" protested Rafi. "Never!"

"Are your steeds so well trained," asked Porphredo, "that they can descend a vertical ladder down a hole only as wide as a man?"

"My lord," said Rafi, "we must not consider such a route."

The Mirza held up his hand. "We have come this far, Rafi. So long as the horses can be looked after, I am willing to go on foot."

"The horses can be sent back to Devidurga where they will be well cared for," said Porphredo.

"Then someone shall have to return to the village with them," said the Mirza.

"I will go, my lord," said Sabur.

The Mirza nodded. "So be it. Return to the village and guard the horses for us. If Jaimal should somehow find his way there, lie to him about where we have gone, for we can no longer trust his intentions. Porphredo, is there some way word can be sent to your hidden city, if the army comes this way?"

"There would have been," Porphredo replied dryly, "had you not released all the doves. If any should return to the village, you may use one of them. Otherwise, we must take our chances. Sri Sabur, if you follow the hoofprints we left you should be able to return to Devidurga safely."

As the men dismounted and took their necessary belongings off the horses, Porphredo rerolled the false rock over the tunnel door and latched it in place. *What can have happened here? I fear it is something terrible. Tchai, I should never have let her return without me. If she has gone mad, poor Enyo cannot handle her alone. Has Stheno given orders that I may not return to Bhagavati? If so, she shall regret it.*

Prabaratma sat humming and rocking back and forth beside the lotus pond, filled with joy. What wonders awaited! The Mahadevi had summoned the generative power of Bhagavati to her palace. All the unmarried girls. Such *shakti!* And they would be wedded to the divine power, Earth combined with Heaven. Soon, soon, the forces of male energy would come to Bhagavati and penetrate the walls of the palace—Ah! What a divine explosion, like that of a burgeoning seed-pod. The destruction that leads to Creation.

Just now, Prabaratma had delivered a message, in secret, to the Golden One, the Divine Offering. The sky-daughter, Aditi, wished to meet the foreigner tonight in the Sacred Garden at the rising of the moon. Prabaratma could not sort the meaning of this event to come, but there was a rightness to it. Over and over he thanked all the divine powers for allowing him to be present at this time and in this place. He could sense the movement of great forces around him, even though he could not see their source, much as the ripples on the lotus pond might suggest the large fish who swim hidden beneath.

XVII

DIAMOND: This stone, also called Adamant, is clear and brilliant, yet its nature is a mixture of good and evil. In the East, a decoction of this stone is used to bring virility and long life. It is said that to wear this stone wards off plague and pestilence, and confers strength and courage. However it also brings one to walk without sleep at night, and a stone of poor quality will bring upon the wearer sorrow, lameness, illness, and misfortune. Some say the diamond is a source of sin, or that it is only so bright as the virtue of its owner....

What can he want now?" asked Padre Antonio Gonsção of Gandharva as they approached Commander Jaimal's tent, lit golden by the waning evening sunlight. Gonsção, Estavão, and Carlos trudged wearily, for the army had travelled day and night the last twenty-four hours, stopping only for prayers and meals. At least they had been able to sleep somewhat in the rocking, bumping entertainer's cart. And it seemed the commander was finally willing to let his army make camp and rest for a while.

"His invitation was quite conciliatory," said the musician, "but that is no guarantee of his intentions." Gandharva was guided by the silent girl who seemed to be with him everywhere now.

The guards at the door to the tent indicated that the girl could not enter with them. She started to protest, but Gandharva patted her hand and spoke to her gently. She pulled the *shal* of her sari down over her face and sat obstinately on the ground at the feet of the guardsmen. The guards seemed to think this mildly amusing and they allowed her to stay.

As Gonsção entered beside Gandharva, he asked softly, "I mean no insult, but why do you keep that poor creature by your side these days?"

"Let us say I have realized that I owe her a great debt," said Gandharva, "and therefore I have become her protector. In turn, she serves as my eyes, as well as pleasant companion."

By way of paying his debt, he takes advantage of the girl. And the wanton child allows him to. What a strange sense of propriety these people have. It is no wonder the Church is having difficulty taking hold in this land.

The commander's tent was not as large or well-apportioned as the Mirza's had been, although Gonsção thought he recognized some of the Mirza's furnishings. The commander himself stood in the center and bowed to them in welcome. He was dressed in a clean, plain cloth coat, trousers, and turban. Jaimal seemed thinner, however, since the last time Gonsção had seen him, and his expression was less proud and more uncertain. He gestured to two servants who brought warm, damp towels of scented water with which Gonsção and the others could wash their face and hands.

When they had finished and the towels were taken away, the commander beckoned for them to sit on soft cushions near him. The servants returned with covered dishes from which steamed the aroma of spiced chicken. Clove tea was poured for Gonsção. His stomach rumbled, for he and the other Goans had been given little to eat in the past few days. Gonsção reached for one of the dishes. "You do not suppose, Gandharva, that he means to poison us?"

"It would be insulting to even suggest such a thing," said the blind musician. "But given that he nearly killed you before and chose to forebear, I think it unlikely."

The commander seemed to sense the reason for Gonsção's hesitancy. He gestured to a servant who removed a portion of rice from each dish, which Jaimal then tasted. He then gestured and spoke at them again.

"He asks," translated Gandharva, "that you partake freely of his hospitality and he apologizes that his former misunderstanding has made you cautious."

"Thank him for us, then, for his kind generosity," said Gonsção and he nodded at Carlos and Estevão that they should also feel free to eat. They did so with gusto and Gonsção could not blame them.

When the meal had finished and they had again washed their hands on warm towels, Jaimal began to speak.

"He says," translated Gandharva, "that as you are both Men of the Book, and revere the same prophets, that he regrets that he has allowed enmity to come between you and him. He says the loss of the Mirza and then the native woman Porphredo had distressed him into momentary madness. The Mirza's trail has now led us further into empty wilderness and he has not returned and now the commander is uncertain what to think. Perhaps the Sufi for mysterious reasons of his own, or because his dreams commanded him, has killed the Mirza and the old woman. Or perhaps the Begum Porphredo, heaven forbid, had fooled us all and killed the Mirza herself to destroy the expedition."

"Please tell the commander," said Gonsção, "that I had grave doubts about the old witch from the beginning, and that I would not be surprised if she proved duplicitous."

Gandharva gave him an odd frown and then spoke at length to Jaimal. Gonsção sighed, realizing he had no way of knowing how accurately the musician repeated his meaning.

Jaimal sighed as well and Gandharva translated his next words, "Perhaps, although he would feel shamed if it were true. Or perhaps the Mirza and the others who rode with him fell prey to tigers or bandits, or other calamity that has nothing to do with our expedition. He confesses that he feels lost, without guidance other than Allah. He asks that if you have advice to offer, he will gladly set aside his prejudices and listen."

Gonsção paused, almost swayed by the Mughul's humbler demeanor. *But Gandharva has said his Queen of Life and Death has no wish to meet an army, nor would I wish the* muçulmanos *to learn of the* pulvis mirificus. *Why does it seem to be my fate to need to lie or misdirect for a greater cause?*

"You may tell him, Gandharva, that again we have more in common that we thought. My party, also, has lost the member who knew where we were headed. Without the fair-haired Englishman, we are as much at a loss as the commander. I, too, have lost someone to whom duty bound me, the little monk whom I thought of nearly as a son. Both of us have cause to grieve and cause to feel lost but for the guidance of Heaven."

As Gandharva translated, the Mughul commander stared intently at Gonsção and chewed upon a fingernail. Jaimal then replied, "Then we are alike, indeed, and I ask your forgiveness that I have overlooked our similarities. Please allow me to make amends to you by accepting this gift I now offer. As it is unfair to keep you here suffering our misfortune with us, I will give you all horses and provisions so that you may return to Bijapur and tell our sad story to the Sultan. He can, no doubt, see that you are sent safely home to Goa."

Estevão leaned toward him and said, "Padre, perhaps we should reconsider and accept this generous offer. Perhaps Carlos and I, we could find some work to do for the Sultan in Bijapur after all. Who can say when the Mughuls will change their minds about us again? It is better than dying in an ass's skin, *sim?*"

Gonsção held up his hand. "I will forgive your loss of heart, Estevão. But I will not leave while Timóteo is still unaccounted for. I could not forgive myself for abandoning him."

"This is noble of you, of course, the commander says," Gandharva translated, "but you must consider the possibility that the boy no longer lives. You could wait the rest of your life for him."

"My faith," said Gonsção, "encourages hope. So, although

you may be correct, unless you can provide proof that my hope is groundless, I will continue to believe that Timóteo lives."

"Of course, of course you may," said Jaimal, raising his hands. "I wish I had proof to offer you, either way. As Allah is my judge, I hope you are right and the boy may be found."

Gonsção paused with a new thought. "Commander, if you are willing, as it seems, to allow us to leave the confines of your army, and give us horses and provisions, would you think it ungrateful of us to use these to search on our own for Timóteo? A few men on horseback can cover more ground in shorter time than five hundred on foot. That offer I would accept."

Jaimal's mood visibly brightened. "That is a splendid idea. I should have thought of that myself. Of course you may search—I will even offer three of my best men as escort to give you assistance! Consider it done. All will be ready for you in the morning."

After the pleasantries and the good-nights, Gonsção left the tent in considerably better spirits. Just outside the tent, the girl stood and reattached herself to Gandharva's arm.

Like a barnacle to a ship's hull she clings to him, thought Gonsção. *Well, Gandharva must say good-bye to her soon. For surely she will not be coming with us.*

When they had walked some distance toward the entertainer's wagon, Gandharva said, "Why did you accept the commander's offer?"

"Is it not better that we will have horses and provisions? Will this not aid our escape?"

"Yes, horses. And three of Jaimal's best men to watch us. Do you not see what he has done? He suspects you know the location of the hidden city and has set you free in hopes that you will foolishly lead him to it. Which, it seems, is exactly what you want to do."

"Nonsense," said Gonsção. "Surely we can outwit or overpower three men."

"They will be armed, we are not. They are well trained

whereas, if you will pardon me, your men are malnourished and weak. I am blind. And Pramlocha here cannot fight at all."

"Her? You are not thinking of bringing that girl with us!"

"I owe her a debt," Gandharva said firmly. "As you are duty-bound to your lost little monk, I am bound to her. I cannot abandon her."

Gonsção could not fault the musician's sense of duty, but he could not help recalling that barnacles on a ship's hull hindered its passage through the water. *In our case, to be slowed in our flight could prove to be our doom.*

Thomas waited in the dark shadows beside the gated entrance to the sacred garden. Again he had to leave Timóteo behind, with instructions on what lies to give Enyo or Queen Stheno should they ask for him. The boy was greatly displeased and Thomas could not blame him.

When the mad priest arrived with Aditi's written message, Thomas had wondered if it was a trap. But the mad priest had insisted that Aditi herself had given it to him, with instructions that Stheno must not know of it, Thomas accepted his word. *Mayhap my hunger to speak with Aditi again was too great, and I too readily believed him. Mayhap this is a ruse, by which the monstrous queen will learn my willingness to wed. No matter. She would learn it e'er long.*

He heard movement in the garden and saw a female figure approach in the pale moonlight. She was not veiled so she was certainly not Stheno. And she was not small and stooped so she was not Enyo. It was Aditi, and as she came close and unlocked the iron gate, Thomas nearly leapt over the spiked bars to embrace her.

"Thank you!" he said into the softness of her hair. "Thank you for meeting with me again."

"Shhh." Aditi pulled back with a finger across her lips. "Not so loud. We do not know who may hear. Do you speak Portuguese?"

"No. I fear I learned but a word or two while in Goa."

"Ah, well. We must chance the Greek, then, and hope no one overhears us. Come." She took him by the hand and led him further into the garden.

"Why did you suggest this place? It will offend Enyo, if she learns I have trespassed here."

"Because the Mahadevi never comes here. Enyo believes it is out of guilt, or because the Mahadevi will not accept that there is a greater goddess than she. But you are not trespassing, Tamas, for if you are truly given to the Lady of Beasts, then you belong here."

"These trees," Thomas said, noting the cypress and the oaks, "they are sacred in Europe but do not grow in this land."

"Enyo says these plants were brought from far, far away, and this garden formed in the shape of a distant, ancient shrine. That pond represents a lake, and those little columns there a temple. Those mounds behind the trees are hills and mountains. The real shrine must be a beautiful place."

"Or once was. Who knows how long ago Stheno saw it."

"True." Aditi pulled him into the darkness beneath a broad oak. "Now let us speak of you."

"Of me? There is little to say, unless I can avoid this false marriage to your Mahadevi."

"What is it you fear?"

"Is it not plain? She told me she believes that one who truly loves her can gaze upon her face and not die. I cannot love a creature such as she, so the day she bids me look upon her to prove my love . . . that day I die and join the statues in the crypt."

Aditi nodded. "They are not truly dead, you know. That is why Prabaratma looks after them. If any one of those statues, as you call them, is painted or bathed in the Mahadevi's blood, it will return to life."

"Oh greater crime is this!" breathed Thomas. "She has the power to revive them but she does not."

"Now and then, she does. But if you return to life a man

whose family are all dead and gone, he is a stranger to the world he is reborn into. Such people do not fare well in their new life."

"I saw some statues in pieces. Is there—"

"There is no hope for them," Aditi said bluntly. "Once in pieces they cannot be revived."

"Then I am guilty of murder. Aditi, while I was down there I, without intent to, knocked one over."

"Do not blame yourself, Tamas. Many fall, due to earthquakes or other things."

"Why aren't they wrapped then, or better cared for?"

"The Mahadevi thinks little of mortal life. Compared to her, we are all just ants."

"Another reason I shall not marry her!"

"Shh." Aditi was silent a moment.

"What is it?"

"I thought I heard someone in the bushes. No, there is nothing now."

"Can you help me to flee, Aditi? We could return to Bijapur, you and I."

Aditi laughed. "Tamas, have you forgotten there is a Mughul army between here and there?"

"We could go around it. There must be a way, Aditi."

"And what of the little monk?"

"Surely he could come with us."

She turned away and by the moonlight, Thomas could see hesitation and reluctance in her face. "This is my home, Tamas. I do not wish to leave it. I have been a stranger in the outer world for so many years. Here, I have a place. I belong."

"Being servant to a creature like Stheno?"

"And beloved daughter to Enyo and Porphredo, and princess to the good people of Bhagavati. But you would have me leave and become servant to you."

Thomas opened his mouth and shut it again, not knowing how to respond.

"Where you come from," Aditi went on, "do they welcome strangers, those who look like me?"

Thomas had to admit she was wise. Immigrants to England from the Continent were often treated with mild suspicion unless they were of noble birth. Strangers from elsewhere, Africans and Asians were, at best, thought of as curiosities. *If I brought Aditi home to London, Master Coulter would explode with apoplexy and deny he ever knew me. My father . . . well, who can say what that unfathomable man would do?* "No," he said at last.

"I thought not. Besides, I am several years older than you. That may not matter now, but some day it would. I think you should set aside all thought of replacing marriage to the Mahadevi with marriage to me."

Thomas turned away from her, now finding the beauty of her moonlit face painful to behold. *All that she says is good sense and are even thoughts that I, myself, have pondered. Wherefore should this wisdom seem so harsh?*

"And I think you should not be so swift to flee Bhagavati," Aditi continued. "Prabaratma insists that you have an important part to play in events to come."

"Prabaratma? Enyo says that old priest is mad."

"Perhaps. But I have known him many years, and there have been times his visions were true ones. Even madmen may speak truth sometimes. I believe there must be purpose in your being here." She strolled closer to him, almost flirtatious. "Do you know, I nearly killed you on our long journey? Several times, in fact. I had such a terrible time deciding if you should be stabbed or poisoned."

Thomas looked sharply up at her. *Does she now make cruel jests to drive the knife home in my heart?* "Did you? But yet I live. Surely you are more skilled an assassin than that, my lady."

"Every time I thought on it, or made the attempt, something stayed my hand. Circumstances, sometimes. A fond emotion, other times. I have often wondered at it. For it was my duty as the Mahadevi's daughter to keep you from learning her secrets. Yet, here you are. Despite the efforts of the Orlem Gor and the Mughuls and me to stop you, here you are."

"My comrade, Lockheart, once said much the same thing.

That Fate seemed to have grabbed me like a mother hound her pup and drags me where she will."

"So you see."

"Aditi . . . deny me if you must, but understand that I will not submit myself to marriage—"

"Shh! Listen. There are three days until the wedding. Much can happen in that time. Great changes. I sense it. If you must, I can always find you a hiding place in the palace on the day of the wedding. I know the secret passages well—I explored them all as a child. Be patient and watchful. The gods hold us in their hands like augur bones. We must wait and see which way we are tossed." She turned her head at another rustling from a nearby bush. "I must go." She ran off without another word.

With a heavy sigh, Thomas ran back to the iron gate, but slowed as he passed through it. *What matter if I am seen or not? If my fate is in the hands of gods, what occurs henceforth is by their will. Wherefore should I have a care? Wherefore should I strive against the divine powers that compel me?*

Thomas plodded to his quarters and opened the door, determined to not leave the balconied room again until forced to. "I have returned, Timóteo. Timóteo?"

The boy was not there.

Timóteo ran down the long, torchlit ancient hallway, his little, worn prayerbook clutched in his hands. *It must be now. Bom Deus, help me do what I must do before the gorgon commits so great a sin and dooms Tomás with her. Let me save her for you while I can! Let me be brave this time and not fear her.* It was good, in a way, that Tomás had abandoned him again, for the *inglês* would only have tried to stop Timóteo if he could.

After the audience with the queen, Timóteo had napped in the heat of the day. He had had disturbing dreams. He dreamed the palace was filled with beautiful girls, everywhere he looked, like the Isle of Venus described in *Os Lusiados*. He dreamed he floated above them, their faces turned to him like flowers to the sun. And he flitted from one to another, bringing the word of God to each, and they had raised their willing, accepting arms to him and his being was filled with joy.

He had awakened to a wet and stained sheet and a profound sense of shame. *It was a dream sent by the Devil to tempt me from my purpose. Or a warning from the angels. What the Dama Stheno plans must not happen.*

Though lost, Timóteo steered his feet in the direction that the servant Enyo had admonished them not to go. He tried not to look at the stone idols that sat over doorways—their blissful smiles seemed to be mocking him, laughing at him. Whenever he saw one of the blind priests sweeping a corridor, Timóteo would go up to him and ask in Kannadan, "Where is the Rani Stheno? Where is the Mahadevi? Take me to her, please."

But the priests would either not understand him or would back away with words of warning. Finally Timóteo found one he recognized, though it did not reassure him. In a small courtyard garden, under an *asoka* tree, he found the mad priest Prabaratma humming and chanting vedas to himself. *At least he understands some Kannadan. But will I understand him?*

"Please, holy sir," Timóteo said, although it unsettled him to call this mad pagan holy, "I wish to speak with the Mahadevi. Can you tell me where she is?"

Prabaratma smiled and bowed, murmuring in a babble of words like water running down a street. Timóteo could only comprehend a word here and there. "The Mahadevi . . . yes . . . in the heart . . . in the mind . . . speak through the vedas . . . fills the world, the sky."

Timóteo steeled himself to patience, though he wanted to shake the man. "Can you lead me to her? I want to see her."

The old priest stopped, his breath catching in his throat. He held out broad brown hands and gently touched Timóteo's face and neck. He murmured again, his voice filled with wonder.

"Please, will you take me to see her?"

Prabaratma stood and bowed very low. He placed a hand atop Timóteo's head and whispered what may have been a Hindu blessing. Then he grasped Timóteo's wrist and shuffled ahead, pulling Timóteo along.

Timóteo followed willingly as the old priest led him down many more corridors until they reached an antechamber. On one wall was a painting of a Hindu goddess, nude but for a loincloth, her tongue lolling out and her many arms holding swords. Timóteo turned his face away from the obscene image, wondering why the eyes hadn't been painted in. His gaze came to rest on a stone tiger crouching and snarling beside a doorway with a beaded curtain. *Were you once flesh and blood, mighty cat?* Foolishly he wondered if it were the same tiger he had chased away with rocks on the road to Bijapur. But there was much dust on the tiger's back and the statue had clearly been in place a long time. On the other side of the doorway was a bronze bull with a crescent moon between its horns. It had clearly never been living, but it spoke mutely of ancient myths and civilizations. Timóteo wished he could have seen the land and times in which it had been made.

The old priest went through the beaded curtain and spoke to someone beyond. Timóteo felt a shiver when he heard Stheno's voice reply.

Prabaratma reappeared in the doorway and beckoned for Timóteo to enter. Timóteo swallowed hard and walked in, his heart pounding. It was difficult to tell how large the inner room was, for silk draperies and screens of carved wood and thin, translucent jade were placed everywhere, at odd angles to each other. The air was pungent with the perfume of hibiscus and the smoke of the oil lamps hung on the walls. There were no windows he could see. Shadows rippled and shifted on the screen to his left and he heard the sound of wind through dry leaves.

"So, little monk of the Orlem Gor," said Stheno in her odd Latin, "I am told you have come to . . . see me."

Her dark-honey voice sent tremors of more than fear down Timóteo's spine and he was reminded uncomfortably of his afternoon's dream. "I . . . I have." He clutched his prayer book tighter. *Bom Deus, help me. Give me courage.* "I must talk with you."

"You must? Well. It must be urgent to bring you to me at this late hour."

The sinuous shadows on the jade screen moved as Timóteo heard her stand and approach him. He stared in awed fascination.

"So," she went on, "I am here. You are the companion of my husband-to-be, and I will not deny you an indulgence. What do you ask?"

"Um . . ." Timóteo was suddenly uncertain how to begin.

"Does it concern Tamas?"

"No. Yes. Well, him and you. And your people. But I am here to save you, most of all."

"To *save* me? What a charmingly naive notion. From what, child, would you rescue me?"

"From yourself. From your lack of knowledge. You are dooming yourself, Domina. And you will doom Tomás's soul, too. You must not have this . . . marriage with the girls."

"What can you be thinking? That I would . . . oh, what a filthy-minded little monkey you are. It is to be a divine marriage. The girls are to become priestesses. I will not touch them. I am no Sappho. I have tried women and, while they are pleasant, I can assure you I much prefer men."

The implications of what she said set Timóteo's thoughts spinning and he fixed his gaze firmly on the flame of an oil lamp ahead of him. "That . . . that doesn't matter." He took a deep breath. "I have come to bring you knowledge of Christ, the only begotten Son of God, through whom all mortal souls find salvation."

She laughed and Timóteo felt his resolve begin to wither. "This is useless information for me, little monk, for I am not a mortal soul."

Timóteo tried again. "Though you may have been born a demon—"

"I was born, child, mortal as you. I have, however, changed somewhat since then."

"Then there is hope, Domina! Accept the Savior and His Holy Church into your heart and he may take the serpents from your head and the evil from your soul! You need not be a gorgon any longer."

"Now there is a word I have not heard in a long time. Gorgon. So you know my nature. How comes a good Christian boy to know of the ancient myths?"

"My . . . my grandfather knew the old stories and told them to me."

"How gratifying that certain lies have so long a life. How long have you known what I was?"

"Since before I left Goa, I learned it in . . . the Santa Casa." *Bom Deus, let her not trick me into breaking the Rule of Silence.*

"Ah, yes, the Santa Casa, the Orlem Gor. My daughter spent much time in Goa and has told me much of your bloodthirsty temple."

"It is not like that!"

"What service did you perform there, little monk?"

"I . . . I was an advocate. I counselled guests of the Santa Casa to freely confess their sins and thereby be forgiven and return to the grace of God."

"Yes. Guests. Some friends of my daughter were guests in your Santa Casa. Hakim Zalambur. And the Domina Serafina. And Magister Bernardo De Cartago. Did you minister to any of these?"

Her voice held an edge like a knife and Timóteo wondered whether it would be better or worse to keep silent. "I spoke with . . . the Domina. And Magister De Cartago."

"And yet they are all dead. Your ministry seems to have had poisonous effect."

"No! The Domina Serafina confessed and lives." Timóteo suddenly clapped his hand over his mouth to prevent more words from spilling out. *Deus forgive me. I have broken the Rule.*

"And Tamas, he was under your care too, was he not?"

"Yes. And he freely accepted God in his confession."

"A confession secured by torment, hanging him from his arms until his shoulders came undone, Aditi tells me. One will admit to many ridiculous things under such pain. You must be a very naive boy not to have seen that your so-called Holy House exists only to terrorize the populace and make money for itself."

"Those are lies! You must not think such things of the Santa Casa. You have only heard bad stories told by evil people. The Santa Casa is a place of compassion, where those who are blinded by sin may learn their faults and give themselves up to the love of God."

"Compassion? Love? You have a twisted sense of those emotions, I see. Are you one of those who takes pleasure from inflicting cruelty upon others?"

Timóteo remembered the Grand Inquisitor Sadrinho bent over the Domina Serafina as she lay bound with wire upon a rough wooden board. The hunger in the Inquisitor's eyes as he stroked her arm and petted her hair and gently coaxed the confession from her . . . "No! I only asked them to confess so that they would not need to suffer pain! You misunderstand the Santa Casa. All who serve there are men whose hearts ache for the sinners who come to us, and we worship a loving God."

"A loving God. From what I have heard of your Christos, he sounds nothing like Krishna or Eros. Do you think your God could even love me?"

Hope rose again in Timóteo's heart. "Yes! That is why I am here, Domina. He will listen to you and forgive you if you will but seek Him."

"I have petitioned many gods and goddesses over the centuries but none have answered my prayers and taken this curse from me."

"That is because they are false gods, Domina. There is but one True God and He will forgive and bless you."

"That would be a forebearing god indeed. You are dedicated, for one so young. Your Holy House must have prized your service. But we are in my holy house now, and we will do things my way. You say your god is a loving deity. Very well, let us put it to the test. As I told Tamas, anyone who looks upon me without fear and with love in his heart will not be turned to stone. So I will make you a wager, little monk. I will allow you the chance to see me, as you wished. You may call upon your god for assistance. If you meet my gaze and are not harmed, then I will accept your god and your faith and your bloodthirsty temple as my own. Do you agree?"

Timóteo's mouth felt dry. This was the very chance he had hoped for, yet he wavered. *But is it not the sin of Pride to expect Bom Deus will protect me? The Padre said I should not dare too often the intercession of the angels. But if I now back away, the gorgon will laugh at me and her soul will be lost forever.* He swallowed hard again and said, "Yes, Domina. I accept."

"You are brave, little monk. I will give you some moments to prepare yourself."

Timóteo knelt and prayed desperately. *Bom Deus, hear me. Help me. I do not do this for my pride but for her soul and for You. Let me save this woman for You. Give me the strength to withstand her gaze. Remove her curse and turn her heart toward Your love. Amen.* He crossed himself and stood. "I am ready."

"So soon? Very well."

He heard one of the screens move aside and the soft sursurrance of silk. Timóteo closed his eyes a moment and breathed out, trying to empty his heart of all fear. Though he tried to think upon his faith and his duty, he also knew he was about to gaze upon an ancient legend, a wonder of Olympus. He opened his eyes again and saw her sari-draped form emerge from behind the nearest screen. She turned and stood, bare-headed before him.

She was beautiful, in the way Timóteo had always imagined creatures from his grandfather's stories. And the serpents waving to and fro on her head seemed . . . natural there, as if there could be no more fitting frame for her face, nothing else that could contain such unearthly beauty. He could easily worship her. *Bom Deus, what am I thinking?*

Her eyebrows rose and a smile played about her full lips. "Well. I am impressed. I had not thought to take so young a lover, but, then, you will last all the longer." She reached up with one hand and, with a gentle tug, released the upper portion of her sari from her shoulder. The silk slid off her ample breasts like a serpent from an anthill and Timóteo's gaze was suddenly riveted there.

"No, Domina, you do not understand. It is not I . . . not I who . . ." His heart quickened and again he felt a swelling in his groin. He blushed and his hands and feet felt cold and suddenly he felt an overwhelming fear of an unexpected sort. *Bom Deus, no, do not let me think these things!* His breathing became shallow and he looked back at Stheno's face, knowing that fear was beginning to show in his eyes.

Her gaze now held a feral hunger and her smile was that of a tiger seeing prey. The snakes on her head whipped around to face forward, their tongues flicking the air. The irises of Stheno's eyes began to glow red and Timóteo's feet felt colder. His stomach began to sicken and there was an ache in his bones.

"No," he whimpered, "Bom Deus, forgive me, I cannot do this!" Timóteo flung his arm before his face and turned to flee. But something hindered him and instead he was falling to the floor, agonizing pain creeping up his legs.

XVIII

BANYAN: This fig tree grows in the Indies, and bears large leaves and red fruit the shape of cherries. It is said that if its seed falls upon another tree, the banyan will strangle its host as it grows. A decoction of the fruit will draw forth fluids that gather from ailments of the chest and throat. A salve made with its sap gathered from the stems and leaves will remove warts. Paste made from the cooked flesh of the fruit will shrink boils. The Hindoos consider the banyan a tree of vengeance as well as symbolic of knowledge. They believe it is dedicated to their pagan god Shivo, and one who cuts down a banyan is said to be cursed thereafter with the destruction of his family....

By the late morning, Stheno could wait no longer and she went to the palace courtyard, just within the front gate, where the girls were being assembled. She had dressed herself as an old woman, in plain dun sari and *shal*, her face veiled. She hoped to wander, unnoticed among them, and hear their hushed gratitude at being the generation selected to be Divine brides, to hear their worshipful awe of the Goddess they were to serve.

But her pace slowed as she reached the archway to the courtyard and gazed out past the lotus ponds. *How can there be so few? Is Enyo gathering them somewhere else and she has not told me? Yes, my people have some hours left to bring their girls, but there are scarcely one hundred girls here when there are surely at least five hundred unmarried virgins in Bhagavati!*

She continued as she had planned, walking among the girls nearly unnoticed. To her growing dismay, many of the girls she saw were lame or disfigured, or diseased. Some rocked and muttered to themselves, suffering ailments of the mind or spirit.

Do my people intend that I should heal these creatures? Or have they so little respect for me that they send their worst as offerings and not their best?

Stheno paused near groups of girls who were gossipping. She overheard them whisper to one another about how a sister or a cousin was withheld from the conscription, and married in secret during the night to any available, suitable man or boy. Some men, they said, were taking several wives, so that the girls would not be delivered up to barren imprisonment with the Goddess. Only the ones who could not be readily married off had been sent to the Palace to be the Mahadevi's brides.

Stheno sagged back against the wall, clutching the cloth of her sari tightly in one fist. *My own people cheat me! They deny me their best daughters so that they can have more children and overcrowd themselves still more. And they dare whine to me that I must solve their problems. Fools! What duplicitous fools!*

Stheno shuffled to one corner of the courtyard where a tall, beautiful girl of high-caste—Brahmin probably, Stheno thought, judging from her fine clothes and many gold necklaces—was holding court. *So I am sent at least one pretty maid. I must learn who her family is and reward them.* Stheno stood nearby and listened.

"Papa says there are only old women and blind priests serving in the Mahadevi's palace. Now that Princess Aditi is back, and brought foreigners with her, more servants are needed and that's why all the girls were sent for. I don't intend to be anyone's servant. I shall befriend Princess Aditi and she will become so fond of me that we will rule Bhagavati together."

Oho, thought Stheno. *So you were sent to me because you are too ambitious and willful to be a proper Hindu wife. Fair enough. With the proper encouragement, I can harness your will to my uses.*

"But what about the Mahadevi?" said another girl of clearly lesser caste. "We are supposed to become divine brides of the Goddess, my family said, and it is She whom we will serve."

A conspiratorial gleam appeared in the Brahmin girl's eyes and she leaned down to speak softly to the others. Stheno had to creep closer to hear what was being said.

"Have you ever seen the Mahadevi?"

"Of course not! To look upon her is death. Everybody knows that."

"Very clever, don't you think?" said the Brahmin girl. "We are ruled by someone we never see. It could be one of the old women giving the orders for all we know."

"That's not true! My father has been to the palace when She held audiences and he says She looks just like the idols."

"Her shadow, you mean," said the Brahmin girl. "Listen. My mother has spoken to a cousin of mine who used to be a dancer until she went blind. This girl, Mother says, now dances behind the Mahadevi as a pair of the Goddess's arms. That image that our fathers have seen on the screen . . . is a fake! The Mahadevi is just a story to make us all obey—"

"Shhh! That old woman is listening to us!"

Stheno stared at them from behind her veil, feeling her eyes grow hot. *So. My people no longer believe in me. Have I kept myself hidden for so long that they have forgotten?*

"So what?" said the Brahmin girl. "She is just a low-caste servant. You!" she said to Stheno. "Why are you eavesdropping on us?"

Stheno shuffled forward and said in her best ancient crone voice, "Beware, child. Beware how you blaspheme against the Mahadevi, for She has eyes and ears everywhere and hears all you say."

A trace of uncertainty crossed the Brahmin girl's features, but it was swiftly replaced by a haughty stare. "You may believe what you like, old woman. But my people are priests, whose lifework it is to study the *vedas,* and they know what the true faith is."

Can she lie so boldly? thought Stheno half in admiration, half in horror. *Or are she and others like her ignorant of what the priests who serve me know?* "The Mahadevi does not care if you are of high-born caste, child. The divine truth does not live in the ancient, scrawled words of self-proclaimed learned men. The gods do not live in their prayers alone."

The Brahmin girl raised her nose with a quick intake of breath of insult and fury. The other girls gasped and covered their mouths. "Now it is you who blaspheme, old woman. How dare you say such things about your betters! If my father could hear you, he would have you whipped or even banished. No, the gods do not live in ancient words, they live in their heavens where they belong, not on earth."

Drawing herself up, Stheno spoke in something approaching her real voice, in Brahminic tones, "Would he now, insolent child? Do you dare threaten someone you know nothing of?"

The Brahmin girl wavered, but the presence of the other girls seemed to prevent her from backing down. "Are you mocking the way I speak, old woman? Do you know the great penalty for pretending you are from a higher caste than your own? Now go and fetch us water and some food or I will pull the veil and clothes off you and show the world your ugly wrinkles."

A couple of the girls giggled nervously behind their hands.

Oh, yes, thought Stheno as a raw eagerness that was almost hunger built up inside her. *Do that. Pull the veil from my face and receive the surprise you would earn. A pity your terror and remorse would be so brief.* Stheno could feel her eyes grow hotter and her little ones beginning to shift restlessly beneath her veil and turban. *But no. Let it not be here, not now. Some of the innocent girls would be harmed and the town might be panicked such that they will send no more daughters to me. I will not have a bull-headed mule of a girl ruin my wedding.*

"I will go," Stheno said, darkly. "But watch your tongue in future, girl, for you may not know to whom you speak." As Stheno turned away, she heard nervous laughter behind her and felt a rain of twigs and little stones on her back. Barely holding her rage in check, Stheno entered the coolness of the dark corridors and hurried to her inner sanctum.

How many more will be like them? Stheno thought coldly as she flung the beaded curtain aside. *Will I be hounded throughout my own home, afraid to show my face to stupid, ignorant, willful children—the few my oh-so-loving people deign to send me—just so that Enyo will be content that I am giving unused room to my people. My people—who no longer believe in me.*

She stepped into her bedroom and a priest leaped out from behind a screen. "Great Mother, I must speak with you!"

Stheno jumped back in surprise. And then she screamed at him, a wildcat screech of rage. She regretted that he was blind, for her anger could have no effect other than making him cower on the floor, hands over his ears.

"Great Mother, forgive me! I just . . . it is . . ."

He was not one of her usual lovers and she could not remember his name. He was one of the fanatics who had gouged out his own eyes so that he might serve in her palace. "How dare you lurk in my room to spring out at me! I should have your tongue, ears, and balls as well as your eyes for this!"

The priest flung himself prostrate on the floor. "Forgive me!"

"Explain to me why the good people of Bhagavati are only sending me their ugly, lame, sick, and willful daughters."

"Great Mother?"

"Why?!"

Trembling, the priest sat up. "Please . . . Great Mother . . . understand. And forgive them. They are not immortal, as you are. For them . . . family is all. It is their immortality. Those who have only daughters . . . for you to take them . . . it is worse than sentencing them to death. For you condemn the family to oblivion. No children. No grandchildren. Their daughters will not know the gentle love and guidance of a husband. It is wrong that they disobey you, Great Mother. But the sacrifice you ask . . . it is too much."

"What of my sacrifice, giving up my home so that they do not crowd themselves? Ingrates!"

The priest bowed his head. "Forgive us, Great Mother."

"And you. Why did you leap out from behind my screen, nearly frightening me into killing you?"

"I tried to give the message to your demon, Enyo, but she would not hear it. Yet, because of your instructions to us, I felt it was important you should know."

"You are babbling. What should I know?"

"That last night, against your orders, your daughter Aditi met with the foreigner Tamaschinri in the Sacred Garden. I could not understand their words, but they seemed to speak as lovers do."

Stheno felt the warmth of her rage cool into a cold knot in her stomach. "So. Even my daughter defies me. She whom I took in as a vagabond orphan and taught more than the daughters of sultans or kings ever learn." And Tamas—she had heard his objections when the wedding was announced at the audience with the town elders. Had Tamas lied too when he implied that the bond of marriage was necessary for him to love her fully?

"It is time," she said calmly to the priest, "to give my people a reminder of who I am."

"Great Mother?"

Stheno unwound her sari and let it fall at her feet. She removed her *choli* bodice and her underskirt until she wore only a loincloth across her hips. She pulled off her veil and gently unwound her turban. One by one, her little ones, the myriad brown serpents, popped forth and flickered their tongues, undulating freely around her head. She could sense their relief and joy at no longer feeling restricted.

Stheno went to a cedar box on a nearby table and pulled out from it a necklace of cat skulls. She hung this around her neck, letting the bones dangle over her bare breasts. From another box, she took a ceremonial knife with an ivory handle and hung it by a leather thong over her left thigh.

"Great Mother? Why are you silent?"

"It is time to let my presence speak, rather than my words. My people no longer believe in me. It is time for the Goddess to walk among them again."

The priest's face blanched in horror. "Great Mother . . . no! Please . . ."

"Go and warn them if you like. But I will walk this day and remind them who I am."

The blind priest got to his feet and blundered out of the room, feeling his way. Stheno followed him, stopping outside the chamber to look at the fresco of Kali as if gazing into a mirror. She bent down and removed the lid from the paint-pot the artist had left. Dipping in two fingertips, she placed them on the unfinished eyes of Kali, giving pupils and a semblance of life. "Through the eyes, one sees the soul," she murmured. Stheno smeared the remaining black paint from her fingers in streaks across her thighs and continued her walk.

At the courtyard, she was rewarded with the screams and shrieks of the girls as they scattered before her like peacocks confronted with a tiger. Stheno held her head high, not meeting the gaze of anyone in particular. If her visage brought ill effects, she did not notice it. She heard the warning bells begin to sound, first from within the palace, then carried throughout the city, accompanied with the cries, "The Goddess walks! The Goddess walks!"

Stheno smiled, enjoying the warmth of the sun on her bare skin, on her little ones, as she passed through the great bronze doors of the palace, down the basalt steps into the city of Bhagavati. Padding barefoot down the rutted stone streets, she reveled in the wails of fear, the running feet, the cries of "Get inside! Get inside!" In her peripheral vision she saw men and women fling themselves to the ground, arms over their heads, attempting to avoid her terrible gaze. Some ducked into cloth-covered doorways, slammed closed the wooden shutters on windows.

How glorious this is! To walk freely, unveiled again through my city, among my people. I must do this more often.

Stheno turned down an alleyway toward her right, a dusty track lined with the rickety wood houses of the poorer castes. Something small and dark blocked her path and she looked down.

It was a child. A chubby, naked little boy of no more than two years stood staring up at her, one finger in his mouth. His eyes were full of curiosity. Stheno's serpents turned their heads forward to view this odd creature who dared to stare openly at them. Perhaps it was the movement of the serpents, or something in Stheno's expression that suddenly distressed the child. His brows shot up with fear and his little mouth dropped open, lips quivering, and he gasped in a deep breath preparing to scream.

All of the serpents on Stheno's head thrust forward, hissing. Stheno's eyes grew hot, but instead of averting her gaze she let the long-suppressed sensation grow within her, devouring the sight of the terrified child. The warmth flowed from her face to her chest and down into her loins until she nearly shuddered with the surge of power and heat. A grunt of triumph escaped from her throat.

The little boy's skin turned from brown to ash-grey, flowing rapidly from from his feet to his head. His imminent shriek became only the whistling of air through a stone flute. His eyes glazed over, milky white and sightless.

After a moment, Stheno shuddered again and sighed. Her little ones drooped, relaxing against her cheeks and shoulders.

A wail of grief came from off to her right and a woman came running out of a nearby hovel. Holding part of her sari over her face, the woman flung herself to the dirt at Stheno's feet.

"Mighty Kali! Great Mother Durga! Why have you cursed us? Please, I beg you, restore him! Give me back my son!"

"It dared to gaze upon the Mahadevi. It was only a child," said Stheno. "Have you no others? You are surely young enough to make more. It seems I cannot stop you people from breeding."

"I have no other sons, Great Mother. And you have taken my daughters from me. Please. Give him back his life."

"There are so many children in Bhagavati. Your elders have complained that you are running out of room. Why should I restore this one?"

"All the world's children are yours, Great Mother, so surely he seems one of many to you. But he is my only son. Without him, who will learn the family trade? Who will support me when I am old? Who will make his father proud and give us grandchildren? The loss of one is nothing to you, but he is everything to me. Please. Give me back my son. I will offer you whatever sacrifice you ask for this."

Stheno wavered, and said, "Your faith and courage has impressed me, woman. Therefore I will give you a chance to regain your precious child. I have learned recently that my people have forgotten me. I am now thought a tale told to frighten children, my existence no longer believed in. That is why I walk this day, and that is why I turned your son to stone—he has paid the price for Bhagavati's forgetfulness. Therefore, here is how you may redeem him. Place your son in the central square where all may see him and remember my power. Every day, you will stand beside him and tell the story of what has happened here to all who will listen. After seven years have passed, come to me again, and if you have done well, I will return his life."

"Seven years . . ." sobbed the woman. "But, Great Mother, so much can happen in seven years. I myself might be dead before then."

Irritated, Stheno snapped, "Then you must pick someone in your family to speak in your place if you die. See that it is done, or the boy has no hope. Now move aside or I shall turn you to stone as well."

The woman crawled back and Stheno continued on, deliberately unhurried down the winding alley. To follow any street in Bhagavati to its end led eventually to the mountain rock wall, and the tunnel entrances that led down toward the valley of the Krishna River. The tunnels had entrances to secret passageways that passed under the city and through the palace. Once in them, Stheno could go anywhere unseen and unhindered and pop out to surprise the unwary. *My people will know again what it is to have a Goddess who lives among them,* thought Stheno and she smiled.

* * *

Thomas wandered the empty corridors of the palace, vaguely aware of alarums in the distance. Timóteo had not returned to their quarters during the night. Thomas had seen no sign of him and was unable to make himself understood to the few priests he encountered. Enyo had been frantic, trying to deal with the girls being brought for Stheno's abominable wedding, and had not seen Timóteo. Thomas desperately hoped the boy was merely hiding somewhere to watch the girls come in.

From up ahead, he heard a rhythmic booming, deeper than a drum, like the titanic footfalls of some giant. *Dear God, let there not be more monsters in this place.* Against his better judgment, though fearing that Timóteo might be nearby, Thomas headed toward the sound.

He turned a corridor to see the plaster on one wall bulging in, struck by blows behind it. There was a final, mighty crash and a portion of the wall fell in. Thomas flattened himself against the opposite wall, ready to run if some new creature of legend burst in.

But it was human arms that brushed away the plaster from the opening, and a man who emerged from the hole, albeit dust and dirt-covered like some gnome out of the earth. The man brushed himself off and looked around blinking and Thomas realized he recognized him.

"Andrew! By my soul!" Thomas rushed up to him and nearly embraced the Scotsman.

"Thomas? Tom! 'Tis you indeed! Then we have been led to the right place. Art well?"

"Well enow, though I could wish for better. And you, how did you find this place?"

Out of the hole stepped the old woman Porphredo, only somewhat more grey, from the dust, than she had seemed when Thomas saw her in the Mughul camp. Instinctively, Thomas took a step back from her, now knowing that she also was a creature out of legend. She regarded him a moment and then inclined her head, saying, "Greetings to you again, Hibernian. Please excuse our unusual arrival, but the entrance that you took was closed to us."

There was shouting and muttering within the hole in the wall. Porphredo turned and spoke toward it in Persian. Then, to Thomas's shock, the Mughul Mirza Akbarshah emerged, sword drawn, followed by two soldiers and the Sufi Masum. The Mirza saw Thomas and his brows rose, as he murmured something.

Thomas stepped back. "Andrew, did you bring the whole of the Mughul army with you?"

"Nay, lad, just these four who come seeking justice and enlightenment. And safety from treacherous men, if our guide's word may be trusted." He glanced sidelong at Porphredo.

The old woman began to speak and then paused, frowning. Then the frown transformed into a stare of alarm. "The alarm bells . . . the Mahadevi . . ." She looked at Thomas. "Despotas, what has been happening here? Where is Enyo?"

"I do not know what the bells mean, madam, but your Mistress is gathering virgin girls from the city for a bizarre form of nuptials, which I am also compelled to attend. Your . . . sister is it? Enyo has her hands full with the penning of the women in the courtyard, the last I saw of her."

"Ai! Madness has overtaken her. I should never have let her return without me. All of you, you must barricade yourselves in a room at once! For your safety!" She repeated her message in Persian for the Mughuls.

They argued with her, but Porphredo hurried to a nearby door and opened it. "In here! At once! You are all in great danger!"

"What do the bells mean?" Thomas demanded, as the Mughuls were undoubtedly asking also.

"The Goddess walks unveiled, if that means anything to you," Porphredo said, darkly.

Thomas felt the blood drain from his face. "It does, madam," he said quickly and strode through the open door, pulling Lockheart with him. The Mirza watched them and followed, ordering his men to enter as well.

The room was small and lit only by a narrow window high in one wall. It appeared to be used for storage, though what it contained was covered with a thick blanket of dust. Bats fluttered among the beams in the ceiling.

The door slammed shut behind them. "You would be wise to bolt it," Porphredo called through the door in two languages. "I or my sister will be back soon."

"What is this folderol, Tom?" asked Lockheart.

"If what she says is true," said Thomas, "then we are indeed in danger. Her mistress is a gorgon, Andrew, posing as a goddess. Her visage will turn all who look upon her to stone. 'Tis true! I have seen those who have suffered her gaze. If the chance arises, I will show you the crypt in which her ensorcelled victims dwell."

"Were it not for the fright in thy face, lad, I'd say you'd heard too many of Timóteo's fancies. Speaking of whom, is he here as well?"

"Until yesternight, the boy was with me and well. But I have not seen him since and now I begin to fear the worst."

The Mirza walked up to them and spoke.

"He asks, lad, whether this be trick or trap and what danger it is that you and Porphredo fear. Shall I tell him what you have just bespoke me?"

"You may as well. I see no need to lie for the monster. Best that he and his men know so that they may protect themselves."

"Art certain that is what we want?"

Thomas felt a chill in his stomach. "I care not that the Padre and the Santa Casa fear the Mohammedans gaining what knowledge may be found here. As I have told you, I have never wished a man dead, most surely not for his faith. Tell them."

Lockheart made an almost imperceptible shrug and began to speak to the Mirza. Thomas heard a word like "gorgon" among it, and felt relieved that at least some of the truth would be translated.

* * *

Porphredo hurried down the corridors, every bone and muscle in her legs and back protesting. Bad enough that she had walked for hours with the Mughuls up a narrow, pitch-black, dirty tunnel not knowing if she would find it fallen-in ahead, or have it fall in upon them. But now to be home at last to discover that Stheno had once more slipped her rational tether to cause who knew how much destruction and death. *One curse was not enough—the Fates must send me another atop another.*

She entered an open, gravelled area to the north of the main palace courtyard. The area, where normally horses were exercised, was now filled with huddled, frightened children. They shrank away from Porphredo in fear and she nearly blundered into a woman emerging from behind a column. Porphredo grasped the woman's shoulders for balance and to give warning when she noticed the blue eyes.

"Aditi!"

"Porphredo!"

"It is you, our little Aditi. Though you are not so little anymore, are you?" Porphredo gazed for a moment proudly on what a handsome woman her charge had grown into. "Are you well? Did you recover fully from your—"

"My death? Yes, dear Porphredo, I am fine. But all is not well here, as you see. Have you spoken to Enyo? Have you heard?"

"I have heard the bells and they tell me enough. And are these the girls the despoina intends to be her brides?"

"They are, poor things."

"Wherever did Stheno get such a horrid notion?"

"She said it was your idea."

"Mine? I never suggested any such thing."

"She said you wanted her to give part of the palace as living space to the townsfolk. In a way to . . . cut down the population increase, Stheno ordered all marriageable girls to be brought to the palace to live."

"She doesn't intend to blind them all, does she?"

"The Mahadevi has not said so to me, but who knows what she intends?"

"And now she has gone mad entirely and walks unveiled. Do you know where she is?"

"Somewhere in the city. Enyo has gone to try to stop her. I have gathered the girls here and I hope that the Mahadevi does not choose to pay us a visit."

Porphredo considered running after Enyo, but her legs nearly gave out at the thought. "I do not suppose there is any reason given for why the Mahadevi should punish her people so?"

"I have not spoken to the Mahadevi since yesterday morning, but there are some possibilities. The townsfolk have been disobeying her, sending only their flawed daughters and quickly marrying the rest. One of the girls here told me that the mayor's daughter blasphemed the Mahadevi in front of another, veiled old woman, who must have been the Mahadevi herself in disguise."

"Yes, either of those would be enough to sting her pride. We can only hope Enyo catches her before too many are . . . harmed." Porphredo sagged back against the column and slowly sat on the ground with a moan.

"*Aya* Porphredo, are you all right? You are so pale, and you smell of the grave."

"You always were such a complimentary child. I am tired and dirty. Would you be so kind as to fetch an old woman some damp towels, some water, and some food? I will watch your charges for you—they seem to fear me enough to be obedient."

"Of course, *aya*. You rest and I will return soon." Aditi hurried away and Porphredo realized she should have to tell her soon about the Mirza and the others locked up in the storage room. And how would Stheno, in her madness, react when she learned she had new, uninvited guests? Porphredo regarded the miserable, frightened girls nearby and sighed. She wished she had words of reassurance to offer, but none came to mind.

XIX

POPLAR: This tree hath two forms, the White and the Black. Both bear heart-shaped leaves and long, narrow catkins. The bark roughens as the tree ages. Tea made from the winter buds eases coughs, while bathing in the tea heals wounds and burns. An infusion of the root heals stomach ailments. The ancients wrote that Heracles travelled to Pluto's realm wearing a crown of poplar, and in that infernal place the leaves were scorched above and silvered below with his sweat. Thus were the leaves of the White poplar made, and thus did the tree come to signify continuance beyond death. The Black poplar was once sacred to pagan goddesses of the earth and if used in fortunetelling, signified that the seeker was without hope....

The Mirza Ali Akbarshah studied the face of the golden-haired westerner, seeking signs of treachery. *He is a very skilled pretender if the fear he shows is false. But his story! That the queen we have sought is no more than a monster of Iskandr's time. I will not have come all this way to tell my emperor such a thing.*

The Mirza noted that Masum had walked up behind him. But the Sufi stood, uncharacteristically silent, with his head cocked like a curious puppy. *Poor man. If what the westerner says is true, Masum will find no Great Sophia or beauteous Bilqis here.*

Rafi and Awwal were poking among the items in the storage room, lifting blankets that released clouds of dust. "My lord," said Awwal, "I see glints of gold within these chests. Perhaps Commander Jaimal was right and there is treasure to be found here after all."

And what further hatred will that arouse should word get back to him? thought the Mirza, ruefully.

A woman's voice echoed through the room. "Treasure indeed, depending on what you seek."

"Someone is in the walls!" said Lakart.

The Mirza and his men instantly drew their swords, all but Masum, but as the Mirza could not tell from what direction the voice came, he found himself turning in wary circles.

"It would seem I have uninvited guests," the voice went on. "I wonder how you found your way here." Her voice was low and beguiling, like the best courtesans of Lahore, but with an undercurrent of power and menace. She spoke an ancient, elegant Persian. The Mirza found himself desiring the owner of that voice, as well as fearing her. *Perhaps what the keeper of the nameless shrine said is true—this is a daughter-in-law of Shaitan, who has fooled the yellow-hair into believing she is some other demon.* The Mirza looked at Masum but the Sufi was merely staring at the walls in wonder.

At last, the Mirza recovered himself enough to respond. "I am the Mirza Ali Akbarshah, sent by the Shahinshah Emperor Akbar to seek a queen with the powers of life and death. If you are her, I greet you in his name. Your servant, Porphredo, guided us here."

"Ah, Porphredo. You must have had a compelling reason to convince her to bring you to my hidden city."

"I come to learn of your kingdom and offer alliance with the great Empire of Akbar. One of my men comes seeking justice, for the death of his brother which may have been caused by your sorcery. Another comes seeking the answer to philosophical mysteries. What should we call you and why do you not show yourself?"

"What to call me?" she mused. "I am the Mahadevi. I am Kali, the Giver and Destroyer. I am the builder of cities and the slayer of armies. I was formed in the image of the Lady of Beasts and to gaze upon my face brings death."

The Mirza noticed that Lakart's mouth had dropped open, face pale and eyes staring dumbstruck at the wall. *Does the northerner fear her more than I? I thought him a braver man.*

"You may call yourself a goddess," said the Mirza, "but I recognize no god but Allah. Understand this and give me another name by which to address you."

"Where have I heard this before?" murmured the voice in the walls. "No matter, I have heard so much foolishness over the centuries. You are welcome to my city of Bhagavati, Mirza Akbarshah. You may call me 'Majesty' or 'Queen Stheno' if it suits your sensibilities better. You arrive in time to attend my wedding. My groom stands among you."

The Mirza and his men turned to stare at Tamas. After Lakart's swift translation, the young yellow-hair blanched and shook his head.

"Ah, he is modest," said Queen Stheno, "but he will do his proper duty when the time comes. Now I must go see how the rest of the preparations are going. And I must tell Porphredo to find you better quarters. We will speak again soon."

The Mirza thought he heard movement beyond the wall. "Majesty?"

Rafi could no longer contain himself. "What about Mumit? There must be justice for Mumit!"

The Mirza reached over and touched Rafi's shoulder. "She is gone. We will bring the matter of your brother up first thing when we next speak to her." Although the Mirza dreaded encountering the owner of that voice again.

Masum fell to his knees and began to pray. The Mirza fought back a desire to join him.

Thomas felt deeply embarrassed under the stares of the men around him. But worse was Lockheart, who gazed at him with the intensity of a man who has been told he must take a medicine that will likely kill him. "Groom to the image of the Lady of Beasts," Lockheart said softly. "Though I might drag my feet, you have guided me more sure to my destination than the stars that accompany the moon on her night's voyage."

"Andrew, surely you cannot think that this creature is the goddess whom you serve? I tell you she is a gorgon, a mere demon, though immortal with powers of life and death, 'tis true."

"Demons are but gods defrocked, my lad. Stripped of their sanctity by faiths who have no room for any god save one." Lockheart looked sidelong at the Mughuls.

"That's as may be, but I'll not bow down and worship Stheno. Whatever utterance she may have made, you must understand that she is mad. Even her servant says so. There is little of reason in her words. You must take no import in them."

"Import there must be, lad, for you and she have imported me to this place. But I must drink my fill here, for from this port there'll be no sailing home, for the bottle be stopped and all hope drowned."

Thomas wondered if Lockheart had loosed the bonds of reason himself. *Though he cannot be all gone if he still plays upon words.* "Andrew, whatever you may think her, we will escape this place. I do not plan to stay."

"Oh, aye, escape will come. Swift and sure when time is ripe."

"Andrew, you affright me in this vein. And I now become concerned all the more for Timóteo, if he has found her thus. Damme, I should have asked her whilst she was here. I pray you pardon me, Andrew. I will continue my search."

"Certes. I will come with you."

"No! Stheno will not harm me, as I am her groom-to-be, but she may think less kindly on blundering strangers. Keep you safe and close here, and I will send a servant here anon." With a bow to the Mirza, Thomas unbolted the door and ran out, glad to put the energy of his fear to some purpose.

* * *

Padre Antonio Gonsção dozed in the hot noon sun on the bench atop the entertainer's wagon, leaning against the ornate railing. He had been warned by the blind *vina*-player that too much time with head bared to the sun could lead to madness and death. But Gonsção preferred riding above most of the dust kicked up by the men and horses. And the smell of which he preferred to the more earthy and sensual scents and the close company of women inside the cart below where Carlos and Estevão rode. *And I am not meant for Death just yet—had I been, my resurrection would never have been permitted.*

A shout rose up passed back through the unorganized ranks of elephants, horsemen, and foot soldiers. Slowly the army column slowed. *Of course,* thought Gonsção. *It is time for their noon prayers. Their faith brings them to choose an unlovely spot for stopping.*

They were in a flat dry treeless plain that showed signs of periodic flooding. A brown ribbon of river had been winding nearer to them as they had traveled further south and east. Now it was but some yards to their south, although in the rippling hot air it still seemed, at times, a mirage. Far down the river were some dark shapes that might be trees that might denote a village. Beyond the river, stony hills marched in serrated ridges one behind another.

The cart rocked with movement and Gonsção turned. He was disappointed to see the Hindu girl who had hung on Gandharva's arm coming up the ladder. She hurried over to sit close beside him. Gonsção flinched and wanted to move away, but he was in a corner and felt trapped.

The girl put on a broad, but false, smile. She said in Latin—in the cadence of one who has been taught words without knowing their meaning—"Tempus est. Nunc imus."

Gonsção had questions but knew it would be useless to ask them of this girl, with whom he shared no language. He nodded curtly to her and followed her as she went back to the rope ladder and descended.

The back doors of the cart swung open and Gandharva leaned out. "We must hurry. While they are at prayers."

Gonsção glanced behind the blind musician and saw Carlos and Estevão dressed in the flowing, garish scarves of the Hindu whores. "What shameful nonsense is this?"

"A disguise, Padre," said Carlos. "Come in and put this on—you drape it over your head and wrap it around you." He flung out a long wide piece of blue silk that glittered with gold thread.

Gonsção began to object, but Gandharva said, "We have no time for theological argument. This is the only way we will turn aside their notice long enough. Swallow your pride and beg forgiveness of your god later."

Reluctantly, Gonsção climbed into the cart and accepted the garish clothing. The Hindu girl tucked and tugged with expert hands on the silk to drape it right. In the dimness of the cart, Gonsção saw with dismay that two of the Hindu prostitutes were now wearing the *soldados'* clothes and helmets, and had painted black on their lower faces to resemble beards. The fattest of the girls wore a long white wool robe, similar to Gonsção's. "They will never fool the Mughuls," Gonsção grumbled.

"They need not fool them long," said Gandharva. As the call to prayer rang out across the army, Gandharva hopped out of the cart, *vina* slung across his back, and he took the Hindu girl's arm. She carried a large covered basket on the other arm. "Now," he said softly. "Walk slowly with me. We are just the girls stretching our legs and taking a piss by the river. Laugh like women if you can, but not too loud."

As they left the cart, Carlos and Estevão did rather convincing giggles that shocked Gonsção.

"Very good," said Gandharva. He said more in a louder voice in a different language, stretched with a big smile, and allowed the girl to lead him toward the river.

Gonsção bumbled along beside the musician, not knowing how to walk like a woman, nor wishing to. *Lord forgive the things I must do to serve your will.* "What do you plan to do when we reach the river?"

"Do you see two rocks that look like bathing elephants?"

"There are two large boulders in the river near the bank, yes."

"We head for those. Do not look behind us and do not speak to me again until we are there."

Gonsção remained silent but felt his back was terribly exposed, as if hundreds of pairs of eyes were watching him.

When they were halfway to the rocks, the Hindu girl said something in Gandharva's ear and he stopped. He took the *vina* from off his back and left it on the ground.

"You are going to leave your instrument?" Gonsção asked softly. "I have never seen you without it."

Taking the Hindu girl's arm again, Gandharva said, "I have fostered the illusion that the *vina* is my life precisely so that I may someday leave it. If Jaimal's men see it, they will believe I have not gone far." He continued walking to the river.

The girl led them around and behind a cluster of man-high thorn bushes. They were now out of sight of the Mughul army. She pulled out of her basket more long silken scarves, and tossed these into the air and over the bushes.

"If we are lucky," said Gandharva, "those behind us will think we are bathing. There should be very tall reeds ahead of us, between the elephant rocks."

"There are," said Gonsção.

"You and your men must search among them. If my message arrived at Devidurga, there should be small rafts hidden there."

Gonsção slogged into the water, Carlos and Estevão behind him, and he pushed through the reeds and grasses. He hoped there were no serpents lurking there. Sandflies and gnats swarmed around his face.

"Over here! Here they are!," Estevão called out.

"Shhh! Hurry and climb on. They are but a few boards wide, but if you wrap your arms around them, they will carry you across. Pramlocha!"

The girl took his arm again and led him down to the water. As Estevão shoved a raft about three-foot square toward them both, Gandharva and the girl grabbed on.

"Surely she is not coming with us!" said Gonsção.

"Did I not tell you I owed her a debt?" growled Gandharva.

"And I need her guidance. Now. Push off across the water. Hurry."

As Gonsção did so, he asked, "Would this not have been better at night? They will be able to see us when we are out in the open river."

"At night is when they would expect our departure and we would have been more closely watched."

"Ah. You are very perceptive, for a blind man."

"My thanks. So are you. Now do be silent and swim!"

Ignoring Gandharva's implied insult, Gonsção kicked with his legs and moved his raft far enough into the brown water to be caught by the river's current. It was not as swift as he feared, but it took much work with his feet and one arm to get any lateral distance across the river. The swirling water was colder than he expected and swiftly seeped into his wool robe. Carlos was having trouble guiding his raft and rammed, spinning, into Gonsção who gripped the *soldado's* sari and held onto him until Carlos could balance himself better on his planks of wood.

They were nearly to the rocks on the far bank when there came shouts from behind them.

"The Mughuls have seen us, Padre!"

"Paddle hard as you can and do not look back!" said Gandharva.

By good fortune, an eddy of current caught their rafts and flung them amid the boulders and reeds of the far bank. Gonsção let go of his raft and let it continue downstream. As he helped Carlos from his, Gonsção could not help one glance across the river.

Mughul horsemen were riding up to the opposite bank, pulling bowls from their backs and nocking arrows to them. A whirring went past Gonsção's ear and an arrow shattered against the boulder beside him, just above his head.

New energy in his legs, Gonsção clambered up the riverbank and crouched behind the boulder. Carlos and Estevão swiftly joined him. "God help us if they can cross the river," he gasped.

"Where is the blind man?" asked Carlos.

Gonsção swallowed his fear and peered around the boulder. Gandharva and the girl had just arrived at the bank and she was struggling to help him up onto the bank. There came another rain of arrows and the girl arched her back, pain and shock in her eyes.

"Pramlocha?" said Gandharva.

"Madre Maria," cursed Gonsção and he scrambled out from behind the boulder, grabbed them both and pulled them with him into the shelter of the rocks. He laid the girl down on the ground and saw that the arrow had gone through a lung. She was gasping horribly and blood leaked from her mouth.

"What has happened?" said Gandharva. "Is she all right?"

"She is pierced by an arrow," said Gonsção. "She will likely not live long. I am sorry."

Gandharva's brows wrinkled with sorrow a moment, then smoothed. Softly, he said, "We must leave her, then."

Gonsção had been about to suggest the same, but the surprise of hearing the pagan musician say so shocked him into contrariness. "You would abandon this girl like you did your *vina?*"

"If she bleeds, she will leave a trail that can be followed."

"Can the Mughuls cross the river?"

"The horses cannot. The river is too deep and swift. But the elephants might. It will take them a little time to realize that and bring them so we must not stay any longer."

"What is he saying, Padre?" asked Carlos. "We are not going to just leave her here, are we?"

Gonsção said to the musician, "Your queen can revive the girl if she dies, can she not?"

Another rain of arrows pinged off the rocks behind them, scattering wood shards into the hillside ahead of them.

"Of course, of course," said Gandharva, "assuming we could get her to Bhagavati."

"Then we will. You have brought her this far because you owed her. Your debt is not discharged. We will bring her with us. Carlos, can you carry her?"

"I think so, Padre."

"Estevão, you will take Gandharva's arm and guide him. Gandharva, where is the trail we are to take?"

"Look for the sign of a coiled serpent in the rocks higher up on the hillside."

Gonsção translated this for the *soldados* and Estevão said, "I see one, Padre. Over there."

"Then let us head for it."

As Estevão took Gandharva's arm and Carlos crouched and slung the wounded girl across his shoulder, Gandharva said, "I have misjudged you, priest of the Orlem Gor. May your generosity not bring death upon us all."

Thomas slowed his pace, the afternoon heat sapping his strength, even though the air in the stone corridors of Stheno's palace was cooler than outside or in the storage chamber. The hallways were more deserted than ever—even the ubiquitous priests with their straw brooms were gone. And there had been no sign of Enyo or Aditi, no one to tell him where Timóteo might be.

He rounded a corner and stopped. Leaning against the wall near a wooden door, was the old blind priest who had left offerings for Thomas the day he had arrived. *What was his name? Praba-something. Did Enyo not say he was mad?* Thomas wondered if he should tiptoe past the priest or take a different way.

But the priest suddenly stood up straight and turned his sightless face toward Thomas. "Ah! Tamas. Tamas." The priest smiled and beckoned to him.

Does he have more vision than I thought? It is as though he were expecting me. Ah, well. Perhaps Timóteo left a message with him for me, although I can think of no less helpful messenger. With a sigh, Thomas walked up to the old man. "I am looking for Timóteo," he said, slowly and carefully in English, and then "Exquiro Timóteo, um, flamine de Orlem Gor?" Thomas inwardly winced at his mishmash of languages, but he had no idea how to make himself understood to the priest.

The old man continued to smile and bob his head and indicated the wooden door beside him. "Tamas. Tamas." He opened the door and beckoned again.

"Is Timóteo in there?"

Still grinning and nodding the old man went through the doorway. Thomas started to follow him, and then paused. Beyond the doorway, dimly lit by rush tapers on the wall, were stone stairs leading down. Memories of the dungeons of the Santa Casa and the Aljouvar rose into his mind and his heart lurched. *Wherefore it is my fate to be summoned into dark, stygian places?* He smelled damp earth and stone, but no scent of blood, or moans of anguish or other hint of distressed humanity.

The old priest padded down the steps, humming a strange, haunting tune. *Well, I am not forced this time, and if the old man is the only danger I can likely overpower him. And I should learn whether Timóteo is here.* With a sigh, Thomas followed after the priest, careful to leave the door open behind him.

The steps led down into a single, dirt-floored room bare of all furnishing save a squat stone statue set against the far wall. There was no sign of Timóteo.

Praba-something was standing beside the statue and, to all appearances, talking to it. *I should have known,* thought Thomas. *He has but involved me in one of his mad fancies.*

He turned to go back up the stairs, when a hand gripped his wrist. The old priest was surprisingly strong as he pulled Thomas toward the statue.

"What do you want?" Thomas said, exasperated. He did not wish to hurt the old man but he had no patience for humoring him. When they got the statue, however, Thomas paused. The stone figure, unlike those in the crypt, had clearly never been alive. This was a plump, leering, winged creature with a protruding tongue. And serpents for hair. *Ah, 'tis a likeness of Stheno, albeit an unflattering one. No wonder she keeps it hidden in a cellar. Or mayhap it is some other gorgon. Mayhap the famed Medusa herself.*

The old priest mumbled something that was beginning to sound like a religious chant. He placed Thomas's right hand atop the idol and patted it. Then he bent down and took from behind the statue a basket covered with a vermillion cloth. From it, he took out a garland of large scarlet flowers which he placed over Thomas's head. The only words Thomas could catch in the old priest's mumbling were, "Arayani, arayani, arayani. . . ."

Once more I am forced to serve at a pagan ritual. Is this some part of Stheno's abominable wedding?

The priest raised a small clay bowl over Thomas's head and poured a cool liquid onto his hair that smelled of butter. "Sraddha, sraddha," murmured the priest.

"Prabaratma!" someone called out from the stairs.

Thomas turned his head and saw it was Enyo, staring wide-eyed at the priest. She hurried down the steps and walked right up to Prabaratma, railing at him in, presumably, his Hindic language. Prabaratma bowed low but did not seem in the least humbled or ashamed.

"Your pardon, despotas," she said to Thomas in Greek. "As I have warned you, this one is . . . not right in his mind. It seems to be a . . . common malady today."

"All is well. He has done me no harm," said Thomas.

"That is as may be," Enyo grumbled cryptically. She took the garland from around Thomas's neck and flung it at the feet of the statue. Then the little woman grabbed Prabaratma's shoulders and propelled him toward the stairs. The priest meekly began to ascend.

Enyo returned to Thomas's side, scowling. "He should not have brought you here. Neither of you should be here."

"Your pardon, madam. I do not know why the old man brought me down here. I had hoped he would lead me to Timóteo, whom I had not seen since yesterday."

Enyo glanced up at him with sad shock and then ran to the stairs. She called something up at Prabaratma. He gave a singsong reply and Enyo came back. "Prabaratma says your boy is with the priests, and is in their care. What this means, only his addled mind knows."

Thomas sighed, flooded with relief. "Ah. No doubt he is trying to convert them all. He must have become bored with my company and decided to occupy himself with his holy work. This eases my mind greatly. By the way, if you do not already know, your . . . sister is it? Porphredo has returned."

Enyo turned happy, grateful eyes to him. "Has she? Is she well?"

"Yes, to all appearances."

"Where is she?"

"I do not know. She left us in a storage room when she heard the alarum bells."

"Us?"

"Um, she brought a few of the Mughuls back with her."

"Ai! What a terrible time to bring more strangers in! What could Porphredo have thought? What if the despoina sees them?"

"She already has. Queen Stheno is in the palace, apparently lurking between the walls."

"Yes, yes, this palace is riddled with secret passages. She could go anywhere. You are a fountain of news, despotas. I hope the despoina was not driven to greater fury?"

"Not that I could determine. She spoke entirely in Persian, for the sake of the Mirza, and I only understood that which was translated for me. It was made clear that she is determined to go through with this wedding of hers." Inspiration struck Thomas and he asked, "You say there are secret passages? Enyo, I would not marry a madwoman—could you help me escape through them?"

"No!" Enyo clutched at his sleeve. "You must not leave now, despotas. This wedding may be all that keeps her from enstoning the whole city. She is angry that some of her citizens have disobeyed her. If you upset her wedding plans, who knows what she will do? If her wedding, however horrible it may seem to you, soothes her anger and returns her human spirit to her, think of the lives you will be sparing. Perhaps, when all is done, her mind will be turned to other things. She is like a child that way—her attention is easily distracted. You may then escape and forget everything that has happened here. Please, despotas, I beg you. For the lives of hundreds of strangers, please stay!"

Thomas frowned, clenched his fists and then relaxed them. "Very well, madam. You speak most eloquently on behalf of your people. I could not live with my conscience if my selfish actions were to lead to their deaths, or near-deaths." Softly, he heard himself say, "I will stay. For now."

"Thank you! Thank you, despotas. Perhaps it will not be so bad as you think. You might learn much while you are here, nai? Now I must go find my sister. There is so much to tell her."

"Please tell me, madam, before you go, what the meaning of this room and this image are?"

"No," said Enyo. "Forgive me, despotas, but this place is still sacred to . . . some of us. Prabaratma should not have brought you here."

"I see. Forgive me, then, for trespassing, madam. Before I go, can you at least tell me what Prabaratma was doing to me?"

"I cannot be certain what he intended," said Enyo, "but that garland is what the people of Bhagavati place upon animals who are to be particularly honored. Or to be sacrificed."

"Ah. I thank you." His stomach turning sour, Thomas followed her to the stairs and out of the buried chamber.

Enyo found Porphredo in the horse-exercising yard, sitting against a pillar, eating rice from a bowl. "Ah! The young despotas was right. You *are* back!" She rushed to her sister and embraced her tightly, nearly knocking the rice bowl from Porphredo's lap.

"Gently, sister. This food is too precious to me right now to waste even in fondness."

"Oh, but I am glad to see you! You have no idea how chaotic it has been here!"

"I am gaining some understanding of it, believe me."

"I was so worried."

"Enyo, you know there is nothing Stheno could have done to me. Our curse promises us that, at least. We are like those little fishes that swim safely among anemones in the tide pools."

"But what if the Mughuls had torn you to pieces with their elephants? Are you immortal enough to survive that?"

"Why, then, dear sister, every piece of me would have come crawling back to you so that you might stitch me back together. Then I could present quite a sight to Stheno, nai?"

"That is a horrible image." Enyo sighed and sat down against the pillar beside Porphredo. "Ai, what shall we do, sister, what shall we do?"

"What we have always done in times such as these. Wait it out. See that as few people as possible are hurt. How many did Stheno . . . ?"

"Too many. Oh, all right, I don't know. Two citizens that I know of. And a child. A child! Not even two years old."

"Our despoina does not discriminate by age."

"She will never restore them."

"Perhaps, perhaps not."

"That is why the Despoina Euryale left us, don't you remember? She felt so guilty for Despoina Stheno's crimes that she kept giving her own blood to restore those whom she could."

"And sensible, calculating Deino could stand it no longer and got her out of here."

"Ah, Deino. Sometimes I have forgotten we have another sister. I miss her."

"Miss her? We argued with her constantly. She's nearly as devious and wicked as Stheno."

"Yes. But only for the right reasons. I wonder where she is now."

"Her last letter said she and Euryale were headed for a land called the New World. That was . . ." Porphredo frowned and a troubled look came into her dark grey eyes. ". . . a long time ago."

"I wonder if they ever found it. Have you ever dreamed, Porphredo, of running away? Abandoning Despoina Stheno and making our own lives . . . out there?"

"Who would not? But I believe we were cursed to be companions to the gorgons for a reason. Without us, who knows how monstrous Stheno would have become? We stay to keep her human."

"Strange, but I was just telling the golden-haired despotas that he must do the same—stay for her wedding so that she might calm herself again."

"Much is required of people for the Despoina Stheno's sake."

"At one time, our companionships made sense. Euryale is so sweet of nature, she needed a viper like Deino to be nasty for her. Stheno is so . . . thoughtless, she needed you to be her wisdom."

"And Medusa was so pious and serious, she needed you to be her cheerful, sweet friend."

"I suppose. I hardly remember her now. I remember that we cared very much for one another. And she always listened to me. But all these centuries, my kind nature has been wasted in the company of Despoina Stheno."

"I would hardly call it wasted. You are even more her conscience than I. She rails at you because you still poke at those parts of her that feel anything."

"But why couldn't Stheno have been given the 'gift' of death?"

"Which of those sisters do you think more deserving of escaping their curse?"

"Euryale."

"Only because you have forgotten Medusa. Perhaps it is better things happened as they did. Stheno is more than enough for two companions to handle."

"So. How do we handle her now?"

"Wait. Keep her from doing her worst. And hope we can change her for the better."

XX

FIR: There are many evergreen trees of this name, all bearing flat needles and cones that stand erect upon its branches. A distillate of the needles eases pains of the chest, as well as that of the scurvy. A poultice made from the inner bark soothes eruptions of the skin. Some say one may cure the gout by reciting a rhyme to a fir tree at sunset, or by tying a knotted cord on a fir branch. It is a tree of Jupiter, and meant much to the ancients. It was also thought sacred to Artemis, goddess of the hunt. Some pagans worshipped the tree itself and offered sacrifice to it. Some Christians employ fir boughs as scourges for penance. To the Irish, it is a tree of birth and beginnings, and harbors a female spirit. If struck by lightning, however, the fir tree is a harbinger of death....

'Tis like the fabled labyrinth of the Minotaur," Thomas said to Lockheart, as they stopped in an intersection of hallways. Now that evening had fallen, cool breezes blew through the palace corridors, bringing the scent of lotus blossoms and inviting a pleasant stroll.

Enyo had finally led the Mirza and his men to better quarters and Thomas had offered his unused room to Lockheart, so long as Timóteo was going to lodge with the Hindu priests. After resting through the afternoon, the Scotsman's strange mood seemed to have left him and Thomas was glad again for the near-countryman's company. Thomas was careful not to wander too close to the wings off the courtyards where Enyo had told him the girls of Bhagavati were being housed. He did not fear too much that Stheno might pop out with fatal surprise—not if she still wanted her precious wedding.

"Aye, but 'tis a different legend entire who lurks within, you say. I am most curious, lad, as to what proof you have that this Queen Stheno is a cousin of the famed Medusa."

"Sister, actually, or so she says. But I have seen her, Andrew."

"What, and felt no ill effect? How is't possible?"

"In like wise as the hero Perseus. With a mirror. Timóteo had brought it for me. One night when she came . . . visiting, I had propped the mirror just so, such that I glimpsed her countenance and serpentine tresses by moonlight."

Lockheart's expression changed from wonder to scandalized amusement. "She visits you o' nights, eh?"

Thomas felt his face grow hot. " 'Tis not entirely as your imaginings may paint it. She makes herself free with me . . . she . . . whilst I sleep . . . let us say I have not been a willing nor waking lover."

"This grows more and more of interest. No wonder a wedding is nigh."

"Think you I could love such a creature? Nay, Andrew. I would not speak of this matter further." Thomas walked the next few yards in embarrassed silence, and then said, "If truth be told, I have more affection for her daughter."

"Who? Ah, your dancing lady Aditi. She did recover, then?"

"She did, though it took some days. Mayhap you will see her whilst you are here. I am now forbidden to."

"I assume 'twas not so fearsome a sight as when De Cartago was resurrected."

"No, 'twas in the manner of awaking her from long sleep."

" 'Tis a potent powder indeed. I wish I could have seen it."

"I did not use a powder, but Stheno's fresh-drawn blood itself."

Lockheart stopped and stared. "Eh?"

"Truly. You were right, Andrew. The *rasa mahadevi* is indeed blood, though of a demon who only poses as a goddess. The source of the miraculous powder is Stheno herself."

"Wonder upon wonders," murmured the Scotsman. "So it was this Queen Stheno herself who came to rescue her daughter that night."

"Her very self, yes."

Lockheart scratched his beard. "Aye, that explains Mumit. And the unfortunate Joaquim."

"Joaquim? What about him?"

"You did not know? Joaquim is dead, lad. Died that very night, bit about the face by poisonous vipers. Confuted us all as to how he might have gotten such strange wounds."

Thomas shut his eyes and balled his fists. "She invited him into the shadow of the trees for a kiss." *Poor Joaquim. He deserved a better end.* Thomas struck the palm of his hand with his fist. "That . . . monster! Oh, she has much to answer for, Andrew. There is a crypt here that I have seen where she keeps those victims who have been translated into stone. There they await a reawakening that never comes, for she has the power to do it, Andrew, but she does not."

"Aye, now I believe you, lad, with full heart, for I too have seen proof, though I knew it not."

"What's more, there is a pit dug out o' th'earth where she keeps a hideous statue depicting one such as her. One of her priests led me there and attempted a rite of sacrifice upon me."

Lockheart's eyes went wide. "That cannot be right. 'Tis not yet your time."

"Do you jest, Andrew? I was unaware of what was happening until Enyo came and stopped it. Oh, would I were a warrior of Perseus's mettle, I should gladly lop Stheno's head off in a trice."

"Wait, calm yourself, lad. Be of metal more malleable, for gold hath more value than steel. Think what wonders may be gotten here."

"Oh, aye, there are wonders. There is a library in which tomes from the world over and civilizations of ages back to Abraham, but there is no order in it! 'Twould take a scholar a lifetime to study one shelf of it. But Stheno knows not what she has, nor cares. She has the gilded majesty and dross of millennia gath'ring dust in her storerooms."

"Then condemn her not so soon, lad, for at least she had the sense to gather it. Were I to live a thousand years, who can say what volumes of knowledge I would forget, or what I would think important? And there is the greater wonder of Stheno herself, and the life-giving blood in her veins. You yourself have said you have devoted your life to easing the ailments and pains of others as steadfast as any physician. See you not the possibilities in this?"

"What do you suggest, Andrew? That I capture her and tap her sap as though she were a maple tree? At great risk to my own life as well as others? Or perhaps I should present her as a gift to Her Majesty Elizabeth, a curiosity for her court? There'd be no need for royal sculptors then. You'd find busts with no greater likeness than Stheno's handiwork."

"Tom, Tom, you are twisting yourself into stranger knots than a trollop's bedsheet. Calm yourself and be of better cheer."

" 'Tis easier said when you are not to be her bridegroom on the morrow. Ah, here . . . here is another of her strange fancies." They had come upon one of the iron gates leading into the sacred garden where Thomas had met with Aditi the night before. "If Enyo speaks aright, this is a copy of some holy garden on the Continent. 'Tis thought sacred, yet Queen Stheno ne'er visits it." Thomas pushed on the gate and found it open. "Come, Andrew, and have a look at this."

Lockheart followed, asking, "Are we not trespassing if this is thought holy ground?"

Thomas nearly ran over the well-tended path through the oaks and the cypress. "I care not, nor I suspect would Stheno. Come, Andrew. See. That pond there is meant to be a lake and those hummocks to be mountains, those columns there a temple." He heard a groan behind him and Thomas turned.

Lockheart had sunk to his knees, his eyes wide and face pale as if he'd been struck a mortal blow. He murmured something in Greek too soft for Thomas to catch."

"Andrew, what's the matter now?"

"So," the Scotsman sighed, "it is to be here." He ran his fingers over the gravel of the path as if caressing it.

"What is? What is all this to you?"

"I know this place, Tom. 'Tis a shrine in Italy."

"Dedicated to your . . . our goddess?"

"The very same. Oh, that its image should be here, ruled by the image of Artemis, a queen of life and death. And rebirth."

Thomas found the return of Lockheart's odd behavior somehow calmed his own inner storms of fear and anger. "You expected to discover . . . this?"

"Not this, no. Merely a sign. But there can be no greater sign than this." Lockheart stood, dusting his hands off on his breeches. "I thank you, yet I thank you not for showing me this."

"Andrew, what is't distresses you?"

"My own foolish fondnesses and the vagaries of Fate, lad—these distress me. Never own a heart with wishes if you would be content. I shall tell you all anon. But, come, a bridegroom must have his rest upon his nuptial eve. Let us hie back to our quarters. I would not look longer upon this green and pleasant place than I must."

"As you will." As Thomas passed by him, Lockheart grasped his shoulder. There was fear and terrible hope in his eyes. "I once chastised you for resurrecting the Padre. I apologize most heartily."

"No, you never did, Andrew."

"Did I not? I thought it, then. You say you never wished a man dead."

"I say it still."

"Save for the gorgon."

"She is not of mankind."

"Well. I once thought such philosophy foolish in you. I think it no longer. I pray you do remember it—and yet . . ." He frowned and squeezed Thomas's shoulder, as if wishing to force some humour from his flesh.

Thomas winced. "Ow! Andrew, do remember I am but somewhat healed."

Lockheart removed his hand. "Your pardon. Let us go."

Porphredo waited in the darkness. She would have rather slept, but sleep would have to wait. Together with Enyo and Aditi, they had managed to get the girls of Bhagavati bedded down for the night. Two hundred girls, even frightened and submissive ones, had been much for three women and a few blind monks to manage. Especially when matters of family and caste dictated who could not sleep next to whom. *Ah, the challenges you give us, despoina.*

Porphredo heard a sound, a scraping of wood on stone and a soft susurrance like wind in bare boughs. She smiled.

She saw the glimmer of a rush taper, lit from one of the incense-brazier coals no doubt, on the translucent screen in front of her. The glow became lighter as an oil lamp was lit. When she heard the rush taper blown out, Porphredo pulled the screen aside. "Good evening, despoina."

With a shriek, Stheno jumped back, her breasts bobbling, her serpents frantically whipping about her head unable to find a target to focus upon. Stheno's eyes glimmered red briefly, then faded. "Porphredo!"

"Ah, you remember me. I was so afraid you had forgotten. I know how age taxes the memory."

"What do you want?"

"What, no 'Welcome back, Porphredo'? No, 'How was your stay with the Mughuls, Porphredo'? No, 'It is good to see you, Porphredo'? My, how swiftly affections can fade in just a few days."

Stheno brushed aside a few serpents that had drifted in front of her eyes, much as a woman might with annoying strands of hair. "Why should a queen ask any of those things of her servant? I gave you a task. I trust you have done it. Now you have returned. If you expect more, you must swallow your pride and remember your place."

"Ah. I expected to find a queen upon my return. Instead, I find that Bhagavati is being menaced by a monster. If you will point me in the direction of the missing queen, I will gladly give my full report of the Mughuls to her."

Emotions warred on Stheno's face, but Porphredo could not tell which was winning—rage or chagrin. "You are supposed to be wise, Porphredo. You should know better than to mock when you do not understand the situation."

"Well, that is part of why I am here. I have gotten a very interesting impression, from what I have seen and heard. You misunderstood my suggestion, and chose to only give rooms in the palace to unmarried girls. You misunderstood your people, and became angry when they tried to preserve their families. You misunderstood why they were willing to defy your proclamation. And no doubt you misunderstand why your little reminder to them of your godhood might have been a mistake."

Stheno stood straighter, regaining some composure. "I think I am not the one misunderstanding. Your task was to see that the Mughuls did not find us. Yet here you bring some of them straight to Bhagavati. What am I to think of this willful treason?"

"Ah, you have already seen my gifts to you, despoina. I brought the Mirza, because I know how you love dallying in foreign intrigue. He brought his men over a little matter of justice that might interest you. I have brought a man from a northern country we have never heard of. And there is a Sufi. I know how much Sufis amuse you."

"They are amusing once, and I had my fill a long time ago. What do you intend I do with this Mirza? If I keep him here or kill him, questions will be asked and his emperor may send more after him. How dare you endanger all we have built this way?"

"I was hoping," Porphredo said mildly, "that you would come up with a more creative solution than death or imprisonment.

I had hoped that you would welcome the chance to be part of the wider world, more of a leader, rather than a spider who sits at the center of a web, waiting for whatever comes to her. Think on it, despoina. Is it better to be a goddess, feared and worshipped by a few, or to be a queen admired by thousands, known to kings and emperors throughout the civilized world. Would you rather your kind remained monsters of legend? Or would you prefer to become renowned for your true skills, throughout history? Would you—"

"Very well! You have made your point." Stheno crossed her arms and began to pace the small chamber. "But I tell you, though you may not understand the reasons, that my walk and my wedding are necessary." There was a wild glint to Stheno's eyes that Porphredo recognized as doubt. "You speak of history, and legend, but those are cold things, Porphredo. Athena may have withered up your flesh and bones, but my heart and flesh have been well preserved. You can have no understanding of what I want."

"Ah, yes," said Porphredo dryly. "Love. *Eros.*"

"Hah. You think of it only as a joining of flesh, but it is a joining of spirit I seek."

"May I humbly submit, despoina, that you are going about searching for it in a most peculiar fashion."

"And what do you suggest, old hag?"

"As the ancient poets say, love flees like a deer when pursued. Wait patiently, and it comes to you—though often from a source unexpected and unlooked for."

"I have waited centuries, Porphredo. I will wait no longer." Her tone was soft and dramatic, yet Porphredo heard genuine pain in it. But after staring at the lampflame for long moments, Stheno turned briskly and said, "Have you no more important thing to do than nag at me?"

"No, despoina. It is my most important task." Porphredo knew, however, that Stheno had lost patience with listening, and turned to go.

Porphredo paused, however, at the beaded curtain and said,

"Whatever else, despoina, strive not to be a goddess, but a queen. You have the skill to become a great one. Be a queen."

Padre Antonio Gonsção leaned against the heavy wood panel and slowly pushed it open. Every muscle in his body ached from the flight from the Mughul camp. Through the afternoon and into the night, he, the *soldados,* and Gandharva had scrambled over rock-strewn paths that threaded among boulders and through canyons. They allowed themselves only some minutes of rest at a time, driven on by fear of pursuit, hampered as they were by a blind man and a now-dead girl. The last portion of their mad run had been through an ancient tunnel that had been carved out of the mountain rock. Much of it had been stairs or upward sloping ramps, through which they had had to grope their way in utter darkness. Gandharva's lack of sight was no hindrance then.

Gonsção would not have thought himself capable of such physical exertion when he had begun this journey from Goa. *Truly the Lord can confer miracles upon those who need them.* At last, he had pushed the panel aside far enough to squeeze through.

"What do you see?" Gandharva asked behind him.

"There is much candlelight," said Gonsção, blinking from the brightness. "It is a large chamber . . . . Ah. There is a large idol against the wall to our left. It is surrounded by candles and votive bowls."

"Oho. So that is where we have entered," said Gandharva. "This is the main temple to the Mahadevi, near the center of Bhagavati. We are not far from the palace. Do you see anyone?"

"No," said Gonsção. "There is no one here that I can see." He tried not to stare at the horrific, obscene pagan idol that filled the wall, with her many arms, her outlandishly enormous breasts. *How can anyone be thinking of divine matters when staring at such a . . . thing?*

Gandharva pressed past him into the room and called out something loudly.

"Shhh! Why do you announce our presence?" hissed Gonsção.

"Do not be afraid, priest of the Orlem Gor. I am known to most of the brahmins of Bhagavati—I have played at many of their temple functions. They will gladly assist us if I ask it."

But there was only silence for answer in the temple.

"Strange," Gandharva went on. "Very strange. There is always someone here, if only an acolyte or two."

"Padre!" called Estevão, from inside the tunnel. "May we come out now?"

At Gandharva's nod, Gonsção said, "Yes, you may come in. It would seem we are safe."

Carlos and Estevão shuffled in, carrying the dead Pramlocha between them. They placed her gently upon the stone floor.

"Tell me," said Gandharva to Gonsção, "What is the aspect of the goddess? Is she fearsome or benign?"

"I beg your pardon?"

"The statue," Gandharva persisted. "Is it smiling or scowling?"

Gonsção glanced at the idol and said, "Scowling like the most fearsome wild beast I have ever seen."

"Hm. That does not bode well. You said there were offerings left to her. What are they?"

"Whyever do you want to know that? Shouldn't we be moving on?"

With exaggerated patience, Gandharva replied, "Because we might learn something of what we will encounter. If you please."

Gonsção took a couple of steps closer to the idol. "I do not recognize these things. There are . . . large red flowers. And a golden liquid that perhaps could be oil. And rice."

"And there is much of it, you say?"

"Yes—many bowls fill this side of the room."

"Those things are sometimes offered at weddings. Must be a big wedding in town. Perhaps the mayor's daughter. Still, I am amazed there is no one here offering prayers for the couple."

"It may be very late at night," said Gonsção. "I have lost track of the time."

"That should not matter," said Gandharva.

"Do you intend that we rest in this place?" asked Gonsção, "or may we now leave here?"

"No, no, we will go. But there is one more thing to be done here. Since you are closest to her, I would ask another favor. Between the Mahadevi's legs, you should find a vial of the *rasa mahadevi*. Please get it, so that we may have some for Pramlocha, and we will be on our way."

Gonsção stood and turned to face Gandharva. "No."

"What? Come, come, this is no time for squeamishness. If she is to be saved, we must have the *rasa mahadevi.*"

Despite his weariness, Gonsção felt as though a rod of iron had solidified in his soul. "No. I will not touch that substance."

Gandharva sighed heavily. "What did you have us bring her for, then? Are you mad? Did you want us to be captured by the Mughuls?"

"I had her brought so that she might be buried with dignity according to the customs of her people."

"Her people are in Bijapur!" said Gandharva.

"Do I understand him correctly, Padre," asked Estevão, "that the miraculous powder is here and that we can bring this girl back to life?"

"Yes, but I will not imperil my soul by retrieving it."

"Then tell me where it is, Padre, and I will get it."

"Do you think I have less regard for your soul than mine own? No, my son. She has fled this world to whatever doom her pagan life has earned her. Let her rest in peace."

"But if she is revived, Padre, she might be convinced to leave her pagan faith and save her soul."

Gonsção sighed. "Thus does one begin the slide down the slope of virtue, by the use of a tool of Evil in the name of Good."

"It brought *you* back," said Carlos.

Gonsção closed his eyes and brought his hands to his forehead. "It was without my knowledge or consent and had it been possible to ask me, I would have rejected it."

"Then let me fetch it," said Carlos, "for I killed a man in Goa and my soul is doomed already. My shirt is stained with this girl's blood and I heard her last sobs as she died upon my back. Let me help her."

"There is much yet you might do to earn forgiveness," said Gonsção. "And returning her life by wicked means will not wash away the stain on your soul from your crime."

But Carlos ignored him and turned to Gandharva. "Where is it—the powder? *Ubi . . . est . . . rasa mahadevi?*"

"It will be in the idol's crotch," said the blind musician. "Our Mahadevi has a sense of humor."

Too weary in body and spirit to stop him, Gonsção watched sadly as the young *soldado* vaulted over the votive bowls to stand at the feet of the statue. Carlos felt around the area Gandharva suggested, at last pulling out a small canister. It was in the shape of a phallus.

"A sense of humor, indeed," said Carlos. "Too bad Joaquim is no longer with us. This is his sort of humor."

Gonsção turned his face away in disgust. *Madre Maria, how easily corruptible is the heart of Man. Give me the power to destroy the source of this powder, which brings temptation as great as gold or flesh.*

In slow, awkward Latin, Carlos asked Gandharva, "We give . . . to her . . . it now?"

"No, no. Let us wait until we are in the palace where we may revive her in greater comfort. She can wait another few minutes, I think. Come, let us continue."

Carlos and Estevão picked up the dead girl's body between them. Gandharva directed which way the entrance to the temple might be, and Gonsção staggered wearily behind them.

After a short chain of cloth doorways, they emerged into the night at the top of the temple stairs. Gonsção beheld before and below them a huge plaza drenched in moonlight. On three sides of the square were semi-pyramidal buildings that seemed alive and crawling with carved animals and human figures in frozen movement. In the center of the plaza, a statue of an elephant reared on a platform. At the far end of the plaza was a crowd of people standing or kneeling on a broad set of steps that led up to a pair of shining doors in a high stone wall. Beyond the wall was a hill, or some amorphous construction built upon a hill, Gonsção was unable to tell. The people on the stairs were carrying lamps or candles and were wailing and weeping. It was a scene out of nightmare. To Gonsção it seemed some circle of Hell had been transported to Earth.

Gandharva clicked his tongue. "I do not like the sound of this at all. Let us go find out what has happened."

Gonsção had no wish to descend into so alien a place. Even Bijapur, by comparison, now seemed at least of familiar, human scale and design. This hidden city could only be for the comfort of demons. Nevertheless, Gonsção numbly followed his men and Gandharva as they tottered down the temple steps.

By the stone elephant, they came upon a lone woman who stood beside a child-sized statue, weeping. Gandharva had Gonsção lead him over to her and spoke with her for a while. Her voice was reedy and rasping as if she were ill, or had been shouting for many hours. At last, Gonsção's patience was tried too far and he interrupted. "What is she saying, man?"

Gandharva tilted his head. "We have arrived at a bad time, priest of the Orlem Gor. The Mahadevi is not Herself, or rather She is a different aspect of Herself. I have heard of times when She was this way, and they are never good. Still, I must fulfill my duty and take you to Her for She has demanded it. I feel pity for your soldiers, for they seem of good heart. I hope She will show them mercy."

"But you do not pity me?" asked Gonsção.

"There is little point in that," replied Gandharva. "Come. Let us finish our journey and then we may all rest. Lead me to the palace steps."

"They are crowded with people."

"I will take care of that."

Gonsção took hold of the musician's elbow and guided him to the mass of petitioners.

Gandharva called out something in a foreign tongue. The people grew silent and turned to stare at him. He raised his arms and spoke again. The people gathered up their candles and lamps and silently moved aside, creating a pathway for them up the palace steps to the bronze doors.

Gonsção was reminded of the Biblical parting of the waters, but the comparison did not comfort him.

"Has a way been made?" Gandharva asked.

"Yes. The steps before us are clear."

"Then let us ascend."

As Gonsção went ahead, the blind musician's hand upon his shoulder, the great bronze doors at the top of the steps slowly opened. A cold dread filled him as he approached the dark portal, yet he kept his legs moving, one foot after another.

XXI

LOTUS: This water lily is the most sacred flower of all the East. It hath large, round leaves which float upon the water, and bears flowers with many petals white or rose in hue. It bears its seeds in a broad, round pod. All parts of the plant may be eaten, most particularly the root. Chewing of the lotus leaf will ease weakness due to heat and women's complaints. Grinding of the seeds into a tisane makes a healthful tonic. The flower hath been a symbol of beauty, the womb of creation, fertility, procreation and preservation of life, resurrection and immortality. It is worn as a good luck charm, or used as a cure for lovesickness. Its blossoms are also thought to be receptacles for the soul, and its petals are used to wrap food offerings for the dead....

Thomas sat on a gilded, canopied platform overlooking a central courtyard of Stheno's palace. Before him, hundreds of girls in saris of scarlet, vermillion, magenta, and gold knelt, heads bowed, facing away from him. A cool, gentle wind billowed their garments, giving the illusion of ripples on an ocean. *A sea of blood,* Thomas thought sourly.

The courtyard was in the central, oldest portion of the palace. The part, Enyo had told him, that had been an ancient temple when Stheno had first arrived in Bhagavati. Indeed, the walls were carved of the very basalt of the mountain, and the dancing human figures that adorned them from ground to top were worn almost indistinguishable by centuries of wind and water. It reminded Thomas of those enstoned souls in the crypt and he suppressed a shudder.

Uncomfortable in his cloth-of-gold tunic and turban, Thomas gazed beyond the far wall of the courtyard to where the pale moon was setting into a bank of distant clouds. *Were you truly my protectress you would have prevented or would undo this travesty.* Thomas had to consider, however, that if his father and Lockheart and others of their cult were wrong, then the event before him might be just retribution from an angry Christian god.

He sat between Enyo on his right and Prabaratma on his left. He supposed they were sitting in place of father and mother, though he could think of no stranger parentage than a mad Hindu priest and a legendary crone. *This event entire is madness. To save the lives, mayhap, of many I will sit and suffer this rite. But somehow, some way, I will ensure that for Stheno there will be no bliss on her wedding night.*

Prabaratma began burbling happily beside him, gesturing out toward the courtyard. The priest was wearing only a *dhoti* loincloth and a necklace of a single strand of sapphire beads that tangled in his long white beard. His grey and black hair hung in a thick plait down his back. Over and over Thomas heard him say the word *shakti.* Thomas leaned closer to Enyo and asked, "What is he saying? What is *shakti?*"

Enyo frowned. "It is difficult to translate. It is the female power of creation. It sounds like he is having visions again."

"You mean the ability of bearing babies? But this is to be a barren marriage—I thought that was the very idea of bringing these girls here rather than letting them marry men. As for me, I do not intend to get Stheno with child."

"It would seem Prabaratma believes this event is a sign of a greater birth. A new goddess. A new world. Although I have made no real study of the Hindu faith, I understand such cycles of rebirth are common in their thought."

"Ah." Thomas decided it was best not to comment further on Prabaratma's madness, preferring not to give offense. He was beginning to sense that paganism was more complex, however, than bowing down before idols or dancing while wearing bedsheets on moonlight nights.

The wall to the north side of the courtyard quadrangle had a second-story gallery. It was filled with brown-skinned priests wearing magenta jackets and garlands of flowers, milling about. Some appeared to be praying. Thomas thought, now and then, that he glimpsed Timóteo among them, sitting pale and still.

The gallery on the south wall, opposite the priests, held the Mirza and the other Mughuls, Lockheart, and musicians. One of whom he recognized. "Gandharva? Could that be—"

"Gandharva!" said Enyo, "Is he here?"

"Is that not him, with the other players?"

"Ah! Yes it is! Oh, I am so glad he returned in time for this. He would have been so disappointed to have missed it."

"That man is everywhere. But how comes he here? The last I saw of him was in the Mughul camp. Perhaps he arrived with the Mirza's men, but he was not with them when they came through the wall."

Enyo smiled. "Our Gandharva has unexpected talents. It is possible he returned on his own."

"He is talented indeed. I do not recognize some of the instruments the musicians around him hold."

"Ah. Well, they are mostly drummers and flutists of the Madiga caste—playing for weddings is what they do. There is also a percussionist from Pegu who plays upon bells and chimes with his mallets. And lyres and sistrums from our homeland. I am pleased to see the despoina has not forgotten."

Thomas thought he detected the fog of fond remembrance in Enyo's eyes so he said nothing. Below them, he could see the tall, stately Porphredo moving among the girls, now and then bending down to speak to one of them. On the opposite side of the courtyard, beautiful and elegant in an emerald-green sari, Aditi was doing the same. Thomas sighed as he watched her, wishing it were she whom he would be joining in this ceremony. *Her rea-*

sons for turning me aside were just, but my heart remains a fool and listens not to wise discourse.

A trilling of pipes and rattle of drums began suddenly, startling Thomas. At no signal he had seen, the musicians began a lively if not altogether comprehensible tune. Priests who had been standing by the northern entry into the courtyard turned and began to walk the periphery, chanting loudly, often in discord with the music. Thomas wondered if it was Stheno's hurried preparations that had led to such soul-jangling clashes of sound or if this were a common part of Hindu rites.

When the Brahmins finished their walk, returning to where they had stood, the great long horns that Thomas had heard in Stheno's throne room began to intone. Again, one atop another the horns added layer of sound until Thomas thought the very stones should tumble from the courtyard walls. *Verily, it must have been such horns as these with which Joshua brought down Jericho.*

A new group of priests, clad in white, entered from the east. They carried among them a palanquin, on which rode a four-armed wooden idol seated upon a tiger skin. The idol's face had an extra eye in its forehead and above that was a crescent moon. Its torso was grey with smeared ash, and snake skins had been tied around its neck, which was painted blue. The idol wore nothing else but a garland of scarlet flowers. An enormous black phallus protruded from its groin.

"Those are priests of the Jangam caste," Enyo explained, "and they are carrying an image of Shiva, which is the male aspect the despoina is taking on for this ceremony."

"And what sort of god is this Shiva?"

"He brings good fortune, prosperity, and increase. He is a teacher of the arts and healing. He is also the Lord of Sacrifice, destruction, and resurrection. All too appropriate for our despoina, I fear."

"I see." Thomas would have laughed were he not so personally entwined in the proceedings. The priests carried their idol out through the large archway in the western wall and disappeared. Thomas glanced up at the sky and noticed that the clouds were noticeably higher than they had been. He watched them for a moment, noting that they were approaching at swift speed and growing darker and fuller. A gust of wind tugged at his turban and on the air Thomas scented a hint of rain.

"This part is the *lagnam,*" Enyo was saying when Thomas redirected his attention to the courtyard. The Jangam priests had returned, without their idol, and had begun to move among the kneeling girls, placing a strand of black beads around the neck of each, and a gold ring on the second toe of each girl's right foot. "There are several forms of marriage the Hindus recognize," Enyo went on. "For example, the Brahma, which is a marriage of those of equal caste. Or the Daiva, where a daughter is given to a priest as his fee for services rendered. There is the Prajapatya where a girl is wed despite the fact that she offers no dowry. . . ."

"And what sort of wedding would they call this?" Thomas asked.

"I am not sure," Enyo mused, "though perhaps it is closest to Rakshasa. Marriage by capture."

As the Jangam priests continued their tedious work, the Brahmin priests returned, carrying small bronze braziers. These they placed in a row in front of the dais on which Thomas sat. The priests sprinkled something over the braziers' coals and Thomas smelled an interesting tang on the smoke. *Hemp, mayhap. Or hashish. Ah, well. 'Twill make the tedium more pleasant.*

The daylight began to noticeably darken and the wind blew stronger and more chill. " 'Twould seem a storm is blowing in," said Thomas.

"Ai, no! A winter monsoon on this day of all days. That such a rare thing should happen now. And yet . . ."

"And yet?"

"Shiva is also known as the Lord of Storms."

"Appropriate, then," said Thomas with growing, vengeful pleasure. "Our despoina can hardly be disappointed."

He heard a rumble that went on too long for thunder. Something was emerging from the western archway—something big. A huge wheeled cart came forth, bearing another image of Shiva exactly like the first, but many times larger than the idol the priests had carried—nearly four times the size of a man.

"Amazing!" said Thomas. "It is as though the first idol has grown."

"Wait," said Enyo.

The music stopped and the great figure brought its many hands together and executed a slow bow. A susurration of wonderment and awe swept among the girls. Thomas felt his mouth hang open.

"It's a puppet," Enyo confided with the tone of a child who knows a magician's secret. "Our despoina herself controls it with ropes. She is hidden in a hollow in the back. She has used this at several festivals in the past, but so long ago none of these children remember."

"Ah. Is she not afraid of . . . being seen?"

"Hm? Oh, she is covered. And it is the nature of these rites that the faithful see only the divine image and not its manipulator."

Prabaratma stood and made a loud pronouncement. Pipes trilled and drums rolled for a moment. Then a man stood beside their dais and declaimed.

"That is the *gamabhojaka,* the mayor of Bhagavati," Enyo explained. "He is representing the father, if you will, of all the girls of Bhagavati here. He is offering them to Shiva."

A loud, low voice boomed in response from beneath the huge idol, startling Thomas again.

"Speaking tubes," said Enyo. "The ancient priests used them and taught our despoina how."

"Impressive," muttered Thomas. Thunder that was not drums or cartwheels rumbled in the distance, and Thomas thought he saw a flicker of lightning in the approaching clouds. "It would seem Lord Shiva is impressed as well."

The Shiva-puppet sat up and opened its arms as if gesturing

to all assembled in the courtyard. Again the eerie, god-like voice spoke from beneath its cart.

"She . . . he is making the marriage promises. That the girls will be properly instructed in their faith, that they will know wealth and comfort, that they will not be betrayed, that they will know . . . chaste and immortal love."

The wind began to blow hard and steady. Thomas had to hold onto his turban, and the purple canopy above them flapped and fluttered dangerously. Others in the courtyard began to look up with concern and comment to their neighbors.

An oddly flustered-sounding Shiva spoke again.

"She . . . he says that he, Lord Shiva, welcomes the life-giving rain, and offers it as a wedding gift to the city of Bhagavati."

Thunder boomed again, closer.

A middle-aged woman, holding her sari with one hand, came around the right side of the dais. She tried to place a cup of yellow rice on the brazier directly in front of Thomas. But the wind picked up the cup and scattered the rice with ease. With a frown of consternation, the woman nonetheless turned and with one arm upraised addressed the idol.

"She represents the mother of the girls, as she is the mayor's mother," said Enyo. "She is offering the blessing that the union be . . . well, the usual term is fruitful. Ah, she says successful."

The wooden Shiva began to speak again.

And then the storm hit.

Great gobbets of water mixed with mud struck Thomas in the face and spattered all around him. The canopy overhead was ripped away and vanished into the gale-blown rain. Thomas could barely see around him. He heard the screams of the girls, and Prabaratma laughing and crying "Shiva! Shiva!" He felt Enyo clutch his arm, and protectively Thomas helped her climb down the platform with him.

Just as they were behind the dais, a flash of light momentarily blinded him and great peals of thunder rang as if Heaven were cracking open and falling to earth.

"Despoina! Porphredo!" cried Enyo and she tried to turn back toward the courtyard, but Thomas put his arm around the old woman's shoulders and pulled her toward the nearest archway. They ran into the labyrinth of corridors on a tide of shrieking young women and shouting priests.

The wind howled and played hob with clothing, but there was relative calm in the protection of the palace hallways, and the thunder was muffled. Enyo detached herself from Thomas's grip and went over to the nearest gathering of girls to reassure them. "Ever the mother hen," Thomas murmured.

With a sigh of release, Thomas walked off in the opposite direction. He wanted to laugh, to dance down the hallways praising Shiva and every other god of storms he had ever heard of. "There has been no wedding, there will be no wedding," he said to himself, smiling. "The gods themselves have rebuked the Mahadevi, for there are greater gods than She!"

He turned a corner and saw a familiar movement—someone in a robe entering a doorway. The door remained open and lamplight spilled from it. Curious, Thomas walked up and peered around the door.

"Salve, Magister Chinnery," said Padre Gonsção, pale and wan as a baleful ghost.

"Padre?" said the stunned young *inglês* as he took a couple of steps into the room. "You are here too?" His red-and-gold wedding jacket was drenched and spattered with mud. His golden hair was plastered down over his eyes and face. To Gonsção he resembled nothing so much as a bedraggled puppy.

"*Felicitas,*" Gonsção said with a slight, mocking bow. "I would have attended your wedding, but . . . I was not invited."

"I am sure . . . that is, had I but—" the young man put his hand to his mouth and did not complete the sentence. Instead he asked, "How . . . when did you get here?"

"In the early morning. I was led here by your friend the blind musician."

"Gandharva? Yes, I saw him but . . . why would he bring—"

"Me? He needed help." Gonsção gestured toward a pallet on the floor where a familiar girl lay. "Her name is Pramlocha. Perhaps you remember her. She was one of those unfortunates that rode in the entertainer's wagon which you so often visited."

"Yes, I think I remember her."

"She is recovering from a fatal wound. I tried to dissuade Carlos from using the *rasa mahadevi* on her, but he was determined. Now I can only pray for him."

"So Carlos is here too."

"And Estevão."

The young man laughed in disbelief. "Did you bring the whole Mughul army with you as well?"

"They were hot on our heels but we evaded them. With good fortune this rain will wash away whatever trail we might have left."

"The storm is a double blessing then," sighed Tomás.

There was an awkward pause. Gonsção finally asked, "I trust Timóteo is here also and well?"

The *inglês* nodded. "The last I knew. I thought I glimpsed him at the wedding, and I've been told he's been staying with the priests, converting them no doubt."

Gonsção hid his relief, not certain whether to believe him. "Well. Good. I shall be glad to see him again and to hear of his progress."

"So will I."

There was another awkward pause. "I see you have been doing well for yourself," Gonsção said at last, pointedly. "You have managed a marriage with the fabled Queen of Life and Death."

"There has been no marriage," the young man growled. "Nor will there be if I have any say in it."

"Oh. All is not well?"

"You have come at a bad time, Padre."

"So I have been told. But I have not been permitted to choose the time. I am here. Now."

The *inglês* nodded again.

"So," Gonsção went on with studied casualness, "have you, at last, found the source of our mysterious *pulvis mirificus?*"

"I have."

"Will you tell it to me, or must I delve for it myself?"

After a momentary pause during which Tomás studied him, the young man said, "Let us have truth for truth, Padre. I will reveal it to you if you will answer a question for me."

"Truth for truth, then. What would you ask?"

"Did you murder Aditi?"

Oh. "No," said Gonsção, relieved that he could, to a point, be truthful in this. "I did not. If you must know, she killed herself. There was a misunderstanding. I wished to talk with her, but my sin is that I frightened her. She ran herself against Carlos's sword before . . . before I could stop her."

A cold, dubious smile grew on the young man's lips. "Truly?"

"I would swear to it upon the Holy Book. Now, to your truth."

"Very well. The source is, indeed, powdered blood. The lifeblood of the queen who reigns here, Queen Stheno herself."

"The blood of a woman?"

"No ordinary woman, Padre. She is immortal."

"With such blood, I assume she would be. But, then, she cannot be human, can she?"

The *inglês* smiled again. "As for the rest, I will let you delve for it yourself. But I warn you, you may be shocked at what you learn."

"After a career in the Santa Casa, Magister, you might understand that I am difficult to shock."

"Even so," said the young *inglês.* "Even so."

Gonsção sighed. "Well, then. I look forward to having my horizons broadened. Will you introduce me to your queen?"

"I do not wish to speak to her myself. But I will send word that you have arrived."

"You sound as though you do not love this Queen Stheno, Mistress of Life and Death."

"Let us say, Padre, that our goals are no longer as dissimilar as they might have been. Now if you will pardon me, I wish to change from these sullied clothes. Perhaps we will speak again soon." With a sketched bow, Tomás departed.

"How very strange," Gonsção murmured to himself. He then realized that he had not asked Tomás how to find Timóteo. Hearing footsteps outside his door, Gonsção ventured into the corridor to see if the young *inglês* might still be there. He was nearly bowled over by a group of girls in wet saris as they hurried along, herded by the tall, old witch Gonsção had met in the Mughul camp.

"So, Domina Porphredo. This is where you disappeared to."

The old woman glared at him and guided her charges into a room opposite his. She shut the door behind the girls, then turned to face Gonsção. "Gandharva told me he had brought you. You should return to your room. It is not safe to wander about the palace now."

"Not safe? Because of the storm?"

"Because of Queen Stheno. You come at a bad time."

"So I have been told."

"She has become unstable. She may go about unveiled and to look upon her face is death. There is no telling what damage she may do now that her precious wedding was disrupted. I wish you and the rest of your expedition had listened to me and never come near us."

"Listened to your lies? Domina, I must tell you that your vanishing from the Mughul camp nearly cost me and my men dearly. The Mughul commander believed we had murdered you, and sentenced us to death."

The old woman's eyes went wide. "I am . . . very sorry, *flamine.* In my life, it has been difficult to remember the consequences my actions can have. I assure you, my intent was to save lives, not destroy them. I am glad to see you have evaded the commander's sentence."

"Gandharva somehow managed to change the commander's

mind. You should be warned that your ruse may have failed completely. The Mughul army brought us to the Krishna River not far from here. At that point, we escaped, but we were seen. I do not know if the army has followed our trail or not."

Porphredo inclined her head. "I see. I will inform the queen when I can." She turned to enter the room into which she had herded the girls.

"Wait! If you could please tell me where I could find Brother Timóteo. I have not seen him since my arrival and I am anxious to learn if he is well. I was told he is with the priests."

"The monastery is in the southeast corner of the palace. If you take this corridor all the way to the end," Porphredo pointed away from them, "you will find it easily. But again I must advise that you be careful."

"I have faith and prayers for protection."

"That may not be—"

"*Aya* Porphredo!" A young woman in a green sari came around a corner behind her.

Gonsção felt the blood drain from his face, as if he were seeing a ghost. "You."

Aditi stared at him a moment, then said in accented Latin, "Welcome to Bhagavati, priest of the Orlem Gor."

Gonscao felt himself lose balance and he leaned against the wall beside him. "Of course. The *rasa mahadevi.* You were revived." *And no doubt Senhor Chinnery knows the story from your lips and knows where what I told him were half-truths.*

She nodded once. She exchanged a few words with Porphredo in a language Gonsção did not know.

"I congratulate you," Gonsção said, trying to regain his composure. "You and your cohorts have been more clever than I expected. Please tell me, on whose behalf do you come seeking the miraculous powder."

Aditi tilted her head, frowning. Then she took two steps toward Gonsção. "I did not come seeking, priest of the Orlem Gor. I came home. I live here."

"This . . . is your home? You are well acquainted with the immortal queen then?"

A cold smile spread across Aditi's face. "She is my mother."

"Ah." Gonsção felt his stomach turn over.

"She is eager to meet you, I hear." Aditi walked back to Porphredo and the two of them went into the room, shutting the door behind them.

Gonsção sagged against the wall for a moment. Then he stood and straightened his cassock. *So. I have no reason to expect kindness from this queen, if Aditi speaks the truth. Yet I have not yet been arrested or thrown into her dungeons. Perhaps she will hear my side of the story. Perhaps I will live long enough to accomplish what I must.*

Gonsção began to walk down the corridor toward the monastery. It was now deserted, the only sound being the distant rumble of thunder and the moaning of the wind through the hallways. *Perhaps I can get Carlos's sword—no. Being so visibly armed would cause alarm. A dagger then. To let her blood so that none can use it. But if dried to powder it is still efficacious . . . no. I cannot let it remain. Fire. Yes, that might do it. There are many open flames and coal-filled braziers about the palace. It is stone, so I cannot burn the building itself. I must await my chance, find the queen surrounded by flammables. But how do I ensure that she does not escape? Perhaps by dying with her.* Scenes of a great conflagration, in which Gonsção nobly holds an imagined Queen of Evil to the flames, succumbing only after she screams her last, filled his mind like smoke.

And yet, a part of him wondered at such murderous thoughts. His work with the Santa Casa only prepared him, at worst, to damage men's flesh in order to change their mind. He had never purposefully set out to take the life of anyone. *Will I be forgiven this most heinous of sins, because of the greater good it serves? Or will my soul be sent to perdition for it, my only comfort being that I will have saved the souls of so many others?*

Porphredo had been right, the Hindu monks' chambers were not hard to find. Once in the proper region, Gonsção had only to follow the chanting and the scent of sandalwood incense. He was not hindered as he wandered through the large connecting rooms—but, then, as the priests were blind they were possibly not aware of his presence. Each room contained low pallets on the floor, with sandals and food bowls neatly placed beside each. The walls were covered with colorful hangings decorated with unreadable script.

As he was about to depart the fifth chamber he walked through, he heard someone cry, "Padre!"

"Timóteo?" Gonscao saw the boy in a far corner of the room, lying on a raised platform covered with a blanket. He rushed over to him.

"Padre, is it really you?" Timóteo was pale, his hair was matted, and there were dark circles around his eyes.

"It is I," Gonsção sank to his knees beside the platform, taking Timóteo's hand. It was cool to the touch. "Have you been ill, my son? Have you the fever?"

"No, Padre, but . . . but you must forgive me, Padre. You must hear my confession."

"Why? What could you possibly have done?"

"I have sinned . . . the sin of pride, Padre. You warned me. You said I should not dare the intercession of angels."

"Pride is a very human failing, my son. I am sure it is easily forgiven. But how did your pride make you ill?"

"I . . . I spoke to the queen. I tried to bring her the word of God."

Again Gonsção felt a sinking feeling in his gut. "Timóteo. I have been told this queen is dangerous. That to look upon her face brings death."

"It is true, Padre. But she said that if one looks at her with love, he will live. I thought that if I filled my heart with the love of God, it would save me. It did . . . it almost did! I saw her! She is beautiful. In a way. But it was not enough. I grew afraid. I tried to run, but I fell." Timóteo stared down at himself and stopped speaking.

Gonscao patted his hand. "But your faith did not fail you, Timóteo. You are alive. You are only sick and you will recover."

"I . . . I do not know, Padre. They might have used the powder on me. I fell in the queen's chambers. And I woke up here."

Gonsção grew cold with anger at the thought of Timóteo subjected to the evil of the *rasa mahadevi. That such a pure soul should be tainted . . .* "Did you dream, my son?"

"Dream? No, I remember no dreams, Padre."

"How long have you been here with the monks?"

"Several days, Padre. I lost count how many."

"Then I do not think they have used the powder on you. I have observed its working, my son, both inside and out. You would be healing faster if they had resurrected you with it. Be glad for your sickness, therefore. It shows you are still innocent of their evil. Come, the smell of this air cannot be good for you. I have a large room. Come stay with me and we can pray together and talk more."

Gonsção grasped one side of the blanket and lightly flung it off the boy.

"No," Timóteo weakly protested and he tried to re-cover himself.

"Are you cold, Timóteo? It is warmer in my chambers. We can bring the blanket too, if you like." Gonsção picked up the blanket to drape over his arm. And then he saw Timóteo's legs, which ended at bloody, bandaged stumps at the ankles. "Deus carus," he whispered. "What has happened to you? Where are your feet?"

Timóteo was starting to cry. "Be . . . beneath the pallet, Padre."

Slowly Gonsção bent down and looked under the pallet. There, tidily placed like the monks' sandals, were two perfect stone feet. Gonsção pulled them out from under the pallet. He ran his hands over the smooth stone, formed more real than any sculptor's skill could create. "What sorcery is this?"

"I told you, Padre. The queen . . . she is a gorgon. Truly. I saw the snakes on her head. Her gaze turns people to stone. But I only turned partway."

"The queen did this?"

"It was my fault! I was too foolish."

"No, Timóteo. You are blameless. But fear not. This evil queen will pay. We will see to you it. You and I."

XXII

PEARL: This beauteous stone of pale lustre is found in the sea, though in the East it is said to grow within elephants, or that it is the spittle of dragons. Others say the pearl grows from tears and therefore brings tears to those who wear it. "Salt of pearl," or pearl dissolved in lemon juice, is a potent medicine, easing all manner of fits, and an antidote to snake venom and other poisons. Powder of pearl is oft used in love charms. Some describe the gates of heaven as being made of pearl, and to the Mohammedans, the Third Paradise is made entirely of pearl....

The Mirza Ali Akbarshah stepped through the open, polished-wood doors into a cavernous room. Masum entered behind him. They had managed to avoid the rush of women and children by slipping into side corridors and moving away from the sound of voices. But they had become separated from Rafi and Awwal, and in the labyrinthine passages of the palace, had lost their way.

The Mirza gazed at the enormous stepped dais to his left, the many scarlet-painted pillars that were at least three times as tall as a man, the polished black marble floor, the huge bronze braziers. "It would seem," he said to Masum, "that we have discovered where the Queen holds her *durbar*. Or perhaps it is a *harbis* shrine. That screen up there could hide either an idol or a throne."

Masum looked around, wide-eyed. "It would seem too austere for a Hindu shrine. Perhaps it is of another faith."

"Perhaps our mysterious queen has invented her own, just as the Shahinshah Akbar has done." The Mirza started to cross the room, then sighed and sat on the second step of the dais. He adjusted his turban and rubbed his beard. "I find I am in need of your counsel, Masum."

"I am here to serve Your Highness in all things," said Masum, still turning his head this way and that, gawking at the chamber.

"Then help me to understand what we have seen here. What this Queen Stheno is. I have decisions to make and I am finding them difficult."

"How may I guide Your Highness's thoughts?"

The Mirza sighed again and peered up at the darkness obscuring the roof of the chamber. "This place . . . the entire matter is not as I had envisioned it. Instead of arriving in proper form to offer peace and alliance with my emperor, we steal in like thieves, and make demands not offers. It is no wonder she has not received us formally."

"Perhaps, Lord, she has merely been distracted with her own affairs, and will speak to us in time."

"Yes, her 'wedding.' What do you make of that, Masum? I have heard of strange Hindu rituals, of course, but never of this one."

"Nor I, Great Mirza. But it had . . . there was . . ." Masum gestured with his hands as if scooping sand and then stopped with an embarrassed grin. "Forgive me, Highness. It is not a thing I can put into words."

If you can scarcely articulate it, thought the Mirza, *how am I to understand it?* "Given the storm that fell upon us," he said, "it would appear that Allah Himself disapproved."

"Perhaps," Masum said softly, frowning.

"Did my eyes deceive me, or was that horrid wooden idol not struck by a lightning bolt?"

"My eyes were too dazzled, my lord. I could not say."

"Ah. Never mind, then. But I am a general and a diplomat, Masum, not a philosopher. Tell me how I am to explain this . . . queen to my emperor. Should he deal with her as with other *harbi* rajas and ranis? Force her to pay a tax to keep her pagan faith, but otherwise respect her rule if she will but do him homage and respect his laws? At least he need not fear her kingdom as a military threat. Have you noticed that we have seen no armed men in the palace? Nor have I seen any in my glimpses of the city itself. Either this queen is certain that her hidden city is safe from discovery—"

"Or she has no need of any army," Masum finished for him.

"Yes. And that implies a queen of extraordinary peace."

"Or extraordinary power."

"Ah," said the Mirza, "now we come to another matter. What if this queen is more than a human woman? What if she is a sorceress? What if she is a demon? What if what the Englishman said is true and she is a creature out of the ancient tales? I have no experience with such things. Truly, I would claim to not believe in them. And yet, I saw the hand of stone. And Mumit."

"Indeed, my lord, we have been privileged to witness wonders."

"But what terrible wonders these are, Masum. Should I permit my emperor to learn of this creature? What if her existence causes him to decide to become a pagan of Iskandr's sort? You have doubtless heard how suggestible he is. I would be branded a traitor by every sheikh in Lahore for turning him from the True Faith."

"I think," said Masum, "that, should you return to tell the tale, that you must trust your emperor's heart to guide him. He is known to be wise throughout Sind, and he is a seeker of Truth. Surely there can be no sin in revealing to him the wonderful variety of Allah's creations."

"And if it is true that it is her blood that has the power to return life to the dead," mused the Mirza, "then alliance with her is of vital importance. We must learn who else has the secret, and how to control it. The emperor himself will want some for his own use. And here is another thing . . . is it spiritually wrong for him to do so? If Allah the Merciful has decided it is his time to be summoned to Paradise, is it wrong for the emperor to retain life through such a means?"

"Surely," said Masum, "this is a matter for sheykhs and *pirs* to discuss thoroughly. I am not sufficiently learned to offer an opinion. They may well decide such a gift is antithetical to God's will and opposes Him. Or they may decide that such a gift, like so many other resources the Great Provider gives us, is intended for mankind's wise use. I cannot say."

And would such a decision be made for spiritual or political reasons? thought the Mirza, cynically. *What help are you, Masum, if you will not offer any guidance?* "And what of you, Masum? Have you found what you expected? Will you find your great Sophia, your fount of wisdom, here? You said once that you were on our journey to be a witness. What do you expect to see?"

"I have already seen it," Masum replied, gazing oddly at the screen atop the dais. "But I believe I mistook my purpose. I am here, perhaps, to give—not to receive."

"To give what? Do you intend to offer yourself as councilor to this queen?"

"In a small way, perhaps."

"Remember what happened to the nameless shahid, if his tomb-keeper was correct. Remember Mumit."

"You wonder at the things which are great, my lord," said Masum, "while I wonder at the things which are small. You marvel that this woman is a creature of amazing powers, while I marvel that amid this wondrous power there is yet a woman."

"You puzzle me, Masum. There is nothing to marvel about women, who only keep the home and give birth to children."

"There it is. The giving birth."

"What has that to do with this queen? Or us?"

"We have witnessed the conception," Masum said softly, almost whispering. "The joining of the male and female principles.

What remains is the birth. Precisely what is born may be determined by what we do here."

The Mirza felt as though he ought to shake his head to clear it of philosophical fog. He put his hands to his temples. "Perhaps I am too practical a man," he said at last. "Perhaps it is a sense I lack, as those men who cannot perceive the colors red or green. I hear you speak but cannot place meaning to the words."

"Do not trouble yourself, Great Mirza. Perhaps it is only my foolishness, and my words mean nothing. All will be as God wills."

"Yes. No doubt. I tire of this place. Let us go see if we can find Rafi and Awwal."

"If you please, Highness," said Masum, "I would like to remain and contemplate this room for a while."

The Mirza stood and sighed yet once more. *Perhaps I will think more clearly when out of his company.* "Very well. I will come look for you once I have found the others."

"Thank you, Great Mirza."

As soon as the Mirza vanished through the doors, Masum ascended the steps of the dais. He stopped on the second step from the top. "I trust I find Your Majesty well and in all things content?"

There came a sharp clack from behind the screen. "How did you know I was here?" Queen Stheno's voice was less alluring and more alarmed, this time.

"As I told the Mirza, I notice the small things. His thoughts were turned inward, toward his confusion. Mine were turned outward, toward the beauty of this place."

"I . . . I thank you. But were all your words to the Mirza said for my sake, since you knew I was listening?"

"You ask if I changed what I said because of my audience? No, I would have said nothing different."

"Hm. In answer to your first question, no I am not well, I was singed by the lightning. And I am in no way content."

"Your . . . wedding was most . . . spectacular, Majesty."

"There has been no wedding," she growled. "The gods see fit to curse me and disrupt my life yet again. No doubt Porphredo will tell me that Nemesis struck because I dared to pretend I was a god."

"All souls are godlike, for the Divine informs all of creation with itself. It cannot be that you are cursed by Heaven, Majesty. The human soul curses itself by denying the love and compassion that rains from Heaven. This is why the gods of the pagans are . . . incomplete. They lack the aspect of divine love."

"Love? Hah! What do you know of it? I have spent centuries . . . but never mind. It is part of my curse, I am sure, that I am forever denied it."

"It can only be, Majesty, that you deny it to yourself. If you will permit me, I would like to tell you a story."

"A Sufi tale?"

"No, it is not exactly a Sufi tale. It is a folktale I heard long ago, but you might find it pleasing."

"I doubt it. But it may distract me. What is your tale?"

"It is called The Princess In The Tower, and it is simply this: Long ago, in a faraway kingdom, there lived a princess. She was but one of many, for her family had been blessed with many children. Although this girl had beauty of her own, for reasons that were never made clear, her family declared her the ugly one and would tease her by running from her, or taunting her. Because she knew no other life, the princess believed it herself, and covered her face in shame. At first, she was kept separate from the other women's quarters in the palace. But as the myth of her ugliness grew within the family, eventually her father had her locked away in a tower in which there were no mirrors or windows, so that no one need look at her. The princess willingly went into her prison for by this time she could not even bear the sight of herself.

"In time, the family forgot about her, except as a story told to frighten babies. The princess languished in the dark tower, drinking only the dew that gathered on the walls in the morning and eating only honey brought by the bees, or berries dropped by the birds who nested in the eaves.

"One day, an earthquake shook the tower, and a piece of the roof fell to the floor. Through the hole in the roof, the sun shone in, filling the once-dark tower with radiant light.

" 'Oh, Lord of the Heavens!' the princess cried, 'do not shine on me, for I am ugly and unworthy of your glory.'

"And a voice called down to her, 'Unfortunate child. I caused the earthquake so that I might shatter the walls and see you.'

"The princess replied, 'But I am not worthy!'

" 'Nonsense,' said the heavenly voice. 'My warmth belongs to all, and no aspect of creation is ugly or unworthy in my sight. Step into the light and let me warm you.'

"The princess obeyed and saw a great golden face beaming down at her through the hole in the roof. She stretched up her arms to him and let his warm light flow all around her. She smiled and began to dance, whirling slowly in place. So light had she become from her fasting that she dissolved into golden specks of shimmering dust. Such joy did she feel in the light of Heaven, that she floated up out of the tower on the beams of sunlight, freed from the cruelty of the world at last.

"So, whenever you see sunlight slipping into a dark place, look closely and you will see the golden dust that is the princess dancing."

Masum waited through a long silence.

At last, Queen Stheno cried, "But . . . but this is honey-soaked tripe! Fit only for the ears of children. Who could subsist on dew and berries? No one dissolves in the light of the sun." More softly, she added, "No heavenly hand has broken the dark tower of my existence."

"Perhaps it has," said Masum, "but you turned away from it."

"Oh, I see now. You are trying to proselytize me, like so many other fools who have come here."

Masum raised his hands, even though she would not see the gesture. "I will not tell you what truth to believe. I am only a seeker, myself, though it is my hope that you will seek the Divine Light as I do. I only meant to suggest that your tower need not be so high, nor as dark as you think it. Or that you need not be its willing prisoner."

"Hah."

"Allow me to prove it, Majesty. Let me look upon you."

"Are all you mortals mad? Have you all a wish to die? Or is it your pride that spurs you to dare the gorgon's gaze? That foolish boy of the Orlem Gor tried it and did not succeed."

Masum paused. "He . . . the boy . . . he is not dead, is he?"

"No. But he is no longer as whole as he was. Do not make the same mistake."

"I do not feel it is a mistake, Majesty," said Masum as he began to step around the screen. "Rather, it is my calling. It is my purpose in being here." At the edge of the screen, he turned and gazed upon the immortal queen.

She sat slumped upon her throne, a brooding frown upon her beautiful face. The brown serpents that framed her face lay quiet and docile. "Ah, what a wonder you are," breathed Masum. "The northerner Lakart called you the image of the Divine, and surely there is some truth in what he says."

Slowly she looked up and their gazes met.

Masum smiled, feeling a warm glow in his heart.

Queen Stheno stared, dismay crossing her features. "No. Surely the gods mock me. That an unworthy clod of dirt such as you should be the one to gaze on me."

Masum sank to his knees before her. "Truly, I am unworthy, and I know not how I am spared. But unworthy as I am, please accept my humble gift of chaste love and spiritual friendship." Masum reached forward toward one of her serpents, and ran his fingers under its chin. The creature rubbed against his hand like a kitten, its tongue gently flicking against his skin.

"No!" Stheno stood abruptly and staggered, knocking over her throne and sending the screen clattering down the steps of the dais. She bared her teeth in a grimace of disgust, while her serpents milled about her head in confusion. "No! What further humiliation is this?"

"Humiliation is not possible," said Masum, "when a soul willingly submits to the design of the All-Knowing."

"Madmen," Stheno growled. "Only madmen and mystics with their minds half elsewhere can look upon me with so-called love. I have been tricked! Duped by the gods into having hope. But no more." She whirled and strode away down the dais steps.

Half in admiration and in sorrow, Masum watched her go. He felt no inclination to move, now that his purpose had been completed. He did not know if he had been successful, for the meaning of the Divine Light eluded him, just as the shining stars were forever out of reach. And yet, he thought he had seen a tear upon Queen Stheno's cheek. And eyes often will water when they feel the first touch of Light.

He did not know how long he had knelt in meditation before he heard the voices behind him. They were whispering loudly in Persian.

"There he is!"

"No. That is the Sufi who has misled him."

"Let us have words with him anyway."

Masum heard their footsteps pound up the dais and he turned. The two were horsemen of Jaimal's retinue. Masum had seen them before but did not remember their names. The men had their *talwar* swords drawn and approached with fear and anger on their faces.

"You. Where is the Mirza?"

"I do not know," said Masum, mildly. "Does your arrival mean that the rest of the army is here as well?"

"Not yet. We are the advance. But the rest will be here soon."

"Fool! Why do you tell him this? He will only report it to the Mirza." The soldier on the right advanced another step and placed the tip of his sword beneath Masum's jaw. "Tell us everything or we will kill you. Where is the treasure?"

"Treasure is everywhere," said Masum. "If you mean gold

and silver, I cannot tell you, for I do not value these things, therefore I do not notice them."

"Useless idiot. Where is the Queen of Life and Death?"

"She is here," Masum said, placing his hand over his chest. "But I do not know where she has gone. Take care when you seek her, for you will find more and less than you desire."

"Stop spewing the mystic offal, Sufi heretic. Where is the Mirza?"

"I tell you honestly, I do not know. He is somewhere in the palace, that is all."

"Let us leave him," said the other horseman.

"No. He will tell the Mirza we are here. We must kill him."

"But he is a holy man!"

"He has misled the Mirza. Let him answer to God for it."

"But we must answer for his death."

"Brothers in the Faith," Masum said, "I believe that I have done that which I was sent upon this journey to do. My Path has come to its end. Let my life be at its end as well. If you feel it is the will of Allah, do what you must. And may the All-Knowing give you blessing."

This seemed to take the horseman aback and he hesitated. "Of course. It is what we must do."

Masum turned back and faced the direction in which Stheno had departed. He bowed his head. "Then so be it."

"May your soul find Paradise."

The swordpoint was taken from Masum's jaw and the men behind him stepped back. He heard the swoop of the blade as it swung through the air, up and then toward him. Masum felt a sting at the edge of his neck. And then he knew nothing more.

XXIII

JUNIPER: This tree bears many small, flat leaves in manner like unto a fir. It brings forth small yellow flowers in late summer, and its bark is a roan hue. Its green berries ripen after two years to become black. Eating the berries aids digestion, and eases the rheumatics and gout. Oil of the berries soothes aches of the joints, as well as pains of tooth and gum. Care must be taken, however, for it may also inflame the skin. Breathing the steam of the berries boiled in water will cure infections of the lungs. A poultice of the boiled leaves will cure snakebite. It is believed that the juniper and the rowan tree cannot grow beside one another–if they are planted so in a garden, one will die. If boughs of each are brought into the home, the house will be destroyed by fire. Yet juniper boughs protect stables from lightning and evil spirits. The Welsh say he who cuts down a juniper tree will soon be cut down himself....

You have been very quiet, Timóteo," said Padre Gonsção as he handed the boy a copper bowl filled with water. "Are you in pain? Do you feel ill?"

Timóteo took the bowl and sipped from it. "My ankles, they ache, Padre. And it is very strange, but my feet itch. Even though I know they are not there and I cannot be feeling them."

"It is simply that you are not used to them being gone, my son," said Gonsção. He took the one wooden chair in the room and brought it closer to the ornate, ancient couch on which Timóteo lay. Gonsção sat on the chair and said, "What did you do while you stayed with the Hindu priests, while you were recovering? Did they try to teach you their ways?"

"No, Padre. They hardly ever spoke to me. Although I think they prayed for me, in their own way. That is not bad, is it?"

"I am sure it does no harm, though I expect it does little good."

"Oh. Anyway, I had a lot of time to think."

"What did you think about?"

Timóteo stared down into his water bowl a long time before replying. "Padre, what if we are wrong?"

Gonsção felt a constriction in his chest. "Wrong about what, my son?"

"About . . . about everything." Timóteo looked up at him, eyes full of concern and a little fear. "What if the world . . . is not as we are told . . . in the Bible? There are no gorgons in the Bible. Only in the ancient stories of the Greeks and Romans. The Bible talks of angels, but I have never seen one. But I saw her. The gorgon. She is real."

So. thought Gonsção. *What I feared must come has come at last.* Gonsção remembered when he was Timóteo's age, the doubts, the questioning. Gonsção had dared mention it to his father only once and still remembered the terrifying fury with which his father had harangued him. Gonsção never spoke of it again, and in time his doubts faded or were explained away. *Timóteo deserves better. I shall not rail at him as if he had just stolen the neighbor's gold.*

"And if we are wrong," Timóteo continued, his hands anxiously writhing in his lap, "then all those people in the Santa Casa . . . all those whose souls we were trying so hard to save . . . then . . . then, they were tortured and suffered . . . for nothing!"

Gonsção quickly reached over and grasped Timóteo's arm. "Peace, my son, peace. It is understandable, Timóteo, that questions should come to your mind, given what you have experienced. But I am glad you have chosen to speak to me of this, for sometimes only the maturity of years can make certain mysteries clear. And, in all honesty, I cannot conceive of the world being other than the way our faith teaches us."

"Nor I, Padre, but—"

"Shhh. Let me continue. Before joining the Santa Casa, I

was something of a scholar. My father had me tutored, hoping I would become more than a lutemaker such as he was. I learned something of the lore of the ancient pagans. Such a cold, unhappy world they imagined. A world controlled by the whims of childish deities who toyed with the lives of mortals for sport. No redemption for mankind . . . only uncaring Fate that locked Man into his doom.

"No, Timóteo, if the rightness of a thought may be known by its beauty, then the myths of the pagans must be false. Surely a world so wondrous as ours could not be the work of their squabbling gods. I could not accept that such a thing be true."

"But, then, how do we explain the gorgon, Padre?"

"Oh, it may well be that the ancients encountered such creatures. And then they invented stories, myths, to explain them. I have heard tales of faraway peoples whose eyes and mouth were in their chest, or who had but one leg and one foot. Perhaps the gorgons are simply a bizarre race of people no longer as numerous as they once were."

Timóteo stared at him a moment, and then said, "A race that can turn people to stone. Whose blood brings the dead back to life."

"Well, yes, those are most unusual properties. Perhaps her people carry some . . . disease that petrifies the flesh at her touch. Ah, listen to me. Now I sound like Senhor Chinnery. But you see, my son, it is not that a gorgon's existence proves the ancients were right—only that they chose to explain them in terms of their stories."

"I see. But she did not touch me, Padre. She only looked at me. And let me . . . see her. And then her eyes glowed and her serpents all hissed at me and I was afraid. It was when I was afraid that I began to change."

"Then perhaps she may be explained in terms more terrifying, my son. The Bible does speak of sorcerers and demons. We must consider the possibility that she is one of these."

"Why would a demon want a kingdom on Earth?"

"Because it cannot rule in Heaven or in Hell. Perhaps she

takes the guise she does for the very purpose of testing our faith. We must consider that as well."

"Oh. What are you going to tell Domine Sadrinho about her?"

"I have not yet decided."

"Are you still going to . . . to . . . kill her?"

Gonsção paused. "If I can."

"But the Santa Casa does not kill, Padre."

"The Bible says one must not permit a witch to live. Sometimes a small evil must be done to ensure a greater good."

Timóteo looked down at his hands. "What if, in the Santa Casa, we were doing a great evil, Padre? Even if we intend good, is it not still great sin?"

Gonsção frowned, uncertain what more to say. "God surely knows the reasons for our actions and judges accordingly. Surely he will find no cause for blame in you. Sleep now, my son. Do not let your mind become fevered with these questions. Rest in the comfort that the world is still as you believe it—it has not turned upside down."

Timóteo nodded and lay back on the couch. But a slight frown remained on his features, even as he closed his eyes for sleep.

Gonsção patted the boy's shoulder and stood. There was a narrow archway leading from the room out onto a wide, sheltered balcony that ran the length of the building. Gonsção walked out onto the balcony, even though the morning's storm remained, now as a steady, leaden rain. There was not much of a view, therefore, but Gonsção hardly minded. He had seen as much of Bhagavati and its horrific queen's palace as he ever wanted to.

He leaned back against the wall, letting what few drops that flung themselves under the sheltering roof strike him. The hiss and patter of the rain was soothing, and lent a fresh, sweet scent to the air. Gonsção breathed deeply and sighed, only now realizing what a balm he needed for his cares.

Did I argue so long with Timóteo because I, myself, needed convincing? Do I begin to doubt all I have ever learned? Perhaps that is the greatest danger in this evil queen—to make men doubt themselves and the world they have come to know. Madre Maria, have mercy. Give me the strength to keep hold of the truth.

After a while, Gonsção became aware of another sound within the rain—the sound of a woman weeping. At first it had been so soft he thought he had been imagining it. Soon it was loud enough to be clearly real, and nearby.

Gonsção turned his head and saw a woman emerge from another room onto the balcony. She was dressed entirely in black, from head to toe, even her face veiled.

A Muslim woman. So, the muçulmanos *are here as well. How much do they know about the* pulvis mirabile? Gonsção was hesitant to go to her, knowing that Muslims often did not approve of their women talking to men who were not relatives. *Still, I must learn what I can.*

Gonsção approached her, and then realized he might not have a language in common with her. Nonetheless, he said in Latin, "Good woman, why do you weep? Can I be of assistance?"

The woman stopped suddenly, apparently noticing him for the first time. She straightened up until, Gonsção noted, she was taller than he. Her carriage changed as well, no longer bent under the burden of sorrow but filled with a radiant rage. "You. You are the priest of the Orlem Gor, are you not? Gandharva brought you."

"I am," said Gonsção, taking a step back. He noted that the Latin the woman spoke was of the ancient, classical pronunciation. He also noted a subtle shifting of the veil over her head, as if something alive lay beneath. "Deus carus," he breathed.

"You are the one who killed my daughter."

"You . . . you are . . . the queen who rules here? Your daughter lives, and she was never harmed by my hand. If she has told you otherwise, then you have been misinformed."

The dark, veiled figure stepped toward him. "She lives because my blood restored her. I saw her body when it was without life. I saw the horrible wound on her neck. She says you are the cause of it."

Padre Gonsção took one step back and then another and another, suppressing a desperate urge to flee. He now had no doubts that she was a demon, and he felt ashamed at his sudden lack of courage. He tried to mutter prayers, but his tongue would not obey. He reminded himself that his duty was to destroy this creature, yet his only weapon was a dagger and he was caught unprepared. "I . . . did not give her that wound, Madam."

"Did you not? No matter. I hear you priests of the Orlem Gor are skilled at unintended deaths."

Gonsção backed up more, the rain pelting on his head and back, until he was stopped short by the stone balcony railing behind him. He looked over the edge. It would be a two-story fall to the flagstones below, sufficient to break limbs or the neck if one's fall were fortunate. *I might overpower her, for surely I am stronger, and throw her off. Even if I fall as well in the process, I might ensure her demise and thus fulfill my purpose. But that will leave Timóteo defenseless. I can only hope Senhor Chinnery has sufficient charity left in him to look after the boy.*

The veiled queen stopped a few feet from him. The wind billowed the black silk such that her shape was indeterminate, as if she were constantly changing form before him.

"Do you intend to harm me, Majesty?" Gonsção said at last. "This is unjust. I came here invited, in good faith. Will you not offer me a trial?"

"No. I tire of human ritual. I tire of all things human. I have been a fool to expect anything worthwhile of mortals. I am an immortal and will take those liberties that gods may take."

"Then you fool yourself, Majesty, or you lie. There is but one god." Gonsção took the dagger from the sheath at his side and held it vertical, so that the hilt and guard made a cross.

The creature laughed in a tone that hinted of madness. "What do you intend to do with that little stick? Did you not hear me say I was immortal? You might make me bleed, but I will not die. I cannot die."

"One of your kind has been known to die."

"Ah. So your little boy monk has told you my nature. Yes, my sister Medusa was granted that gift for her piety and goodness. As it happens, I lack those qualities." Her hand reached for the veil over her face.

Why do I hestitate to act? Why should I believe her? "I am not afraid of death, Madam. I have walked through that dark doorway and returned. I only live because a powder of your dried blood was administered to me, without my knowledge or consent."

Her hand stopped. "You show an amazing lack of gratitude to the one who saved your worthless life."

"I did not ask to be revived, Madam. It will not trouble me to leave this mortal shell behind and begin that journey again."

"Ah. You know, it is an interesting thing. But my priests and philosophers tell me that when I turn someone to stone, the soul remains, trapped, unable to leave. I believe they may be right, for those few times I have chosen to do so, the petrified ones return to life quite quickly. It would seem what I do is the proverbial fate worse than death."

Fear and anger joined forces within him. "And you would do such a horrible thing . . . to one who is scarcely more than a boy?"

"You mean your little boy monk? I turned him away at first, but he begged and pleaded so earnestly that I had to give him his chance. He nearly succeeded, as well. I think, had he been more worldly, there might have been hope for him. I could see his adoration for me. He would have made a charming lover in a year or two."

Disgust overwhelmed Gonsção and he lunged at her with the dagger. But she nimbly stepped aside and grabbed his wrist.

"Jealous, priest? Aditi told me she thought you had no love of women. Is that why you keep the boy near you? Is he your catamite?"

"Foul demon, begone!" Gonsção cried as he pulled his knife hand out of her grip and stabbed the blade into her middle. She gasped and went rigid. Gonsção grasped her arms and pulled her to the balcony railing.

"You . . . fool. . . ." With one hand she gripped his shoulder while the other tore at her veil. But before she could reveal herself, Gonsção hoisted her over the railing and toppled with her over the side.

The fall took longer than he expected. He had tried to keep them both head-down, but the queen twisted and fought him in the air. He struck the flagstones on his back with her atop him.

He heard the crunch of bone as his back hit, and then his head and elbows. For a moment all went black and then, to his horror, consciousness returned. With it came a numbing ache and he was unable to move. A weight on his chest lifted and he saw the veiled queen looming over him, her face just above his. *Too short a fall. Neither of us is dead. I have failed. God forgive me.*

She tore the veil from her face at last, revealing features contorted with rage. She screamed at him, the serpents on her head, a few of which lay limp and crushed against her cheek, writhed and hissed, their little red eyes glowing.

Able only to stare at her terrifying face, Gonsção felt a great heat in his chest, followed by intense cold. It spread outward from his ribcage to his limbs. He could not breathe. His heart stopped. His throat grew rigid and he choked. His tongue and cheeks grew numb. A milky whiteness obscured his sight. And then he knew nothing more.

Porphredo strode down the corridor, carrying an empty amphora. The warm mineral waters of the subterranean hot springs would do the despoina's injuries good and Porphredo hurried, the sooner to bring Stheno ease. The late afternoon light that managed to penetrate the palace was dim from the gloom of the passing storm. Porphredo hurried around a dark corner and felt a blow that knocked the amphora from her arms, and nearly knocked her down. The jug shattered on the floor and Porphredo staggered back but was caught by the small figure in front of her.

"Oh! Oh! Porphredo! I'm so sorry."

"Enyo? Dear sister, what is the matter?"

The smaller old woman's eyes were wide with fright and her face was pale. "Terrible, terrible things! Where is the despoina?"

"She is in her chambers, resting. She has been hurt."

"Oh, no! Not her too!"

"Fear not, Enyo. It is nothing dire—she had a long fall and has a broken arm, a cut in her side and some bruises, and you know how fast she heals. What do you mean 'too'?"

Enyo swallowed and grabbed her wrist. "Come see."

Porphredo allowed herself to be led to a nearby corridor where a man lay sprawled in a pool of blood beside the wall. On the wall, in that same blood, was painted words in Arabic—"Allah akbar."

"By Hecate," Porphredo breathed, "who has done this? This is one of the Mirza's men. Awwal, I think his name was. Has the other one gone mad?"

"There is more," said Enyo, panic rising in her voice. "Further up that way is one of the girls. She looks much like this one. And in the throne room . . . oh, Porphredo."

"What is it?"

"I know you were fond of him. It is . . . the Sufi. Dead also."

"Masum?" Porphredo whispered. "Who . . . how? If Stheno has done this—"

"No! He was . . . beheaded. She never carries a sword."

Porphredo paused to still the wail of grief that threatened to escape her. "We must learn who did this."

"Would the Mirza kill his own men? And a girl?"

"I cannot believe it." A sickening fear grew inside her and Porphredo. "Enyo, get the girls to a safe place. Remember the storage room the despoina had cut into the stone beneath the Peacock Garden? There are no secret passages into that room. Take them there."

"Very well. What will you do?" asked Enyo.

"We must not waste time talking. Just go." As her sister hurried off, Porphredo ran to the north wall of the palace, and the observation tower that stood nearly in ruins at its western edge. It was the one place on the palace grounds from which one could see down into the valley of the Krishna River. Gasping from the run and from clambering over the fallen stones, Porphredo made her way to the cupola of the tower. At one time, sentries had been stationed there, but after centuries of no need, Stheno no longer bothered.

The wind was strong at the top, though fortunately the storm had passed. Porphredo smelled wet earth . . . and something else. Burning, damp wood. She looked to the north, and saw tendrils of smoke rising in the valley. The village of Devidurga was burning.

There was movement on the hillsides, like ants crawling up an anthill—to be seen at this distance meant what she saw was large, or numerous. *Elephants! Despite my efforts, Jaimal's army has found us!* Porphredo stared at the approaching columns in stunned immobility. Then she came to her senses and hurriedly picked her way back down the tower staircase.

She grabbed the first half-blind priest she came across as he was sweeping the courtyard below. "Sound the alarm horns! Go! At once!"

The priest meekly tilted his head. "W-why, holy demon? Does the Goddess walk again?"

"We are under attack, you fool! And the Goddess must walk to save us if we are to have any chance. Now go!" Porphredo shoved him in the proper direction and he shambled off. *Too slow, too slow. The elephants will be at the palace gates before the people of Bhagavati are warned.* Porphredo rushed on, despite the burning in her lungs and muscles from unaccustomed effort. It distracted her from the guilt she felt at having failed and brought this trouble upon them all.

She entered the dark corridors, heading for Stheno's rooms when she stopped. Up ahead she heard the echoing clash of swords and men shouting at one another in Persian.

"Traitor! Where is the treasure!"

"I am not the traitor here. Put down your swords and listen to me!"

The Mirza. Porphredo approached the sound and peered

around the corner of a connecting corridor. The Mirza was backed against the wall, holding his sabre at ready, facing four other armed men. One man, Rafi perhaps, lay dead at his feet. She could see the attackers were preparing to rush the Mirza. *He cannot withstand them all.* Porphredo stepped into the corridor and called out, "Highness! What is the meaning of this? Do you need assistance?"

They all turned to look at her.

"Begum Porphredo, run!" cried the Mirza.

"Silence, traitor!" One of the swordsmen struck the Mirza's blade from his hand and grabbed the collar of his *jama.*

"It is the witch who tricked us!" said another.

Porphredo vaguely recognized them. But instead of following the Mirza's advice, she stepped slowly forward, drawing herself up, painfully, to her full height and most regal carriage. "What is the meaning of this? Why do you bring this violence to our peaceful city?"

"Tell us where the treasure is and take us to your queen, or we will kill you and the Mirza." Two of the men came up to her, swords at ready.

Porphredo held out her hands. "Peace, my lords. Of course you may come see my queen. You have passed the test, have you not?"

"Test? What test?"

"She is lying again."

"Not everyone may find Bhagavati," Porphredo went on. "Only the bravest and most clever. You have thus proved yourselves. Come. My queen will be honored to meet you."

"No tricks!"

"I swear to you by all that is holy, you will meet her," said Porphredo. "If you please, follow me." She turned and with a serenity she did not feel, she strolled toward Stheno's lair.

She heard the Mughul swordsmen scuffle behind her, pushing the now-captive Mirza along with them. *Great Mother, guide me. The Mirza is my guest—I invited him here. Let me not have led him to his death.*

Porphredo ignored their continuous threats and questions until she had led them to the beaded curtain. "If you will but wait here a moment—"

"No! We do not trust you. We will come in with you."

"As you wish."

Stheno called out from the inner room, in Greek, "Porphredo? Did you bring the mineral water? Who is with you?"

Porphredo replied in Persian so that the Mughuls would understand her. "O mighty queen, we are graced with the presence of some noble lords from afar who demand audience with you. I beg you give them your attention."

Still in Greek, Stheno said, "If this is one of your taunts, Porphredo, it is ill-timed and unwanted."

"It is a serious matter," said Porphredo, still in Persian. "I beg you respect these gentlemen and give them audience."

One of the Mughuls shouted, "Hear us, O treacherous queen. We have the traitor Ali Akbarshah at the point of our swords, and our armies surround your city. You had best speak with us and surrender your treasury and your lands to us, or we will raze your city and your palace to the ground."

"This man speaks the truth. I beg you, Majesty," Porphredo said, "to *see* these men."

There was a pause and then, in Persian, Stheno replied, "Ah. Of course. Please bring them in."

Porphredo bowed to the Mughuls and gestured toward the curtain. "You may enter."

"You first."

"As you wish." Porphredo passed through the beaded curtain and into Stheno's chamber. A translucent chalcedony screen stood between the doorway and the bed on which Stheno lay. The light from the oil lamps did not throw her shadow on the screen. Stheno stood aside to allow the men behind her to enter.

"You must excuse our begum," Porphredo said to them, "for she has been recently injured and is not fully dressed to receive visitors." She glanced meaningfully at the Mirza who gave the most imperceptible of nods.

"We do not come as admiring courtiers," said the leader of the Mughuls, "but as soldiers." He stepped forward and with a sweep of his sword knocked the screen aside.

Stheno looked pale and startled a moment. Then she rose from her bed, gaze fixed on the Mughul. Her little ones faced forward, first with curiosity, then hissing with hate.

The Mughul managed to stagger back two steps, breathing "*Allah have mercy . . .*" before Stheno's gaze stopped him and his body transformed to stone. The others barely had time to gasp before their throats were stilled. It was over in moments. Only the Mirza, who had firmly shut his eyes and turned his head, still stood in living flesh.

"Idiot," grumbled Stheno, and she punched the lead Mughul with her uninjured arm. He fell to the floor and crumbled into a thousand pieces. "Idiot, idiot," she continued as she pushed or punched the remaining petrified men. The sword that had been at the Mirza's neck fell away with the man who held it. The Mirza stood alone in a pile of bone and flesh-shaped rubble.

"So, Porphredo, what shall we do with this one?" Stheno put her hand under the Mirza's bearded chin, as if to turn his face toward her.

"Be merciful, Stheno," said Porphredo. "He came in good faith, as an ambassador, at my invitation. He means you no harm."

"Mighty Begum," said the Mirza, a slight tremor in his voice, "let me help you. There are many in Jaimal's forces who may yet be loyal to me, and will obey my orders over his. Give me a horse and let me ride out to them. I will do all I can to stop this attack."

"How do I know you will not simply run away?"

"I would rather die than prove myself such a coward, great Begum. I would be too ashamed to show my face to my emperor or my family ever again, were I to do such a thing."

"Ah. Yet you are not brave enough to look at me?"

"Despoina!" Porphredo said, "We do not have time for your little games! We have a city to defend. The Mirza is an honorable man. Trust him and let us get on with what we must do."

"Someday, Porphredo, I will have your head for your insolence. Very well. Be off with you and give him a horse."

"If I may suggest—" Porphredo began, but Stheno held up her hand.

"No. This is all your fault, Porphredo. I will listen to you no more, but go my own way. I presume this is one time you and your simpering sister will not object if I go for a walk." She threw a *shal* across her shoulders and disappeared through a small side door that led into the secret passageways.

XXIV

FURZE: This little spiny shrub, also called Whin or Gorse, grows in Scotland, and is evergreen. Because it brings forth flowers of yellow color, its name means "fires," for the hills seem aflame when it blooms. Because it blooms in any season, dire portents are seen when the furze fails to flower. Chewing the seeds cures ailments of the internal organs, and eases obstructions of the bowels. Furze is burned upon Midsummer Eve as a sacrificial charm to protect crops and cattle. Worn on the clothing, it may help one find that which is lost, or keep one from stumbling. However, to bring furze into one's home is surely to invite in death....

Thomas stood in the cool silence of the underground chamber, staring at the ugly stone idol. "She is not so comely as the original, but as you see there is a likeness."

"Aye, lad," said Lockheart, running his meaty hands over the rough stone with surprising gentleness. "Though this one has lions for her companions in place of hunting hounds, in form there is much similarity." He held up the silver medallion he wore on a chain around his neck and looked from it to the statue.

"I meant with our good Queen Stheno, but no matter." Thomas had changed out of his wedding garb and back into the same shirt and slops he had worn since leaving the Santa Casa in Goa. He felt much more at ease.

" 'Twas good of you to bring me here, knowing that the queen might object."

"I no longer care if it dismays her. I rather hope it does. She may hate me, for aught I care."

"Hmm. I understand wherefore you would not have her as a lover, but I would not feel so free to make an enemy of her, were I you. This is the very stone, you say, where that Hindoo priest did try his rite with you?"

"Aye, wherein he dealt with me as though I were a lamb for sacrificial slaughter. Pay it no mind. They all say he is mad."

"The madness of mystics oft bears an uncanny truth. Somehow this Brahmin knew of your importance."

"Aye, no doubt Queen Stheno told him so. Are you finished, Andrew? I would be gone." Thomas looked around him sourly. "From this place entire."

"Would you?" asked Lockheart. "Is there naught more for you here?"

"Nothing. I brought Aditi home and she has received the benison of her mother's blood and a new life. That was my purpose in obeying Queen Stheno's summons."

"Think you so?"

"Oh, very well. There was my curiosity to be satisfied. Now I fear I know more than I ever wished."

"You would have preferred to remain an ignorant fool?"

"Truly, I would. What need had I to know what madness men may fall prey to? Or woman or other . . . creature."

"For me, I would love Truth, no matter how ill-formed her shape." Lockheart patted the idol's head.

"Mayhap it is you should look upon the gorgon, Andrew. She says whosoever loves her will not be transformed by her gaze."

"But if she loves me not, what then? Nay, lad. I shall not chance it. I am content to worship from afar. But if, as you say, nothing more remains for you in this place, mayhap 'tis time to speak of escape."

"Escape?" Thomas's heart leapt at the thought and he

glanced around him once more to ensure no one was nearby to overhear.

"Was I not plain? To leave this place for good and all, lad."

"Your pardon. 'Twas so fair a word, it stayed upon my tongue. Have you a plan?"

"I do. What say you we meet in the sacred garden on the morrow at dawn?"

"Aye, a goodly thought. There we will not be interfered with."

" 'Tis a most fitting place. Have we a pact, then?" Lockheart held out his right hand.

Thomas paused a moment. "Should we . . . let our thoughts be known to anyone else? Timóteo, perhaps?"

"Nay! He has the good Padre to look after him. This plot is but for you and me, lad. Give it tongue to no one, else it be spoilt. Speak no fond farewells, nor even hint in jest what we may do."

Thomas sighed and reluctantly nodded. "Very well." He took Lockheart's hand and grasped it. " 'Tis a solemn pact. On the morrow at dawn in the oak garden."

Lockheart's face was an unreadable mix of expression, and Thomas wondered at how one man could seem pleased, not pleased, terrified, and exalted all at once. "Well done, lad. There and then shall we meet."

Must needs be a plan of much daring to spark such fires within him. "There and then. Mayhap I will chance another visit to the library. There is a work or two uncared for by the mistress here that might find more attentive a home elsewhere."

"What, would you now turn thief, lad? Did your master teach you no better? Nay, take no chance, take nothing that might be noticed or missed. Do nothing to put our plan in peril."

Thomas sighed. "Very well. Doubtless you know what is best. I would leave this chamber, howsomever. Something in it minds me of my nightmares."

"Go, then. I would yet stay and meditate a while." Lockheart turned back to the statue and laid his hands on its head, shutting his eyes.

Feeling quite dismissed, Thomas walked up the stone stairway to the door at the top. He glanced back once at Lockheart standing before the idol, intent in prayer. *How strange a man is he. Will I e'er understand what tides ebb and flow within him, or should I be grateful that I do not?* Thomas stepped out the door and shut it, only to see Enyo, pale of face, running down the corridor toward him. *Damme, now I am for it. She will rail at me for again committing sacrilege. What will I tell her?*

"Despotas Chinnery!" Gasping and wheezing, the small old woman ran up and grabbed the sleeves of his shirt. "Come with me. We need your help and you must get to safety!"

Then Thomas noticed, faintly from a distance, he could hear the deep Tibetan horns. "What is it, Enyo? Does your mistress walk unveiled again?"

The old woman shook her head and paused to catch her breath. "We are under attack. The Mughuls. They have come. Through the hidden passages. They are in the palace!"

Thomas stepped back and glanced about him, almost expecting the Mirza's horsemen to come bursting through the walls. "Where? How many?"

"We do not know. Please! Come with me! Some of the girls have been injured and need care."

"Very well, madam. Lead on." Thomas followed after Enyo, his thoughts again in turmoil. *Will this new calamity hinder my escape or better my chance? But if my aid is needed, what right have I to flee?*

As Andrew Lockheart heard Thomas's footsteps departing up the stone steps, he took a deep breath and tried to ease his troubled spirit. Gently he ran his hands over the ancient stone image. *Fair Dian, though not so fair in this guise, Lady, forgive me for nearly turning from my duty. You have given sign enough that this is the place. Now give me strength for what I must do tomorrow morn.* He stood in silent meditation for long moments, then felt the idol beneath his hands shudder and begin to move.

With a gasp, Lockheart stepped back. In the dim light, he saw the statue sliding slowly backwards, revealing beneath it a square, stone-lined pit. The base was hollow. A cool wind drifted up from the pit, implying a subterranean passage beneath. Lamplight flickered in the hole and something began to emerge—Lockheart saw the heads of several small brown snakes rise up through the opening. They flicked their tongues toward him and Lockheart firmly shut his eyes, knowing what must surely follow.

He heard soft, feminine grunts of exertion or pain or both, and heard someone breathing in front of him. "*Tis ekei?*" asked the Queen Stheno in Greek. "Who are you? One of the Mughuls?"

Lockheart willed himself to courage, and replied, "No, despoina. I came with the Mirza's party, but I am of another land. I was the travelling companion of your suitor, Thomas Chinnery, and came to do you honor."

"Oh. Is that why you are in our most sacred shrine?"

"It is, despoina. Please believe me, I meant no sacrilege, for I, too, am a worshipper of the Lady of Beasts. Here is my proof." With eyes still closed, Lockheart held out to her the silver medallion.

He felt the tug on the chain as she took it in her hands. "A pretty token. So She still finds gullible ones even in this day and age. I hope She is kinder to you than She has been to me. But surely you did not come all this way, at such risk, to kneel before an ugly statue."

Lockheart paused, wondering how much to reveal, even to her. "I came to perform a sacred duty, despoina. I did not know that I would find it here, but the signs are clear. Your garden is a copy of Diana's sacred grove at Nemi, and here you are, the image of the goddess."

"I seem to be attracting mystics as rotting meat does flies. It baffles me, the stories that have spread since I and my sisters were cursed to look as we do. I suppose you will want to gaze on the gorgon as well, to test your faith."

Lockheart smiled. "No, despoina. I am not worthy, nor have

I the courage to withstand your gaze. I am content to have been in your company and heard your voice."

"Hm. You are the wisest of the visiting mystics. Therefore, let me give you my blessing."

He felt her hands tucking the medallion back into his shirt. Her fingers lingered, running over his chest. She drew near, her warm breath on his face. Her hands travelled upward until they rested on his cheeks. Suddenly, he felt warm lips on his, and warm, sinuous bodies wriggling over his forehead and scalp. After a few moments, she pulled away and Lockheart let out his breath in a deep sigh. "Thank you, despoina. When I die, it shall be as a happy man."

"That is good, for I must now warn you you are in danger. The Mughul's army has penetrated our defenses and has slipped into the palace. You must be on your guard."

Shall my goal be so near to be thwarted by common war? "Again, I thank you, despoina. I shall take all reasonable care. I have faced danger many a time before and know its face well."

"Good. Then I have a favor to ask of you. Find the boy monk Timóteo and take him to safety in the lowermost chamber in the Peacock Wing. The boy is helpless as he is and his padre is . . . no longer able to look after him."

"I see. May I ask, despoina, why you care for the fate of the little boy monk?"

"Because he once looked at me. And thought I was beautiful. Go now, and do not stay in my presence, for I am unveiled and I intend to use my dreaded gaze on any Mughul I find."

"Understood, despoina. Yet . . . there is one thing more."

"What? Be quick."

"Should all go well with the battle, I would ask you to come to your sacred garden an hour after dawn tomorrow. I will be doing a rite there, with Thomas. If you think kindly on me . . . you will understand what I would wish of you."

"You mystics take such pride in being mysterious. Very well. I cannot promise, but if I can I will be there."

"You honor me, despoina." Lockheart bowed to her. He turned but did not open his eyes until he was sure she was behind him. He ran up the stairs, his spirit buffeted by hope and dread.

Enyo pounded on the square door of rough wood. "Let us in! I have brought Despotas Chinnery!"

Thomas heard a bolt slide back and the door opened.

Aditi peered out. Thomas was amazed that she could seem lovely and haggard at the same time. "Enter. Hurry."

Thomas half guided, half pushed Enyo through and the door was slammed shut behind them and the bolt thrown across.

The scene in the unfinished storeroom rended his heart. Girls filled the dirt floor, some weeping, some moaning, some rocking silently in the corners. The scent of blood and fear choked the close air and Thomas was forcefully reminded of the Aljouvar, the grotto prison in Goa.

Aditi touched his shoulder. "It is good you are here. Many were trampled when we tried to rush them to safety. A few have knife wounds from encountering Mughuls. Some of them . . . were ill-used. I must go and find the rest."

"Wait! Aditi, you cannot. The Mughuls."

She frowned. "Demons take them. I must find the other girls." She threw back the bolt and slipped out the door.

Enyo closed and bolted it after her. "She always was a brave child."

Thomas sighed, for a fleeting moment considering whether to chase after her. Then he looked back at the storeroom floor and remembered he had more important business.

He went from girl to girl, speaking in soothing tones and relying on Enyo to translate. He tried to learn the injury of each and bandage those he could. Slippers and sandals served for splints, saris became slings and tourniquets. His experience as erstwhile surgeon aboard the *Whelp* gave Thomas the courage to do what he could, though there was little to be done for those girls who shied away from his touch, holding their legs tightly closed despite the blood on their thighs.

Thomas remembered the apprentice riot of Candlemas Eve, the first year he had worked for Master Coulter. It was not uncommon, of a holiday, for the older apprentice boys of London to run amok, attacking the whores in their workhouses, as well as any female unlucky enough to be on the street undefended. Master Coulter had brought in whatever girl victims he spied from the shop window, and Dame Coulter and his daughter Anna had soothed and treated them. One of them died in the shop, Thomas recalled, and a couple of others doubtless wished they had, for they had been so disfigured by beatings that what life they had left was ruined.

Lord or Goddess, whichever rules this world, wherefore have you so little mercy for the female sex? Are their lives not burdened enough by their nature? Thomas let Enyo help those who could not accept his help and he moved on.

There came a pounding at the door, and Enyo called out, "Who is it?"

"I bring another to sanctuary!" Lockheart shouted beyond the door.

Thomas nodded at Enyo and she pulled the bolt aside. Lockheart strode in, Timóteo in his arms. Thomas stood and went to them, stepping carefully over the wounded. "Is he well, Andrew? What have they done to him?"

"Not they, but she. Our brave little monk has faced the gorgon, but did not escape unscathed. His beloved Padre had worse luck and now adorns a palace courtyard."

Ah, thought Thomas with a touch of sadness. *The Padre's form now matches his heart. Yet, I regret the passing of the man he once was.*

"If you will but pardon me," Lockheart went on, "I'm off to find weaponry and slay some Mohammedans."

"But, Andrew," Thomas looked around and lowered his voice, "what of our plans for the morrow? Should we go?"

"All is still in readiness—at best, this battle shall cover our deeds."

"But if you are killed before then—"

Lockheart put on a hearty grin. "Nought will harm me, lad. I have received the blessing of the goddess. 'Tis you must take care until dawn." The Scotsman clapped Thomas on the shoulder, then let himself out the door.

Thomas turned back to Timóteo. "So, little brother," he asked in Latin, "how have you been?"

"I have no feet anymore, Tomás. They turned to stone. That is why I could not find you again. I looked at her, Tomás. I told her about the love of God. But I grew afraid."

Thomas squeezed Timóteo's arm. "You are a very brave and foolish boy. I am glad you yet live. But she . . . she transformed the Padre?"

Timóteo looked down at his lap. "I did not see it. But I heard it. They argued on the balcony. Then they fell. I think . . . I think the Padre was trying to . . . trying to kill her. Like he said he would. Brother Andrew told me he saw the Padre had been turned to stone. After he fell."

Thomas said, "The Padre had sworn to destroy the source of the *rasa mahadevi*. I almost regret that he did not succeed."

"Why?"

Thomas blinked, startled. "But, Timóteo, do you not understand? There is no place in the world for such power as she possesses."

Timóteo stared at him. "You begin to talk like the Padre."

"Yes, yes, I suppose I do. But—"

"But why can there be no place in the world for her? Does God not create mysteries all the time? Why must we destroy that which is strange, and beautiful and powerful?"

Thomas paused. "I do not know, Timóteo. Perhaps because such a creature makes us poor mortals seem so small and weak by comparison. Now I pray you pardon me. I should return to caring for these poor unfortunates."

Timóteo took a pouch off his rope belt. "Look, Tomás! I have a few herbs still that I gathered while we travelled. There are some betel leaves. And champa flowers, but they are dry now. And—"

"Thank you, Timóteo. You would make a fine apothecary. Your grandfather De Orta would be proud of you."

Timóteo beamed.

"I will take the betel. If you have something that would make a soothing poultice, we will find something to grind it to powder with."

Another pounding sounded at the door, and Porphredo called from the other side, "Open, Enyo! I have found more lost sheep."

Enyo sighed and pulled the door open again. Three girls ran in, silent, eyes wide with fright.

"I found them hiding in the library. They are not hurt. Ah, apotekos. Good. I have brought something for you." Porphredo handed him a roll of undyed cotton cloth and a bottle that smelled strongly of dead plant matter. "This is a salve the priests often use," she said.

Timóteo pointed to the bottle and said, "I know that smell. The priests used that on my ankles."

"As they seem to have saved your life," said Thomas, "I will value this medicine highly. Thank you, Porphredo. Have you seen any signs of battle outside?"

"I have done my best to avoid it, despotas. But the Mirza has been given a horse and he rides to where the main army stands. He believes he may dissuade them from attacking the city. As for the palace . . . I will say only that there are more statues in the corridors than there were this morning."

"What is she saying, Tomás?"

"That your beautiful queen is making herself useful by transforming our enemies."

"So, you see? She is not evil, she is helping us. And she can bring any statue back to life again when she wants. She said so. Maybe she will bring back the Padre, yes?"

Porphredo gave the boy an unreadable stare, then got up and went over to Enyo. Thomas saw her pass a small vial to Enyo, saying, "If any should die." Enyo nodded and tucked the vial into her belt.

"Ah. The *rasa mahadevi,*" he murmured. "Of course. If these are the brides of the goddess, do they not deserve her greatest gift? Mayhap with the most injured, it would do well to kill them and then administer the powder so that they are more fully healed—" Thomas realized what he was saying and he stopped and shook his head. "Do you not see, Timóteo, onto what terrible paths such temptation leads us?"

The boy did not reply. Thomas sat beside him and began to tear the cotton cloth into bandage strips.

The Mirza Ali Akbarshah crouched over the neck of his unfamiliar horse and waited in the dark for the portal ahead of him to be opened. The stench in the tunnel was stifling. *What sort of queen is it who allows her people to live like rabbits? Is this their punishment for some crime, or are they the wrong caste? At least they may fight to defend their homes if I fail and the tunnels are breached.*

With a rumble, the contraption that sealed the tunnel opening was rolled aside and the Mirza pressed out, there being barely room for him and his horse to squeeze through. He blinked in the sudden light of the setting sun.

His horse picked its way along a narrow ridge at the side of a hill. He came to a cliff top overlooking a narrow canyon below. There was Jaimal, sitting on the Mirza's elephant, directing a crew of men who were prying at an iron-barred wood door set into a cliffside. The vines that must have once concealed it had been hacked away.

The Mirza held up his hand and, as loud as he could, shouted, "Allah akbar!" All work stopped and all the men's faces turned to him. "Peace be upon you, my good lords," the Mirza continued. "I pray you, cease your attack. Lay down your weapons, for the queen who rules within is a queen of peace and would have sociable relations with our emperor. She is willing to share all her knowledge and wisdom with us. There is no need for battle."

The men turned to one another, murmuring in amazement. Jaimal looked pale and did not speak.

"What of the treasure?" someone yelled up at him.

"The treasure of her wisdom will be freely given to all," the Mirza replied. "The Shahinshah Emperor will be pleased with what we learn here, and will surely reward those who have made the arduous journey to secure this peaceable alliance."

"You see?" Jaimal said at last, "The traitor lies even now, claiming there is no treasure so that he may have it all."

"No!" cried the Mirza. "My goal has never been treasure. I am not moved by greed. It was to enrich the treasure of the mind that moved the Emperor Akbar to send us upon this journey, and if we now peaceably treat with the queen of Bhagavati, he will be well served."

"Remember," countered Jaimal, "that this so-called queen of peace sent a sorceress who lied to us and transformed Mumit into stone. And now Ali Akbarshah has become her willing servant and orders us to peaceably go to our deaths."

Much as he wished to hurl accusations back at his treacherous lieutenant, the Mirza did not know how many men had changed their loyalty or still respected Jaimal and therefore he modified his words. "You see that I come among you alone and unarmed. Your fears are understandable, but you are mistaken. The Shahinshah Emperor is renowned for his conquests and this queen was afraid we would do just what you are attempting now. She feared us, and so she did what she could to protect her people by misdirecting us. The death of Mumit was an accident."

The murmuring among the men below was approaching a low roar and the Mirza could see disagreements and shoving matches beginning among some of them. He began to hope.

"See how the witch queen has deluded him!" said Jaimal. "We were warned by the wise keeper of the ziarat that the queen we sought was a daughter-in-law of Shaitan, a beguiler of men and a mocker of the Faith. See what she has done to our once noble Mirza. Does such a creature not deserve to be conquered?"

The men quieted and the Mirza felt himself being weighed in their gaze. *What might I say that will finally sway them to my side?* "The gracious Queen Stheno is no minion of Shaitan, and will gladly welcome you all respectfully into her city as guests. But be warned. She does have power beyond that which we understand. I have told her you are honorable men, not barbaric thieves and brigands. She has given me this chance to prove your worth. But if you should prove me wrong, and enter her city as rogues do a wealthy man's house, then she will have no recourse but to protect her people and city. Consider well that you may all meet the fate of Mumit."

These words clearly had effect for the men became silent again and backed away from the door in the rockface. Jaimal leaned back and spoke to someone behind him in the *howdah.* A bow with nocked arrow emerged from beneath the *howdah* canopy, and aimed at the Mirza.

"Be wise, Jaimal!" cried the Mirza. "Do not—" But his next words were stopped by the arrow that plunged into his chest. The Mirza tried to raise his hand, tried to take another breath, but he could not. Another arrow struck, and he felt an immense sorrow as he toppled from the saddle. He only reached the fourth name of Allah before his life was gone.

XXV

MISTLETOE: This plant only grows upon other trees, in particular, the Oak, where it is said to be brought by lightning and thus has become a symbol of life brought from death. It bears pale, waxen berries and leaves which are evergreen. Betimes it is called Holy Cross Wood, for it grows in that shape. Mistletoe is called an all-heal, with power to cure almost any ailment known. Yet care must be taken in its use, for the juice of the berries, in too great amount, is poison. A tisane of the powder of the dried berries will ease all manner of palsy and spasms. If the plant is found with birdlime, a poultice of the two mixed will heal sores. The ancients thought mistletoe protects one on journeys to the underworld. It is oft a talisman to banish evil and prevent witches from entering. Pagan folk ascribed to it great magical power, and gathered it before their most potent sacrifices....

From the private herbal of
Mary Coulter
London, 1603

Thomas awoke at the boom of the storeroom door. Porphredo and Aditi had entered, Aditi now wearing armor of padded leather studded with leather plates. Her hair was bound back in a long plait and she wore a short sword at her side. As he slowly fought for wakefulness, Thomas noticed the unfortunate brides of Shiva were mostly sleeping, as was Timóteo, and a heavy calm hung in the air. The little brother had worked hard through the night, helping however he could. *Rest well, Timóteo. At least we have done good deeds this night, you and I. May God weight these toils of yours in balance against your service in the Santa Casa. Fare you well.*

Thomas stood and went to Aditi. "What hour is it? Has the sun risen?"

"Not yet," she sighed, "but very soon." She wearily rubbed her face.

Thomas realized he had been wishing that dawn had passed and with it his need to decide whether to meet Lockheart as planned. Now the decision was upon him and it rended his heart to have to abandon those who needed his help. "How goes the battle? Surely this new garb you wear does not mean you intend to fight?"

"Not if I can help it," she replied with a faint wry smile, "but I am no fool either. Better to have some protection against flying arrows even if one is running away. Yet I fear for our people . . . they are in need of a leader to guide them. One they can see among them without danger." She gazed speculatively upon Thomas for a moment.

"I am no warrior," Thomas said. "You might be better served by the Mirza, or even Andrew Lockheart. In mind of whom, I was to meet him at dawn in the sacred garden . . . on a matter of some import. Can you tell me if it is safe to go there?"

Aditi frowned at him and did not reply.

Porphredo said, "The palace seems to have been cleared of its infestation, although you must take care for the new-scattered rubble on the floors. The battle is now in the city itself, and I fear our queen's talents will do as much harm as good for the citizens of Bhagavati."

"Why do you need to go to the sacred garden? Why now?" demanded Aditi.

"Your pardon, Aditi, we do not mean to defile it. Rather it seemed it would be a safe place for meeting. That is all." Thomas went to the door and threw back the bolt before his traitorous tongue revealed more.

But Aditi followed him. At his shoulder, she asked softly, "You are leaving us, aren't you?"

"Ummm . . . why think you such a thing?" Thomas felt himself flush and his hands begin to tremble.

"Your eyes betray you. Well. We are not your people, and this is not your battle. I will not compel you to stay. Go. And may the Lady of Beasts, or whoever, watch over you."

"Godspeed, Aditi." Thomas gazed on her a moment, then lightly kissed her cheek. He swiftly pulled open the door and shut it after him before an unmanly tear should course down his face. He heard the bolt slam home behind him.

Thomas ran through the corridors, lit grey by the predawn light. His conscience had been pricked by Aditi's words and the more he ran, the more he wondered if he ran from himself and his true duty. The smell of smoke hung in the air. He dodged as well as he could the piles of anatomical rubble, trying not to identify the piece of hand, nose, bone, or organ it might be. *Damme, I wish I could flee this place of horrors. But am I not the true cause that all this has come to pass? Had I not followed Aditi into Goa, had I not confessed to the Inquisition and offered to lead them to the* rasa mahadevi, *had I not agreed to travel with the Mirza's army for Aditi's sake—Bhagavati might have remained safely hidden, its queen not stirred up like an angry bee, its people happy and at peace. Better I should have died in the Aljouvar, or of the scurvy aboard the* Whelp. *Rather I should have died in my mother's womb, rather than she die in bearing me. No. No, I must tell Andrew to go on without me. I must stay and attend to what I have wrought.*

He had taken one wrong turn after another, yet—from the rosy quality of the light—he reached the iron gate of the sacred garden just as the sun had begun to rise. The gate was ajar and Thomas swung it open and stepped onto the main path. There on the path before him lay a hand-and-a-half longsword. It was clearly old but preserved well with no stain of rust upon it.

"A beauty, is't not, Tom?" Lockheart called out from somewhere amid the oak and alder trees. "Methinks 'tis Norman make. This queen collects all things."

"Indeed. Though I hope my healing shoulders may permit my use of it. Could you not have found me a smaller blade? Such a burden may hinder escape."

" 'Twill serve our purpose. Merry Christmas. Take it up."

Thomas crouched and, with both hands grasped the hilt and lifted it. The sword was not so heavy as he feared and his shoulders protested only a little at the weight. " 'Tis well balanced."

"I am pleased to hear it," said Lockheart, still hidden from view. "Put it to a test. Say, knock that branch of mistletoe from off that oak branch to your right."

Something in his words sent alarum bells ringing amid the dross of Thomas's memory, but he was too weary to understand why. "Wherefore do you keep from my sight?"

"All will become clear. See to the mistletoe, lad."

Thomas stepped over to the oak and swung the sword at the small green herb overhead. The blade whistled through the air and took down the mistletoe, oak bough and all. " 'Tis a goodly sharp weapon," he said. "Though I fear using it I may cause more damage than I intend. 'Tis well the battles in the palace are ended."

"Not quite, m'lad. One battle yet remains to be fought."

Thomas turned as footsteps approached on the path. There was Lockheart, wearing only a loincloth of leaves save for the silver medallion which hung upon his chest. The rest of his body had been smeared with mud and on his head lay a crown of branches that resembled a rack of stag's antlers. Lockheart also held a longsword and it was leveled at Thomas's waist.

"Hah! Andrew, what means this foolery? Have you gone mad?"

"Rites done in the name of the gods oft seem a form of madness, Tom. The goddess we serve demands a most serious rite of us now. 'Tis for this that I followed you from England. 'Tis for this that your father raised you as he did. We serve the Huntress of the Grove of Nemi. And now, as she has done since antiquity, she asks a sacrifice."

Thomas backed away. "You . . . you cannot be . . . we are civilized men, Andrew, not god-fearing barbarians!"

Lockheart's serene expression did not change. "Men call barbaric the ancient wisdom they deny. Have we not found in this hidden city proof of that? Yet though you choose not to have seen it, the signs are there for any who observe closely. Through your mother's line you are descended from Roman nobility, a pontifex in fact, amusing as that may be. Your ancestor a precursor of the Pope. Your birth was the cause of your mother's death. So it was with mine, lad. The Furies who haunt your dreams are there with a purpose. And here we are in the image of the Grove of Nemi, where the image of Artemis dwells." Lockheart saluted him with his sword. "Welcome, Orestes."

Thomas felt chilled to his bones. In the myths he had studied, Orestes was doomed to die in the grove of Nemi as expiation for his mother's death. "My father put you up to this?"

"Nay, lay no blame on him. This is my sacred duty. I was born to this as you are."

"But . . . but this place is but an image, as you said. It is not the proper place. Is this to be a mock battle?"

"There will be naught to mock about it. One of us will not leave this grove alive."

Dear God. He means to slay me as a sacrifice to Diana. That is why he took such note of Prabaratma's attempt to do the same. What sort of man is this who can befriend me for so long, only to slaughter me as though I were a sheep? Thomas swallowed and gripped his sword tighter. "The only 'escape' you spoke of then, when you summoned me here, is a most final one?"

"You have it neatly, lad."

"Have some sense, Andrew!"

"Never have I been more sensible. The air of this morn is sweeter than any other in my life."

"Then let me smell such sweetness a little longer. Let us defy the gods, you and I! How can we worship such a cruel deity who demands the blood of healthful men?"

Lockheart continued to step toward him, without answering.

"What if . . . what if I lay my sword down and refuse to fight? Will you be such a cad as to slay an unarmed foe?"

Lockheart stopped. "I pray you, do not force me to kill you like a dog, Tom. This must be an honorable fight."

"And I thought you a friend," Thomas growled. He looked around him for a way to flee. "What wrong have I done you that you may dispatch your duty so coldly?"

"No wrong at all, lad. I am grown most fond of you. Twice upon our journey I almost turned from my duty and left you to another fate."

"Then, in the name of that love, turn again!"

Lockheart shook his head and, swiftly raising his sword, swung it, the point passing inches from Thomas's neck. "Oh, come and defend yourself, lad. Do not make it too soft a fight." He swung again and Thomas leaned back and deflected the blow with his own sword. The clash of blades sent a jarring into his shoulders that renewed their aching.

"I have not slept much, Andrew. This is no fair fight."

"I've not slept at all, lad. I kept vigil, as the knights of old were said to do. We are more than even." Lockheart's sword clanged again against Thomas's, nearly knocking it out of his hands. "Oh, do try to fight like a man."

"As you wish." Spurred by fear and anger, Thomas swung his sword.

Lockheart easily parried it. "Better. But your aim wants practice. Did you learn nothing from our forays with good Captain Wood?"

"I had a lighter sword and pistols then." Thomas raised his sword, but Lockheart swung first, knocking his blade aside. On the backswing, he cleaved a thin line of red down Thomas's chest.

Thomas staggered back against a tree, hissing with the sting of the cut. A part of his mind uselessly began reciting the sort of poultices he ought to apply to it. "You have wounded me. Let this fight be to first blood and I will gladly concede to you the victory."

Lockheart shook his head. "Death can be the only end. Death to bring forth new life." The Scotsman swung his blade again and Thomas ducked. A chunk of tree bark and trunk came away where Thomas's head had been.

Dear God, he is truly mad, and truly means to kill me. With grim determination, Thomas picked up his sword and swept the air before him with it. Back and forth, like a haying scythe, Thomas swung the blade until it hummed. To his satisfaction, he drove Lockheart backward along the path, the Scotsman only managing the lightest of parries.

"Oh, ho! A goodly effort, lad! Keep it coming! Yet another! You have the spirit of it now."

Angered by Lockheart's teasing humor, Thomas ignored the aching in his shoulders and the cut on his chest and swung the blade faster and faster. The path turned ahead and Thomas hoped Lockheart might lose his balance. *If I can but wound him such that he cannot fight, then this madness need go no further.*

They came to the bend, and Lockheart did, indeed, stumble around the roots of a tree. But as Thomas aimed for where Lockheart's arm might be, the Scotsman flung his own sword aside and walked, arms overhead, straight into the arc of Thomas's blade.

Thomas's sword cut deep into Lockheart's side and the Scotsman fell, with a groan, to the ground. His crown of branches tumbled from his head. Set off balance by momentum, Thomas stumbled forward, tripping over Lockheart's legs. This only drove the sword in deeper and Lockheart screamed.

Thomas let go of the hilt and rolled onto the path. The sword fell over, of its own weight, out of Lockheart's wound. A crimson river of Lockheart's blood began to flow past him. Panting, Thomas gasped, "Forgive me, Andrew. I fear I have killed you."

" 'Tis as it should be, lad," grunted Lockheart. "Well done."

"You walked into my blow."

Doubling up with pain, Lockheart growled, " 'Twas I who had to die lad. You are the next priest of the grove of Nemi. 'Twas you who must kill me."

"But . . . wherefore . . ."

"Had I asked, 'Tom, dear lad, would you slay me?' would you have willingly done it?"

"No!"

"No. Your life has been healing. I had to trick you to't." With blood-smeared fingers, Lockheart removed the silver chain from around his neck and tossed the medallion at Thomas. " 'Tis thine now. Return to England, and thy father shall receive thee with honors and teach thee all thou dost need to know. Remember this day well, for someday thou must do what I have done."

Thomas reached for the silver pendant, then drew his hand back. "No. I will not. Never."

"Aye, thou wilt. In time. Thy death is Hers as well as thy life. Agh! What . . . pain. Thou must finish me, Thomas."

"I . . . I cannot."

" 'Tis no kindness to let me suffer."

"I have not the surgeon's skill. I would only slip and cause greater suffering."

" 'Tis a simple matter. The sword is heavy. Let it fall to my neck. 'Twill be enough." He spasmed and coughed blood. "Swiftly, I pray thee!"

Thomas got to his feet and picked up his sword, now slick with Lockheart's blood. He dragged it to where Lockheart lay. With a grimace, the Scotsman tilted his head to present a better target.

Thomas wanted to shut his eyes, but he dared not miss. As he, at times, had had to do in Master Coulter's shop, he deadened his senses to the sight and smell, fixing only on the task that needed to be done. "Farewell, Andrew." He lifted the sword and let the blade fall against the Scotsman's neck. It bit deep, and another tributary gushed into the red sea upon the path. In moments, Lockheart's eyes emptied of life.

Thomas stood riveted, unable to move. A churning in his stomach warned him that he would soon be reacting all too violently to the sight. He heard footsteps behind him.

"Tamas! What is this? What have you done?"

Thomas froze even more and dared not turn around. "Queen Stheno. Majesty. I . . . he attacked me. This need not concern you."

"This man asked me to attend a ritual here."

"The rite is over. Leave us."

"I see. Well, I am hardly one to judge—"

"Don't you have a city to defend?"

"But I have done so, Tamas. There are few invaders left in Bhagavati. Alas, the city burns and many of my people have died. But the worst is over. There will be much rebuilding to be done. I will need someone at my side to help me. The . . . brides of Shiva, they will all be needed at home now. But we may have another wedding, Tamas. You are no mad mystic. You are my golden one. My Adonis. I still choose you."

Thomas gritted his teeth. "I do not choose you."

"Do not be afraid, Tamas. Even your little monk was able to gaze upon me for a time. Surely my love for you—"

"No! I have seen your crypt. I have seen what you did to Timóteo. I cannot love a monster. A murderess."

"It would seem we have that sin in common."

"I did not wish it! He . . . asked me for this."

"That is always the way it seems, nai? They come to you begging for death. You understand, you see? What other lover but you could understand me? Come, let us rebuild Bhagavati and be great and terrible monarchs together."

"No!" Unthinking, Thomas raised his sword and spun. He kept his eyes open just long enough to note the juncture of Stheno's neck and shoulder. He shut them as the blade sliced through her flesh. But he had seen enough to note the startled surprise on her face.

When the arc was complete, Thomas let the sword fall from his hands. He heard loud hissing falling to his right. He felt a warm splash upon his face and chest. His mouth was open and so he tasted blood. Her blood. As the horrible burning spread down his throat he remembered: *a serpent's bite to one who breathes*. . . . To the living, her blood was poison. Lightheaded, as if in appreciation of a marvelous jest, Thomas sank to his knees. *Dian shall have my death sooner than she thought—my reign as priest of Nemi has been short indeed.* Spots floated before his eyes. His muscles failed him and he fell over onto warm, sticky mud. He thought he heard the rush of leather wings, and the cries of "Murderer! Murderer!" were the last sounds in his ears.

Prabaratma stood on the palace parapet, his arms outstretched. Below him, fire roiled in shimmering scarlet and gold, bright against black columns of smoke. Tears filled his eyes and, for a moment, his clouded sight seemed to clear. He looked up to the sky and saw, towering over Bhagavati, the titanic crimson form of Kali: her many arms gracefully waving, skulls draped about her waist, her eyes aglow. Her long tongue protruded hungrily from her bloodstained lips. Her feet danced down upon the burning houses, collapsing them. Her many hands caught up fleeing souls and flung them to the earth or to the sky. Her dance was Destruction and she laughed.

"Welcome, Kali Durga!" Prabaratma cried. "You who bring doom and renewal of the world, welcome!"

He thought he heard the rattle of tambours and the pounding of drums from the city below him. "Hear the music, Kali Durga? It is your sacred song." Prabaratma swayed to the rhythm. He heard the wails of spirits freed from their earthly bondage sing in discordant chorus around him.

The figure of Kali came closer, her gaze fixed upon him. Two of her long arms reached toward him, fingers curled in beckoning. "Join with me," he heard her whisper. "Join with me in the dance."

Prabaratma was filled with a joy greater than he had ever known. "For this was my life created. I come, Kali Durga."

He stepped forward and felt suddenly light. A glow like the sun surrounded him, the sun's hot breath warming him. He spun, his arms wheeling around and around. "See me, Kali! I dance for you. See me dance! See me dance! See me da—"

* * *

Thomas's first awareness was of a taste of old blood in his mouth. He worked his tongue and his lips.

"He wakes," a woman above him said in Greek.

Thomas's body gave a violent shudder. And then he opened his eyes. He lay on the ground, but no longer in the garden. There seemed to be a cliff beside him, and the charred shells of houses nearby. Many people were gathered around him. He gazed up and saw the armored figure of Aditi standing over him. "Am I not . . . in paradise, then?" he said thickly.

Her gaze was cold and inhospitable. "The less you say, the better. I do not want to know who murdered whom, or in what order, or who was more deserving. Or who pushed Prabaratma off the wall. We brought you back because we could and others spoke on your behalf. Bhagavati has lost its queen so I must fill her throne and do her duty. You must go. Go back to your distant England and never speak to anyone of what you have seen here."

Thomas sat up. "As you wish," he managed to croak.

"Good. Gandharva and these two others will guide you through Sind as far as they can. You will take the boy monk, Timóteo, with you."

"But—" two Hindu men grasped Thomas's arms, not roughly, and lifted him up. They led him to a mule, already laden with bedroll and waterskins. Beside it stood a burro on which Timóteo sat.

"Welcome back, Tomás," the boy said, his eyes a little wary. "Look, they gave me a special saddle I can sit on. Um. How are you feeling?"

"I do not know, yet," Thomas replied as the Hindu men helped him onto the mule. He managed to sit in the saddle without falling over.

"Give him time, little monk," said Gandharva, who, without his ever-present *vina*, sat on a pony beside the boy. "It takes time to be fully alive again. I should know."

Hesitantly, Thomas began, "How long was I—"

"Seven hours, I think they said. Have mercy, good Aditi. Poor Tamaschinri has just returned from his very deep sleep."

"I want him gone," Aditi said.

And wherefore not? thought Thomas. *I slew her mother. Will she ever forgive me, I wonder?* He felt strange, as though he should be somewhere else. Yet if he had journeyed to some other land beyond the Styx, he could not remember it. But also he felt at peace, as if a great burden had been lifted from his back.

He felt a tap on his right knee. Thomas looked over and saw Porphredo standing beside his mule. She held up a leather pouch to him. "Here are a couple of books from our library. They concern herbal lore, but they are quite old, and I cannot guarantee their accuracy."

"Thank you, Porphredo," Thomas breathed, taking the pouch reverently in his hands.

"A parting gift," she said with a shrug. "You suffered much to find us, you should not leave empty-handed, nai?"

"What will you do now, you and Enyo? Should I not send help from Bijapur for you and your city?"

"No, though I thank you. You see what sort of help foreign kingdoms would send us. Enyo and I will endure. It is what we do." With a slight bow, the old woman departed, her grey sari fluttering in the wind.

Aditi mounted a large, spirited black horse, a jute sack in her hands. The sack contained something spherical and lumpy, and a red stain discolored the bottom of the sack. Thomas quickly realized what the sack contained, and what Aditi intended to do with it. *Perseus used such a weapon after he slew Medusa. What courage and iron will Aditi must have. God help what Mughuls remain in Bhagavati.* As she rode off into the smoke-shrouded city, Thomas said to Gandharva, "You know, I think Aditi will make a very fine queen."

EPILOGUE

MAY, 1602
LONDON, ENGLAND

Thomas Chinnery sat at his desk, counting out and recording the day's receipts. He noted that the supply of Turkish poppy would be running low soon, as well as the betel leaf and Florentine orris root. It was time to send letters to those merchants he had met on his way home from India to arrange for replenishment of his stock.

With a sigh, he leaned back in his chair. *'Tis good to see the shop yet prospers.* Thomas had feared that, with the recent death of Master Coulter, the clientele of the apothecary shop might go elsewhere for their medicaments. But Thomas was reassured to see that "Coulter & Son" was doing as well as ever.

"Thomas?" His wife, Anna Chinnery, came in, her black skirts billowing before her like galleon sails filled with wind.

And may her cargo have safe voyaging, he thought. *Thank God Master Coulter lived long enough to see me return, give consent to our marriage, and know there would be a grandchild.* Thomas smiled up at her and kissed her hand. "What may I do for thee, my bounteous beauty?"

She smiled a little, as if not sure how pleased she should allow herself to be. " 'Tis not what thou might do, but what I bring thee."

"Even better." He teasingly tried to pull her onto his lap.

She laughed and fended him off with featherlight blows. "Enough, Tom. A messenger has come with another missive from your father."

Thomas's smile abruptly left his face. "Burn it like the others."

Anna sighed and stamped her foot. "But Thomas! Has this quarrel not gone on long enough? Will you not at least read—"

"No. We have discussed this before, Anna. I'll nothing more to do with him. My duty to him was discharged back in India and there is an end to it."

"But what harm can it do to read his letter? Here, I shall open it and read it to you."

Thomas grabbed her hand with more force than he intended and she winced. "Your pardon. Anna," he said carefully, "have I not said that I have reason?"

"Aye, but you will not share it with me. Your father has had no word from you since your return. You forbade his attendance at our wedding, nor sent him word that he hath a grandchild coming. I should like to know what foul occurrence has cleft a son from his father so!"

Steeling himself to patience, Thomas replied, "Foul enow that no more ears should hear it. That he is ignorant of my affairs is no concern to me."

"It is to me! Are we not told in church to honor our fathers and mothers? And of the grace of forgiveness?"

"My father cares naught for our church, and some matters are beyond forgiveness."

"Then if those hold no argument, what of your father's wealth? There might be an inheritance someday that your obstinacy will deny us. Think of our child, Thomas!"

Gritting his teeth, Thomas replied, "I do think of the child. If we are blessed with a boy, my father must never meet him." He took both of her hands in his. "Anna, the church also teaches that wives should honor their husbands. Honor me in this. Ask no more about the rift betwixt me and my father. I do not wish thy lovely ears to hear what horrors I would tell."

"Oh, your horrors and mysteries! You think me but a child!" She threw the folded, sealed parchment onto his desk, then stomped away through the doorcurtain back into the shop.

Thomas sighed. *Must innocence be only the province of children?* He picked up the letter. Its red wax seal was embossed with a female archer flanked by two dogs.

The Widow Coulter bustled in from the kitchen behind him, skirts flouncing and grey hairs escaping from under her cap. "What was the clamor, Thomas?"

"Anna brought in another missive from my father." Thomas held up the letter.

"Ah." The Widow Coulter snatched it from his hand. "It will go in the fire straightaway."

"Thank you." Thomas followed her into the kitchen, wondering how she could be so understanding and her daughter not. But as it had been Dame Coulter who had encouraged him to go to India rather than Italy, as his father had wished, Thomas suspected she knew more about his family secrets than she ever revealed.

Timóteo sat at the trestle table that nearly filled the little kitchen, bent over a book. Leaves and twigs, roots and flowers were strewn about the table before him.

"How fares the work, Tim?"

"It, uh, it fares him well, Tomás," Timóteo said, his English still uncertain. "The Domina Coulter, her book is good, I think, but many a word here I do not, eh . . ."

"Understand?"

"Ai. That."

Thomas grinned at him. Though he had had doubts at the beginning when they left Bhagavati, he was now glad Timóteo had come to England with him. Timóteo was able to help the Widow Coulter with writing her herbal, a project that kept her from wallowing in grief after the Master's death. Still life was not easy for a dark-skinned, crippled boy in London—particularly a Catholic who had been training for the priesthood. So Thomas kept him mostly indoors, where Timóteo remained a great asset to the shop.

"Thomas," Anna called from the doorway.

Thomas braced himself for another round of pleading. "Yes, Anna?" He turned and saw her eyes were wide and her face pale. He rushed to her side. "What is't? Art thou ill?"

She shook her head. "Two foreign ladies have come into the shop. They have an . . . ill-formed child with them. They asked for you, but there is something about them. They affrighted me."

Thomas stroked her cheek. "Peace, my girl. Thou knowest thy condition makes thee prone to such frights."

"Tush!" said the Widow Coulter. "You'd do no better with half a stone of child squirming in your belly. Go and see to your customers, Thomas."

"Aye, Mother." With a rueful smile Thomas went through the curtain into the dim, aromatic shop.

In the middle of the cluttered room, beneath the stuffed crocodile, stood two women, one tall one short, in black dresses, veiled in black. Between them stood another, of a child's height, but with a head too large. It held onto the women's hands for balance. They were like three dark shadows come to animate life.

Thomas had heard of infants whose heads swelled from disease or after injury. They usually died shortly thereafter. If these women sought help for their charge, he feared there was little he could do for them. "Good even to you, ladies. How may I serve you?"

"Does he not look fine?" said the shorter one, in Greek.

"Nai," said the taller one. "Success and marriage have agreed with him."

Thomas felt dizzy and grabbed onto the nearest shelf, setting the bottles and jars a-rattle. "Enyo?" he whispered. "Porphredo?" His heart dropped to the floor as memories flooded back.

Porphredo removed her veil and smiled at him, creasing her long, leathery face. "Greetings and good wishes to you, despotas."

"Accept my greetings as well, and my joy at seeing you happy," said Enyo, removing her veil.

The third person, between them, did not remove its veil. Thomas stared. "Who . . ."

"I greet you also, beautiful Tamas," said the creature, with the voice of a child. But the intonation was quite mature.

"Stheno!" Thomas whispered. "It . . . you cannot possibly—"

"Did I not tell you I was immortal? I cannot die, the gods will not let me. Even after so able an effort as yours. Only my sister Medusa was granted that blessing. Was that your new wife we saw just now? She is rather pretty. And carries a child, too. You have done well for yourself."

Thomas stepped slowly toward the curtained doorway. *Dear God, she has come for revenge. What do I do against a foe who cannot be killed? I must tell Anna and the others to run for it out the back. But Timóteo cannot—*

"Do not be afraid, Tamas. You think I have come to punish when I have come to forgive. I will not harm you or your family. I wanted you to know that, perhaps, you have done me a great favor. You have given me, you might say, a chance to start anew."

"Oh," was all Thomas could say.

"We have been travelling," said Enyo, "and learning much about how the world has changed. We are searching for our sister Deino, and the despoina's sister, Euryale. While in Paris, we mentioned you to a Frankish doctor and he told us of your prosperity. We wanted to come and offer you our felicitations."

"I . . . I see. How is Aditi?"

"Quite well, the last we saw of her," said Porphredo. "She rules what is left of Bhagavati and there is hope it may someday prosper again. She is making good use of her connections with Sultan Ibrahim."

"She tore down my palace," Stheno grumbled. "Ungrateful daughter."

"Only some of it," chided Porphredo. "She chooses not to rule as a goddess."

"Hmpf." The misshapen Stheno let go of Porphredo's hand and rummaged around beneath her veil. "I have brought you a gift, Tamas. Alas, it is too late for a wedding present. Consider it then, a birthing gift." A small, plump hand emerged from beneath the veil and held something out to Thomas.

Cautiously, Thomas approached and saw that she held a square wooden box. Thomas managed to take it without touching her hand. "My . . . my thanks."

"You are most welcome, Tamas. Use it wisely."

"We should go," said Porphredo. "Our journey leads us on, far from here."

"May blessings fall upon your wife and your offspring," said Enyo, replacing the veil over her cheerful, dark eyes.

"May many good years follow," said Porphredo, draping her veil again across her features.

"Be prosperous and fruitful," sighed Stheno. "Do not forget me." The three women turned and walked out of the shop. The bell over the door rung their departure.

Thomas did not move from where he stood. "Do not forget you? Never fear, I cannot, much as I would." He looked down at the box in his trembling hand. A caduceus was carved in the top. He opened it. On a bed of pale silk lay a small, opalescent bottle. Thomas did not need to open the bottle to know its contents. He slammed the boxlid shut.

The rasa mahadevi. *I cannot escape its temptation, no matter how far I run. What if . . . what if I were to use it, here? I might do what no other apothecary can. Were I to use it carefully, secretly, perhaps it might bring great prosperity. Anna is full of care that we might someday become poor. Would this substance insure against it? With judicious use, Anna and the babe might not want for anything.* His fingers closed over the box.

But then he remembered the visits he got upon his return to England. Questions from the firm of Master Bromefield about the fate of the expedition. Questions from the Royal Court itself. He had told them all that the ships had been wrecked off the coast of India, which at least was true and Portuguese sailors could confirm. He told them that pirates had taken him to Goa where he had spent time in the Governor's prison, which was also true. But he had said nothing of his journey into the continent. He sensed the authorities were suspicious of his tale, he being the only survivor, but they could lay no blame on him and so he was let about his business unmolested. But not unwatched.

A sudden increase in his wealth might be noticed and remarked upon. The questioners might come round again. One slip of tongue or action and . . . well, the accusation of sorcery was easily made these days. He imagined himself standing in a courtroom dock, facing scowling judges and clergymen. He imagined a hangman's noose. He imagined Anna, widowed and penniless, frightened to show her face on the street, even to beg, because of the shame he would bring upon her.

No. This will not be.

"Thomas?" called Anna from the kitchen. "Is all well?"

Taking a deep breath, Thomas strolled casually back into the kitchen. He walked straight to the hearth and, squatting down beside the kettle, tossed the little box onto the coals, beside the ashes of his father's letter. "Fear not, Anna. All is well."

"Who were those women? Where were they from? What did they want? What did you just banish to the flames?"

Thomas stood, wiping his hands on his breeches. "They were

old herbwives, from Greece, I think. They wished to offer me a substance of dubious value and gave me a sample. But the cost was too dear, so I shall not keep it."

"What of the misshapen child with them?"

"No more I may do for her, but she will recover—after some time and growth. Now," Thomas clapped his hands together, "I find I am famished. What's for supper?"